I0582116

THE VOYNICH CODEX
VATICAN SECRET ARCHIVE THRILLERS
BOOK ELEVEN

GARY MCAVOY

LITERATI
EDITIONS

The Voynich Codex

Vatican Secret Archive Thrillers series - Book 11

Copyright © 2025 by Gary McAvoy

All rights reserved. No part of this publication may be reproduced, distributed, or transmitted in any form or by any means, including photocopying, recording, or other electronic or mechanical methods, without the prior written permission of the publisher, except in the case of brief quotations embodied in critical reviews and certain other noncommercial uses permitted under current copyright law. For permission requests, write to the publisher at the email or postal address below.

Hardcover ISBN: 978-1-954123-73-1
Paperback ISBN: 978-1-954123-72-4
eBook ISBN: 978-1-954123-71-7

Library of Congress Control Number: 2025914215

Published by:
Literati Editions
PO Box 5987
Bremerton WA 98312-5987
Email: info@LiteratiEditions.com
Visit the author's website: GaryMcAvoy.com
R0526

This is a work of fiction. Names, characters, businesses, places, long-standing institutions, agencies, public offices, events, locales and incidents are either the products of the author's imagination or have been used in a fictitious manner. Apart from historical references, any resemblance to actual persons, living or dead, or actual events is purely coincidental.

All trademarks are the property of their respective owners. Neither Gary McAvoy nor Literati Editions is associated with any product or vendor mentioned in this book.

This book contains original and copyrighted material that is not intended to be used for the purpose of training Artificial Intelligence (AI) systems. The author and publisher of this book prohibit the use of any part of this book for AI training, machine learning, or any other similar purpose without prior written permission.

The author and publisher do not endorse or authorize the use of this book for AI training, and shall not be liable for any damages arising from such unauthorized use. Any unauthorized use of this book for AI training is strictly prohibited and may violate applicable laws and regulations.

The author and publisher reserve all rights, including but not limited to, the right to seek damages and injunctive relief, against any person or entity that uses this book for AI training without prior written permission.

If you wish to use any part of this book for AI training, please contact the author and publisher to obtain written permission.

BOOKS BY GARY MCAVOY

The Pompeian Betrayal

The Medici Heresy

The Voynich Codex

The Devil's Symphony

The Hildegard Seeds

Covenant of the Iron Cross

The Apostle Conspiracy

The Celestial Guardian

The Confessions of Pope Joan

The Galileo Gambit

The Jerusalem Scrolls

The Avignon Affair

The Petrus Prophecy

The Opus Dictum

The Vivaldi Cipher

The Magdalene Veil

The Magdalene Reliquary

The Magdalene Deception

PROLOGUE

TOLEDO, SPAIN – 1526

Under flickering candlelight, Sister Juana de la Cruz Vazquez y Gutiérrez knelt beside the freshly plastered monastery wall, etching symbols into still-damp stucco. Her slender fingers moved deftly, guided by decades of study, devotion, and quiet courage. Each line and symbol represented more than mere decoration; they were the distilled essence of wisdom, protection, and faith, etched deliberately beneath mundane disguises.

She paused momentarily, listening anxiously. The monastery's silence was absolute yet oppressive. Recent news had reached Toledo that Inquisitors in nearby villages were conducting ruthless interrogations, branding sacred botanical practices as witchcraft. Juana's sisters had grown fearful, many abandoning their studies or burning their manuscripts.

1

Yet Juana refused to despair. With quiet resolve, she continued engraving zodiacal symbols beneath faded frescoes, her movements delicate yet deliberate. Her cipher was guardedly designed, visible yet hidden, preserved for those wise enough to decipher her intentions.

Footsteps approached suddenly from behind, urgent and soft. Juana turned abruptly, pulse quickening, relaxing as Sister Isabel appeared, anxiety etched across her young face.

"Mother Juana, Father Tomás was arrested today," Isabel whispered, voice trembling. "They found his herbal manuscripts and have accused him of heresy."

Juana closed her eyes briefly, feeling grief tighten her chest. Father Tomás had been a gentle man, wise and compassionate, undeserving of such cruelty.

She touched Isabel's hand reassuringly. "We must not falter, daughter. Our knowledge is sacred—given by God to heal, not harm. If fear silences us now, future generations lose truths they may desperately need."

Isabel nodded slowly, eyes fearful yet determined. "Then we continue."

Juana turned back to her work, engraving a symbol of Virgo interwoven with vine leaves—a subtle nod to the Majorcan mystic Ramon Llull's botanical allegories of purity and regeneration. Her whisper was fierce yet reverent: "May God forgive those who silence truth—and guide safely those who seek it."

CUBAS DE LA SAGRA, SPAIN, 1533

Juana de la Cruz moved intently through her quiet monastery cell, candlelight flickering across sparse furnishings and shelves filled with treasured books. Her breath quickened anxiously as distant shouts and pounding footsteps echoed through stone corridors—the heavy footsteps of Inquisitors, men bearing suspicion and judgment, readily approaching. She and her sisters had remained resolute over seven years of constant suspicions and danger. But now she knew the time had come to separate truth from truth, to keep the wisdom she had gained from the Inquisitor's hands.

She clutched tightly a bundle of parchment sheets, fragments hastily torn from her diary, each filled with secret botanical ciphers and spiritual symbolism preserved over decades. Juana's hands trembled slightly, sensing imminent danger. Her sisters had warned that Inquisitors now openly accused her of heresy, condemning as demonic the botanical wisdom she held sacred.

Juana moved toward the cell's stone hearth. Laboriously removing loose stones near its base, she revealed a small hidden cavity painstakingly carved months before. She pressed the precious diary fragments inside, praying fervently for their safety.

"Forgive me, Lord," she whispered, sealing the stones again tightly, hiding away the fragile parchment. Her heart ached fiercely, knowing her knowledge would now lie incomplete, its secrets protected but fragmented. "Let them remain safe until people's hearts become wise enough," she prayed softly.

Suddenly, her door burst open, shattering the cell's calm. Two imposing Inquisitors strode inside, eyes harshly judgmental.

"Sister Juana, you will come with us immediately," the elder man commanded coldly. "We have orders from Toledo. Your writings and teachings are under suspicion of grave heresy."

Juana stood up, meeting his gaze firmly. "I speak only what God's creations reveal. What wisdom I share is for humanity's good, not harm."

His eyes narrowed sharply. "That remains for the Church to determine."

As the Inquisitors led her roughly from the cell, Juana glanced back once, her gaze lingering anxiously upon the hidden cavity. She whispered silently, desperately praying that future seekers—ones pure in spirit and humble in heart—would rediscover what she had so carefully hidden. The truth she protected was too powerful, too easily corrupted, for humankind's hands as they were now.

Her prayer remained unspoken yet fervent: that someday, people might approach such wisdom responsibly, always humble before its mysteries.

THERE ARE mysteries that history guards jealously, veiled in whispers, concealed beneath ink, hidden in the weave of parchment. Among them, none has so persistently defied scholarly inquiry as the curious codex known since 1912 as the *Voynich Manuscript*.

Although no single official name for the manuscript survives from before that period, there are several key facts and historical clues that point to its pre-Voynich provenance.

In the seventeenth century, the manuscript is believed to have been in the possession of Emperor Rudolf II of the Holy Roman Empire, who reigned from 1576 to 1612. Scholars once proposed the manuscript as originating in Rudolf's famed library in Prague, renowned for its collection of alchemical and magical texts. Rudolf, a passionate collector of curiosities, was known to employ cryptographers and alchemists, and his court attracted intellectual adventurers from across Europe. However, the manuscript's origins predating Rudolf by over a century suggest he gained it rather than commissioned it.

According to a 1666 letter by Marcus Marci, a Bohemian scientist and physician, he believed the manuscript to be the work of Roger Bacon, the thirteenth-century English Franciscan friar and polymath. This association led to the manuscript later being loosely referred to as the "Roger Bacon Cipher" or "Bacon Manuscript." Bacon had an acute interest in languages, alchemy, and secret knowledge. Early theories suggested he might have created the manuscript as a cryptic alchemical text.

In 1912, a Polish antiquarian book dealer named Wilfrid Voynich discovered the manuscript while browsing through a cache of old books and manuscripts at the Villa Mondragone, a Jesuit college near Frascati, Italy. The Jesuits were discreetly selling off part of their library to raise funds, and Voynich was granted access to the collection.

Among the materials, he found a mysterious, illustrated manuscript written in an unknown script. Captivated by its odd botanical drawings, undecipherable text, and apparent antiquity, he purchased it along with other items. He later named it the *Voynich Manuscript* and spent the rest of his life attempting to decode its contents and trace its origins, believing, as others have, that Roger Bacon may have authored it.

This perplexing volume was immediately recognized as extraordinary. Its pages whispered in unfamiliar symbols, adorned with intricate drawings of enigmatic plants, celestial diagrams unlike any known astronomical charts, and figures that seemed to float through a surreal, half-remembered world. But most remarkable was its text —lines and lines of fluid script, elegant yet indecipherable, dancing like echoes from a vanished tongue.

For over four hundred years, historians, theologians, linguists, cryptographers, and even artificial intelligence experts have attempted to unravel the *Voynich Manuscript's* mysteries. All have failed. Radiocarbon dating in 2009 pinpointed its creation between 1404 and 1438, placing it squarely in the early Renaissance—thus ruling out Roger Bacon, who had been deceased by a century, as its creator. Its vellum pages, aged to a warm, honey-gold, were crafted from calfskin, carefully prepared and expensive, suggesting importance. But who created this manuscript, and why, remains maddeningly elusive.

Theories have blossomed like wildflowers in an untended garden. Some have suggested it was a medicinal manual, encoded to protect precious pharmacological secrets. Others speculated it was an elaborate hoax, concocted by a medieval trickster with sufficient resources and creativity to deceive even the most astute scholars. Still others saw in its baffling text and surreal imagery a coded mystical treatise, perhaps the lost work of an alchemist or an early Renaissance philosopher, cautiously preserving heretical knowledge.

Yet another, more recent, theory suggests a Central or Eastern European origin, possibly in the circle of mystics or herbalists working discreetly in medieval convents or hidden communities. These communities, blending folk wisdom, pagan tradition, and early scientific inquiry, might have sought refuge from persecution by encoding their knowledge in a script understood only by initiates. It is precisely this possibility—a sect of clandestine herbalists and spiritualists—that resonates powerfully in recent scholarship.

Indeed, beneath all of its varied theories lies a tantalizing possibility: the *Voynich Manuscript* might indeed encode genuine knowledge, deliberately obscured. It is neither gibberish nor deception, but a carefully constructed cipher designed to guard truths deemed dangerous or subversive by powerful authorities of its day. The intense efforts spent in decoding it—through statistical analysis, linguistic comparison, even attempts at computerized decryption—strongly suggest that the manuscript's language, dubbed Voynichese, contains underlying structure indicative of meaningful content.

In 2017, a researcher claimed that the manuscript's language was a form of medieval proto-Romance, encoded in abbreviated and symbolic forms. This theory, quickly contested by the scholarly community, nevertheless reignited interest, pointing toward the Iberian Peninsula or Southern France—regions historically rife with secret religious orders, herbalist traditions, and alchemical practice.

Here, the historical shadow deepens intriguingly. Could the manuscript be the legacy of an obscure medieval sect known as the Hesperides? Named after the mythical garden in Greek legend where immortality-granting apples grew, these purported followers, rumored in obscure medieval texts, were said to cultivate rare plants believed capable of healing mind and body. Their symbol —a tree bearing golden fruit—strikingly aligns with some mysterious plant illustrations in the manuscript itself.

7

Might the *Voynich Manuscript* be the surviving testament of their suppressed wisdom?

One thing remains clear: the manuscript has defied decoding precisely because it seems layered—its illustrations, symbols, and text forming not just one cipher but multiple, nested within each other, each key dependent on botanical knowledge, celestial alignments, linguistic subtleties, and, perhaps, spiritual or symbolic understandings lost to modern interpreters.

Yet, historical records hint at one other intriguing possibility, scarcely noticed. Isabella of Portugal, wife of Holy Roman Emperor Charles V, is briefly mentioned in historical footnotes for her patronage of alchemists and herbalists, particularly for commissioning rare medicinal texts—texts that were subsequently banned during the Counter-Reformation. Her connection remains tenuous, yet historically plausible. Isabella, renowned for her intelligence, commissioned works exploring the intersections of faith, healing, and natural philosophy. Could the manuscript have passed quietly through her hands, deemed too dangerous for the Church's comfort?

As centuries passed, the *Voynich Manuscript*'s allure only intensified, drawing generations into its tantalizing web. It became the ciphered Mona Lisa, a literary sphinx challenging humanity's understanding of itself and its own past. And though scholars despair at its undecipherability, every so often, whispers surface—of newly discovered marginalia, faint palimpsests beneath the script, or partial translations suggesting profound botanical and spiritual insights. Each whisper reopens the chase, promising revelation just beyond reach.

When no buyer could ultimately be found, its final owner—rare book dealer Hans P. Kraus—relinquished the manuscript, donating it in 1969 to Yale University's Beinecke Rare Book and Manuscript Library, where it rests today—enshrined in glass, its secrets still sealed, its silence undisturbed.

THE VOYNICH MANUSCRIPT has survived the flames of religious zealotry, evaded the scrutiny of countless intellects, and guarded its truth fiercely beneath layers of symbol and ink. But perhaps its most vital secrets are not merely medicinal or botanical, nor only linguistic or cryptological. Perhaps, beneath all the encoded layers, it harbors something infinitely more powerful: a secret about human memory, a revelation about the spirit, hidden in the quiet whispering of ancient parchment.

What truths might yet awaken in those prepared to understand its long silence?

And what might those truths unleash upon the world, for better or worse?

BRUGES, BELGIUM

The medieval city of Bruges was wrapped in a shroud of fog, its canals whispering secrets as Hana Sinclair stepped from the taxi onto the rain-slicked cobblestones. The early morning air was saturated with scents of river water, old brick, and distant bakeries just warming their ovens. Hana paused, inhaling deeply, savoring the distinct, layered atmosphere of the Belgian city she had always loved, though her visit today wasn't for pleasure.

Drawing her coat tighter around herself, Hana crossed Markt Square, dominated by the imposing belfry, its Gothic pinnacle thrusting defiantly upward into the mist. At this early hour, the Markt Square was still mostly deserted, the first rays of dawn casting pale gold reflections across its puddled surface. As she made her way through narrow, winding streets lined with stone-fronted townhouses and shuttered cafés, her footsteps echoed faintly, mingling with distant sounds of shopkeepers readying their wares.

The auction house lay just beyond Burg Square, an unassuming stone-fronted building bearing an ornate bronze plaque: **Van Den Broeke & Sons: Antiquarian Booksellers since 1847.** She had frequented auctions in more glamorous settings—Paris, London, Rome—but this small, prestigious house held a reputation for uncovering manuscripts others overlooked. And today, Van Den Broeke had something rare enough to entice collectors, historians, and reporters—such as Hana—from across Europe.

Inside, the lobby was warmly lit, lined floor to ceiling with polished wood shelves crammed with leather-bound volumes, gilt-edged bindings gleaming under discreet lights. A solemn-looking receptionist, an older man with neatly groomed white whiskers and wire-rimmed spectacles, checked Hana's credentials silently before gesturing toward the main auction hall.

Within, the space was compact yet elegant, rows of carved wooden chairs already half-filled with scholars, collectors, and a smattering of journalists murmuring quietly in various languages. At the far end stood a raised podium framed by heavy velvet curtains. A long oak table displayed the items up for bid, each resting upon velvet cushions beneath carefully directed lighting.

Hana selected a seat near the rear, positioning herself to observe discreetly. Her eyes wandered across the assembled crowd, noting a few familiar faces—specialists from the British Museum, the Bibliothèque Nationale de France, and, intriguingly, one of Genetica Therapeutics' archival researchers, recognizable from a recent symposium on historical botanical medicine. Hana's pulse quickened subtly. *Why was the once-disgraced Alton Blackthorn's company interested in today's sale?*

She quickly flipped open the catalogue, scanning the listings. The manuscript of interest to her this day was item twelve, described simply as *"Codex Hesperides, Southern France or Northern Spain, circa 1450."* A scribbled footnote, provided by the auctioneer, stated: *"Margins annotated in Hebrew script, referencing Roger Bacon Cipher MS."* That alone had compelled Hana to journey here. References to this yet-undeciphered *Bacon Cipher Codex*, now referred to as the *Voynich Manuscript*, would certainly add flavor to the article she had in mind about this auction.

Promptly at nine, a smartly dressed man with gray-streaked hair ascended the podium. "Welcome, ladies and gentlemen. I am Antoine Van Den Broeke, and it is my honor today to present some extraordinary pieces." His voice, rich and cultivated, carried the particular diction of generations of booksellers. The early lots passed without excitement—rare atlases, illuminated texts, early printed incunabula—until at last, Van Den Broeke gently lifted the modestly sized, leather-bound codex into the light.

"This," he declared reverently, "is Lot Number Twelve. An intriguing medieval herbal manuscript, estimated at mid-fifteenth century origin, probably southern France, though possibly Iberian. Of particular interest are marginal annotations in Hebrew script, referencing botanical and zodiacal symbols famously associated with the Roger Bacon Cipher Manuscript, today known as the *Voynich Manuscript*."

A wave of whispers swept through the hall, tension elevating palpably. Hana straightened slightly in her seat, pen poised.

"Opening bid, five thousand euros," Van Den Broeke announced.

Bidders erupted instantly. Voices rose rapidly—ten thousand, fifteen, twenty. Hana noted Blackthorn's researcher bidding aggressively, the idiosyncrasy of it tightening her stomach. Bids climbed higher, quickly passing thirty thousand. Suddenly, a bespectacled older woman, representing the British Museum, declared, "Forty thousand euros," prompting murmurs and temporary silence.

Blackthorn's man hesitated briefly, muttering into a phone pressed to his ear.

Hana recognized the move—someone important was directing him remotely. She swallowed uneasily.

"Forty-five thousand," he said finally, nervously adjusting his tie.

The auctioneer inclined his head toward the woman. She shook her head, conceding. "Forty-five thousand euros, once, twice—"

Hana scribbled furiously, capturing every detail—then something compelled her to glance up once more. The auctioneer paused, squinting curiously at a card handed urgently from behind the curtain. "A late absentee bid has just been received," he announced. "Sixty thousand euros."

Gasps rippled around the hall. Blackthorn's representative paled visibly, hesitated, then shook his head, abruptly turning to depart. The auctioneer's gavel fell decisively. "Sold to absentee bidder, sixty thousand euros."

Hana released a breath she hadn't realized she was holding. *Who had placed that decisive, secretive bid?*

As the crowd dispersed, Hana moved quickly toward

the podium. Van Den Broeke was wrapping the manuscript in protective linen.

"Excuse me," she ventured, flashing her press credentials. "Hana Sinclair, *Le Monde*. May I see it briefly before delivery?"

He eyed her credentials carefully, then nodded. "One moment, Ms. Sinclair." He then peeled back the linen cover, revealing parchment pages whose ink was delicately faded, with botanical illustrations faintly visible. Carefully, Hana scanned the margins, her eyes tracing the Hebrew annotations.

Her heart jolted. In faded Hebrew script, one annotation stood out distinctly, ink darker, letters precise:

"See Roger Bacon Cipher MS fol. 89v. Hesperides formula?"

Hana blew out a breath. *Someone long after the creation of this codex had inserted this reference, but why? And what was this Hesperides formula about?* The word resonated with her, vaguely familiar, yet cryptic. Before she could process further, Van Den Broeke recovered the manuscript, saying, "Delivery will occur tomorrow. The buyer prefers privacy."

"Who purchased it?" Hana asked eagerly.

"I'm afraid confidentiality prevents—"

"Please," she insisted, pleading with her eyes, "it's important."

He hesitated, clearly sympathetic, then lowered his voice. "An organization. One representing the… a church."

"The Scriptorium Vaticanum?" she asked, recognizing he had stumbled, nearly saying the Church.

He looked surprised. "Why, yes. Do you know it?"

She did. The Scriptorium Vaticanum was a covert acquisitions branch within the Vatican Secret Archives, discreetly authorized to obtain rare manuscripts bearing potential theological or historical significance.

Hana thanked him hurriedly, thoughts racing. Why was the Vatican secretly acquiring an obscure manuscript linked to *Voynich*? Did Michael know anything about this? And why had Blackthorn's company risked public exposure to try to obtain it?

She slipped out into Bruges' damp streets, heart racing, mind alive with speculation. As she moved quickly toward her hotel, the city's enchanting medieval veneer seemed suddenly more sinister, shadows shifting subtly in corners. Instinctively, Hana glanced behind her. A man in a dark coat lingered near a shop doorway, apparently uninterested, yet she sensed his eyes tracking her movement. Anxiety surged.

Only last year, she and her fiancé, Father Michael Dominic, had faced off against Blackthorn's Zentara Biogenics in his attempts to destroy the seeds of a medicinal herb that could have destroyed lives under his hands or saved lives if ethically employed. Hana's relentless journalistic pursuit of the truth, with Michael's help, had brought down Blackthorn. Her resulting articles in *Le Monde* had shed light on the man's heinous behavior. Somehow, he had survived the scandal, but she had no doubts he blamed her for his downfall. Would he really send someone to exact revenge at this late date? The very fact that she had seen one of Blackthorn's researchers at the auction was enough to give her pause. She checked behind her again. The man in the dark coat still stalked her, though at a distance.

She forced herself to slow, calmly blending into tourist groups crossing Markt Square. Reaching her boutique hotel, she quickly ascended to her room, locked the door, and pulled out her phone to call a familiar number.

"Michael," she said urgently when he answered. "We have a problem."

Across hundreds of kilometers, deep in the quiet of the Vatican Archives, Father Michael Dominic replied, concern rising instantly in his voice at the urgency in hers. "Tell me."

"The Vatican—specifically the Scriptorium Vaticanum —just secretly purchased a manuscript at auction here in Bruges: the *Codex Hesperides*, linked explicitly to the *Voynich Manuscript*. More interestingly, Alton Blackthorn was represented there, his proxy desperately bidding for him by phone."

Silence fell briefly before Michael spoke gravely. "I feared as much. That manuscript may hold the key to secrets the Church once tried very hard to bury. But if Blackthorn is associated with it..."

"Exactly," Hana agreed tensely. "So, were you involved in the decision to acquire the Codex today?"

"Yes, I did authorize the acquisition, at any cost. Although the Scriptorium Vaticanum is a separate unit, it falls within the operational parameters of the Apostolic Archive. I didn't realize you were going to be attending the auction, or we could've discussed this beforehand." Their specialized careers, hers as a French journalist and his as prefect of the Vatican Secret Archives, kept them frequently separated. Yet many times their individual tasks had crossed, giving them opportunities to work together. That was, in fact, how they had first met. "So, are you coming home soon?"

"Yes—but as it happens, I think I'm being followed."

"Well, that's not something I want to hear... Stay where

you are, Hana. Karl and Lukas are nearby, in Antwerp. I'll have them join you within a couple of hours." Michael's voice turned resolute. "Strange timing, though. Maybe related to Blackthorn, since his people certainly know who you are."

Hearing Michael's reassurance relieved her. The seasoned Swiss Guards were trusted allies, remaining calm and capable even in the most perilous situations. "Thanks," she whispered.

Hanging up, she sat heavily on the hotel bed, thoughts spinning. Outside her window, Bruges' ancient streets lay quiet, cloaked in misty twilight, secrets hidden in shadow. A centuries-old mystery had begun to stir once more, bringing danger, intrigue, and perhaps revelations humanity wasn't yet prepared to handle.

What started as another interesting article for *Le Monde* now swirled with intrigue. Her journey had just begun—and with it, she realized, so had the danger.

VATICAN CITY

Alone with the fear for his fiancée and the weight of the task coming his way by courier tomorrow, Michael stepped away from the desk, taking several steadying breaths. The tranquility of the Vatican Archives, usually so comforting, now felt weighted with danger. The Hesperides manuscript, its cryptic annotations, its dangerous implications—all pointed toward escalating peril. He knew Alton Blackthorn's ruthlessness all too well from the recent Hildegard von Bingen affair. The collapse of Zentara had destroyed countless lives; Michael wouldn't allow history to repeat itself. And he certainly would not let his fiancée be put in danger yet again.

He pulled out his phone and called Karl Dengler. The Swiss Guard answered immediately, voice crisply professional.

"Father Michael?"

"Hi, Karl. I assume you guys are still in Antwerp?"

"We are, yes. About ready to head back this afternoon."

"Well, you'll have an interim mission before returning to Rome. Hana's in Bruges and seems to have a tail on her, possibly—in fact, probably—by direction of Anton Blackthorn, that scoundrel from Zentara. That's only an hour from where you are now. Could you give her some support and make sure she returns home safely?"

"You bet, Michael. We're on it."

Ending the call, Michael stood patiently for a moment, contemplating the darkened aisles stretching away, filled with secrets too perilous to share openly. The *Voynich Manuscript* had defied human understanding for centuries, safeguarding secrets potentially powerful enough to threaten spiritual, historical, and scientific worlds. Might the *Hesperides Codex* cast light on the *Voynich Manuscript*?

Now, drawn inexorably into the orbit of Alton Blackthorn's ruthless ambitions, whatever secrets it held demanded protection, resolution, and clarity. Michael was well aware of the stakes they faced in terms of knowledge, power, and lives, if the past was any measure.

Closing his eyes briefly, he offered a silent prayer for courage, guidance, and protection.

Then, shoulders squared with determination, Father Michael Dominic moved swiftly to secure the Archives—and brace for whatever storm was coming.

CHAPTER
TWO

BRUGES, BELGIUM

The shadows of early evening settled over Hana's hotel in Bruges, draping its historic facade in hues of twilight. Warm lamplight spilled from the windows, casting soft reflections on the damp cobblestones below. Inside her modest second-floor room, Hana paced restlessly, anxiously awaiting Karl and Lukas's arrival. Father Michael's earlier warning haunted her thoughts: *Blackthorn knows what we have.*

Pausing at the window, she carefully scanned the quiet street, her gaze lingering suspiciously on a dark-haired figure standing across the street near a café entrance. He appeared casual, yet his posture felt alert, controlled—too intent for a mere bystander.

A sudden, firm knock startled her, and she spun toward the door, heart racing. "Hana? It's Karl," came a familiar voice, warm yet urgent.

Relieved, she hurriedly unlocked the door and opened

it wide. Karl stepped in swiftly, followed closely by Lukas. Both men wore civilian clothes, their posture vigilant and controlled. Karl immediately softened, seeing Hana's anxious expression, and warmly clasped her shoulders.

"You all right?" he asked, his voice full of genuine concern. "Michael called and told us everything."

"I'm fine, Karl—just shaken," Hana replied softly. The Swiss Guard's comforting presence eased the tension from her shoulders. He was more than just a capable protector; he was family—her cousin, someone who had watched over her since childhood.

Lukas crept toward the window, glancing warily outside. He turned slightly, eyes alert. "Someone is watching from across the street. Dark jacket, near the café."

Hana nodded nervously. "He's been there all afternoon."

Karl's expression hardened protectively. "We saw at least one more down the street. Blackthorn's agents don't play games. We'll move you now—get your things quickly."

Hana pointed to a suitcase and her laptop bag near the bed. "Everything important is ready."

Lukas smoothly gathered her belongings while Karl squeezed Hana's arm reassuringly. "Don't worry, we won't let anything happen to you," he whispered warmly. "Michael has arranged protection at a Vatican residence nearby."

With Lukas carrying her suitcase, Karl cautiously checked the hallway before signaling for them to follow. The trio descended the narrow staircase, footsteps hushed against the worn wooden steps. As they reached the small lobby, Hana caught the curious gaze of the elderly concierge, whose eyes followed them reflectively, perhaps sensing trouble but saying nothing.

Outside, twilight deepened into the soft darkness of early night, the ancient city settling into silence. Karl led confidently, Lukas close at Hana's side, their strides brisk and purposeful. Crossing Markt Square, its Gothic spires stark against the dimming sky, Lukas abruptly murmured, "They're behind us—two men."

Hana's pulse surged. Glancing back quickly, she saw the dark-haired man from the café rapidly closing the distance, joined now by another in a hooded jacket. Karl's voice tightened but remained calm: "Move faster. Stay close to us, Hana."

They quickened their pace, weaving hurriedly into a narrower street lined by centuries-old buildings, shadows deepening around them. Suddenly, from a side alley, another figure emerged, blocking their path forward. Hana stopped sharply, heart racing.

Karl instinctively stepped in front of her, shielding her with his own body. Lukas moved smoothly beside them, his stance rigid and ready.

"Hand over the woman, and no one will get hurt," growled the dark-haired man in English, advancing slowly from behind, his heavy Flemish accent controlled but menacing.

Karl straightened defiantly, his tone steely yet protective. "And I'd say just back off, or someone *will* get hurt. You're not taking her anywhere."

Hana's breath quickened as she clung to her cousin's arm.

The aggressor's eyes narrowed impatiently. "You really want to do this the hard way?"

Karl didn't flinch. "You'll regret trying."

Without further warning, the man lunged forward. Karl reacted instantly, deftly sidestepping while using the attacker's momentum to send him sprawling onto the cobblestones. Lukas rapidly engaged the second assailant, parrying punches with calculated precision. The narrow street erupted into chaos—shouts, muffled blows, the sharp scuffing of shoes on pavement.

A third man surged forward, catching Hana's sleeve and wrenching her toward him. Panic exploded in her chest as she twisted desperately, kicking fiercely at his shin. "Karl!" she cried urgently.

Instantly, Karl spun around, his fist connecting solidly with the assailant's jaw, knocking him backward. Freed, Hana stumbled toward Lukas, who quickly shielded her while Karl regained his stance, vigilant and fiercely protective.

The attackers, momentarily beaten back, hesitated.

Karl drew himself up, commanding authority radiating from his stance. "Last chance," he warned fiercely. "Walk away."

The dark-haired man spat angrily, wiping blood from his lip. "We'll see each other again soon enough," he threatened coldly before signaling retreat. In moments, the street cleared, leaving only silence and the echoes of their rapid, fading footsteps.

Karl immediately turned to Hana, his eyes softening with concern. "Are you all right? Did they hurt you?"

"I'm okay," Hana assured breathlessly, still trembling from adrenaline and fear. "Thanks to both of you."

Karl gently cupped her elbow, steadying her. "Come, quickly. More will likely follow."

They resumed their swift, cautious pace, Lukas continually scanning behind. Minutes later, they arrived safely at a stately old building near the canal, the quiet diplomatic residence marked discreetly by a small bronze Vatican crest. Karl pressed an intercom beside the heavy wooden door, exchanging brief, quiet words before the door swung open to reveal a serious-faced Vatican attendant.

Inside, warm lamplight illuminated polished wood and antique furniture. Once the doors locked securely behind them, Karl visibly relaxed, guiding Hana toward a private sitting room off the entry hall. Lukas set down her belongings, securing the perimeter instinctively.

Karl sat down beside her on a velvet sofa, eyes gentle yet serious. "Hana, this is getting worse quickly. Michael told us Blackthorn is in operation again, and we know he blames you for losing Zentara Biogenics. We must move cautiously."

Lukas nodded, joining the conversation. "We'll stay close. No one gets through again."

Karl's voice softened as he continued, "Tomorrow morning we'll travel together back to Rome. Once we're there, we'll have Vatican resources fully behind us."

Hana nodded, calming gradually under Karl's steady gaze. "Karl, thank you. Truly. I just don't quite understand why Blackthorn would pick now for revenge or jeopardize his newfound freedom by even thinking of it."

Karl stood, offering her a reassuring embrace. "We know the man is ruthless, and being vindictive comes right along with it. Try to get some rest. We'll stand watch tonight."

Hana hugged him tightly, grateful for his strength. As he and Lukas moved toward the door, she settled back onto the sofa, listening to their quiet voices murmuring just outside.

The room's quiet soon enveloped her, easing her anxiety. Yet as her heartbeat slowed, Hana realized with sudden, chilling clarity how dangerously determined Alton Blackthorn had become. A year ago, he had sought the seeds secreted away by twelfth-century Benedictine Abbess Hildegard von Bingen, expecting them to bring him fortune. Instead, Hana's reporting of his activities had undermined Blackthorn's illegal efforts, which ultimately led to his downfall. Now, with the attempted purchase at the auction, it appeared he seemed determined to uncover something valuable from the Hesperides Codex. Likely, his simultaneous intention was to prevent Hana from thwarting his new efforts as well. And at the heart of it, she wondered: could this manuscript truly hold secrets similar to what they discovered a year ago?

Pulling a wool throw around herself, Hana lay back, eyes closed but mind alert. Outside, Bruges whispered through the darkness, hiding dangers she had only begun to glimpse.

CHAPTER

THREE

VATICAN CITY

Michael Dominic adjusted his reading glasses and leaned closer to the illuminated manuscript lying before him, delivered this afternoon by secure courier. The dim solitude of the Vatican Secret Archives provided a familiar, comforting embrace, the air cooled and filtered by the climate-control systems humming unobtrusively in the background. Rows of towering wooden shelves filled with cataloged volumes surrounded him, each spine bearing the silent dignity of centuries.

Michael's fingers lightly traced the vellum page laid open on the desk. The ink, though slightly faded, still carried a clarity indicative of meticulous craftsmanship. This was the *Hesperides Codex*—the one hurriedly delivered by courier from Bruges under the discreet guidance of the Scriptorium Vaticanum.

The annotations caught his immediate attention: marginal notes delicately inked in Hebrew, neatly penned, perhaps hurriedly, by someone deeply knowledgeable. Michael's Hebrew was fluent, yet deciphering this script proved challenging; it was cramped, archaic, the handwriting an ancient Sephardic cursive rarely encountered in modern academic circles.

He leaned back slightly, removing his glasses and rubbing tired eyes. The Archives' subterranean tranquility had always allowed him to think clearly, but tonight unease persisted. The mention of the *Voynich Manuscript* and "Hesperides" troubled him. He had learned over many years that manuscripts acquired secretly by the Vatican often harbored truths the Church found uncomfortable—truths that others would exploit, or worse, kill to suppress.

A soft footfall echoed from the adjacent hallway. Michael glanced up as his assistant Ian Duffy emerged from between two towering shelves. The tall, slender Irishman nodded, his bright red hair subdued by the gentle lighting, his posture alert.

"I locked the Archives' outer doors," Ian murmured, glancing toward the manuscript. "No interruptions. Penetration attempts on our servers have tripled since that codex arrived."

Michael exhaled knowingly. "Blackthorn?"

Ian nodded grimly. "Undoubtedly. His digital fingerprints were all over it. He knows what we have. He must suspect its importance."

Michael turned back to the manuscript. "Whatever this manuscript holds, Alton Blackthorn is willing to risk everything to obtain it."

Ian leaned over Michael's shoulder, studying the manuscript's dense margins. "Any idea why?"

Michael pointed to one of the Hebrew annotations. "I believe the key is here. Look at this."

Ian squinted, gently tracing the faint letters with his fingertip. "'*Voynich* folio eighty-nine verso.' And this strange phrase—'Hesperides formula?'"

Michael nodded. "Exactly. The *Voynich Manuscript* famously resists interpretation, yet here is a direct reference, clearly connecting this codex to the Bacon/Voynich book. This note suggests something powerful hidden within the Voynich's botanical illustrations. Possibly an encoded recipe, an alchemical formula—something medicinal and dangerous enough to warrant secrecy."

"Dangerous enough to kill for?" Ian murmured skeptically.

"Perhaps," Michael replied soberly. "Historically, medical knowledge and spiritual truths have often been conflated. A plant-based compound, one possibly capable of extensive healing, might be seen as miraculous, even heretical, threatening existing power structures. Blackthorn knows this."

Ian shook his head, sighing heavily. "Blackthorn's past isn't pretty. Zentara collapsed under fraud charges, leaving countless lives ruined. If he's resurfaced, you can bet it's not for philanthropic reasons."

Michael stood, stretching stiffly. "That's right. Blackthorn's pharmaceutical ambitions are global, aggressive. Imagine what a unique botanical medicine, historically obscure and scientifically undocumented, might offer someone driven by greed."

Ian frowned. "If this manuscript references *Voynich*, we need access to our own *Voynich* facsimile. Immediately."

Michael smiled slightly. "You anticipated my thoughts. Bring it here."

Ian disappeared down an aisle, returning moments later carrying a large, leather-bound volume with gilt lettering: *Voynich MS – Yale facsimile*. He set the heavy book next to the *Hesperides Codex* and opened it delicately to folio 89v.

Both men stared silently at the intricate illustration: an unfamiliar plant drawn with fluid strokes, possessing twin roots colored distinctly red and green. Surrounding the plant were lines of the manuscript's elegant yet incomprehensible Voynichese script.

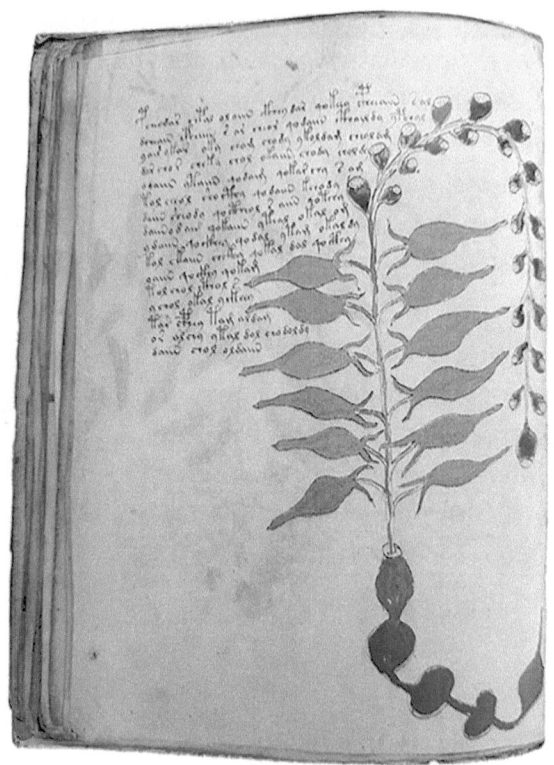

Michael leaned forward, examining the subtle botanical details. "This plant—have you seen anything like it?"

Ian shook his head slowly. "No botanical reference matches strictly. Possibly symbolic?"

Michael considered this. "Botanical symbolism often encodes alchemical processes—red for spiritual awakening, green for healing or renewal. The *Voynich Manuscript* might not merely illustrate real plants. It may encode alchemical stages."

"So the Hesperides formula," Ian suggested, "could reference combining these two symbolic states—red and green—for spiritual or medicinal purposes."

Michael nodded gravely. "The Hesperides were

mythical guardians of golden apples, conferring immortality. Perhaps these illustrations represent not immortality literally, but profound regenerative properties —a botanical medicine believed miraculous."

Ian's gaze returned to the Hebrew annotations. "But why Hebrew? Was a Sephardic scholar involved?"

Michael paused thoughtfully. "Perhaps Jewish scholars, expelled from Spain and later France, carried secret botanical and alchemical knowledge with them. Encoding their discoveries cryptically would ensure the survival of their knowledge amid religious persecution."

Ian glanced at him sharply. "Meaning this manuscript could represent suppressed knowledge fleeing the Inquisition—potentially revolutionary medicine the Church feared?"

Michael inhaled slowly, nodding. "Exactly. Knowledge too powerful, dangerous, and perhaps sacred, to leave openly accessible."

Silence fell, both men recognizing the gravity of the moment. Michael carefully flipped another page in the Hesperides Codex, revealing additional annotations—lines of Hebrew interspersed with small drawings of zodiac symbols and lunar phases. He peered closer, tracing symbols meditatively.

"These zodiacal symbols," Michael murmured, "represent preparation timings, perhaps harvest or extraction aligned with lunar phases. The complexity is astonishing."

Ian exhaled slowly. "So, whoever encoded this had deep botanical, astrological, and alchemical knowledge."

Michael nodded. "Indeed. And why someone as ruthlessly ambitious as Blackthorn would covet this knowledge. Imagine a proprietary medicine based on lost medieval compounds—he could corner the global market. But imagine the cost if he twists something sacred into something exploitative."

Ian straightened, his voice firm. "In which case, we must protect this knowledge."

Michael smiled faintly, encouraged by his friend's resolve. "Yes. But first, we must decode it ourselves. Safely."

Ian's phone suddenly buzzed discreetly. He glanced at the screen message, frowning. "The Archives' security system just flagged unauthorized entry attempts at the outer gate. Someone wants in badly."

Michael felt urgency tightening his chest. "Blackthorn's agents?"

Ian nodded grimly. "That would be my bet. They're attempting electronic overrides. Whoever it is knows exactly what we have."

Michael closed both manuscripts. "Secure these immediately in the vault. Let's shut down all external networks—full lockdown. We'll make it impossible for them."

Ian quickly gathered both volumes, nodding resolutely before disappearing down the shadowy aisle.

CHAPTER
FOUR

VATICAN CITY

Hours later, the Vatican lay silent beneath the blanket of night, its maze-like halls illuminated softly by antique sconces casting gentle halos upon the richly frescoed ceilings. Father Michael made his way briskly through these quiet corridors, his footsteps echoing against polished marble. As prefect of the Vatican Secret Archives, Michael had walked this route countless times—yet tonight, summoned urgently by Cardinal Severino, each step seemed weighted with an ominous uncertainty.

Cardinal Giovanni Severino, Vatican Secretary of State, was a man both respected and feared. To be called privately to his chambers, especially at this late hour, suggested matters of utmost gravity. As Michael ascended the staircase toward Severino's private apartments, he felt an uneasy tightness within his chest.

A young priest met Michael at the ornate double doors. "His Eminence is expecting you," he said serenely, opening one of the heavy wooden panels.

The cardinal's study was richly appointed, its walls lined with towering shelves filled with theological treatises, ecclesiastical histories, and rare texts spanning centuries. A fire flickered in the hearth, casting dancing shadows. Behind a broad mahogany desk, Cardinal Severino sat silently, his distinguished silver hair catching the firelight.

"Come in, Father Dominic," he said benignly, beckoning with a frail but authoritative hand.

"Your Eminence," Michael replied respectfully, approaching and taking a seat before the cardinal's expansive desk. The older man studied him with penetrating eyes, their sharp intelligence undiminished by age.

Severino's gaze lingered thoughtfully before he spoke, his voice deceptively mild. "Father Dominic, I've heard reports about a recent acquisition from Bruges. A document apparently connected with the *Voynich Manuscript*."

Michael offered a quiet, reflective nod. "Yes, Eminence. We believe it may hold significant historical and botanical insights. Possibly even spiritual significance."

The cardinal's brow knitted slightly, his eyes narrowing. "Father, I appreciate that you know the Church's long history regarding manuscripts of questionable origin—particularly those involving botanical alchemy or spiritual mysticism."

"I do," Michael acknowledged cautiously.

"Then I commend you," Severino continued evenly, "for seeing the necessity of securing such texts, to shield them from prying eyes. Manuscripts of such unknown origins can often present dangers far greater than their apparent scholarly value. Your efforts to protect whatever is in this manuscript by consigning it to the Vatican Archives are appreciated. I assume you have already fortified it in a secure area?"

Michael paused, choosing his words carefully. "With respect, Eminence, my intentions are both to understand and protect whatever knowledge might be hidden within its pages. The *Hesperides Codex* explicitly references the *Voynich Manuscript*—an artifact that is notoriously indecipherable yet, to some degree, historically significant. It would be irresponsible to ignore such a discovery."

Severino's expression hardened slightly. "Irresponsible? Father Dominic, this Church has spent centuries shielding humanity from certain truths—truths capable of sowing spiritual confusion, even heresy. You are a respected scholar; you must recognize the perilous nature of certain forms of knowledge. I would strongly caution you against pursuing this matter further. Some paths are best left untrodden."

Michael hesitated, sensing the cardinal knew more than he was revealing. "Is there something specific about this manuscript that troubles you, Eminence?"

For a moment, Severino regarded Michael silently, as if debating internally how much to reveal. Finally, he rose from his chair, sauntering to a tall bookcase behind his desk. Selecting a leather-bound volume, he opened it tenderly, turning pages until he reached a bookmarked section. He placed it deliberately in front of Michael, tapping the page softly.

"Here," Severino murmured, "notes from the Secretariat's archives. Read them attentively."

Michael leaned forward, reading the handwritten lines of faded Latin script. His pulse quickened with each translated word:

"1453, Southern France—heretical botanical texts seized from convent of St. Geneviève. Sect calling themselves Hesperides, cultivating plants said to induce visions, restore memories, and heal ailments through ungodly rites. Texts burned by order of the Holy See. Surviving followers fled persecution, scattering manuscripts throughout Europe. Vigilance required against future attempts to revive these heresies."

MICHAEL RAISED HIS EYES SHARPLY. "This sect—the Hesperides—they believed their plants granted spiritual and physical healing?"

Severino nodded solemnly. "Indeed. They mixed alchemy, herbalism, and mysticism into a volatile heresy. Such ideas, once rekindled, might spread dangerously. Your manuscript from Bruges directly references these Hesperides. I must say again: abandon this investigation."

Michael drew a deep breath, processing what he'd heard. "Eminence, I fully grasp your concerns. But consider that others outside the Church are also pursuing this knowledge. Powerful interests, like Alton Blackthorn, who might misuse such discoveries."

The cardinal's eyes narrowed. "Ah, Blackthorn. Zentara Biogenics once promised medical miracles, yet delivered only scandal and ruin. We are aware that he has returned, and he is even more dangerously ambitious. His presence concerns us greatly."

"All the more reason," Michael argued tactfully, "that

36

the Church should understand exactly what we possess. Ignorance leaves us vulnerable."

Severino sighed heavily, sinking back into his chair, suddenly appearing very weary. "Father Dominic, when I first joined my order decades ago—a Jesuit, like yourself— I believed firmly in the absolute clarity of faith, in the necessity of safeguarding believers from dangerous truths. But the Church—our Church—has evolved, struggling endlessly with which secrets we keep and which we must share. Yet some truths are undeniably dangerous. The Hesperides manuscript, whatever else it could offer, might well embody perilous knowledge capable of upheaval."

Michael paused, then inclined his head pensively, his tone respectful yet resolute. "Your Eminence, I promise discretion and utmost caution. But abandoning this inquiry now, by not understanding what we safeguard, could place others in harm's way. Blackthorn's pursuit confirms that danger is already upon us."

Severino studied Michael intensely, silent for several heartbeats. Finally, he exhaled slowly, nodding reluctantly. "Very well. But tread cautiously, Father Dominic. Keep this strictly contained. If the Hesperides formula is indeed real —if the manuscript genuinely unlocks what remains hidden in the *Voynich*—then its implications extend far beyond mere botanical curiosity."

Michael inclined his head gravely. "I understand."

Severino nodded approvingly. "Good. Trust those closest to you—but trust few others. As we've seen before, Blackthorn's reach is wide, his methods brutal."

The cardinal rose, signaling the meeting's conclusion. Michael stood respectfully, bowing his head. Severino extended his hand, clasping Michael's warmly yet firmly. "You carry a heavy burden, Father Dominic. Remember, the line between guardian and violator of truth is exceedingly thin. Walk it conscientiously."

"I will, Your Eminence," Michael promised sincerely.

Exiting the cardinal's chambers, he ambled back through shadowed corridors toward the Archives. His thoughts churned restlessly, haunted by Severino's warnings. The Church had indeed burned dangerous knowledge before, condemning entire generations to ignorance in the name of spiritual safety. Yet Michael understood, perhaps better than anyone, the serious risks of unguarded truth.

The Hesperides manuscript could unleash miracles—or catastrophes—depending upon whose hands unlocked its secrets first. Blackthorn's presence in this dangerous game heightened the stakes dramatically, placing urgency into every careful step Michael now took.

Reaching the Archives, he padded into the comforting silence, moving directly to the secure vault where the Hesperides manuscript lay protected. Retrieving the vellum-bound volume, he opened it, staring thoughtfully at the delicate Hebrew script lining its margins, whispering promises and threats from the shadows of history.

Cardinal Severino's voice echoed in Michael's mind, an uneasy yet necessary caution against the shadows he now pursued.

Gazing at the illuminated pages before him, Michael felt the weight of centuries press upon his shoulders.

CHAPTER
FIVE

VATICAN CITY

I an Duffy had long believed that the Vatican Secret Archives had a life of their own, a silent, watchful presence that revealed their treasures only when the seeker's patience and persistence had been fully tested. Today, deep beneath the Apostolic Palace, amid labyrinthine corridors lined with ancient tomes, his theory was again being proven true.

It was early morning, yet within these hidden chambers beneath the Vatican, time had a habit of fading away. Ian rubbed his tired eyes and set aside yet another dusty volume. He stood, stretched, and cast his gaze across towering wooden shelves brimming with manuscripts, papal correspondence, and centuries-old ledgers. Each spine bore secrets, whispering silently of forgotten histories.

His search, prompted by Father Dominic, had led him here—into the dimmest corners of the Archives, guided only by instinct and scant historical references. Father Dominic had tasked Ian with finding any references to what the cardinal had shared with him: anything from the mid-1500s in southern France, potentially related to a herbarium or the convent of St. Geneviève. Cardinal Severino's warnings had only lent urgency to this quest, heightening Ian's awareness that time was slipping dangerously away.

Running slender fingers along the shelves, Ian paused suddenly, eyes narrowing. An oddly bound ledger, tucked into the shadow of two heavy volumes, caught his eye. Its leather cover was worn, cracked with age, faint gold lettering barely visible: *Registrum Herbarum, anno 1527.* Carefully, Ian pulled it from its resting place, feeling its significant weight and solidity in his hands.

He moved swiftly back to his worktable beneath a gentle pool of lamplight. The ledger's ancient clasp was fragile, opening reluctantly with a faint creak. Ian gingerly turned thick vellum pages, each inscribed in a neat yet archaic hand, ink faded to a pale sepia. Immediately, his heart quickened as Latin words appeared—botanical terms, zodiac references, and cryptic diagrams filling margins densely.

Ian leaned closer, reading slowly, translating as he went. The author had diligently recorded plant species accompanied by elaborate zodiacal symbols and celestial alignments. Each plant entry was annotated with lunar phases, times of harvest, and exact methods of preparation.

His pulse quickened as he noticed a detailed illustration of a peculiar plant—two roots intertwined, one inked boldly red, the other green—exactly as depicted in the *Voynich* folio Michael had studied. Beneath the illustration, the Latin notation read clearly: *Radix Gemini. Luna nova. Salutem animae.* "Twin-root. New moon. Healing of the soul."

Excitedly, Ian traced symbols farther down the page, recognizing familiar *Voynich* glyphs drawn precisely beside the Latin notes. This was explicit proof: the Vatican had once knowingly possessed botanical and astrological knowledge directly connected to the mysterious *Voynich Manuscript.* His thoughts raced: Why had this information been hidden away? Had its implications frightened the Church enough to bury the manuscript within these forgotten shelves?

Ian continued scanning pages, finding repeated references to a certain formula: *Lumen Viride.* Its name appeared again and again, emphasized heavily alongside the plant diagrams and cryptic astrological symbols. He whispered the name faintly to himself: *"Lumen Viride...* the Green Light."

He flipped pages faster, curiosity building urgently. The ledger described intricate rituals involving this green compound—ceremonial preparations aligned accurately with lunar cycles. Ian read rapidly, stunned by the depth of detail. These ancient practices were minutely noted, suggesting genuine medicinal or spiritual importance.

Finally, near the end of the ledger, he found an entry with a hurried tone, its handwriting less controlled, seemingly penned under duress:

"Aprilis, anno 1527. Official suppression ordered by His Holiness. Botanical manuscripts seized, censored, or destroyed. Brothers scattered, knowledge dispersed. May God forgive us.

Manuscriptum Hesperidum absconditum est—*The Hesperides manuscript has been hidden."*

READING IT, Ian froze. The Hesperides manuscript—the exact name referenced by Cardinal Severino and now secured in the Vatican. Clearly, this ledger belonged to someone involved in preserving or concealing this controversial knowledge at the time of suppression. What had frightened the Church enough to warrant such dramatic censorship?

As Ian turned the fragile, yellowed pages of the forgotten ledger, the delicate, age-obscured script caught his eye. Leaning closer, he slowly deciphered entries referencing a name he hadn't encountered before: Juana de la Cruz Vazquez y Gutiérrez. Curiosity piqued, he began reading more intently, faithfully transcribing the faint notes into a more readable form.

Then, turning to other research material, he discovered that Franciscan Sister Juana de la Cruz was a fifteenth-century Spanish mystic and influential abbess from Castile, revered for her intense botanical knowledge and deeply spiritual insights. Recognized as both healer and scholar, Juana had devoted herself to documenting rare herbs, their properties intricately linked to celestial movements and cycles. It was likely she had read, or at least been aware of, the earlier enigmatic Roger Bacon Cipher/*Voynich Manuscript* itself. That would explain the similarities in some botanical images. Yet despite her benevolent intentions, Juana had faced suspicion and persecution from Church authorities, who viewed her visionary practices as dangerously close to heresy.

Aware of the growing threats, Juana had apparently

cleverly concealed her findings within an encoded manuscript—the *Hesperides Codex*—designed to protect her invaluable knowledge and subtly challenge the oppressive religious dogma of her era. This *Registrum Herbarum* corroborated that she had secreted the Codex away for safety. Ian's heart quickened as he researched this remarkable woman further, discovering how Juana's writings had eventually spread secretly among trusted intellectual circles throughout Europe, profoundly influencing various scholars, alchemists, and mystics.

Ian's pulse raced with excitement as he realized the potential implications. Here was concrete historical evidence pointing to Juana de la Cruz as the author of the manuscript that Michael and Hana were currently investigating. Carefully transcribing every detail, he meticulously documented the references connecting Juana to the botanical experiments, celestial alignments, and encoded symbolism described in the codex.

Quickly gathering his notes, Ian snapped photos of critical pages, ensuring he captured every detail. Yet as he worked, a subtle unease prickled at his neck. Instinctively, he paused, listening closely. Deep silence filled the archives —yet the silence suddenly felt unnatural, oppressive, as if the archives themselves were holding their breath.

Slowly, Ian rose, stepping around shelves toward the Archives' main door. He froze abruptly. The door was slightly ajar, its security latch overridden. He was no longer alone.

Heart pounding, Ian quickly dimmed his workspace lamp and concealed the ledger beneath a pile of unrelated manuscripts. Then, taking quiet, measured steps, he moved toward the shadows of the shelving, listening intently.

Faint footsteps echoed nearby—someone cautiously yet purposefully entering the deepest Archive chamber. Ian's pulse quickened. Only authorized Vatican personnel could access this section, yet these movements felt surreptitious, calculated, invasive.

He pressed himself flat against a heavy oak bookshelf, holding his breath as two dark-clad figures emerged cautiously, faces obscured by hoods. Despite their being dressed as monks, Ian immediately recognized their tactical bearing, their military footwear—professional operatives, undoubtedly hired by Alton Blackthorn. They silently moved toward Ian's workspace, eyes searching intently. Clearly, they knew exactly what they sought: the Hesperides manuscript or anything associated with it.

A surge of anger mixed with fear tightened Ian's chest. Whatever knowledge this ledger held, it must remain protected. Carefully sliding deeper into shadows, he made a swift decision. He couldn't overpower trained operatives alone, but he could evade them and alert Vatican security.

Using the maze-like layout to his advantage, Ian moved silently toward the opposite exit, avoiding creaky floorboards he knew intimately from years working here. Finally reaching the emergency call box mounted discreetly near the entrance, he activated the silent alarm, alerting security and simultaneously triggering the automatic locking mechanisms within the Archives.

Instantly, heavy doors throughout the complex began sealing, metallic clicks echoing through the vast spaces. Voices erupted behind him—urgent, angry whispers as the intruders realized their predicament. Ian allowed himself a grim smile, stepping into an adjoining corridor, safely locking the Archives doors behind him.

Minutes later, breathless and anxious, Ian found Father

Dominic and Karl Dengler waiting impatiently near the Archives' main entrance, concern etched across their faces.

"Blackthorn's people breached the Archives," Ian reported instantly, catching his breath. "I secured a ledger I discovered—it clearly ties *Voynich* symbols to the Bruges manuscript and mentions the Hesperides suppression. But we must act quickly."

Just as Ian turned back toward the Archive corridor, a distant clang rang out—metal on stone, sharp and reverberant.

Karl's head snapped up. "Someone's forcing a secondary exit."

Michael's brow furrowed. "I thought the lockdown sealed all routes."

Ian shook his head. "All primary doors—yes. But they never retrofitted the oldest ventilation corridor, the one near the sub-vaults. I mentioned it last year during the security audit."

Karl didn't wait to be asked. He was already moving. "Come on!"

They dashed through the adjoining corridor, their footfalls muffled by the thick stones of the Vatican's ancient foundations. The smell of old paper and ozone from the lockdown system lingered in the air, thick as incense.

Rounding a corner, they saw it—the grated archway to the narrow stone channel where deliveries and waste had once moved by handcart. The door there had been sealed halfway, but someone had jammed it with a wedge of archival shelving. Papers fluttered wildly in the draft. Beyond the door, two shadowy forms squirmed through the narrowing space like rats abandoning a sinking ship.

Karl broke into a sprint, weapon drawn—a trained deterrent, not a call to violence.

"Halt!" he roared. "This is sovereign Vatican territory!"

One intruder—tall, lean, and agile—slipped through just in time, vanishing into the night. The second, bulkier, wasn't so fortunate. His backpack caught on the lowering gate.

Michael reached his side. "We've got him!"

But in a heartbeat, the figure twisted free, abandoning the pack and lurching through the last sliver just as the gate slammed shut behind him with a deafening clang.

All three stood motionless, staring at the vibrating door.

Karl exhaled sharply, frustration creasing his jaw. "Too close."

Michael bent, retrieving the dropped pack. Inside, a tablet blinked to life briefly before shutting down—encrypted, but revealing a symbol unmistakably tied to Blackthorn's biotech firm. And nestled beneath it, a slim, weatherproof file containing photos, maps, and what looked like infrared scans of the Archives' deepest vaults.

Ian's voice was icy now. "They were mapping the Archives. Planning something bigger."

Michael nodded grimly. "This wasn't theft. It was reconnaissance."

Karl looked toward the sealed doorway. "In any case, we'd best assume they'll return—with better tools and worse intentions."

Michael stood slowly, his voice low and certain. "We'll be ready. I'll alert Cardinal Severino. We have undeniable proof now that Blackthorn is after these manuscripts. I'm guessing the attack on Hana somehow fits with that as well, not purely revenge. Our next steps must be decisive."

As Karl moved to secure the perimeter further, Ian turned back toward the Archives doors, adrenaline ebbing slightly. Tonight's revelations had shattered the Archives' hushed tranquility, unveiling secrets long buried yet dangerously potent.

Meeting Michael's steady gaze, Ian realized they now stood at the crossroads of truth, danger, and responsibility.

Whatever secrets the *Lumen Viride* formula guarded, the Church had once buried them deeply—yet now, centuries later, they had emerged powerfully into the present, demanding answers, courage, and caution.

Father Dominic clasped Ian's shoulder warmly. "Well done, Ian. Tonight, you've shown bravery and wisdom. But it seems our task is only beginning."

Ian nodded gravely, accepting the heavy truth. "I understand, Father. Whatever happens next, I'm with you."

Together, they stood in silence, steeling themselves for the storm about to unfold—one that might reshape faith, knowledge, and history itself.

CHAPTER
SIX

VATICAN CITY

In a modest, quiet room deep within the Vatican's administrative wing, Sister Teresa Drinkwater sat before an array of glowing screens, her habit illuminated faintly by the digital displays surrounding her workspace. Known affectionately throughout the Vatican simply as Sister Teri, the Pauline nun had long overseen the Vatican's complex digital systems, confidently safeguarding the delicate secrets entrusted to her care.

Tonight, however, her usual serenity had given way to growing unease. She frowned at the rapidly shifting data streaming across her primary monitor, her eyes narrowing with suspicion as lines of code quickly flickered by. For several hours, Teri had been monitoring subtle but persistent attempts to penetrate Vatican firewalls—attacks that were increasingly aggressive, well-targeted, and worryingly sophisticated.

Something was wrong. Very wrong.

Reaching decisively for her headset, she hastily contacted Ian Duffy.

His voice was tense when he answered. "Teri? Any update?"

"More attempts at unauthorized access," she replied. "They're intensifying. And whoever's doing this isn't a casual hacker—this feels orchestrated. Professional."

Ian's sharp exhale crackled through the line. "You think it might be Blackthorn's people?"

"Likely," she confirmed grimly. "The pattern matches known techniques used by Zentara Biogenics before its collapse. Whoever is behind this is highly trained—ex-intelligence, military, corporate espionage. This isn't amateur work."

Ian's voice tightened. "Can they breach us?"

Teri hesitated briefly, running her eyes swiftly across diagnostic screens. "Not yet—but they're probing methodically, looking for weak points. They clearly know we've digitized catalogues of recent manuscript acquisitions."

"Specifically, the Hesperides manuscript," Ian muttered darkly.

"Yes," Teri confirmed. "That's their main target. Access attempts spiked significantly once the Scriptorium registered it digitally."

Ian sighed heavily. "Hold the line, Teri—I'll alert Father Dominic and Karl immediately."

"Understood," Teri responded firmly, her fingers promptly initiating countermeasures to strengthen firewall layers.

Minutes ticked by painfully slowly as Teri continued to analyze the attack patterns. The Vatican's digital archives were among the most heavily secured systems globally, yet tonight she sensed vulnerability as never before.

Finally, her door opened quietly, and Father Michael entered alongside Ian and Karl.

"Teri, talk to me," Michael urged gently. "What exactly are we facing?"

She gestured at her screens. "Advanced cyber-penetration tactics. Extremely professional, relentless, coordinated. Blackthorn's people, undoubtedly. They're using precise algorithms to bypass firewall protections, searching systematically for our digitized records referencing the *Hesperides Codex* and *Voynich Manuscript*."

Karl folded his arms, expression grim. "Have they gotten through?"

Teri shook her head reassuringly. "Not yet, but they're methodically probing every angle. I've reinforced the firewall layers multiple times. However, it's not just the digital penetration that worries me—they've clearly had internal assistance, someone who understands our system architecture intimately."

Karl glanced sharply toward Michael. "An internal informant?"

Michael's jaw tightened. "It wouldn't surprise me. If you recall, Blackthorn has penetrated Vatican ranks before."

Teri nodded solemnly. "That's my fear. Whoever assists them knows our system intricacies, our catalogue protocols, and—most worryingly—the exact timing of recent manuscript acquisitions."

Ian's voice hardened. "They knew the moment we brought the Hesperides manuscript into our digital catalogue. That's chillingly specific intel."

Michael sighed heavily. "Who else but someone in the

Vatican would know exactly what to target and when? The acquisition was authorized by Cardinal Servino, who would have discussed it with the Curia. That covers a wide number of people, unfortunately. Teri, can we track this internal leak?"

Teri hesitated slightly. "Possibly. I'm running advanced monitoring software now, flagging internal logins, cross-referencing access points. But if they've hidden their tracks cleverly—"

"Do your best," Michael interjected.

Teri smiled briefly, appreciating his unwavering support. "I'll find them."

Karl stepped forward, voice determined. "In the meantime, strengthen all physical and digital security measures immediately. Any internal leak compromises both our safety and the manuscript's secrecy. We can't afford further breaches."

Teri nodded readily. "Agreed. I'll escalate security protocols immediately—implementing biometric access controls, multi-factor authentications, and full lockdowns on sensitive files."

"Good," Michael approved firmly. "Whatever it takes."

As Karl and Ian moved quickly toward the exit to reinforce physical security measures, Michael lingered attentively, gazing at Teri's screens with troubled eyes. "Teri, did you uncover anything further about Blackthorn's new venture?"

She nodded seriously, pivoting toward a secondary monitor displaying corporate logos and complex data trails. "Blackthorn founded a new pharmaceutical company after Zentara collapsed: Genetica Therapeutics. Publicly, it focuses on groundbreaking treatments for cognitive disorders, memory enhancement, and neurological therapies. But privately, Genetica has aggressively acquired obscure botanical research labs, purchasing rare medicinal plant collections—especially medieval herbal manuscripts, alchemical texts, and ethnobotanical records. Anything related to rare plants or unusual pharmacological formulas."

Michael's expression darkened. "They're trying to corner a lost historical remedy—a botanical compound, perhaps a formula, something like *Lumen Viride*? If Blackthorn succeeds, he could potentially monopolize a potent treatment or exploit it in a dangerous manner. The Church once suppressed such knowledge because of its perceived dangers."

Teri leaned forward intently. "Then we must stop him. We can't let the likes of Blackthorn get hold of knowledge like this. He'd commercialize or weaponize it."

Michael's eyes conveyed quiet understanding. "And that's why we trust you to guard our digital frontiers, Teri. Without your vigilance, we'd be completely vulnerable."

She smiled faintly, determinedly. "I'm on it."

He squeezed her shoulder warmly before turning to leave, his quiet footsteps echoing away. Alone once more, Teri stared at her screens, her determination renewed. Tonight's digital siege confirmed her worst fears: someone inside the Vatican had betrayed their sacred trust.

Hours passed unnoticed, a blur of keystrokes and security reinforcements. Finally, as dawn's gentle light crept into the sky outside her narrow window, Teri noticed a subtle yet critical anomaly appear suddenly on her screen. Her heart quickened—an internal Vatican user, identified only as *"Archive_LVL3,"* had accessed highly restricted manuscript data exactly at the timestamp matching the external penetration attempts.

"Gotcha," she whispered fiercely, quickly tagging the profile for further investigation.

She immediately called Michael, who answered through a yawn. "Teri?"

"Father Dominic, I've identified our leak—an internal Archives-level account just accessed restricted files aligning exactly with external attacks. The infiltration matches perfectly. I can trace this further."

Michael's voice sharpened. "Excellent work, Teri. Follow every lead rigorously and discreetly. Let's catch this traitor now."

She nodded unflinchingly. "I'll handle it personally, but it will take some time. And Father, this confirms conclusively that Blackthorn is moving rapidly. He's closer than we realized."

Michael blew out a breath in exasperation. "Then we must move faster still. Whatever formula lies within the Hesperides manuscript and *Voynich*'s symbols, we must decipher it before Blackthorn's forces do."

Teri hung up, steeling herself for action. Her fingers moved deftly across the keyboard, implementing the final layers of protection around their fragile digital sanctuary.

Outside, Vatican City gradually awoke beneath a dawn sky glowing with gold and amber hues. Yet within her small room, Sister Teri knew their peaceful façade now concealed a deepening storm.

But whatever lay ahead, she vowed silently, her resolve hardening as her screens continued their vigilant watch— she would guard the Church's secrets fiercely, unyieldingly, until the very end.

CHAPTER
SEVEN

MADRID & TOLEDO, SPAIN

The private jet—a sleek Dassault Falcon 900 bearing the Saint-Clair family crest on its gleaming white fuselage—lifted off smoothly from Rome's Fiumicino Airport, climbing rapidly into the crystalline Mediterranean sky. From her comfortable seat near the window, Hana watched the Roman landscape recede, dissolving into a patchwork of fields and ancient roads, then disappearing beneath clouds tinged golden by the morning sun. When her grandfather passed, he left his extensive and lucrative banking empire to her. However, unlike some beneficiaries who inherited substantially, Hana's devotion to her career as a journalist continued regardless of her newfound wealth. She did, however, appreciate the benefits of private travel, serving as a true asset when it came to "getting the story," wherever that happened to be in the world.

Michael's voice interrupted her thoughts with, "I could get used to this."

She looked at him, puzzled, and he grinned. "A private jet to take us wherever we need or want to be? What an amazing benefit you have, Hana."

"Well," she said cautiously, "maybe you need to get used to it. We are engaged after all, and this will eventually be as much yours as mine to use as you wish. There will be various benefits when we are married," she added coyly. She saw the hint of a blush on his cheeks as he glanced ahead at the others on the plane. The Pope had only recently given his blessing to priests who wished to marry. It had taken little time for Michael to ask for Hana's hand. But setting a wedding date had been difficult for them for many career and personal reasons. In the meantime, the church still expected a certain degree of decorum from those priests who chose to marry. Michael took his vows and the church's preferences to heart, and they avoided openly displaying their relationship.

Nearby, Karl and Lukas sat silently as if relaxed, but Michael knew their minds were constantly alert despite the tranquil surroundings. If they had heard the flirtatious banter, they had the discretion not to react.

"Oh, I don't know," he tried to recover with a smile. "I'm rather used to my benefits as a Vatican priest. My 200 square-foot apartment, including laundry services and endless hours in the archives, is a pretty rewarding life just as it is." Yet even as the playful words escaped his lips, his eyes took in the serene and loving face of his fiancée, and he knew how much he loved her and wanted them to be together.

They smiled softly at each other, knowing their time

together would come, even as they turned their attention back to their earlier work.

Father Michael sighed and began to leaf quietly through his notes, as he became, again, absorbed in the mysterious paths of botanical alchemy they were pursuing.

Hana leaned back, feeling the faint vibration of the powerful engines beneath her feet. Though accustomed to travel, this journey felt different—urgent, weighted with the significance of ancient mysteries threatening to erupt into the present. It had been mere days since Bruges, the attempted theft within the Vatican, and now the revelations from the digital attacks on the Vatican Archives. Everything seemed to rush forward relentlessly, compelling them toward Juana de la Cruz's Monastery of Santa María de la Cruz in Cubas de la Sagra, a village between Toledo and Madrid.

Michael glanced up from his notes, sensing her unease. "We'll land in Madrid in less than two hours. Then a quick train to the monastery," he reassured her.

Hana nodded. "Do you really believe Juana's monastery still holds something tangible? It's been nearly five centuries."

Michael smiled faintly, confidence mingled with caution. "Manuscripts and sacred texts aren't always confined to parchment. Often they're etched in stone, concealed in architecture—especially something as delicate and controversial as Juana's botanical alchemy."

Hana's curiosity sharpened. "And you're certain the zodiacal clues from Ian's ledger lead directly to Toledo?"

Michael set aside his papers, leaning forward slightly. "Ian's ledger clearly referenced Juana's monastery, noting an astrological sequence corresponding precisely to *Voynich* symbolism. It can't be coincidence. Juana practiced in nearby Toledo, famously blending mysticism, theology, and herbal medicine, until the Church intervened. She left subtle clues behind."

Hana studied him closely. "And Blackthorn—he'll have made the connection too."

Michael's expression darkened slightly. "I'm afraid so. Sister Teri confirmed last night that Genetica Therapeutics recently purchased old monastic property records across Castile. Blackthorn knows exactly what he's looking for, and where. We can just hope we are one step ahead of them at this point."

The aircraft sped onward, sunlight shifting subtly as they crossed the azure expanse of the Mediterranean toward Spain. Soon, the Iberian coastline emerged, a narrow ribbon of ochre sand and green hills dotted with villages. Within minutes, Madrid sprawled beneath them, a tapestry of streets and plazas glinting beneath the midday sun. Hana felt a brief moment of calm amid their rising tension.

On landing at Barajas Airport, they quickly transferred to a waiting limousine, navigating Madrid's bustling streets toward Atocha Railway Station. The midday crowds moved fluidly, unaware of the delicate historical web drawing this small party toward Toledo. Within half an hour, the high-speed train carried them swiftly south across the sun-warmed Castilian plains toward the ancient city.

The moment they stepped off the train in Toledo, Hana felt the city's historic gravity settle around her—a powerful aura of time layered thickly over narrow cobblestone streets and sandstone walls baked golden in the afternoon sun. Toledo rose above the River Tagus, its clustered towers and rooftops shimmering faintly beneath the deep Spanish sky.

Outside the station, a middle-aged priest, Father Emilio, awaited them patiently beside a dark SUV bearing the discreet insignia of the Archdiocese. He greeted Michael warmly, eyes kind yet guarded. "Welcome to Toledo. I've secured the monastery grounds. You'll have the privacy you need."

Michael thanked him gratefully, and they drove upward through winding streets lined with whitewashed houses and blooming geraniums cascading from balconies. Eventually, they reached the crumbling monastery of Santa María de la Cruz, its medieval arches entwined in ivy, sunlight filtering placidly through ancient, broken stonework.

Entering quietly, Hana immediately felt the weight of history in the shadows and dust. A courtyard opened before them, enclosed by faded frescoes and slender columns. Weeds and wild herbs sprouted from crevices, their fragrance drifting faintly in the warm air.

Michael guided them toward the main cloister, his notebook open, eyes scanning mindfully. "Ian's ledger mentioned Juana concealed a zodiacal map somewhere near the central chapel."

Hana followed him closely, stepping gingerly over cracked paving stones. The chapel was smaller than she had expected, its roof long since collapsed, open to the deep blue sky above. At the far end, partly obscured by rubble and ivy, stood a stone relief—a circular zodiac, its carvings worn but unmistakable.

"This is it," Michael breathed, stepping quickly forward, brushing dirt and moss away with his fingers.

Hana moved beside him, camera already capturing every detail.

She traced the zodiac signs vigilantly. "Strange," she murmured, her brow furrowing. "The signs are out of traditional sequence. Scorpio's positioned at the zenith."

Michael examined the carving intently, eyes alight with realization. "Scorpio represents regeneration in medieval astrology. Perhaps Juana deliberately emphasized it to symbolize rebirth, healing—exactly what *Lumen Viride* purportedly offered."

Hana retrieved her notebook and a printed copy of the *Voynich* zodiacal folio. Placing it beside the carving, her breath caught sharply. "They match exactly," she whispered. "Look—each constellation aligns perfectly, marking nodes that must represent plants or medicinal stages."

Michael traced the symbols intently. "It's not just astrology. It's a botanical and alchemical calendar. Each constellation symbolizes the ideal harvesting and preparation conditions, aligned squarely with lunar phases."

He paused, tracing an inscription along Scorpio's edge, barely discernible beneath centuries of erosion: "*Sub rosa viridi, lumen sequitur.*"

"'Under the green rose, the light follows,'" he translated smoothly, exchanging an intense glance with Hana. "The rose symbolism indicates secrecy. Juana was guiding initiates conscientiously, deliberately hiding powerful knowledge."

Behind them, Karl and Lukas patrolled soundlessly yet attentively around the perimeter, eyes scanning continually for any disturbance. Karl approached cautiously, voice low but urgent. "We have observers—two men with cameras near the eastern ridge. Lukas is circling to intercept if necessary."

Hana tensed, anxiety flaring. "Blackthorn's men?"

Karl nodded grimly.

Michael's jaw tightened. "How did they know...?" He shook his head. "Hana, we need to document this quickly. We may not get another chance."

Hana painstakingly photographed each detail, while Michael sketched accurate diagrams, noting every glyph and alignment in his field notebook. Their urgency grew as Karl watched closely, his radio murmuring quiet updates from Lukas.

Within minutes, Lukas returned, face grim but composed. "They withdrew once they knew we'd spotted them. But they were professionals—armed, trained."

Michael exhaled slowly, closing his notebook. "Then we have less time than we thought. Blackthorn understands exactly what's at stake."

Hana looked around the chapel once more, feeling history resonate powerfully within its walls. "So, where does this map lead us next?"

Michael studied the zodiac again. "It's a sequential map of sacred preparation sites. Each node likely represents another location, another step toward completing the formula. Maybe where ingredients are to be found? Maybe some process we don't yet understand?"

He traced again Scorpio's prominent position. "The first step—harvesting or initial preparation—will likely align with the lunar cycle in Scorpio. But these nodes are useless without something to—" Michael looked up. "Of course! The key to the locations had to be kept separately, for safety. Ian's ledger... I think that the ledger he found might identify where Juana would have directed her initiates."

Hana nodded resolutely. "Then we should return to Rome immediately. And trust that Ian's ledger will provide the clarity we need."

As they left the monastery grounds, shadows lengthened faintly across the ancient city, amber twilight bathing Toledo in gentle warmth. Yet Hana felt no comfort in its beauty now, sensing the looming threat posed by Alton Blackthorn and the historical weight of secrets that had brought them here.

Glancing back once, she saw the ruined chapel bathed in golden light, serene yet silently powerful, its secrets still guarded beneath stone and time. She felt certain Juana had left them more than merely clues—she had left a message, a challenge, a formula, a sacred truth waiting centuries for the right hands to unlock.

Hana shivered slightly, pulling her coat tighter as Karl guided them toward the waiting SUV. A storm was gathering, powerful and uncertain—but she felt no hesitation, no doubt.

VATICAN CITY

Sister Teri sat silently within her softly illuminated workspace deep within the Vatican, her usually steady hands trembling slightly. Her screens flickered, displaying encrypted data streams she had fully traced through layers of compromised networks.

She expelled a breath as realization hit—Genetica Therapeutics had deliberately infiltrated the secure data systems of one of the largest humanitarian relief charities, Global Aid Alliance, secretly using their infrastructure to mount increasingly sophisticated attacks on Vatican networks.

Teri felt her stomach tighten, cold dread gripping her. Global Aid Alliance provided emergency medical support, refugee assistance, and humanitarian aid globally. Disrupting their operations—even if only intended to negate the attacks from Genetica temporarily—could harm thousands of innocent people. Yet doing nothing meant the Vatican's critical systems and invaluable archives could suffer irreparable damage.

Her mind raced, the ethical implications overwhelming. "Dear God," she murmured, eyes closing briefly. "How can I choose between the Vatican's safety and innocent lives?"

Her heart pounded with anguish. She reached for her secure phone, hesitating briefly, then dialed Ian's private number. "Ian," she began urgently as he answered immediately, "We have a severe ethical problem. Genetica's attacks are routing through Global Aid Alliance's infrastructure."

Ian paused before responding, his tone confused at her inaction. "Teri, we need immediate intervention. Can't you do that?"

She nodded slowly, her voice heavy with dread. "But intervention means disabling the charity's global network temporarily. Thousands could suffer immediately from that interruption."

Ian hesitated, now clearly troubled. "I understand. But if the Vatican Archives are compromised, we risk a major breach."

Teri's voice tightened with an emotional yet resolved

determination. "I know. I just wish there was another way."

Ian responded solemnly, recognizing the immense weight she carried. "You realize, don't you, that this may be exactly why they chose that far-reaching humanitarian organization as their Trojan horse? It was to put us— assuming we discovered their digital pathway—in this exact situation, making us face this ethical dilemma. They don't care about the consequences, but they know we would. This is on them, Teri, not you. I trust *your* judgment. You know how to navigate these digital platforms and do it quickly. Trust in yourself. I'll stand by your decision—whatever it is."

She let out a quick breath, gripping her phone tightly, tears forming in her eyes. "Pray for me, Ian. Pray that I make the right choice."

CHAPTER
EIGHT

ROME & VATICAN CITY

K arl Dengler adjusted the small handheld sensor
as he prudently swept it along the interior of
Hana Sinclair's jet, his eyes focused on the
device's softly glowing screen. Beside him, Lukas Bischoff
methodically inspected the aircraft's paneling and
upholstery, hands deftly searching every crevice with
practiced efficiency. The two Swiss guards worked well
together, not just as fellow soldiers but as life partners.
Such relationships were not unheard of in their careers, but
discretion remained imperative. Only their closest friends
realized their commitment to each other ran deeper than
even the normal camaraderie of protectors of the Vatican
and the Church's hierarchy. Today, they worked tirelessly
to grasp why some of those dear friends were in danger
from Alton Blacktorn.

The Dassault Falcon 900, securely parked within a
guarded hangar at Rome's Ciampino Airport, had

returned only hours before from their tense journey to Madrid. Karl and Lukas, determined not to overlook even the slightest vulnerability, worked with thorough precision. The recent incidents had heightened their vigilance beyond routine precautions.

"Anything?" Karl asked, pausing briefly to watch Lukas's progress.

"Nothing obvious yet," Lukas replied, running fingertips deliberately along seams in the leather seats. "But Blackthorn's men are pros. They wouldn't leave anything in plain sight."

Karl nodded thoughtfully, turning toward the cockpit. As he passed the galley compartment, the sensor's soft beep suddenly intensified, rapid pulses indicating an anomaly. He halted immediately, eyes narrowing.

"Lukas—here," he murmured. "There's something."

Lukas promptly joined him, retrieving a small toolkit from his pocket. Karl stepped aside, allowing Lukas to expertly pry open the panel beneath the coffee maker. Within seconds, a tiny metallic device no larger than a coin fell into Lukas's waiting palm.

"Tracker," Lukas confirmed grimly, scrutinizing it closely. "High-frequency GPS transmitter. Probably activated remotely."

Karl sighed heavily, examining the sophisticated bug with wary concern. "Blackthorn knows everywhere we've flown."

Lukas secured the tiny device into an evidence bag, shaking his head gravely. "He's always one step ahead. But now we know what we're dealing with. We'll run a full frequency scan of the hangar and Michael's apartment tonight, just to be safe."

Karl clasped his partner's shoulder, smiling warmly.

"Good idea, Lukas. If Blackthorn has other trackers in Rome, we'll find them."

As they exited the jet, Karl's thoughts turned inward. The unique nature of Blackthorn's espionage unsettled him. It was a disturbing escalation—and one he would have to share with Father Dominic.

MEANWHILE, in the quiet shadows of the Apostolic Palace, Father Michael Dominic entered Cardinal Severino's private chambers with cautious respect. The cardinal sat waiting at his broad, mahogany desk, the room softly illuminated by dim lamps and flickering candlelight.

"Your Eminence," Michael greeted the Secretary of State, bowing his head respectfully.

Severino gestured kindly toward the chair opposite him. "Please, sit. I understand your journey to Toledo proved... enlightening."

Michael took the offered seat, nodding seriously. "Indeed, Eminence. The monastery of Juana de la Cruz revealed remarkable details. Her zodiacal carvings correspond directly to the *Voynich Manuscript*'s astronomical diagrams, distinctly encoding particular botanical rituals. There is no doubt now that she was the author of the *Hesperides Codex* and that the *Voynich Manuscript* had influenced her. It appears Juana was preserving both a botanical and a spiritual alchemy— possibly even a sacred knowledge—that aligns closely with historical Christian mysticism."

The cardinal's eyes narrowed as if preoccupied. "Sacred knowledge? In what sense?"

Michael leaned forward, voice lowering slightly. "Juana's writings emphasize an extensive theology of healing. She integrated herbal medicine, astrology, and prayer into a unified practice, suggesting not merely physical healing, but spiritual regeneration—an almost resurrection-like symbolism connected to the zodiac."

Severino regarded Michael with quiet intensity. "Resurrection symbolism is inherently powerful, Father Dominic. Such doctrines, though spiritual in intention, have historically been perceived as dangerously heretical."

Michael raised an eyebrow briefly, signaling agreement. "Exactly why Juana and her followers concealed their knowledge so thoroughly. And now, centuries later, Alton Blackthorn seeks to exploit it commercially."

The cardinal sighed, contemplating this. "You've proven your point. But tread cautiously, Father. History reminds us that the boundaries between heresy, science, and spirituality are perilously thin. The Church must guard truth, but also stability."

"I understand," Michael acknowledged cautiously. "But Eminence, hiding such knowledge indefinitely is impossible. Blackthorn's aggressive pursuit of the *Lumen Viride* shows the danger already upon us."

Severino nodded reluctantly. "Then we must prepare ourselves—and safeguard these documents wisely. Trust few, Father Dominic."

Michael rose, slightly bowing again. "I promise caution. But inaction is no longer an option."

As he departed the cardinal's chambers, Michael felt deeply unsettled yet determined. He now clearly understood Severino's warnings—the knowledge Juana had preserved was transformative, volatile, and dangerously enticing. Safeguarding it would test them all.

. . .

WITHIN THE DIGITAL nerve center of the Vatican, Ian Duffy leaned intently toward the glowing monitors. Beside him, Sister Teri rapidly entered new security protocols, her fingers flying across the keyboard with practiced ease—though the steady rhythm masked a deeper turmoil beneath her focused expression.

"We've blocked most external access attempts," she murmured, scanning rapidly scrolling data streams. "But Blackthorn's team keeps adjusting their methods. They clearly have internal help."

Ian frowned, leaning in closer. "Can you isolate internal access patterns—track which accounts repeatedly access sensitive manuscript data?"

Teri nodded solemnly, eyes never leaving the screen, yet her heart remained burdened by an unresolved ethical conflict—one she had privately uncovered earlier, involving the compromised networks of Global Aid Alliance. Each keystroke felt heavier, knowing the humanitarian organization's infrastructure was still unknowingly facilitating Genetica's aggressive cyber-attacks against the Vatican.

"Yes, but whoever it is knows our architecture intimately," Teri replied, masking her deeper concern. "They've concealed their presence skillfully—though every digital mask leaves subtle traces."

She paused suddenly, eyes narrowing sharply as data cascaded before her. "Look here," she indicated, pointing to a series of logins highlighted prominently on her screen. "This account—'*Archive_LVL3*'—accessed restricted files multiple times last night. Always briefly, discreetly."

Ian's expression hardened with immediate seriousness. "Who owns it?"

"Supposedly dormant," she answered, tapping

commands rapidly to confirm her findings. "But clearly someone has reactivated and misappropriated it. Each login coincides with Blackthorn's external digital penetration attempts."

Ian exhaled tensely, visibly disturbed by the confirmation. "Then we've found our mole. Can we pinpoint a physical location?"

Teri hesitated slightly, her fingers momentarily suspended above the keyboard. To do that would require backtracking through Global Aid Alliance's system, something she hesitated to do. Her mind flashed briefly back to the compromised humanitarian network and the grave ethical implications that still haunted her. She hadn't yet made her choice: to act decisively, protecting the Vatican but harming innocent lives, or to wait, risking catastrophic consequences. Her heart clenched painfully with indecision.

"Not yet," she finally admitted, her voice careful yet steady. "They've routed logins through external proxies. But I'll activate silent tracers immediately. The moment they log in again, we'll know their exact location."

Ian nodded approvingly. "Excellent. If we capture the informant, we disrupt Blackthorn significantly. But until then, we must assume all our movements are monitored."

Teri glanced anxiously at Ian, her expression subtly betraying an additional layer of concern. "What worries me most is their expertise. Whoever this informant is, they're familiar with Vatican procedures—someone inside, someone trusted."

Ian grimaced, acutely troubled by the thought. "I'll brief Michael immediately. Meanwhile, let's reinforce security protocols."

Teri offered a slight, strained smile. "You bet. They won't breach easily again."

As they hastily reinforced firewalls, sealed digital access points, and deployed sophisticated monitoring systems throughout Vatican networks, Teri's internal conflict intensified. Beneath her practiced efficiency lay an unresolved moral question she knew she must soon confront: how far could she ethically go to protect vital historical truths if innocent lives were at stake?

She vowed to herself that the moment of decision was fast approaching—but for now, secrecy was essential. The internal mole threatened their unity and resolve, and she couldn't risk further compromise by prematurely disclosing her ethical struggle.

As Ian finished entering final security protocols, Teri resolved within herself to face the looming ethical choice— soon, decisively, and with careful responsibility. Until then, she would continue silently, burdened by an intelligent moral dilemma that remained hidden beneath her steady, composed façade.

LATE THAT EVENING, Father Dominic met Karl and Lukas outside the Archives, discreetly secluded within the Vatican Gardens cloaked by night shadows. Karl handed Michael a photo of the small tracker discovered on Hana's jet, his voice low and urgent.

"Blackthorn planted a highly sophisticated GPS—he's tracking our every move," Karl explained. "That's why the men showed up in Toledo when we were there." Michael stared grimly at the photo Karl showed him on his phone of the tiny device. He frowned, about to ask where the device was now, when Karl continued, "For at least a while, they will be tracking the jet of a CEO of an Internet company." Karl grinned. "It was being fueled for destinations unknown, and the pilot was friendly enough to show us their aircraft. The engine noise will muffle any conversations the CEO has because of where Lukas placed it," he said, turning to his partner with a mischievous grin. Then he soberly finished, "Of course, Blackthorn will catch on soon enough. But it gives us a bit of breathing room."

"I wish that were the case," Michael said. "Ian just confirmed a serious internal breach—someone aiding Blackthorn digitally has compromised our security."

"In which case," Lukas spoke up, alarm in his eyes, "we must adjust our strategy immediately—strengthen physical defenses, limit all sensitive communications to trusted individuals only."

Michael offered a small, reassuring gesture. "Agreed. Inform Hana discreetly. She needs to know how severe the threats have become."

Karl's voice softened with concern. "She'll be shaken. But she's resilient—she understands the stakes."

Michael gazed up toward the Apostolic Palace, its windows softly glowing beneath starlight. The discoveries from Toledo, the ethical dilemmas raised by Juana's manuscripts, and Blackthorn's relentless pursuit weighed heavily upon him. Yet within him stirred quiet resolve, strengthened by those around him—Karl's watchful protection, Lukas's unwavering discipline, Ian's pedantic intellect, and Sister Teri's tireless vigilance—not to mention Hana's razor-sharp mind and passion for the team effort.

"Then we proceed warily but decisively," Michael said. "Blackthorn seeks to exploit the past—but we'll stand guard, protecting the future."

Karl nodded firmly, sharing Michael's resolve. "No matter what comes, Father—we're ready."

CHAPTER
NINE

VATICAN CITY

I n the sparsely lit archival chamber of the Vatican Secret Archives, Father Michael Dominic spread his notes across the broad oak table, placing photocopies of Juana de la Cruz's zodiacal carvings next to annotated diagrams from the *Voynich Manuscript*. Hana Sinclair, seated beside him, leaned forward, attentively comparing details between the two sets of documents.

"Look here," Michael murmured thoughtfully, pointing toward a zodiac symbol depicting a crescent moon entwined by vines. "Juana explicitly encoded lunar phases —particularly new moons—in her botanical rituals. It's remarkably similar to the alchemical processes documented by Ramon Llull in the late thirteenth century."

Hana's brow furrowed slightly as she examined the symbols. "Llull? The Majorcan mystic?"

"Distinctly so," Michael confirmed, excitement

sharpening his tone. "He was a Catalan philosopher from Palma, Majorca, in the late thirteenth century. Llull's work profoundly influenced medieval alchemy, particularly his concepts linking botanical substances to spiritual regeneration. His writings were controversial— dangerously close to heresy—but widely circulated among religious mystics and scholars."

Hana looked at him. "And you think Juana intentionally built upon Llull's ideas?"

Michael paused, then nodded, pulling another document closer—a detailed medieval engraving depicting Llull's intricate "Tree of Knowledge," symbolizing alchemical transformation through botanical allegory. "Notice how closely Juana's zodiac symbols echo Llull's imagery. She wasn't merely preserving herbal remedies. She was encoding a thorough alchemical theology, a structured path toward spiritual rebirth through botanical preparations."

Ramon Llull's *Tree of Knowledge*

HANA'S EYES widened with realization. "She was hiding sacred rituals beneath layers of astrology and alchemy, hoping future generations might rediscover them safely."

Michael smiled faintly. "Exactly. Juana knew the Inquisition would persecute such knowledge as heretical, just as they did Llull's followers centuries earlier. Her cipher was her insurance—carefully guarded secrets, readable only by those knowledgeable enough to understand."

IN A SMALL CAFÉ just off Toledo's Plaza de Zocodover, Christophe Vaux slowly sipped his espresso, his sharp gaze fixed steadily upon the nervous man seated opposite him. Professor Luis Vargas, a historian from the local university known for his extensive research into Toledo's medieval monasteries, shifted uncomfortably, avoiding Vaux's cold stare.

"I trust your research was thorough," Vaux stated calmly, his French-accented voice edged with subtle menace. Christophe Vaux had been Zentara's lead European research and development operative until its dissolution. He still served Blackthorn, but now in even more clandestine and direct ways. Vaux, like Blackthorn, was not about to fail this time. His penetrating blue eyes and serious, gaunt face left no room for argument as he faced off with the professor. "Your payment depends entirely on accuracy."

Vargas nodded quickly, anxiously sliding a thick envelope across the table. "Everything I discovered is here —documents, maps, photographs. Plus recordings of the Vatican team as they visited Juana de la Cruz's monastery yesterday. They studied the zodiac carvings extensively, especially those related to lunar cycles and herbal medicine."

Vaux thumbed briefly through the envelope's contents, eyes glinting coldly with satisfaction. "And their conclusions?"

Vargas hesitated slightly, swallowing nervously before replying. "They believe Juana encoded an alchemical process—a preparation ritual involving rare botanical compounds. They're certain these rituals match illustrations found in the *Voynich Manuscript*."

Vaux's eyes narrowed, his interest piqued. "Intriguing. What else?"

Vargas shifted uneasily, his discomfort growing. "The Vatican team was thorough. Their interpretation seems historically accurate—though controversial. Juana certainly hid significant knowledge within those carvings."

Vaux leaned forward intently, voice soft yet threatening. "What exactly did Dominic and Sinclair say about the manuscript itself?"

The historian hesitated, clearly frightened by Vaux's intensity. "They mentioned something they called *Lumen Viride*—a powerful botanical formula. They believe Juana's zodiac cipher points directly to specific locations across Europe that somehow involved this formula or knowledge of it."

Vaux smiled slightly, satisfied. "Excellent work, Professor. You've earned your fee. It will be transmitted to you as we arranged."

He stood abruptly, signaling their meeting's end. Vargas rose quickly, relief flooding his expression, leaving without another word.

Alone, Vaux pulled out his phone, dialing out on a secure line. When Blackthorn answered, Vaux spoke quietly but decisively. "Dominic and Sinclair are close. They've linked Juana de la Cruz's monastery directly to *Lumen Viride*, uncovering explicit references to the *Voynich Manuscript*. It confirms everything we suspected."

Blackthorn's response was brief: "Ensure they remain under observation. Our window is narrow. If they decode Juana's final cipher, we risk losing everything."

Vaux's voice hardened dangerously. "They won't succeed. I'll see to it personally."

BACK IN THE VATICAN ARCHIVES, Michael set down the Llull engraving, turning toward Hana, seriously troubled. "Juana's ritual isn't just historical curiosity—it's profoundly transformative. She genuinely believed these botanical compounds could trigger deep spiritual awakening, possibly even experiences resembling resurrection."

Hana exhaled, unsettled by the implications. "That would make it revolutionary—and dangerous."

"Yes," Michael agreed gravely. "Alchemy has always been volatile because it merges physical healing with extensive spiritual transformation. The medieval Church feared alchemy exactly for this reason—any knowledge promising spiritual rebirth challenged institutional control."

Hana met Michael's eyes seriously. "Then Juana was taking immense risks encoding this knowledge."

Michael responded with a slight nod, thoroughly respectful of Juana's courage. "She entrusted future generations with truths she couldn't openly share, hoping they'd eventually be understood responsibly. But now, with Blackthorn pursuing this knowledge of this formula aggressively—"

Hana's voice grew determined. "We have to safeguard it."

Michael closed his notes, determination hardening him. "Exactly. Juana and Llull risked everything to preserve knowledge they believed sacred. We must honor their legacy—protecting these truths from those who'd exploit them."

As the two gathered their notes beneath the gentle glow of the Archives' antique lamps, Michael felt the utter weight of their task. They now stood as guardians of a fragile legacy, entrusted with the spiritual and alchemical secrets that courageous souls had meticulously preserved from centuries past.

CHAPTER
TEN

VATICAN CITY

Ian Duffy rubbed his tired eyes and leaned back from the cluttered desk deep within the Vatican Secret Archives. Before him, yellowed maps, faded manuscripts, and annotated journals lay spread across the polished table, each artifact a whisper from centuries past. His quest had started simply—to contextualize the astrological and botanical ciphers of Juana de la Cruz—but now, threads of history tangled into unexpected, and deeply provocative, revelations.

He reached toward a particularly fragile parchment, gently shifting it into the pool of golden lamplight. Its edges, crisp and brittle with age, threatened to crumble beneath his fingertips. Yet the inked words still carried power, quiet echoes of voices long silenced:

. . .

"ANNO DOMINI 1244—FALL of Montségur. Cathar refugees reported escaping with sacred texts concerning botanical rites and spiritual regeneration. Authorities ordered immediate suppression; manuscripts seized, destroyed, or hidden across southern Europe."

IAN'S PULSE QUICKENED SHARPLY. Montségur—the final Cathar stronghold, whose defenders had famously perished rather than renounce their beliefs—was closely tied historically to a spiritual dualism condemned vehemently by the medieval Church. However, the botanical rites mentioned here were new revelations. Could Juana's monastery, nearly three centuries later, have inherited knowledge from the persecuted Cathars?

He quickly retrieved another sheet, delicately unfolding the delicate vellum. A detailed map showed clandestine trade routes between southwestern France and northern Spain, connecting Occitan towns near Montségur directly to Toledo's region. Beside the route, scribbled in tiny Latin script: *"**Refugium Herbarum**—sanctuary of herbs —guarded by spiritual descendants of Montségur."*

Ian drew a sharp breath, realization crystallizing swiftly. Juana's monastery had been no isolated anomaly; she was preserving a lineage of botanical wisdom that had originated with the Cathars themselves, knowledge violently suppressed, yet discreetly passed through hidden channels.

With careful hands, Ian began documenting every detail. Father Dominic needed this urgently. The manuscript they pursued now bore not just Juana's quiet rebellion—it contained echoes of a much older defiance, a spiritual resilience stretching back to the lingering flames of Montségur.

~

IN THE DIM BACK room of a small, dusty bookshop near Avignon's medieval walls, Christophe Vaux leaned casually against the wooden table, scrutinizing the anxious face of Professor Marcel Giraud. The scholar, thin and nervously polite, shifted uncomfortably beneath Vaux's cold, unwavering stare.

"Professor Giraud," Vaux said, his icy voice intimidating, "I trust you understand how critical accuracy is here. Any omissions could be… unfortunate."

Giraud swallowed nervously, eyes darting toward the locked door. "I've shared everything, Monsieur Vaux. There's nothing else—"

Vaux's hand shot out suddenly, gripping the professor's wrist, silencing him with pain and surprise. Giraud gasped, fear sparking vividly behind his scholarly composure.

"Don't lie to me," Vaux warned, his eyes cold. "Your research into medieval botanical alchemy is well known. Your latest paper mentions Ramon Llull extensively, particularly in the context of alchemy and spiritual regeneration. Tell me exactly what you discovered regarding Llull's influence on southern French monasteries."

Giraud's eyes widened fearfully. "Llull influenced many scholars, mystics, and herbalists, particularly the Cathars before their persecution. They integrated his botanical alchemy into their rites—healing rituals, spiritual transformations—practices the Church later condemned as heresy."

Vaux released Giraud's wrist slowly, satisfied. "And Juana de la Cruz? Did your research confirm direct Cathar influence on her?"

Giraud hesitated, frightened yet truthful. "Indirectly, yes. My research indicates knowledge traveled secretly through Occitan refugees, eventually reaching monasteries in Spain. Juana's rituals closely align with Cathar symbolism and Llull's alchemical concepts. But these historical connections remain theoretical. Unproven. If true, that would change historical perspectives drastically. Juana was cautious, though—she left few clear traces."

Vaux stood abruptly, expression chillingly unwavering. "Thank you, Professor. I trust you'll keep this conversation strictly confidential."

Giraud nodded anxiously, understanding the thinly veiled threat. Vaux exited without another word, leaving the frightened scholar trembling in silent dread.

IN THE SWISS GUARD BARRACKS, Karl Dengler and Lukas Bischoff rigorously reviewed surveillance footage from the Vatican's private hangar and surrounding areas at Ciampino Airport. Each frame of video offered potential clues—subtle gestures, faces partially obscured by shadows, movements repeated too regularly to be casual.

Suddenly, Lukas halted the footage, pointing at the screen. "Karl—there... Look!"

Karl leaned forward, immediately recognizing the figure partially illuminated by hangar lights. "Vaux," he muttered grimly, watching closely as Christophe Vaux briefly conferred with an unknown man before slipping discreetly into darkness.

Lukas nodded gravely. "Blackthorn's man, the same that we confronted at the Hildegard monastery last year, is apparently personally handling Blackthorn's operations now. This isn't mere surveillance—it's active espionage directed from the top."

Karl's jaw tightened with determination. "Then Father Michael must know immediately. Vaux isn't just someone's mercenary—he's ex-Zentara, and we've seen how ruthless he can be. He'll stop at nothing this time to deliver what Blackthorn demands."

FATHER DOMINIC EXAMINED Ian's historical revelations later that evening, seated quietly in his private chambers beneath flickering candlelight. Ian stood silently nearby, awaiting Michael's thoughts.

Finally, the priest set the parchment down, eyes troubled yet fascinated. "Cathar connections to Juana's botanical formula—this explains so much. Her monastery was guarding a knowledge that had defied violent persecution for generations. But the Church's historical condemnation of Cathar beliefs was unequivocal—accusations of dualism, heresy, even sorcery."

Ian nodded grimly. "Exactly why Juana encoded her processes so cautiously. She knew their historical origins—knew what dangers lurked in openly preserving such ideas."

A sharp knock interrupted them. Karl entered quickly, Lukas close behind, their expressions grave.

"Father Dominic," Karl began, "we've confirmed Christophe Vaux is personally leading Blackthorn's field operations. We have direct surveillance evidence linking him to the tracking devices planted aboard Hana's jet. He's actively orchestrating espionage—targeting us specifically."

Michael glanced again at Ian's documents, realization dawning. "Vaux has clearly made the same historical connections we have. My guess is that Blackthorn seeks more than just botanical formulas this time. It is unknown what the effect of this formula is, but I have a feeling that Blackthorne already has an inkling of what it might be. Maybe he has already been working on a preliminary version ot it. Whatever it is, whether a powerful beneficial drug or a biological weapon, he has already determined a way to monetize it. In essence, he plans to commercialize knowledge that has been considered both sacred and dangerous for centuries."

Ian frowned warily. "And monopolize these discoveries, reaping the rewards of it for himself alone."

Michael stood, voice unflinching. "Then we must move decisively. Ian, document every historical connection you can—Juana, Llull, the Cathars—everything. Karl, Lukas, double all security protocols immediately. Ensure that Hana and Sister Teri remain under constant protection. Vaux must not catch us unaware."

Ian nodded firmly. "I'll gather all relevant historical documentation for immediate safeguarding."

Karl and Lukas exchanged determined glances. "We'll secure all entry points—physical and digital," Karl affirmed. "Blackthorn's operation ends here."

As they hurriedly departed, Michael sank back into his chair, troubled yet undaunted. Juana de la Cruz had guarded great knowledge that resonated with centuries of suppressed spirituality—echoes of the Cathar heresy,

Ramon Llull's controversial wisdom, and quiet resistance across generations.

Now, those echoes had resurfaced, entangling them all. The past had cast long shadows, but they must face them directly, protecting sacred truths against ruthless forces determined to exploit them.

Michael reached toward Ian's parchment once more, reverently tracing the faded lines of text. Juana had believed passionately in the sacredness of her knowledge, risking everything to preserve it. Now, centuries later, Michael felt that same quiet courage stir deeply within himself.

IN A DARKENED ROOM, where only one desk lamp cast its light on a freshly printed report, Alton Blackthorn held his phone to his ear as he awaited the response from Christophe Vaux to his pointed question.

His normally stellar henchman offered Blackthorn a heavy sigh before replying, "Yes, I know, obviously the tracker was discovered, and—"

"I would say that is obvious," snapped Blackthorn, malice in his voice. "May I remind you I have no interest in trying to discern the muffled voices of businessmen flying to some technological conference in Budapest." He let a pause play out as he crumpled the report and tossed it across the room. "I thought you had this under control. I need to know exactly what the priest and journalist discovered. I have nearly everything I need to go forward, and can't afford that troublesome pair meddling at this late stage. Did you not understand that?"

Vaux steeled his voice with a confidence he only partially felt. "I have a contingency plan, and it is being done even as we speak. I assure you, I have this handled."

"Don't assure me," Blackthorn hissed. "Just do it."

LATE AT NIGHT, alone in the dim solitude of the Vatican Secret Archives, Ian continued thoroughly examining Juana de la Cruz's manuscript fragments, driven by an intuition he couldn't fully articulate. He had noted subtle irregularities—cryptic annotations hinting at additional documents hidden somewhere else, beyond Vatican walls.

His pulse quickened as his gaze settled on a faded margin note, nearly overlooked in earlier studies:

"*UNDER ROME'S OLDEST STONES, truth slumbers, watched over by martyrs and saints.*"

HIS MIND RACED. "Rome's oldest stones" suggested ancient catacombs, perhaps San Callisto or San Clemente—sites renowned historically for layers of secrecy and symbolism. Ian hesitated briefly, considering whether to share this discovery with Michael and the others. Yet caution prevailed. The recent infiltration attempts by Blackthorn's forces had shown clear vulnerabilities within their circle.

Carefully concealing this new lead, Ian resolved silently: he would pursue this discovery personally, safeguarding its revelation until he understood its significance—and its risks.

ELEVEN

PROVENCE & AVIGNON, FRANCE

The morning sun had risen fully, draping the rolling hills of Provence in brilliant gold, highlighting endless rows of lavender and vibrant sunflowers stretching toward the distant horizon. Father Michael Dominic, freshly dressed in his clerical attire, guided their rented Peugeot through narrow country roads, each turn bringing them closer to the Monastery of Saint-Paul-de-Mausole. Beside him, Hana Sinclair gazed at the countryside, the serenity outside sharply contrasting her inner turmoil.

In her lap were copies of pages from the enigmatic *Voynich Manuscript*, a codex that had resisted decipherment for centuries. The botanical images and strange zodiac symbols seemed to shimmer with new urgency following their recent discoveries. Hana traced her fingers over the ancient illustrations, trying desperately to discern their meaning.

Michael glanced at her briefly, sensing her unease. "We'll find answers today, Hana. I can feel it." They had used the engravings they documented at Juana's monastery, along with the nodes indicated on her map, and then coupled that to what Ian had found in the Vatican Archives. Armed with these clues, they had now arrived at the first location they believed Juana had indicated as the beginning of the ritual she had secreted in her cryptic ways.

"Answers," she murmured, "or perhaps more questions."

The ancient monastery appeared suddenly as the road dipped around a wooded curve. A once-grand structure now stood crumbling, with ivy climbing its stone walls and gaps in the roof allowing shafts of sunlight to penetrate into shadowed interiors. Michael parked near the ruins and stepped out, Hana quickly following. They paused momentarily, taking in the absolute silence surrounding them.

"It's beautiful," Hana whispered reverently, adjusting her scarf as the cool breeze brushed past them.

"Yes," Michael agreed. "Beautiful, but somehow unsettling."

Inside, the air was colder, thick with the scent of moss, damp stone, and forgotten history. Hana moved purposefully through the central cloister, her eyes immediately drawn to a large fresco adorning the chapel's north wall.

"Michael," she called urgently, her voice echoing faintly.

Michael hurried to join her, his own breath catching as he absorbed the sight. The fresco, incredibly well preserved despite its age, depicted an elaborate series of botanical plants intertwined with complex zodiacal symbols: Aries, Taurus, Gemini, each precisely drawn, each plant matching illustrations from the *Voynich Manuscript* exactly.

Hana held up her photocopied pages, comparing them diligently. "It matches perfectly," she breathed, her eyes wide in astonishment.

Michael stepped closer, examining the intricate details. "More than perfect, Hana. This is clearly the first step in the process Juana delineated."

They painstakingly documented the frescoes, Michael meticulously photographing every detail, Hana jotting notes quickly. They moved from panel to panel, uncovering more clues embedded in symbolic imagery: celestial bodies, phases of the moon, cryptic glyphs.

"There must be significance in these zodiac symbols," Michael mused aloud, squinting at the frescoes.

Hana nodded reflectively. "Perhaps they encode specific celestial coordinates or dates?"

Before they could further contemplate, footsteps echoed through the monastery halls. Michael hastily concealed his camera, instinctively stepping protectively in front of Hana. A man emerged, impeccably dressed, looking distinctly academic in tweed and round spectacles.

"Ah! Visitors." The man smiled warmly, his accent vaguely French. "I am Dr. Laurent Fournier, a UNESCO historian. How delightful to see others interested in this marvelous site."

Michael hesitated, his instincts warning caution. "Father Michael Dominic, Vatican Archives. My colleague, Hana Sinclair. We're investigating medieval botanical symbolism."

Fournier's eyes sparkled keenly behind his glasses.

"Indeed? Are you, perhaps, examining connections to the *Voynich Manuscript*?"

Michael exchanged a swift, wary glance with Hana. "Indirectly," he answered.

"An extraordinary puzzle," Fournier continued smoothly, stepping toward the frescoes. "Perhaps we could compare notes? Collaboration might hasten our understanding."

Michael paused, uncomfortable with the stranger's overly familiar tone. Just as he prepared a cautious reply, another figure appeared, steps purposeful and confident—the Vatican Swiss Guard Karl Dengler, his expression unreadable but tense.

"Father Dominic, Ms. Sinclair," Karl interjected with professional formality, eyes locked onto Fournier. "I believe there's been some confusion. My partner just confirmed there are no UNESCO representatives authorized here today."

Fournier's expression faltered momentarily, his confident demeanor breaking to reveal a flash of anxiety. He quickly recovered, smiling stiffly. "A simple misunderstanding, surely. Forgive the intrusion."

Karl remained silent, unwavering, as Fournier hastily exited the monastery.

Michael let out a ragged breath, tension draining from him.

"Obviously one of Christophe Vaux's men," Karl explained tersely. "You should finish quickly. Lukas and I will secure the perimeter."

Returning to their hotel room in Avignon, Michael and Hana accelerated their documentation efforts, the frescoes taking on renewed urgency.

Outside, as twilight descended upon Avignon, Karl and

Lukas maintained their quiet vigilance. Inside, Michael stared out the window, pondering how the fake Dr. Fournier knew where to find them. Were they still being tracked in some way? Or did Blackthorn already know about the locations symbolized in the maps and documents and had assigned men to watch over them? Or to intervene if Michael's team arrived? Either way, he had to wonder what they might find at the location of the next node on their mapped journey. A journey that he and his friends were about to continue, understanding that each step closer to the truth brought them nearer to dangers both acute and unknown.

CHAPTER

TWELVE

AVIGNON, FRANCE

N ight had fallen over Avignon, draping the historic city in a silken cloak of darkness dotted by twinkling streetlamps. Michael sat at the antique oak desk in their modest hotel room, illuminated solely by the soft glow of his laptop and the dim bedside lamp. He had removed his black shirt and Roman collar in an attempt to relax, but his mind remained hyper-focused on their mission. Across the room, Hana paced restlessly, her eyes frequently glancing toward the screen as Michael prepared for a secure video call with Simon Ginzberg.

As the screen flickered to life, the old man's aged but sharply focused face appeared, surrounded by countless books piled neatly around his familiar office at Teller University in Zagarolo, not far from Rome.

"Michael, Hana—good to see you again," Simon greeted them. His expression, though warm, carried a tension that Michael immediately recognized.

"Simon, thank you for joining us again," he replied, leaning forward earnestly. "We've discovered something extraordinary, and we believe your insight will be crucial."

Simon adjusted his thick glasses while nodding. "Proceed."

Michael shared the detailed photographs of the frescoes and *Voynich Manuscript* pages side by side, watching Simon's eyebrows knit with concentration as he examined each scrupulously. The older scholar hummed thoughtfully, occasionally adjusting the angle of his glasses or leaning in closer to inspect specific details.

"Fascinating," Simon murmured after a prolonged silence. "The zodiac symbols depicted here aren't mere decorative flourishes. Look... each constellation aligns accurately with known medieval celestial maps, but there's more. Certain anomalies, minor deviations... They align exactly with particular celestial events known historically but never before documented in standard medieval astronomy texts."

Hana ceased pacing, stepping closer to Michael. "Events not recorded?" she questioned the old scholar.

Simon nodded seriously. "Yes, rare celestial conjunctions and occultations. In modern times, these events have been recognized as occurring in the past through reverse engineering of astronomical observations, backtracking, as it were, looking at the cyclic nature of the cosmos and such. The current scientific community has assumed that the observers in the Middle Ages had never recognized those events because there were no ancient records of them. Apparently, they had seen and made notes of them. My guess is that those events were considered too dangerous, or sacred, or subversive in those medieval times to be recorded. Yet apparently the less fearful and more educated among them, such as the Cathars and later Juana, wanted to preserve this knowledge and deliberately encoded the events into these botanical images and zodiacal signs."

Michael leaned back in thought. "Encoded celestial events... But why?"

Simon's eyes held a mixture of excitement and caution. "Historically, such events were considered messages or omens—portents signaling great changes or dangers. Given the context, the *Voynich Manuscript* might link these celestial alignments to rituals meant to harness the resulting celestial energies."

"Rituals?" Hana interjected, intrigue clear in her voice.

"Indeed," Simon confirmed. "These rituals likely were believed to enhance the potency of botanical substances," he pointed to the many botanical illustrations that wove through the documents, "perhaps for healing, enlightenment, or even more arcane purposes."

Michael felt a chill run down his spine. "Arcane purposes such as...?"

Simon hesitated momentarily. "Medieval scholars often linked botanical alchemy to transformative spiritual practices, potentially dangerous knowledge reserved for initiates. Botanical alchemy usually involved specific seasons, lunar phases, and other celestial events, to enhance growth. However, given the manuscript's secrecy and its exhaustive coding, I suspect these rituals went beyond encouraging plant growth, perhaps into realms they considered mystical or even divine."

Michael exchanged a troubled glance with Hana. "Could that explain the Church's historical suppression of such rituals and practices?"

Simon nodded deliberately. "Most definitely. The

Church historically condemned astrological practices combined with botanical rituals as heretical, often fearing their power could destabilize ecclesiastical authority."

As Simon spoke, Michael's phone buzzed urgently. He glanced down, recognizing Sister Teri's number flashing across the screen. Excusing himself briefly, Michael answered eagerly, heart racing.

"Teri, what have you found?" he asked.

Sister Teri's voice, normally composed, carried an unusual urgency. "Michael, I've uncovered Vatican records dating directly to the Avignon Papacy. Pope Clement VI explicitly suppressed a group of Benedictine monks practicing zodiac-linked herbal rituals in this region. Records suggest these monks claimed to possess profound healing abilities derived from celestial alignments. Their practices were brutally halted and their records destroyed —or so they believed."

Michael felt his pulse quicken, the gravity of her revelation settling heavily upon him. "Teri, these rituals… were they detailed?"

"Only vaguely," she replied. "But annotations and footnotes mention star maps and herbal correlations— distinctly matching what you're describing from your findings."

"Remarkable," Michael breathed. "Forward everything securely."

"I already have," she confirmed reassuringly. "Be cautious, Michael. These documents bear warnings— explicit threats about dangers inherent in such knowledge."

Returning promptly to the ongoing call, Michael quickly updated Simon, whose face had grown more somber.

"This confirms my suspicions," Simon murmured. "These monks discovered something genuinely powerful —knowledge linking celestial events with botanical substances capable of extreme transformations. Such knowledge, uncontrolled, could threaten traditional power structures, including the Church."

Hana leaned forward decisively. "Then we must reconstruct these celestial maps accurately. If we can correlate exact times and locations, we might understand what the monks and Juana de la Cruz sought to achieve. Meaning also what Blackthorn hopes to capitalize on as well."

Simon smiled approvingly. "Excellent thinking, Hana. Proceed with deliberation, methodically. Ian and Sister Teri might assist with tracing further medieval astrological texts and annotations. Their expertise will be invaluable."

Michael quickly contacted Ian, who eagerly accepted the challenge. Within hours, Ian and Teri returned astonishing findings: annotations in the manuscript's margins directly referenced previously unknown medieval astrological texts buried deep within the Vatican Archives. These texts, Ian explained breathlessly, connected specific celestial events with exact botanical ingredients— ingredients faithfully depicted within the *Voynich* illustrations.

The hotel room filled with tense excitement as Michael and Hana assembled celestial maps, botanical illustrations, and historical annotations. Simon guided them methodically, his insights and interpretations unraveling centuries of guarded secrets. The atmosphere became charged, each revelation peeling away another layer of historical obscurity to reveal deeper and increasingly unsettling truths.

Hours later, the intricate puzzle began to coalesce. Michael ran down the discoveries without interruption.

They stood back, surveying a comprehensive celestial map studded with pinpointed events, botanical correlations, and dates spanning decades.

Michael felt a deep sense of awe—and dread.

"Simon, we've unveiled something remarkable," he said to the old scholar after calling him back to report their new findings. "A blueprint for a formula that could offer untold benefits."

Hana agreed cautiously, "But untold dangers as well. We know the basics of the formula now—a huge first step."

Simon, voice calm yet weighty, said, "Clearly, we are on the precipice of knowledge humanity may not yet be prepared to comprehend."

Michael met Simon's gaze evenly. "Then we must ensure it remains protected—known but wisely guarded."

Simon nodded approvingly. "Wisdom indeed, my friend. Wisdom that history demands we uphold."

As their call ended, Michael and Hana exchanged a silent acknowledgment. Each sensed they had crossed an irrevocable threshold. Outside, the stars above Avignon shone brightly, indifferent yet seemingly intertwined with secrets long hidden in the darkness of history.

CHAPTER

THIRTEEN

MONTPELLIER, FRANCE

L ate morning sunlight streamed through the tall
windows of the quaint café nestled in a vibrant
side street of Montpellier, casting pools of warmth
over the weathered wooden tables. Michael and Hana sat
quietly, cups of strong coffee slowly cooling before them,
each lost in contemplation. Spread across the table lay
photocopied pages from the enigmatic *Voynich
Manuscript*, alongside freshly printed maps of
Montpellier's medieval quarter, filled with notations and
highlighted landmarks.

Michael rubbed his temples pensively, the weight of
recent revelations pressing heavily on him. Across from
him, Hana Sinclair tapped her fingers gently against her
cup, her eyes scanning the bustling street outside, vigilant
yet anxious.

Finally, Hana broke the pensive silence. "Montpellier's
medieval university specialized in pharmacology and

medicinal studies. There must be some connection to the botanical secrets we're uncovering."

Michael nodded slowly. "Simon is certain Montpellier holds critical clues—perhaps the key to understanding the manuscript's true purpose. We have a map, so to speak, of the locations that are important to the formula. What we don't actually have, however, is an understanding of this formula's intention."

A shadow flickered briefly across the café window, and Hana stiffened slightly. Michael followed her gaze to see the unmistakable silhouette of Alton Blackthorn's agent lingering just beyond, observing them discreetly from across the narrow street.

"Vaux is relentless. His people seem to dog our every step," Hana murmured tensely, a hint of bitterness in her tone.

Michael let out a sharp breath of disbelief, suppressing frustration. "He's escalating. Sister Teri alerted me that Vaux's cyber-attacks nearly breached Vatican security last night."

Hana's eyes met his reassuringly. "I trust Teri. She'll hold the line."

At that exact moment in Rome, Sister Teri sat at her secure workstation within the Vatican, eyes glued to her monitors. The screens flashed continuously with digital intrusions, aggressive probes deliberately attempting to breach Vatican firewalls.

Teri's fingers expertly traversed the keyboard, deploying countermeasures briskly. "Persistent, aren't we?" she muttered calmly, her focus unwavering as she traced intrusion patterns efficiently. With practiced precision, she rerouted Vaux's attempts into meaningless loops of deceptive data, each maneuver buying crucial time and further frustrating their adversary's efforts.

Satisfied for the time being, the nun took a deep breath, knowing the reprieve was temporary. Blackthorn's operatives were skilled and determined; this was only a brief victory in an ongoing battle.

BACK IN MONTPELLIER, Michael and Hana left the café, senses heightened. Navigating narrow cobblestone streets bustling with tourists and locals alike, they moved quickly toward the medieval university library. Ancient stone buildings lined their path, whispering secrets from centuries past.

They soon reached the towering facade of the historic university library, its imposing stonework speaking to centuries of scholarship. Inside, a hushed reverence pervaded the spacious reading rooms. Rows upon rows of ancient books and manuscripts towered high, their spines whispering silent invitations to explore mysteries long buried in history.

Hana and Michael moved purposefully to the library's oldest section, guided by a detailed map annotated by Simon Ginzberg. They scanned shelves, seeking specific manuscripts detailing pharmacological knowledge closely tied to the *Voynich* illustrations.

"There," Hana whispered excitedly, pulling an ancient leather-bound volume from a shelf. The thick, dusty tome smelled of parchment and aged ink. She laid it upon the reading table and opened it gingerly, pages crackling with the brittle signs of age.

Michael leaned in, eyes widening with excitement.

"These botanical illustrations match precisely with those in the *Voynich Manuscript*," he marveled.

Behind them, a gentle cough startled them both, and they turned curtly. Simon Ginzberg stood there, his elderly eyes twinkling warmly behind thick glasses.

"Apologies, my friends," Simon greeted them faintly. "An old scholar's quiet footsteps startled you, it seems. After speaking with you on the phone last night, my curiosity got the better of me, and I caught a flight to meet with you. I assumed you would be here by now."

Michael embraced him warmly, relief evident in his expression. "Simon, your timing is impeccable."

Simon moved closer, examining the open pages thoughtfully. "Extraordinary," he murmured. "These botanical illustrations are more than merely similar—they seem directly related to our manuscript. The notes here expressly reference celestial alignments, correlating perfectly with our earlier findings."

Hana leaned forward eagerly. "Could these celestial alignments be of practical use in rituals?"

Simon nodded sagely. "Medieval scholars believed celestial events amplified botanical properties, enhancing their effectiveness. These texts indicate highly secretive practices conducted only during specific astronomical events."

As they spoke, the faint sound of footsteps drew their attention.

Simon's eyes narrowed, his demeanor instantly alert.

"We're being observed," he warned, glancing surreptitiously toward the doorway.

The footsteps retreated, echoing down the corridor.

"We should move. Now," Simon instructed urgently, helping Michael and Hana document the critical pages with methodical precision. Every minute mattered as tension mounted.

Leaving the library cautiously, they threaded their way quickly through Montpellier's winding streets, Simon directing them toward a secure, secluded spot for further planning. Each shadow cast by the building-confined alleyways seemed deeper, more menacing now, the threat from Vaux's relentless pursuit an ever-present threat.

"We're playing a dangerous game," Hana noted, her voice tight.

"Cat-and-mouse," Michael murmured grimly.

"An apt metaphor," Simon responded calmly. "Yet even mice can outmaneuver the cat, given strategy and patience."

They moved briskly, skillfully losing their pursuers amid Montpellier's crowded market squares and maze-like streets, each step forward driven by urgency and determination. Yet as they reached their concealed safe location, Michael had a clear sense that their safety would be only temporary.

Settling into the quiet sanctuary of an old, discreet guesthouse, Simon spread their gathered documents across a table, eyes intense with scholarly fervor. "We must understand every detail thoroughly," he instructed patiently. "The answers we seek lie within these texts—answers others seek to exploit or silence permanently."

Late into the evening, illuminated only by dim lamps, they pored over their gathered evidence. Simon's guidance was invaluable, his vast knowledge revealing connections previously unseen. Yet the oppressive sense of danger lingered, a silent companion to their discoveries.

Finally, exhausted but resolute, they concluded their

work for the evening, each acutely aware that their discoveries placed them firmly within Vaux's sights.

Outside, as Montpellier's lights dimmed into night, shadows danced silently, holding their own secrets. The city's ancient streets whispered, foreboding and alluring in equal measure, a fitting backdrop for the unfolding drama where truth and danger interwove inexorably.

~

VATICAN CITY

Father Antonio Ricci stood in the shadowed corridor outside the Vatican Archives, his expression tight with barely restrained frustration. His voice was low but edged with urgency as he spoke to Father Matteo, another younger cleric whose face mirrored discomfort at Ricci's intensity.

"Why does the Church insist on clinging to secrecy?" Ricci whispered harshly, glancing briefly toward the closed archive door. "If what Father Dominic and the others suspect is true, don't people deserve the honesty, the truth about our place in the cosmos?"

Matteo glanced nervously down the corridor, clearly uncomfortable. "Antonio, be very careful. Such matters aren't ours to decide—Father Dominic and Cardinal Severino are handling it with caution for good reason."

Ricci shook his head impatiently, his voice strained but insistent. "Caution? Or suppression? The Vatican's history is littered with truths withheld out of fear. People trust us, Matteo. What happens when they learn we hid knowledge critical to humanity's understanding?"

Matteo placed a calming hand on Ricci's shoulder,

attempting reassurance. "Antonio, please. I understand your passion, but we must trust our leaders' wisdom."

Ricci sighed, visibly unsatisfied. "Wisdom? Or institutional inertia? Humanity deserves the truth, no matter how unsettling it might be. If the Vatican refuses openness, maybe someone else must provide it."

Matteo stepped back slightly, disturbed by Ricci's intensity. "Again, I urge caution, my friend. You speak dangerously. These thoughts could lead you down a path from which there's no easy return."

Ricci's expression softened slightly, but determination still smoldered within his eyes. "Perhaps some risks are worth taking, Matteo. Truth is one of them."

With a lingering glance at the closed archive door, Ricci turned sharply, walking away down the corridor, leaving Matteo visibly agitated by the unsettling resolve emanating from his colleague.

FOURTEEN

MONTPELLIER, FRANCE

The Montpellier Botanical Garden stood proudly in the heart of the city, a sanctuary of lush greenery and vivid blooms protected from the bustling streets by ivy-covered stone walls. Established centuries earlier by visionary scholars, it was a testament to humankind's endless fascination with the mysteries of the natural world. The gardens were bathed in sunlight, with dappled shadows playing softly across gravel pathways as Michael, Hana, and Simon stepped cautiously into the sanctuary.

As they moved along the path, each was keenly aware of the profound historical weight carried by the botanical haven around them. Hana paused frequently, tracing her fingers gently over rare plants, some species thought long extinct yet thriving here under tender care.

"It's incredible," she whispered, admiring an especially vivid flower. "These species match some of the *Voynich* illustrations exactly. How could such accurate knowledge about them have been forgotten or concealed when they still thrive here?"

Simon smiled knowingly. "Many things right under our noses can have significance beyond our understanding. History often buries its most remarkable secrets beneath layers of caution, fear, and misunderstanding. The *Voynich Manuscript* could be one of humanity's greatest forgotten keys to ancient wisdom."

Michael followed, his eyes scanning the area, alert for anything unusual. As they wandered deeper into the gardens, they reached a secluded structure—an elegant Victorian greenhouse affectionately known by locals as the Glass Garden. Its intricate glass panels and iron framework sparkled invitingly under the sun.

Inside, the warm, humid air embraced them, filled with the fragrant scent of exotic plants thriving within the precisely controlled environment. The trio moved methodically along the rows, marveling at the astonishing botanical collection. Suddenly, Hana paused, her attention caught by an aged leather-bound journal displayed in a glass case near the greenhouse entrance. An opening at the bottom of the case, with stiffened ribbons extending out, allowed viewers to turn the parchment pages without damage.

"Michael, Simon," she beckoned. "These journals—they look incredibly old."

They crowded around the glass case, scrutinizing the rigid pages with interest.

Simon adjusted his glasses, leaning in closer. "Remarkable indeed," he murmured. "These appear to be personal records from scholars of Montpellier University during its medieval zenith. Look closely at these illustrations—they seem to match the *Voynich Manuscript*'s botanical drawings in every way."

Hana nodded in agreement, excitement coloring her voice as she photographed each page. "The texts are likely from the scholars who directly influenced or were influenced by the creator of the *Voynich* illustrations." Note the annotations—detailed botanical experiments involving celestial alignments, exactly as we found in the manuscript."

Michael leaned closer, his voice tense with excitement and caution. "These entries describe secret botanical experiments conducted during particular astrological events—rituals designed to harness celestial energies. And here… references to extraordinary results."

Hana's lively green eyes sparkled with intrigue, carefully deciphering the archaic script. "The outcomes of these rituals speak of remarkable healings, transformative visions, and warnings of catastrophic misuse."

Simon groaned, his expression somber even as he took notes. "Such knowledge, if misused, could indeed bring chaos. Perhaps this explains why the Church historically suppressed these practices so fiercely."

As they continued their examination, Michael sensed sudden movement outside the glass enclosure, shadows darting rapidly across the sunlit ground. His pulse quickened.

"Karl warned us to remain vigilant," he murmured, scanning the greenhouse perimeter. "Let's finish up quickly here."

Hana finished photographing the journal quickly, capturing every visible detail possible before casually walking away from the display as if she were just a tourist.

Outside, Karl and Lukas maintained careful watch,

eyes scanning the perimeter. Karl suddenly noticed subtle movements, shadowy figures maneuvering among distant hedges.

"Blackthorn's operatives, I'll wager," Karl murmured, alerting Lukas immediately.

The two Swiss Guards advanced confidently through the shadows, their movements sharp and fluid, each step calculated to remain hushed. Approaching from opposite directions, they spotted two of Blackthorn's men creeping toward the greenhouse's glass-paneled entrance, weapons brazenly drawn.

Karl signaled Lukas with a subtle gesture. Instantly, they converged, moving as one unit. Karl surged forward, catching the first agent by surprise. He expertly seized the man's wrist, twisting suddenly to force the weapon free. The man grunted in pain and swung wildly, but Karl evaded effortlessly, delivering a calculated elbow strike to the attacker's ribs, followed immediately by a thrust to the jaw that sent him sprawling unconscious onto the gravel.

Simultaneously, Lukas confronted the second thug, who tried frantically to raise his weapon. Lukas pivoted in a flash, sidestepping the gun's muzzle, and gripped the man's outstretched arm. With practiced precision, he delivered a sharp strike to the elbow, causing the man to drop the weapon with a cry of pain. He followed up with a knee to the assailant's abdomen, doubling him over, and finished the maneuver by pulling him forcefully downward, pinning him firmly against the ground.

In seconds, both assailants were neutralized, their weapons kicked safely away into the darkness.

Inside the greenhouse, Michael, Hana, and Simon froze, alerted by faint yet unmistakable sounds of struggle—

quick blows, muffled cries, the scuffling of boots on gravel. Tension thickened instantly.

Moments later, Karl appeared in the entrance, slightly breathless but controlled, eyes sharp with urgency.

"Time to move," he commanded firmly, glancing quickly behind him. "We've neutralized Blackthorn's men, but reinforcements won't be far behind."

"We can return tomorrow to finish up what we haven't seen yet," Hana said. Without hesitation, she, Michael, and Simon gathered their notes, then rushed into the protective custody of the waiting Swiss Guards.

They exited the gardens, Simon clutching his notes tightly. The group navigated discreetly toward a safer, prearranged location, the atmosphere tense yet determined. Reaching the safety of their temporary lodging, Simon spread the gathered documentation across the table, analyzing each detail with meticulous care.

"To my eyes, this evidence confirms a great deal," Simon stated gravely. "The manuscript's rituals connect specifically with celestial phenomena, and clearly, the medieval scholars discovered or rediscovered methods linking botanical compounds with singular transformative potential."

Michael's expression was deeply contemplative. "Then we must uncover exactly what transformations they achieved—and why these rituals were deemed dangerous enough to suppress so completely."

Hana nodded, her eyes reflecting determination and caution. "We're uncovering truths perhaps never meant for widespread knowledge. But we must understand them more fully to guard against their misuse."

· · ·

LATE INTO THE EVENING, beneath soft lamplight, the team analyzed each manuscript page, each botanical illustration, and celestial reference. Simon provided invaluable historical insights, his guidance crucial in decoding complex historical references.

Eventually, Simon leaned back, exhaustion evident, yet his eyes shining with scholarly fulfillment. "We've taken monumental steps today," he reflected thoughtfully. "Yet each answer brings new questions—questions we must explore cautiously and wisely."

Michael gave a measured nod, thoroughly aware of their precarious path. "We proceed with caution but determination. History demands no less."

Hana gently squeezed Michael's hand reassuringly, her voice firm and resolute. "We won't fail."

FIFTEEN

MONTPELLIER, FRANCE

Golden late-afternoon sunlight filtered through the antique glass panes of Montpellier's medieval botanical greenhouse, illuminating the intricate network of vines and leaves that crowded its interior. A fragile tranquility filled the air, carrying whispers of centuries past—of scholars, monks, and healers who had walked these same narrow paths, reverently tending the very plants that now surrounded Hana Sinclair, Father Michael, and Simon Ginzberg for the second time in as many days.

Hana crouched low beside a raised garden bed, camera in hand, capturing the subtle, faded carvings on its ancient stone border. These botanical engravings, identical to those they had encountered in Toledo, depicted the same entwined vines and zodiacal symbols. Yet here, the carvings seemed especially detailed, their patterns mysteriously vibrant despite the passage of centuries.

Michael leaned forward, brushing away dust and dirt to reveal inscriptions beneath a trailing vine motif. "Another Llullian reference," he murmured, voice awed. "Look at these symbols—alchemy interwoven with astrological alignments. Ramon Llull's teachings on spiritual alchemy clearly influenced whoever planted this garden centuries ago."

Simon moved closer, eyes sparkling with fascination. "Llull's influence was widespread across Europe. His art was considered revolutionary, as it attempted to systematize spiritual enlightenment through botanical means. Montpellier's scholars frequently engaged in conversations about his theories directly. It makes sense these gardens would encompass such ideas."

Hana stepped forward to photograph a particular set of carvings, momentarily leaning against a thick vine entwining the stone pillar. As she did, her sleeve brushed lightly against a small, delicate blossom, releasing a faint puff of golden pollen that floated freely upward, catching sunlight like tiny sparks. Hana inhaled softly, but her attention focused entirely upon capturing the inscriptions.

Almost immediately, a strange warmth flooded through her, a sensation at once calming and unsettling. She straightened, shaking her head slightly as dizziness momentarily blurred her vision.

Michael noticed instantly, reaching to take hold of her elbow.

"Hana, are you all right?"

She inhaled heavily, closing her eyes briefly. "Just… a bit dizzy."

Michael studied her closely, concern shadowing his gaze. "Sit down for a moment, would you?"

As Hana lowered herself onto a nearby stone bench,

her surroundings subtly shifted. The vibrant greens intensified; colors deepened to startling clarity. Her pulse quickened. Her vision sharpened dramatically, the garden around her suddenly alive with intricate detail, veins within leaves pulsating mildly, rhythmic as a heartbeat.

"Michael…" she whispered, confusion blending with astonishment.

Yet her voice seemed strangely distant, echoing faintly, almost as if someone else had spoken her name from a great distance. Then, abruptly, her vision blurred and shifted again, an irresistible sense of displacement overtaking her consciousness. She was no longer in the greenhouse…

HANA STOOD WITHIN A VAST, luminous cathedral of greenery, its vaulted ceilings composed entirely of vibrant, living vines interwoven with delicate blossoms glowing with internal light. Her breath caught sharply—this place was simultaneously impossible yet vividly real. She glanced down; beneath her feet, a spiral pattern stretched outward, intricate botanical designs intertwined with the familiar zodiac symbols she had photographed moments ago. Her heartbeat quickened. The manuscript symbolism, she realized instantly, was alive and tangible around her.

A gentle voice whispered behind her, warm and reassuring, yet compelling. "Welcome, seeker."

Hana turned instantly, facing a slender figure cloaked in a tunic of shimmering emerald fabric. Though obscured by the hood, the figure radiated quiet authority.

"Who are you?" she asked breathlessly.

The figure raised its slender hands. "I am only a guardian. You are here because you inhaled the pollen of a plant that has been celestially touched, one key among many. You glimpse now what Juana de la Cruz saw, what Ramon Llull himself perceived: that true enlightenment is found not by dominance over nature, but through respectful unity, from the heavens to the earth. As above, so below."

Hana glanced around, senses overwhelmed. "This—this vision—is from Juana's manuscript?"

"Not only Juana's," the figure replied. "She was a guardian too, entrusted with knowledge preserved since ancient times. Llull glimpsed this same unity—Cathars, alchemists, healers, mystics throughout the ages knew of this wisdom: the profound bond between humankind, the natural world, and the stars. They encoded their discoveries, knowing mankind's readiness was uncertain, volatile."

The figure stepped forward slightly, the glimmering virescent tunic rippling smoothly. "But the human race stands again at a crossroads. The formula you seek holds the keys—not merely botanical remedies or spiritual symbolism—but the transformative understanding that all life, human and plant alike, thrives only in interconnected balance with the cosmos. Without embracing this truth, humanity risks severing itself irreparably from the living thread that sustains it."

Hana felt deep urgency stirring within her. "Then the manuscript—its symbols—how can they help us?"

The guardian smiled warmly. "They awaken you, reconnect you. But you must protect them, and soon. Forces are gathering who would distort this knowledge for power, profit, and dominance. Who would use this very connection with nature to violate it, twisting nature to function at the will of the one with the key? Only by understanding this truth first yourselves can you guard it effectively."

Suddenly, the vision blurred again, the guardian fading into a luminous mist, the cathedral of vines dissolving back into the familiar greenhouse.

Hana gasped, breath rushing into her lungs, her vision clearing once more.

MICHAEL AND SIMON were kneeling anxiously beside her, Karl and Lukas standing vigilantly nearby, clearly alarmed.

"Hana!" Michael's voice trembled slightly with relief. "You fainted briefly—are you all right?"

She reached for Michael's hand reassuringly, gripping it tightly. "I saw… I can't explain—"

Simon moved closer, kneeling next to them, his eyes searching the nearby plants. "Did you touch a plant? Maybe inhale its pollen?"

"I … I don't know. Maybe…"

Simon nodded. "I suspect you did. Likely a residual botanical compound used historically in visionary rituals. Describe what you saw."

Slowly, Hana recounted every detail—the living cathedral of vines, zodiac symbolism vividly alive, the guardian's message of unity, balance, and urgent preservation of wisdom.

Simon's expression deepened sympathetically, his scholarly mind contextualizing her visions within a historical framework.

"In medieval mysticism," he explained, "visions induced through botanical preparations were commonly reported, especially among mystics like Hildegard von

Bingen or Llull himself. They believed plants offered sacred conduits—connecting physical reality directly to spiritual truths otherwise inaccessible. Today, they might be considered just hallucinogenic and discounted without regard to whether it is, indeed, connecting the spirit to something greater and outside of itself."

Hana's pulse quickened. "But what does it mean practically, today?"

Michael leaned closer, eyes intense. "Your vision confirms everything the manuscript's hinted toward. Humanity is dangerously out of balance—spiritually, environmentally, socially. Juana's knowledge, passed on through mystics and scholars across centuries, is a crucial reminder that true health, true enlightenment, can only exist through harmony with nature, not dominance over it."

Hana added, "The being spoke of harmony with the cosmos as well."

Michael nodded. "This revelation has drastic implications. Blackthorn's relentless pursuit—his ruthless methods—represent exactly the misuse Juana feared. She knew human nature's endless desire for power would corrupt and exploit her discoveries. Blackthorn's plans, no doubt, include somehow harnessing these botanicals to his benefit without regard to the consequences."

Hana met Michael's gaze steadily, realization crystallizing. "Then our responsibility is more serious than we imagined."

"You bet it is," Michael confirmed. "If we fail to safeguard Juana's wisdom, the consequences could be catastrophic."

Simon nodded solemnly. "Medieval scholars understood human nature's dark tendencies. That's why they encoded their truths. They anticipated the misuse, distortion, and exploitation."

Karl stepped forward, his expression grim. "And Vaux and his men have already shown ruthless determination. They're escalating. We must reinforce every safeguard immediately."

Michael's expression hardened. "We will. But we also need to communicate these insights to those who can grasp their importance."

Hana's voice was firm. "First, we must secure samples of any of the plants I was standing near when I experienced the vision. Then we share these for analysis by trusted researchers. The guardian implied this was only one of many, as if other plants are required as well. We'll honor Juana's courage, Llull's insights, and the Cathars' sacrifices."

Simon rose, eyes bright with determination. "Then I suggest we do that now before Blackthorn moves again."

Hana nodded staunchly, strength renewed. "Agreed. Let's finish documenting and taking samples, then secure everything safely. Blackthorn can't exploit what he doesn't possess."

As they resumed their work beneath the fading Montpellier sunlight, Michael stood wistfully, heart heavy yet extremely hopeful. The manuscript, its complex symbolism, and Hana's visionary exposure illuminated a truth humanity had dangerously forgotten—a truth Juana, Llull, and countless mystics had safeguarded faithfully across generations.

Their task now felt thoroughly clear. They stood not merely as historians or scholars, but custodians entrusted with a sacred truth of the symbiotic relationship between humans, the natural world, and even the stars themselves.

Michael glanced toward Hana, who was photographing the garden's ancient carvings, her determination serenely inspiring. He recognized now the greater implications of Juana's manuscript. It contained far more than mere historical wisdom—it offered people a vital opportunity, a powerful chance to reconnect, rebalance, and renew themselves.

But only if that knowledge remained protected, respected, and wisely shared—exactly as Juana herself had intended centuries earlier, when she first etched careful secrets into stone beneath a watchful, uncertain sky.

CHAPTER

SIXTEEN

AVIGNON, FRANCE

The narrow medieval streets of Avignon twisted crazily beneath the fading Provençal sunlight, their cobblestones still warm from the afternoon's heat. The rental SUV carrying Michael, Hana, Simon, Karl, and Lukas moved briskly through the historic city center, heading steadily toward the ruins of an ancient Benedictine monastery overlooking the Rhône River.

Following their astonishing discoveries in Montpellier, Michael had insisted on this detour. His research had uncovered evidence that medieval Benedictines from Avignon had been custodians of a secret botanical codex—one closely linked to Juana's suppressed traditions.

Much to his chagrin, Karl had still been unable to ascertain how Blackthorn's cohorts were able to efficiently track their movements. But they had. So staying ahead of the game required deft footing and fast work. With Alton Blackthorn and Christophe Vaux's agents uncomfortably close behind, each new location was both a fresh opportunity and an increasingly dangerous gamble. The SUV parked discreetly near an ancient stone wall draped with vibrant bougainvillea, its red blossoms cascading gracefully down the centuries-old masonry. Michael stepped out first, followed closely by Hana and Simon. Karl and Lukas emerged last, quickly surveying their surroundings, scanning every shadow and vantage point with practiced vigilance.

The monastery ruins lay half-hidden by centuries of vegetation and neglect, their crumbling walls and empty arches whispering quiet stories of a forgotten past. Michael approached slowly, reverently placing his hand against a weathered archway, imagining the monks who once studied and prayed within these same walls.

"According to Ian's records," he explained, "the monks here secretly studied herbal texts condemned by the medieval Church. These walls may still conceal valuable inscriptions—fragments of the *Hesperides Codex* itself, or even clues linking Juana's work directly to the *Voynich Manuscript*."

Hana's eyes moved along the stones, searching for hidden carvings or symbols. "If the monks preserved botanical secrets here, they likely encrypted them, like Juana did."

Simon nodded agreeably. "Avignon was an intellectual crossroads in the medieval world. Popes lived here during their exile from Rome, fostering scholarship, but also suppressing dangerous knowledge. It's no accident we've found connections here." He continued to move carefully, making notes in his notebook as he went, as well as taking reference photos.

Michael paused, deliberately running his fingers along

a weathered section of wall. He traced faint lines curiously, his voice sharpened by excitement. "Here—these carvings. They're zodiacal again, unmistakably Juana's symbolism."

Hana crouched closer, photographing the subtle marks, her heart quickening. "The exact symbols we found in Montpellier. It confirms a direct historical connection."

Before Michael could reply, Karl's voice broke the quiet, his tone sharp but controlled. "We've got company... three vehicles approaching rapidly. Take cover immediately."

Instantly alert, Lukas drew his pistol, moving promptly into a defensive position near Michael and Hana. Karl stepped forward, positioning himself strategically near the monastery's gateway.

Seconds later, tires skidded abruptly, three black SUVs halting aggressively on the road nearby. Doors swung open violently, disgorging armed forces who quickly spread out with military precision.

At the center stood Christophe Vaux, calm and predatory, his gaze locking coldly onto Michael's group. "Father Dominic!" he shouted mockingly. "Hand over what you've found, and no one will get hurt."

Michael stood defiantly, his voice calm yet firm. "We both know I can't do that, Vaux."

Vaux's expression darkened. "Very well. Have it your way."

He signaled sharply. His teams surged forward, weapons drawn, intent unmistakable.

"Get to cover!" Karl shouted urgently toward Michael, Hana, and Simon. They scrambled quickly behind a crumbling wall, debris scattering under their feet.

Karl and Lukas moved instantly, positioning themselves tactically. Karl fired first, well-placed shots shattering a nearby headlamp, sending the attackers momentarily scattering. Lukas intercepted an advancing assailant, quickly disarming and incapacitating him with a powerful strike to the chest.

Vaux's personnel pressed their attack, returning fire aggressively. Bullets sparked against stone and ricocheted violently through the ruins. Karl and Lukas moved fluidly, their actions coordinated perfectly. Karl darted between cover, firing carefully aimed shots to keep attackers pinned down, while Lukas strategically maneuvered to outflank their opponents.

He reloaded in a flash, calling briskly to Lukas, "On your left!"

Lukas pivoted instantly, intercepting another attacker attempting to breach their defenses. He deflected a wild strike, then immediately countered with precise blows, disarming and immobilizing his opponent expertly.

Vaux observed coldly from behind, frustration tightening his jaw. Seeing his men falter, he gestured urgently to one agent—ordering him to circle behind the monastery, intending to ambush Michael's group.

But Karl had anticipated this. Signaling to Lukas silently, they both repositioned rapidly, intercepting the attacker as he rounded the corner. Karl engaged first, blocking the assailant's advance with aggressive precision, while Lukas moved behind, expertly incapacitating him. In moments, the attacker lay bound and immobilized.

Vaux's operatives faltered visibly, shaken by their sudden losses. Recognizing imminent defeat, Vaux reluctantly signaled retreat. "Fall back!" he ordered harshly, voice tense with anger.

Rapid footsteps echoed sharply as the remaining attackers fled hurriedly toward their vehicles. Within seconds, engines roared to life, SUVs vanishing down Avignon's shadowed streets.

Silence descended abruptly, punctuated only by the group's rapid breathing. Karl quickly surveyed the area, securing their captive and retrieving discarded weapons. Lukas stood guard, vigilant eyes scanning darkened streets.

Breathing heavily, Michael turned anxiously toward Hana where they had crouched behind a stone wall. "Are you all right?"

She nodded, heart racing but composure returning quickly. "Yes—thanks to Karl and Lukas."

Karl approached at once, expression grimly satisfied. "We have one of Vaux's men secured. He'll provide valuable intel."

Lukas joined them. "We must move quickly, though. Vaux will regroup in no time."

Understanding flickered across Michael's features. "Agreed. But first, we must finish here."

Simon had had his eyes on his notebook as they'd talked and now held it out to them. "Look at this! The zodiac symbols we just found here accurately match Juana's earlier cipher. The monks clearly possessed identical knowledge. And this one inscription translates to 'Herba Viridis,'—the Green Herb—a critical component of the Hesperides Codex."

Michael studied the notes intently, awe sharpening his voice. "Remember the handwritten notation on the side of Juana's Hesperides Codex? It made mention of both Bacon's Cipher and the Hesperides' formula. Then Juana's codex wasn't isolated knowledge—it belonged to a broader, suppressed tradition. Each location we've visited has revealed clearer connections, directly linking her cipher to earlier centuries of secret botanical study."

Understanding flashed across Hana's face. "That means we may be closer than ever to unlocking the *Voynich Manuscript*—each fragment deepens our interpretation. This monastery explicitly connects Juana's traditions to broader medieval botanical networks, exactly what we'd hoped for."

Karl's voice interrupted vigorously. "We must leave now—Vaux won't remain passive."

Simon quickly pocketed his notes. "Then let's move."

Under Lukas's vigilant protection, they quickly exited the monastery, guiding their captive firmly between Karl and Lukas toward their waiting SUV. Michael glanced back once, heart tightening with both awe and urgency. The monastery had revealed yet another profound layer of meaning hidden within Juana's codex, bringing them tantalizingly closer to decoding the *Voynich Manuscript*'s ancient secrets—yet those secrets now risked falling dangerously into Vaux's ruthless hands. Their adversary would no doubt document whatever he could here as well now. Would Blackthorn's people understand its significance as Simon had? Be able to put all the pieces together? Would they gain enough to fulfill their devious efforts? Even if they did, they would still fear that Michael, as well as Hana, would be ready—and more than willing —to stop them.

As Avignon's shadowed streets receded behind them, Michael met Hana's steady gaze. Her determined expression mirrored his own resolve. They had survived Vaux's assault—but only narrowly. Each discovery now increased the danger exponentially, yet also deepened their understanding greatly.

VATICAN CITY

Within her workspace, illuminated softly by flickering monitors, Sister Teri faced a terminal screen, the blinking cursor awaiting her command. Her heartbeat pounded, each breath she drew heavy with tension.

On her screens, the Vatican's security barriers deteriorated rapidly. Genetica's attack grew aggressively intrusive, cascading toward catastrophic data breaches. She had no choice left.

Whispering a quiet, heartfelt prayer, Teri initiated the decisive command. Immediately, the compromised networks of Global Aid Alliance went dark, plunging the charity into temporary chaos.

As soon as she issued the command, a deep stillness settled around her, a terrifying contrast to the digital storm she had just unleashed. Her fingers trembled as she stared numbly at the now-empty screens, the blinking terminals where, only moments earlier, data from Global Aid Alliance had flowed continuously, coordinating urgent humanitarian operations across the globe.

She knew exactly what her actions entailed—there was no comforting illusion of ignorance, no refuge in hopeful naiveté. The implications were immediate and severe, pressing heavily upon her conscience. Without their global network, emergency medical teams would be stranded, unable to coordinate critical interventions in conflict zones. Refugee operations, delicately reliant upon real-time logistics, would falter, plunging vulnerable populations into confusion and further hardship. Relief missions supplying vital food, medicine, and shelter to remote communities would be disrupted abruptly, endangering countless innocent lives now left exposed and unsupported.

Teri closed her eyes tightly, her breath shuddering in painful anguish. Her heart twisted in an ache that felt almost physical as images surged vividly, unbidden—the frightened faces of children whose daily survival depended entirely upon the charity's coordinated support; desperate mothers whose hope had rested upon this delicate global safety net, now suddenly and devastatingly compromised.

The realization of what she had done gripped her with relentless clarity, cold and ruthless in its honesty. No reassuring logic or well-meaning justification could diminish the stark human cost now associated with her choice. The Vatican's critical data, precious and historically invaluable, had been saved, yet the toll exacted from innocents would forever burden her conscience.

She envisioned the impending public outcry, the justified fury from the international community when it learned the truth behind the disruption. Soon—perhaps mere hours from now—news outlets around the world would receive reports detailing the abrupt, catastrophic interruption of humanitarian operations. Headlines would inevitably erupt angrily, condemning the Vatican's apparent recklessness, branding the Church with charges of callousness, arrogance, or worse.

Teri felt tears escaping down her cheeks, their path cold against the warmth of her skin. She knew she would carry these imagined scenes not merely today but for years to come. The reality of lives disrupted and hopes shattered weighed heavily upon her, haunting her conscience with unrelenting intensity.

Yet beneath the ache of guilt and remorse, she understood with quiet, painful clarity that the choice had been unavoidable. To protect something crucial—historical truths that mankind needed desperately, but couldn't yet fully comprehend—she had chosen knowingly, fully aware of the potential damage to innocent lives.

Quietly bowing her head in earnest prayer, the young nun sought forgiveness, her whispered words trembling with genuine sorrow and humility. She hoped fervently that humanity's eventual understanding of the broader truth would, in some small measure, eventually balance the suffering her actions had inadvertently unleashed. Yet even in this silent hope, her heart remained heavy with uncertainty and a subtle moral grief.

LATER THAT NIGHT, Ian found Teri sitting quietly in a secluded Vatican chapel, bathed in flickering candlelight. He approached slowly, noting her bowed head, her shoulders trembling slightly.

"Teri…" The young archivist spoke softly, placing his hand reassuringly on her shoulder. "Are you all right?"

She lifted tearful eyes toward him, her voice barely a whisper. "Ian, I caused suffering—innocent people were hurt because of my choice. How do I reconcile that?"

Ian knelt beside her, his voice gentle yet firm. "Teri, you faced an impossible choice. You acted not from malice but from desperate necessity. A necessity created by Genetica, orchestrated by them specifically to protect themselves at the expense of those humanitarian causes. *They* are the cause."

She let out a sharp breath, eyes closed briefly. "Yet thousands are suffering because of me. Families, children

—victims I cannot comfort or apologize to. The Vatican's mission is compassion, not harm. Did I betray everything we believe?"

Ian shook his head, compassion radiating from his expression. "You protected a greater truth, Teri, one critical to humanity's understanding. Your actions were agonizing, but your heart and intentions remained compassionate. Sometimes, even ethical choices involve pain."

Teri's gaze softened slowly, absorbing his bitter wisdom. She finally nodded, visibly stronger yet genuinely humbled.

CHAPTER
SEVENTEEN

ZÜRICH, SWITZERLAND

I nside the heavily secured underground laboratory beneath Genetica Therapeutics' modernist headquarters in Zürich, Christophe Vaux sat stiffly before a bank of high-resolution monitors. A pale blue glow bathed the stark, sterile space, illuminating his gaunt features as he started the encrypted video link. Moments later, Alton Blackthorn's familiar visage appeared, composed yet subtly impatient.

"Your report, Christophe," Blackthorn instructed tersely, his tone unyielding.

"As I had assured you, my methods have continued to track the priest and the journalist. We successfully followed them and have determined which plant within that monastery garden can produce effects that will benefit your research." His tone was boastful, but an undercurrent of discomfort edged his words.

"And...?" The impatience of Blackthorn's voice sharpened this single word like an early condemnation of whatever Vaux had failed to report.

"Dominic and his group have proven more resourceful than expected," Vaux conceded. "Our recent operation in Avignon—though well planned—was unsuccessful. They escaped unharmed and took one of my men captive."

Blackthorn's eyes narrowed. "Did they uncover anything significant at the Avignon site?"

"Yes," Vaux admitted reluctantly. "The monastery ruins there revealed direct links between Juana de la Cruz's botanical ciphers and medieval Benedictine practices. Dominic is rapidly closing in on the deeper historical origins of the *Voynich Manuscript*."

Blackthorn's jaw tightened slightly, visible even through the digital feed. "Unacceptable. If his people achieve a full understanding before we do, our entire operation could collapse."

Vaux nodded stiffly. "I've reinforced security protocols across all our sites. But Dominic's Swiss Guards are formidable. They seem to anticipate every move we make."

Blackthorn leaned forward intently, voice coldly commanding. "Then be more unpredictable, Christophe. Our investors are growing restless. Securing our laboratories and immediately stopping Dominic are critical to Genetica's success in replicating Juana's formulas."

Vaux inclined his head deferentially. "Understood. I've also increased our surveillance in Rome. My agents have orders to target vulnerabilities in Dominic's support structure. The moment we have another opening, I'll personally oversee the operation."

"Ensure it," Blackthorn concluded curtly. "And what of the operative you allowed them to capture? What danger does he pose to us?"

Vaux's gaunt expression darkened. "I know where he is being held, and he will be no danger to us shortly."

"Very well," Blackthorn replied, disinterested in the details. His image flickered briefly before vanishing, leaving Vaux alone in oppressive silence. He exhaled slowly, tension evident in every movement. Rising, he exited the secure room, resolved that next time, Dominic wouldn't escape.

VATICAN CITY

In the Vatican Archives, Ian Duffy hunched over his workstation, poring over scrupulously obtained classified intelligence reports that Sister Teri's discreet network, including a global network of Vatican diplomatic ambassadors known as *nuncios*, had diligently compiled. Nuncios worldwide often act as informal intelligence agents, gathering political, religious, and cultural information from around the world and reporting it back to Secretariat of State personnel in Rome. Many insiders and journalists covering the Holy See refer to this as the Vatican's "diplomatic intelligence" network.

Files from Genetica Therapeutics had recently been decrypted, revealing more troubling discoveries than anyone had imagined.

Ian quickly scanned through files labeled cryptically as the "Kronos Protocol," frowning deeper with each entry.

His heart quickened as details unfolded: carefully documented biochemical analyses, attempts at synthetic replication of ancient botanical compounds, and detailed chemical structures closely resembling formulas described cryptically by Juana in her manuscripts.

"My God," he murmured, disturbed by the clinical detachment of the notes. Genetica's researchers had clearly attempted to replicate Juana's visionary compound synthetically, often through ethically questionable methods. Many experimental subjects had shown adverse reactions, symptoms of severe psychological stress, and alarming neurological side effects.

Ian quickly flagged critical documents, securing digital copies for Michael and Hana's review. As he scanned further, his unease deepened. References indicated attempts at accelerated production schedules, cutting ethical and safety guidelines to speed replication. He duly noted a recent lab accident, quietly covered up by Genetica's executives—a tragic failure to control botanical potency, resulting in extensive neurological damage.

The truth was clear: Genetica's reckless quest to synthesize and monopolize Juana's formulas endangered far more than academic research. The company threatened innocent lives, desperate in its aggressive pursuit of secrets only partially understood.

Ian leaned back heavily in his chair, unsettled and anxious. He quickly transmitted all critical data securely to Sister Teri. They needed immediate protective measures—before Genetica's unchecked ambition caused irreparable harm.

. . .

IN THE QUIET sanctuary of her Vatican digital workspace, Sister Teri studied the streams of financial data flowing across multiple screens, each transaction illuminating previously hidden networks linking Alton Blackthorn to Genetica Therapeutics' shadowy ventures.

Her fingers flew across her keyboard, tracing financial records through Swiss holding companies, offshore accounts, and shell corporations based in Luxembourg, Liechtenstein, and the Cayman Islands. Patterns gradually emerged—consistent, discreet financial trails prudently hidden through multiple layers of ownership and control.

Teri narrowed her eyes thoughtfully, pausing on a significant series of large wire transfers. These originated from Blackthorn's private holdings, flowing directly into corporations specializing in rare botanical acquisitions and genetic research. Each was fully anonymized, yet with patience, she began linking them to Genetica Therapeutics.

A quiet knock at her door startled her slightly, and Ian quickly entered, concern etched across his face.

"I found something troubling," he explained urgently, sharing his findings about the Kronos Protocol. "Genetica's trying desperately to replicate Juana's botanical compounds, even bypassing ethical standards."

Teri nodded grimly. "That aligns with what I'm seeing here. Blackthorn's invested millions into acquiring rare botanical specimens—he's utterly desperate to control Juana's discoveries. Once he does, who knows what purposes he has in mind. Although we can count greed as being at the heart of it."

Ian's voice grew tense. "Already they've endangered lives, Teri. Human experimentation, unregulated trials— it's beyond unethical. It's criminal."

She exhaled slowly, recognizing the weight of

responsibility now upon them both. "Then we must share everything with Father Dominic. He needs to understand the depth of Blackthorn's obsession—and the danger he poses."

LATER THAT EVENING, beneath the warm glow of candlelight in his modest apartment overlooking the gardens of Vatican City, Michael reviewed Ian and Teri's unsettling findings.

Hana, seated across from him, studied each document closely, her expression seemingly troubled.

"This explains Blackthorn's desperation," she said. "He's convinced Juana's compounds could redefine modern medicine. He'll stop at nothing to commercialize them."

Michael rubbed his temples wearily, unsettled by what he had read. "Blackthorn's greed risks far more than we imagined. He threatens the legacy of the *Voynich Manuscript* itself—its possible purpose as a beacon of careful wisdom, now reduced to mere profit and exploitation."

Hana shook her head adamantly. "Whatever insights Juana and the monks safeguarded, it's knowledge humans aren't yet ready to comprehend fully. Juana encoded the *Voynich* symbolism precisely because she understood humanity's temptations, its endless hunger for power."

Michael leaned forward intently. "Exactly. Juana's entire life was a testament to responsible stewardship. She cleverly balanced revelation and concealment. We must continue her work—reveal enough to awaken the world, yet protect the deeper secrets that still remain elusive."

Hana's eyes brightened. "Perhaps Juana's ultimate

message is simply that: the balance between seeking knowledge and respecting its power. The *Voynich Manuscript* itself resists complete decoding because it's designed to remain tantalizingly incomplete, always inspiring—but never fully yielding—its assumed truths."

Michael inclined his head, greatly moved. "It's a lesson we must heed faithfully. If Blackthorn succeeds in his reckless pursuit, the foresight Juana guarded so faithfully could become humankind's undoing."

The room fell quiet, each of them lost in deep thought. Hana reached across the table, taking Michael's hand firmly. "We can still safeguard her legacy, Michael—but we must act decisively."

He squeezed her hand gratefully, determination returning. "Agreed. Tomorrow, we reinforce everything— physical security, digital protections, historical evidence… Blackthorn's next move will undoubtedly be aggressive. We need to be ready."

As candlelight flickered softly around them, shadows dancing across walls lined with cerebral texts, Michael knew Hana was right. The deeper truths hidden within Juana's ciphers—the powerful wisdom encoded within the *Voynich Manuscript* itself—required vigilant guardianship now more than ever.

Juana had known the risks intimately, had foreseen the world's perpetual struggle between prudence and temptation. She had encoded those secrets, knowing future generations would grapple endlessly with their meaning.

Now, centuries later, Michael felt a certain gratitude for Juana's caution, her foresight, and her quiet courage. Yet he also felt intense responsibility, for Blackthorn's ambitions threatened far more than mere historical curiosity. They threatened the very balance Juana had safeguarded so conscientiously.

Whatever came next, Michael resolved silently—he, Hana, Ian, Simon, Teri, Karl, Lukas—all of them would stand resolutely together, safeguarding Juana's legacy fiercely, ensuring her knowledge remained a beacon of inspiration rather than exploitation.

CHAPTER

EIGHTEEN

VATICAN CITY

Deep beneath the Vatican Secret Archives, the gentle hum of air filters mingled with the soft rustling of pages. Ian Duffy sat hunched over a faded medieval diary, its fragile parchment crackling beneath careful fingers. Beside him, stacks of reference texts and handwritten notes spilled across the heavy oak table, bathed softly in golden lamplight.

This diary, recently discovered among manuscripts hidden by monks centuries ago in Avignon, then secured in the Archives, held promises of profound revelations. Ian exhaled slowly, carefully turning the brittle pages. Tiny lines of text appeared faded yet distinct, inscribed in a meticulous, feminine script. It was unquestionably Juana de la Cruz's handwriting—her words cautious yet determined, filled with the fierce intellect and sincere spirituality that had defined her life.

Yet many of the diary's entries had been encrypted

using a complex cipher, combining alchemical symbolism with intricate zodiacal references. Ian had spent hours painstakingly decoding these fragments, each success deepening the mystery while revealing tantalizing hints.

He adjusted his reading glasses, then peered intently at the newly decrypted passage, reading aloud in Latin, translating into English for clarity:

"To those who follow in wisdom's path, remember always: The keys to Viridis reside not merely in plants nor the celestial spheres alone, but within their sacred union. Observe the heavens at the hour the twin-root blossoms, under Virgo's gaze. When Virgo rules the midnight sky, unite both root and herb beneath the new moon's shadow. Yet beware—the final illumination will elude all but those worthy in spirit."

Ian paused thoughtfully, jotting quick notes. "Virgo, twin-root blossoms, the new moon... clear symbolic instructions, yet intentionally incomplete," he murmured. Frustration edged his voice. Each clue Juana provided seemed to raise more questions than it answered.

He turned to another passage, one more cryptically encoded. After several tense minutes, Ian's pencil stilled as the lines resolved into another translated segment:

"As Llull taught, so must the initiate perceive threefold wisdom: botanical, celestial, spiritual. Without balance, the cipher closes its gates eternally. Yet even I see dimly—the path to the Roger Bacon Cipher remains clouded, its symbols ever shifting, ever hidden from the greedy heart. Future generations

may approach yet never fully reach. Preserve humility, else darkness overtakes wisdom's light."

LEANING BACK INTO HIS CHAIR, Ian sighed in exasperation. The passages were clearly crucial, yet Juana had deliberately obscured deeper instructions. Her diary hinted repeatedly that the Roger Bacon Cipher symbolism was designed for endless exploration, each layer leading to more profound truths.

A gentle knock startled him briefly, as Michael Dominic and Hana Sinclair entered the room.

"Ian?" Michael asked. "Have you made any progress?"

Ian rose, handing Michael his notes. "Fragments, yes. Juana encoded careful instructions—alignments of zodiac signs, botanical references—but explicitly left the core cipher incomplete. It's as if she's teasing us, always promising more yet withholding full revelation."

Hana studied the notes, eyes pensive. "Maybe Juana's intent wasn't teasing, but teaching. Perhaps she believed true wisdom requires persistent questioning."

Michael inclined his head, reading Ian's notes. "Still, Juana hints repeatedly that she had uncovered important truths; yet at the same time, she needed to conceal them."

Ian sighed. "If there are deeper layers, I fear Juana hid them exceptionally well. Every decoded passage raises new questions—yet resolves little."

Michael squeezed Ian's shoulder encouragingly. "Then let's review them again. We might discover more if we work on it together."

. . .

MUCH LATER, Michael set Ian's notes down, exhaling slowly. "Juana understood exactly how dangerous complete revelation could become," he murmured. "Yet she never ceased hoping humanity might someday grow ready."

Hana's gaze softened. "Perhaps she's showing us that such knowledge isn't simply decoded—it's earned through persistent struggle, constant questioning."

Ian nodded steadily. "She expressly states that deeper wisdom is forever hidden from greedy or irresponsible seekers. She believed people must approach humbly, or risk destroying what it is we seek."

Michael stared at the ancient diary, sensing Juana's quiet struggles and personal courage. "Then our task isn't merely to decode—but to preserve a posture of listening, not declaring. Every insight we gain carries responsibility."

Ian nodded, his voice earnest. "Juana plainly connects botanical, celestial, and spiritual acumen. Only when balanced correctly, she writes, can we safely approach deeper truths."

Hana's eyes lit with realization. "Maybe the manuscript isn't incomplete by accident. Juana deliberately structured its symbolism in layers."

They stood silently together, feeling intensely the historical weight of Juana's choices. Her life's purpose had been heartfelt yet risky, courageous yet cautious—guiding humanity toward deeper understanding while vigilantly safeguarding it from its darker tendencies.

Michael drew in a deep breath, fervent respect clear in his voice. "Every mystery we solve reveals yet more complexity. Juana intended it—knowing that only persistent questioning, careful ethical judgment, and deep devotion can lead humans closer to genuine wisdom."

Ian closed the diary, enormously grateful yet humbled. "Then we continue cautiously, always seeking deeper truths in what was intentionally hidden. Juana's foresight protects us even now."

Michael glanced downward, absorbing his words, sensing clearly the deep-seated historical purpose beneath Juana's careful ciphering. Her diary had revealed the lesson mankind most urgently required—courage to seek knowledge, deference to accept limits, and the wisdom to safeguard perceptive truths against reckless ambition.

Standing quietly together in the gentle silence of the Archives, each felt acutely Juana's centuries-old presence guiding their steps. Her experiences, scrupulously protected, reminded them of humanity's responsibilities.

Whatever truths awaited discovery next, each knew firmly their task—to honor Juana's legacy, protect her gifts, and always, humbly, pursue deeper truths.

THE VATICAN'S secrets include that of an underground holding area, a prison of sorts, one might say, where those suspected of crimes can be secured prior to potentially handing them over to the legal authorities. As a sovereign state, the Vatican does not answer to the Italian police. And the Italian police, almost wholly composed of devout Catholics, avoided posing any questions to the Vatican authorities about either their suspects or their facilities beyond the formal paperwork required.

A man with wild eyes and disheveled hair was led in handcuffs from the Vatican holding area late that night to be transported to the nearest Italian police station. Vaux's foiled attempt at the Benedictine monastery in Avignon two days ago had left this one thug in the hands of two determined Swiss Guards. In this case, his crimes, considering they had occurred in the French region of Avignon, meant the man was soon to be transported to the French authorities. Karl, on duty that night, watched as the man had to be pushed into the back of a police van. The man's glare at Karl before they closed the door, spoke volumes of the anger he felt over the lengthy questioning he'd endured already while in the Vatican's custody. Although Karl had learned some things, admittedly, the man knew little of his employer's overall plans or methods. The interrogations hadn't been entirely useless, but not as helpful as the Swiss Guard would have liked. Even at that, Karl's friends in the Italian police assured him that they would continue to question the assailant, their unspoken yet persuasive ways, and pass whatever information they learned on to the Swiss Guard.

It was only an hour later that Karl received a call from his compatriot at Carabinieri headquarters.

The suspect had not survived the transfer to the police station.

Investigations would be held, of course, to determine what had occurred, but it was clear that the man had been well, if frustratingly stubborn, when he entered the van. And when he left, he was decidedly dead. His stomach had purged itself of all fluids from apparently a highly lethal and quick poison that had worked its wonders silently in the confines of the van. The experienced among the Italian Carabinieri had never seen quite the likes of such a poison.

When Karl hung up, only one word came to his mind: *Genetica*.

CHAPTER
NINETEEN

VATICAN CITY

Deep within the Vatican's digital operations center, tucked discreetly behind thick stone walls and layers of reinforced steel, Sister Teri's fingers danced effortlessly over her keyboard. Beside her, Ian sat hunched forward, eyes narrowed in deep concentration, attentively examining streams of encrypted data scrolling across his own screen.

The softly glowing monitors cast halos around the pair as they infiltrated the digital heart of Genetica Therapeutics. Ian glanced briefly at Teri, eyebrows raised in admiration.

"You know, Teri," Ian remarked with mock solemnity, "if you ever tire of Vatican life, there's definitely a future for you hacking into banks or dismantling hostile governments."

Teri didn't look up, but her lips curled into a sly smile. "And if you ever tire of dusty manuscripts, Ian, I hear the local coffee shop needs someone to alphabetize their menu."

Ian chuckled. "Touché, Sis. But seriously, have you ever considered a career as a double agent?"

"Not unless they change the uniform," Teri replied dryly, eyes never leaving the screen. "I don't do black leather jumpsuits."

Ian grinned, tension momentarily easing before he refocused on the encrypted logs. The fragmented data in Genetica's own not-quite-so-secured database wasn't straightforward, but filled instead with cryptic references and partially corrupted files. But Ian's keen historical expertise quickly became evident as he began cross-referencing isolated snippets against his own diligent research notes.

"Teri, I've found something," he murmured intently, fingers flying across his keyboard as he pieced together disjointed fragments.

Teri spared him a glance, eyes twinkling. "Your lucky day, or is it actually skill this time?"

Ian ignored the playful jab, engrossed in decrypting the layered files. "There's encrypted data referencing 'Anno Domini 1427' repeatedly—plus scattered astronomical terms. It can't be coincidental."

"Anno Domini 1427?" Teri echoed, interest piqued. Her fingers briefly slowed as she watched Ian navigate the complexity.

He nodded firmly, excitement sharpening his tone. "Definitely. Cross-referencing that date and location clues within the fragments, I recognized something. Montserrat Abbey, another of the node locations I found in the Archives that corresponded to the engraving in Juana's monastery, keeps appearing alongside references to anomalous celestial phenomena. Hold on…" His voice trailed off momentarily as he decrypted another segment.

Teri leaned closer, curiosity overcoming her usual composure. "Ian, what exactly are we looking at?"

"Genetica had somehow gotten hidden accounts from Montserrat Abbey," Ian replied, eyes intense. "The monks recorded sightings of unusual 'wandering messengers' in the sky, clearly distinct from known astronomical objects. These reports were deliberately concealed, buried deep beneath layers of code."

Teri's eyebrows rose skeptically. "Hidden by whom?"

"Unknown," Ian said, his eyes never leaving his screen. "But here's the kicker—each celestial event they describe correlates precisely with sudden appearances of peculiar botanical symbols as if new plants had just been discovered. And these aren't benign medicinal herbs— they're explicitly marked as dangerous, even toxic."

Teri exhaled slowly, processing the implications. "Deliberately hidden celestial events coupled to toxic plants. You've managed to uncover something seriously troubling. Not to mention that Genetica is already on this same trail."

Ian nodded, downloading the decrypted logs and encrypting them securely. "I'll show this to Michael posthaste."

"Agreed," Teri replied, hurriedly finalizing her sabotage of Genetica's network. "Whatever we've just stepped into, it's much bigger—and darker—than we initially thought."

Ian stood, stretching stiff muscles, determination now mixed with deep concern. "At least we know monks had good reason to keep their eyes on the heavens. They had discovered that certain celestial phenomena triggered new or altered plants. A direct, and distinctly physical connection between heaven and earth. The Church might not have appreciated their findings of this more physical than spiritual connection."

Teri smiled faintly, standing beside him. "Careful, Ian. You're sounding dangerously irreverent again."

He chuckled, though seriousness lingered behind his eyes. "As always, irreverent remains my default setting."

MEANWHILE, seated comfortably at his desk in the Vatican Secret Archives, Father Dominic adjusted the laptop positioned in front of him. After a brief delay, the screen flickered to life, revealing the distinguished features of Dr. Raúl Castillo, seated in a warmly lit study overflowing with antique books and historical artifacts. Castillo, a renowned scholar, was noted for his expertise in astronomy during a multidisciplinary Caltech project. Despite the digital medium, his presence felt welcoming and scholarly, as though Michael had entered his colleague's own library in Barcelona.

"Father Dominic," Castillo greeted warmly, eyes twinkling through his round-rimmed spectacles, "it's always a pleasure. Technology has indeed made our academic world a smaller place."

Michael smiled appreciatively. "Agreed, Raúl—though I confess, given recent events, it also seems to have made it a more complicated one."

Castillo nodded knowingly, his smile turning briefly cautious. "Indeed. So tell me, how can I help with your intriguing research today?"

Michael leaned slightly closer, glancing briefly at notes

spread neatly beside his laptop. "As you know, our investigation into Juana de la Cruz and the *Voynich Manuscript* has increasingly involved references to unusual celestial phenomena. Ian Duffy recently uncovered historical accounts mentioning monks observing strange 'moving stars'—events specifically linked to botanical symbolism appearing in manuscripts shortly thereafter. Have you encountered similar reports in your research?"

Unexpectedly, Castillo's expression darkened slightly, becoming more guarded. "Yes—I have. Particularly striking records surfaced from Montserrat Abbey around 1427. Friars fully documented lights, which they described as 'wandering messengers' traversing the night sky. But these accounts are far more troubling than the innocent curiosities many historians suggest."

Michael's interest sharpened visibly, sensing the shift in Castillo's tone. "Troubling in what sense?"

Castillo adjusted his spectacles, choosing his words with deliberate care. "Officially, as expected, the monks framed these sightings as divine signs. But privately—and these private accounts have rarely seen daylight—they perceived these 'messengers' as hostile entities. Their chronicles describe the lights not merely as puzzling or unfamiliar, but curiously threatening."

Michael felt a jolt of surprise ripple through him. "Threatening? How so?"

Castillo sighed heavily, his intellectual poise momentarily giving way to unease. "They noted strange occurrences coinciding with these sightings. Crop failures, sudden illnesses among livestock, inexplicable ailments within their own community—disturbing phenomena they attributed directly to these 'wandering messengers.'"

Michael sat back slightly. "That broadens what we've

learned about these sightings. What does science have to say about this, if anything?"

"Oh, quite a bit. And yet not much that is conclusive," Castillo said. "As a university dedicated to astronomy more deeply than nearly any other institution in the world, Caltech has a program that can use the cyclical schedules of the planets and stars to deduce the alignments of the heavens in the past. We've used it to go back to various times when such things as crop failures were rampant. We've recognized some potential celestial triggers, yet the general consensus is not clear. Most believe that sunspots, volcanic actions, or other atmospheric issues were more than likely the cause of such anomalies on Earth. But there are those of us still who wonder. Maybe what you have learned will add to our wealth of knowledge. I am counting on you to share, Michael, when the time comes."

Michael saw the quizzical look on the screen, indicating Dr. Castillo's interest in Michael's research. "Most certainly," Michael assured him. "And, thank you for your insights."

Castillo inclined his head, a gentle warmth returning to his features. "My pleasure, as always. Take care, Michael—and tread carefully. Some historical truths, once unleashed, resist being contained again."

Michael ended the call slowly, sitting silently afterward as he contemplated the new uncertainties Castillo had laid bare.

KARL AND LUKAS methodically swept Michael's quarters for surveillance devices. Lukas deliberately waved a handheld scanner throughout the rooms, eyes scanning systematically.

"Found another," he announced dryly, extracting a tiny transmitter from behind a bookshelf and deactivating it. "Vaux's persistence is impressive."

Karl took the device, eyeing it with mild irritation. "If he keeps planting these, we can open our own electronics store."

Lukas's mouth twitched. "Or start a collection. 'Vatican Bugs—Limited Edition.'"

Karl smiled briefly, placing the device securely in a pouch. "Humor aside, let's double security sweeps. Vaux seems intent on invading every private corner."

LATE THAT EVENING, Ian and Sister Teri joined Michael in the Vatican Archives, where they laid out their findings. Ian steadily recounted medieval accounts of monks observing mysterious celestial events, followed closely by unusual botanical discoveries.

Michael absorbed every detail, finally speaking with careful consideration. "If monks consistently recorded these phenomena, we must seriously consider their credibility."

Teri leaned forward slightly. "Father, what if the *Voynich Manuscript* really does encode more than earthly botanical knowledge? Maybe it is meant to document how something in the heavens has a tangible influence on Earth's life?"

Michael blew out a breath, eyes thoughtful yet troubled. "If true, we face extraordinary implications— historically, theologically, philosophically."

Ian leaned back lightly, breaking tension again with dry humor. "In other words, Father, we've gone from decoding ancient texts to chasing medieval UFOs. My career trajectory is fascinating."

Michael chuckled softly despite himself, appreciating Ian's levity. "Indeed, Ian. Next thing you know, we'll find ourselves debating alien theology. Of course, in essence, these events could still be astronomical, something comet-like, asteroid dust, or who knows, and not little green men at all. At this point, 'wandering messengers' could mean anything."

Teri smiled. "That's what keeps things interesting around here, isn't it?"

Michael stood, seriousness returning tempered by the warmth of their camaraderie. "Whatever these truths ultimately reveal—earthly or celestial—we must approach with caution, humility, and open minds."

Ian nodded respectfully. "Agreed, Father. After all, humility is clearly our strongest virtue."

Teri raised an eyebrow. "Speak for yourself, Ian."

UNDER COVER OF EVENING DARKNESS, Ian exited the Vatican, his stride purposeful yet measured. Navigating narrow Roman streets, he reached San Clemente Basilica, its layered subterranean levels offering a complex historical labyrinth. Armed only with a flashlight and a detailed sketch copied faithfully from Juana's cryptic notes, he ventured into the ancient depths beneath the Basilica.

His pulse quickened as the air turned damp and cool. Guided by intuition and scholarship, he navigated ancient frescoes and carved inscriptions until he reached a hidden alcove described faintly yet deliberately in Juana's notes.

Kneeling, Ian ran his fingers along the stones, the grit and dust of ages welcoming his probing touch. He felt carefully along each well-worn stone, first at the floor of the alcove, and then along the walls. His breath caught when he finally felt a movement, accompanied by a light 'tick' sound as the stone rubbed on its neighbor. Now using both hands, he realized several stones adjacent to each other moved as one, like a panel, small but big enough to hide something. Carefully, he removed the loose stone segment to reveal a fragile, concealed manuscript wrapped tightly in aged linen.

Heart racing, he unwrapped the document, scarcely daring to breathe as he shone his light on it. Its pages, remarkably preserved, detailed explicit celestial phenomena. But what caught his breath was direct and clear references to "celestial beings" who had visited ancient Roman astronomers. As he stood, his mouth open, his finger poised over the words that translated, yet again, to "celestial beings," suddenly footsteps echoed suddenly nearby.

Ian froze, extinguishing his flashlight immediately. Hidden in shadows, he saw two figures cautiously approach, unmistakably Blackthorn's operatives, their movements stealthy and alert. They were still in the passageway, their heads swiveling between the pathways at each side as they continued to move forward.

Instinct took over. Ian discreetly concealed the manuscript within his jacket, quietly retreating deeper into the catacomb's shadows. Yet as quiet as he was, his movements could be heard in the cave-like stone labyrinth. He knew instantly he was discovered as he heard footsteps pursue in his direction, forcing him into the labyrinth's narrow tunnels, heart pounding with fear yet determination.

At one point, an alcove provided a dark and secluded place where he could risk a flick of his flashlight only an inch from his map to give him his next direction. Light extinguished again, he now ran down the last passage, making a left, three rights, and a quick U-turn into another tunnel.

Moments later, he had raced up an incline into the major area of the basilica's tunnel system and spotted a rusted, metal door. He rushed through it, closing it quickly behind him, emerging breathless and shaken onto Rome's quiet streets, clutching his precious discovery tightly against him.

CHAPTER

TWENTY

VATICAN CITY

I an burst through the door of the Vatican Secret Archives, breathless and disheveled, startling Father Michael, Hana, Simon, and Sister Teri, who had been anxiously awaiting any news of his whereabouts. Teri had called in for an update, and when she couldn't raise him, she began to worry. Considering the adversaries they faced, any one of their team, if unaccounted for, became a concern to them all. They all felt relieved to see him enter now, yet his condition startled them. His normally tidy red hair was disarrayed, a smear of dust streaked across his cheek, and urgency blazed in his eyes.

"Ian!" Michael stood quickly, concern etched on his face. "What happened? We've been trying to reach you."

Ian leaned forward, placing a worn manuscript onto the mahogany table. "I went to San Clemente," he began, his voice strained yet unswerving. "I found something extraordinary—another manuscript. But Blackthorn's men were there. They nearly intercepted me."

Hana quickly approached him, placing a comforting hand on Ian's shoulder, guiding him toward a chair. "Ian, you went alone? That was incredibly dangerous."

He nodded slowly, catching his breath. "I had no choice. We know the Archives are compromised. Plus you," he glanced at Michael and Hana, "have been surveilled at each location you traveled. I figured that by going alone and not telling anyone, I could potentially avoid that. If anyone had discovered this before us, everything we've worked for could have been lost."

Sister Teri leaned forward, immediately alert. "Did they harm you?"

"I'm all right, just shaken," Ian reassured them, his breathing beginning to steady. "Knowing they can somehow track me as well is most unsettling."

"I'm wondering if that's the case," Michael interjected. "It appears they are already privy to manuscripts that are hinting at the same thing we are following: that there have been celestial events in the past that resulted in unique botanical changes. You found that when you and Teri infiltrated Genetica's own database. So maybe it was a coincidence that some of his people are investigating the same places we are?" Michael looked at the others and received only frowns and shrugs. Who could tell at this early stage? Yet coincidences of this sort obviously didn't settle well with any of them. "So, Ian, what did you find?"

"This manuscript confirms everything we've suspected —celestial phenomena observed historically, just as Juana described. These references directly connect Montserrat Abbey and Juana's diary."

Simon opened the fragile manuscript Ian had retrieved,

his hands trembling slightly with reverence and excitement. He scanned the Latin annotations quickly, his eyes widening with amazement.

"Incredible," Simon murmured, visibly astonished. "This unequivocally references the celestial events we've uncovered, especially those connected to Montserrat Abbey in the early fifteenth century. Look here—'Celestial lights moving with deliberate grace, observed beneath a conjunction unlike any recorded before.'"

Ian spoke up, unable to contain his puzzled excitement at the wording he had found. He pointed to three references, looking up in their faces. "Celestial beings," he said. "Clearly, translations for these phrases indicate 'celestial beings' visited Rome. Nowhere else has a term that indicates an actual entity, not just a light in the sky, visited Earth."

The tension in the room became palpable. Eyes flicked between each of the three phrases as if to discern something other than Ian's interpretation. Then, each person gazed at the others as if looking for validation or a dispute as to this interpretation.

Finally, Michael took a step back, as if to gain perspective, and provided a note of reason, saying, "Clearly the translation is 'being' and it states 'visiting Rome.' But this is the only such reference we've discovered at this point. Let's not jump to the conclusion we all have just entertained. One person's word alone on any subject needs to be taken in light of their possible perceptions. It must be coupled with corroboration and documentation before we can start to assess its reality.

"Yet, this does present a new perspective we have to be alert to as we go forward."

Michael stepped forward again, studying the

manuscript closely. "However, the rest of this confirms what we've been piecing together from Juana's fragments and the *Voynich* symbols. These aren't isolated accounts. They document a historical pattern—repeated celestial visitations, whether they stem from only light sources in the heavens or actual beings standing in Rome, are clearly associated with unique botanical phenomena."

Ian nodded vigorously, now regaining his composure fully. "Exactly. This isn't mythology or mere medieval imagination. This was carefully observed, recorded—and deliberately suppressed. The Church knew, Michael, and feared what public acknowledgment could mean."

Hana leaned in closer, her voice quiet yet urgent. "The being in my vision spoke of how understanding 'thrives only in interconnected balance with the cosmos.' And this manuscript specifically references the spiritual and botanical transformations associated with these celestial events?"

"Yes," Ian affirmed, pointing decisively to another passage. "It describes the exact transformations Juana noted: plants exhibiting miraculous properties, astute spiritual insights experienced by those who witnessed these celestial encounters. This knowledge was intentionally hidden—protected—because of the immense implications."

Michael straightened, taking a deep, contemplative breath. "This revelation escalates our responsibility enormously. We're no longer merely uncovering lost history; we're confronting truths that will profoundly challenge humans. Celestial visitations, potentially contact with something... maybe 'beings'... that influences the minds of men and the plants in the fields. These could be shattering revelations. We must present this knowledge openly yet cautiously."

Ian sat back slowly, visibly relieved yet moved by the gravity of their conversation. "Then our immediate task is clear—developing a careful, deliberate approach to disclosure. Humanity deserves this truth, but they must be ready for its ethical and spiritual weight."

Hana placed her hand over Ian's, offering quiet reassurance. "And Ian, your bravery tonight made all this possible. We owe you our deepest gratitude."

Ian smiled, feeling grateful for her acknowledgment yet humbled by the moment's significance. "Thank you, Hana. But this belongs to all of us—and to humanity. Let's make certain we handle it right."

Michael turned to Simon, his expression contemplative. "This manuscript clearly ties Juana's insights to Ramon Llull's concepts—alchemy as a metaphor for spiritual transformation."

Simon nodded, intrigued. "Llull's *Ars Magna* sought unity of knowledge. He believed that combining knowledge of various fields like, in this case, astronomy and botany, can bring revelations that show relationships otherwise not understood. Many consider his *Ars Magna* to be a precursor to computer science. Perhaps he recognized, intuitively or unconsciously, that humanity's delicate relationship with celestial phenomena could only be fully understood by combining it with other fields of knowledge."

Ian leaned forward eagerly. "These medieval scholars consistently documented experiences linking celestial occurrences with botanical phenomena. Montserrat Abbey's monks, Llull, and Juana—they all encountered something undeniably overpowering."

Hana arranged photocopies of Juana's diary fragments and notes, tracing delicate fingers across the faded script. "Here's what we've decoded so far. Juana describes botanical compounds that must be harvested and combined under specific conditions; celestial alignments are critical."

Michael nodded, scanning the careful translations. "The Virgo alignment, specifically. Juana emphasized the need to combine these herbs precisely when Virgo rules the midnight sky, beneath a new moon."

Simon leaned forward intently, examining a photocopy of Juana's studious sketches. "Fascinating how she insists on absolute precision of celestial alignment. This zodiacal emphasis is particularly intriguing."

Ian, sipping an espresso Hana had made for him, tilted his head skeptically. "I get the spiritual and botanical connections, certainly—but Juana's astronomical focus strikes me as somewhat odd, especially these repeated references to celestial movements that don't match familiar astronomical charts."

Simon's eyes twinkled curiously as he pushed forward another diary page. "That's exactly my point. Look here—she sketches constellations clearly, yet also includes symbols we can't readily identify. It's as though she documented celestial bodies unknown to standard astronomy."

Hana glanced up, her interest piqued. "You think Juana was observing something beyond common celestial knowledge?"

Simon hesitated slightly, tone cautious but animated. "Historically speaking, it wouldn't be unprecedented. Various cultures documented unusual celestial phenomena they couldn't explain. The fifteenth century wasn't exactly known for scientific accuracy—but Juana's precision suggests she was accurately recording something genuine, yet something unfamiliar."

Michael considered this, feeling the weight of responsibility growing. "Then we must reconstruct her ritual as closely as possible, using the best understanding we have. At the very least, it might clarify what she believed she'd observed."

Simon noted, "Juana wasn't the only figure to combine celestial observations with unusual botanical or scientific pursuits. As I'm sure you all recall, you were not that long ago plunged into the bowels of a mountain in Poland. All for the sake of chasing the historical proof of Hitler's intense obsession with esoteric knowledge, advanced technologies, and celestial phenomena—particularly UFOs."

Michael took Hana's hand, both recalling the close call they had with death when they had attempted to infiltrate what ended up to be a stronghold of the Third Reich. They had uncovered the Nazi's secreted cache of not just gold and art, but advanced technology as well.

Simon continued, "Many postwar researchers and conspiracy theorists alike, ever since then, have continued to believe the German *Die Glocke* or 'The Bell' involved anti-gravity power had been provided through celestial or extraterrestrial technology."

Michael sat, absorbing Simon's insights. "While clearly speculative, Simon makes a legitimate point. Juana might have similarly recorded genuine celestial phenomena outside known astronomy, though perhaps interpreted through a medieval, mystical lens rather than modern scientific theory."

Ian nodded cautiously, maintaining intellectual

distance. "Granted, Juana was diligent, not prone to flights of fancy. Still, we must exercise caution. There's a difference between unknown celestial phenomena and outright—dare I say it—extraterrestrial speculation."

Michael smiled knowingly, understanding Ian's caution. "Agreed. For now, let's remain focused strictly on reconstructing Juana's described ritual. If celestial factors genuinely influence botanical potency, Juana's instructions become critical."

They quickly organized materials, reviewing Juana's diary closely. Hana documented each botanical ingredient, creating a detailed checklist. Michael retrieved a large historical zodiacal chart matching Juana's specified dates and alignments. Simon cross-referenced celestial events noted in medieval astronomical journals.

For the next hour, they methodically documented Juana's botanical ritual instructions:

- Identification of rare botanical herbs: specifically, twin-root blossoms (*"Herba Gemina"*), gathered under Virgo's midnight alignment.
    - Exact lunar phase: the darkest hour of a new moon.
    - Botanical preparation instructions: herbs to be dried beneath starlight, mixed carefully at midnight, then steeped in pure spring water until dawn.

Ian frowned as Hana detailed each instruction. "Seems incredibly specific. Almost impossibly explicit."

Michael smiled, understanding Ian's reservations. "True—but Juana considered this precision spiritually critical. It aligns perfectly with her spiritual and botanical symbolism."

Simon added, "And perhaps physically critical too, if genuinely influenced by unknown celestial energies."

Ian chuckled, lightly teasing Simon's enthusiasm. "Simon, if we actually recreate this successfully, I promise I'll personally advocate for a special Vatican bureau of celestial herbology."

Simon returned Ian's dry humor warmly. "Careful what you promise, Ian. You might end up Vatican Minister of UFO Affairs."

Hana laughed, appreciating their lighthearted exchange. "Let's at least try. Juana believed fervently in these rituals. Reconstructing her process might reveal something meaningful—whether spiritual, botanical, celestial... or entirely unexpected."

As their careful preparations continued, Michael discreetly gestured to Ian, stepping slightly away from the group. Ian followed, sensing Michael's thoughtful expression.

"Privately, Ian," Michael began, "I admit some uncertainty. These celestial references trouble me. Juana clearly documented something significant—but inexplicable."

Ian nodded. "I remain skeptical, Michael—but I can't deny Juana's meticulousness. Her astronomical observations seem genuinely puzzling. Still, must we seriously consider extraterrestrial origins?"

Michael sighed, acknowledging Ian's discomfort. "I share your skepticism. Yet Simon's historical references, combined with Juana's odd celestial symbolism, suggest something genuinely unexplainable. Medieval monks were astute observers, not prone to whimsical speculation."

Ian huffed. "Granted. Yet I still find it difficult to embrace extraterrestrial theories fully. Perhaps these celestial anomalies were unusual atmospheric phenomena —meteor showers, comets, or auroras misunderstood by medieval observers?"

Michael nodded. "Possibly. But, Juana explicitly describes celestial alignment precision far beyond mere atmospheric phenomena. Her instructions, combined with your discovery of 'moving stars' observed by several monasteries, strongly suggest genuine anomalies. I will ask my colleague, Dr. Castillo, to run the timings for these events noted by monks through his time back-tracing the astronomical system to see if some known cosmic configurations were present at each event.

"And we can't forget the latest document you found that specifically states 'celestial beings.' That concept needs more substantiating. But Juana's findings are echoed in too many other works to be able to dismiss them."

Ian sighed, for the moment conceding the point. "True enough, Michael. Juana's precision consistently impresses me. If anyone observed something genuinely unfathomable, she would document it rigorously. We owe Juana our due diligence."

Standing quietly beneath the Archives' gentle shadows, they both felt Juana's careful presence guiding their cautious steps. They now carried the responsibility to safeguard knowledge—whatever its origins—against people's perpetual tendency toward exploitation and recklessness.

CHAPTER
TWENTY-ONE

ROME, ITALY

Hana Sinclair stepped down the shadowed sidewalk toward the small Roman trattoria in Prati where she had been told to meet with a confidential Vatican source—one who claimed urgent knowledge of Juana's codex.

The late evening air was crisp, the street deserted, illuminated by flickering streetlamps and the distant glow of Vatican City. An elegant and upscale *rioni*, or neighborhood, of Rome, Prati lies adjacent to Vatican City, and is known for its authentic Roman restaurants and club scene built into Monte Testaccio—a hill composed of discarded ancient pottery.

Clutching her notes tightly, Hana moved quickly, her instincts alert to any unusual movement.

But she never heard the footsteps behind her.

A sudden rush, then strong arms encircled her, a cloth

pressed firmly over her face, pungent with chemicals. Hana struggled desperately, consciousness fading rapidly despite her fierce resistance. Darkness closed in, stealing away all sensation.

HANA AWOKE SLOWLY, mind foggy, disoriented. Her senses returned gradually—first, smell, a musty, herbal scent thick and cloying; then, hearing, the quiet hum of machinery somewhere distant; and finally, vision, blurry shapes coalescing into clarity.

She lay on a narrow cot in a dimly lit room, walls lined with shelves stacked high with jars filled with unrecognizable herbs, vials of strange fluids, and archaic tools reminiscent of medieval alchemy. The air was thick and oppressive, heavily perfumed with botanical essences that made her head swim dizzily.

She tried to sit up, discovering her wrists tightly bound to the cot. Panic flared sharply before she fought it down, forcing herself to take a deep breath. Footsteps approached. The door opened briskly, and Christophe Vaux stepped confidently inside, followed closely by a silent assistant who carried a tray of prepared botanical substances.

"Ms. Sinclair," Vaux said smoothly, his voice coldly courteous. "Forgive the theatrics, but our previous attempts at subtlety have proven ineffective."

Hana's gaze burned fiercely. "What do you want, Vaux?"

He smiled thinly, gesturing casually to the tray his assistant carried. "Simply your cooperation. We've replicated Juana de la Cruz's ritual preparations, or at least something similar. Given your previous experience with just one of the ingredients—and thank you for leading us to it—you're uniquely equipped to reveal the manuscript's symbolism."

Hana strained against her bonds defiantly. "I won't help you."

Vaux's smile faded slightly, his expression hardening. "I'm afraid refusal isn't an option."

He nodded curtly to his assistant. A cloth soaked in a botanical infusion was forced over Hana's mouth and nose. She fought again, but dizziness surged violently. Her vision blurred, consciousness slipping away, and she was lost once more to darkness.

HANA'S EYES fluttered open again, but this time everything had changed.

She stood beneath an alien sky, its colors vivid and surreal—deep shades of violet, emerald, and indigo swirled together, as if the heavens themselves danced to some unknowable rhythm. Above, strange constellations blazed brightly, entirely unfamiliar—arrangements of stars never seen from Earth, forming intricate, compelling patterns, as though ancient secrets connected them across impossible distances.

She stepped cautiously forward, barefoot upon lush, silken grass that glowed softly, illuminating her path. The atmosphere felt oddly heavy yet invigorating, every breath rich with an otherworldly fragrance—a perfume of blossoms unlike anything earthly, sweet yet distinctly powerful, flooding her senses with profound clarity. Ahead, a figure waited calmly, robed in garments that shimmered smoothly, shifting subtly with each slight movement, reflecting starlight in cascading waves of gentle color.

"Welcome, Hana," the figure said, its voice gentle yet resonant. "You are a seeker of hidden truths."

"Where am I?" Hana asked cautiously, her voice awed and confused.

"Between worlds," the figure replied. "This place exists at the threshold of understanding, where visions meet reality. The symbols you pursue bridge worlds known and unknown. It is a sanctuary created through botanical wisdom, a hidden gateway that has existed in quiet secrecy since humankind first looked upward, asking questions of the stars."

Hana stepped closer, her eyes scanning the luminous sky above. "These stars… I don't recognize them. Where is this place?"

The figure's hood fell back slightly, revealing gentle eyes filled with wisdom, eyes ancient yet timeless, carrying the weight of countless generations of carefully guarded knowledge. "Your mind sees through Juana's botanical wisdom, beyond what is merely earthly. These skies belong to another place entirely, far from your world. Juana saw them too—and encoded their mysteries within the manuscript you seek."

"Alien worlds?" Hana whispered incredulously, her mind reeling with sudden implications.

"Other worlds, other stars," the figure corrected gently, the words spoken with quiet conviction. "Throughout history, a precious few have glimpsed this celestial truth— guardedly hidden in plain sight, misunderstood or dismissed as mere myth or madness by generations not ready to accept such philosophical revelations."

Hana hesitated, then moved closer still, driven by curiosity as much as caution. "But why reveal this to me

GARY MCAVOY

now? Why have these visions appeared at this particular moment?"

The figure smiled, a kind and patient expression lighting its face. "Because humanity once again stands at a crossroads. Knowledge can uplift or destroy, depending entirely upon the wisdom of those who wield it. Juana's manuscript was designed to deliver truths in measured increments, awakening you slowly, cautiously, protecting you from yourselves."

Hana took a slow breath, feeling a mixture of reverence and fear. "How could botanical rituals grant visions of such distant worlds? Is there truly a connection between plants and stars?"

The figure inclined its head, eyes glistening thoughtfully. "All life is interconnected, Hana, rooted deeply within cosmic processes that defy conventional understanding. Ancient civilizations recognized this fundamental truth, expressing it symbolically through astrology, alchemy, and botanical mysteries. Juana, guided by intuition and tradition, encoded her revelations within plant and celestial symbols, weaving earnest truths into the tapestry of human history."

"Yet if such powerful knowledge exists," Hana questioned, voice trembling slightly, "why conceal it so thoroughly? Why have humans remained in ignorance?"

"Wisdom must match spiritual readiness," the figure explained with compassion, stepping slightly closer. "Throughout history, humanity's ambition has frequently outpaced its ethical maturity, leading inevitably toward self-destruction. Juana well knew this danger, choosing to protect these secrets until humankind evolved spiritually and intellectually to responsibly embrace them. Even now, many among you are not yet prepared."

Hana glanced again toward the surreal sky above, absorbing every extraordinary detail. "Then what am I supposed to do with this knowledge?"

"Guard it, Hana," the figure urged, earnestness coloring its words. "You and your companions stand now as careful custodians, responsible stewards of wisdom sufficiently complex to transform—or destroy—your world. Every clue you uncover brings humans closer to truth, yet it also amplifies the temptation for misuse. You must proceed with utter caution."

The figure turned its gaze upward, eyes reflecting alien constellations in quiet contemplation. "The stars you see now symbolize paths to deeper mysteries. Some lead to knowledge beneficial and nurturing, others to knowledge overwhelming and destructive. Juana understood this intimately, choosing her revelations carefully, trusting them only to those whose spirits and minds were balanced in wisdom and simplicity of character."

Hana followed the figure's gaze upward, awe-struck by the complexity and beauty of celestial patterns impossible to recognize or interpret. "Can humankind ever fully understand this?"

"Perhaps," the figure replied, tone gentle yet firm. "But understanding and readiness are different matters entirely. The journey toward truth must always respect people's capacity for self-destruction, tempered by compassion, humility, and patience. Juana's manuscript is both a roadmap and a test, revealing just enough to guide without overwhelming. You must honor that delicate balance."

Hana nodded with deliberate care. "I'll remember all you've shown me."

The figure smiled again, eyes filled with quiet

approval. "Then return, Hana, and carry with you a penance of spirit and wisdom. Remember that true knowledge is always balanced upon a delicate edge between enlightenment and chaos. Proceed with caution—and always with respect for mysteries still beyond your comprehension."

ABRUPTLY, Hana jolted awake again, back in the dimly lit laboratory. Her pulse raced as she still trembled from the vivid vision. Before she could fully recover, shouting erupted outside the door, sounds of violence and confrontation. Moments later, the door burst open violently, revealing Karl and Lukas, guns drawn, eyes instantly taking in the scene.

Vaux's assistant turned, grabbing for a weapon, but Lukas fired expertly, dropping him instantly with a nonlethal shot. Vaux himself bolted through a side entrance, disappearing quickly from sight. Lukas ran after him.

Karl rushed forward to cut off Hana's bonds.

"Are you all right, Hana?" he asked, eyes sharp with concern.

"I am now," Hana replied, still shaking as she rose with Karl's firm support. "But how did you find me?"

Karl shrugged. "A group effort. The moment you disappeared, Sister Teri went to work tracing the city's surveillance network. She found footage showing your abduction near the trattoria. From there, Ian quickly ran the license plates and cross-checked addresses tied to Vaux's known associates."

Lukas had returned as Karl spoke, shaking his head. He'd missed Vaux. The two Swiss Guards looked over toward Vaux's fallen assistant, but he, too, was gone and had apparently run back out from where they'd entered while Karl tended to Hana.

Still scanning for further threats, Lukas finished the explanation of locating Hana. "We narrowed it down to this abandoned clinic, which Genetica Therapeutics covertly acquired months ago. Once we'd identified it, thermal scans from *Oculus Petri*, the Vatican's satellite, showed clear activity inside."

Karl nodded, eyes vigilant. "After that, it was just a matter of precision and timing."

Lukas stepped up to support Hana's other side. "We should leave immediately. Vaux will regroup quickly and send reinforcements."

Karl's gaze darkened. "Agreed. Let's move."

An hour later, safely returned to Vatican grounds, Hana sat in Father Michael Dominic's study, wrapped warmly in a soft wool blanket. Michael observed her closely, eyes filled with gentle concern as he passed her a hot cup of tea. He had already passed the point of anger that she would take such a rendezvous without a guard. She knew now, as she should have suspected earlier, that this supposed meeting with an informant served only as a ploy to kidnap her. Now Michael just felt relief at her return.

"Are you feeling better?" he asked, seating himself beside her.

Hana nodded, hands trembling slightly. "Yes, thank you. But I experienced something curious—another vision, Michael. Vaux drugged me with what was apparently his preliminary version of Juana's formula, and the effect was similar to what I experienced in the greenhouse. Even more vivid and strange than before, though."

Michael leaned forward, curiosity tempered by gentle caution. "Can you describe in detail what you experienced?"

Hana took a deep breath, recounting every feature—the surreal sky filled with unfamiliar constellations, vibrant grass glowing around her, the mysterious robed figure describing worlds unknown to humans. Michael listened attentively, eyes widening slightly at each revelation.

"These stars," he asked, voice gentle yet intrigued, "did you recognize any of them... any known constellations, however distorted?"

Hana shook her head, her gaze troubled yet fascinated. "Nothing earthly, Michael. Those skies were completely alien. Stars arranged in patterns I've never seen—not even close to recognizable."

Michael considered her words, his voice quiet. "Juana's manuscript symbols consistently reference celestial phenomena medieval astronomers couldn't explain. Simon mentioned similar historical encounters—monks recording unknown celestial bodies, unusual skies. Events that modern astronomical science can't validate through reversing any celestial cycle we know. Maybe these monks witnessed, just as you did, some other sky altogether—and not that of Earth. Your visions might absolutely align with those descriptions."

Hana exhaled slowly, mind still swirling with intense emotions. "But Michael—are you suggesting my visions are genuinely extraterrestrial? Viewed from some other place, like another solar system?"

Michael's voice remained cautious yet gentle. "Not necessarily. Perhaps what you saw was symbolic, shaped by Juana's botanical compounds, interpreted through your subconscious. Yet..."

He hesitated slightly, choosing his next words carefully. "Juana was thorough. She obviously recorded things she genuinely witnessed—celestial phenomena medieval scholars struggled to explain rationally. If your visions accurately reflect Juana's experiences, then these celestial mysteries may be far more significant than mere symbolic imagery."

Hana fell silent, eyes gazing into the tea steaming mildly in her cup. "The figure I saw specifically warned me—these truths could awaken humanity or destroy it. Juana deliberately concealed her deeper insights, knowing the dangerous tendencies of the human race."

Absorbing the truth of her words, Michael felt intensely moved. "Then Juana understood our capacity for both enlightenment and destruction. Your vision reinforces our urgent responsibility—to protect these truths with due care."

Hana looked up slowly, eyes full of purpose. "Whatever their origin, these celestial visions demand caution. Juana's foresight transcends mere symbolism— perhaps even earthly boundaries. We need to continue with our work on this."

Recognizing Hana's quiet determination, Michael smiled in agreement. However, he also noted the fatigue in her eyes. It might be the result of the botanical drug given to her or the downside of the adrenaline that had pumped through her at being kidnapped. Either way, he recognized that she needed some rest, no matter how determined she was to keep going. "Exactly. Our task is now even clearer. Whatever truths Juana revealed, we must guard rigorously against reckless ambition. But, for the moment, Hana, you need some downtime. Such a traumatic event and your system being drugged, it all takes its toll. You get some rest. Then, when you are up to it, I would like you to give the entire group a full accounting of what you experienced."

Hana appeared about to object, but a weary sigh stopped her refusal. She nodded. "Thanks, I'll take it. Then I'll be more than happy to tell you all about it tomorrow."

They sat placidly together, feeling the weight of history and ethics upon them. Juana had glimpsed strange truths —perhaps even beyond humanity's terrestrial understanding—and encoded them for responsible seekers. Now, centuries later, Hana had been privy to the very type of message that this mystic of a nun had experienced herself. Michael and Hana stood at the crossroads Juana had foreseen, guardians of celestial mysteries humankind still struggled to comprehend.

TWENTY-TWO

VATICAN CITY

Ian Duffy leaned over the illuminated manuscript spread across the table in the private research chamber deep within the Vatican Secret Archives. Around him, ancient texts stacked in uneven towers cast delicate shadows across faded pages illuminated by the soft glow of a banker's lamp. He adjusted his glasses, squinting at the intricate Latin inscriptions inked by medieval scribes centuries ago.

Over the past several days, Ian had methodically expanded his research beyond Juana de la Cruz's manuscripts, delving deeply into medieval records, seeking additional references to the celestial symbolism they now increasingly encountered. The repeated mentions of strange celestial lights appearing across medieval monasteries had troubled him, yet also intrigued him intensely. He struggled between cautious skepticism and growing fascination, compelled to understand exactly what these medieval observers had recorded.

Ian carefully turned another page, pausing abruptly at a small, delicately illuminated passage from a late fourteenth-century monastic chronicler in France. The monk's hand was painstaking yet subtly hurried, as if recording events driven by urgency and confusion. Ian translated the text from the faded Latin:

"Anno Domini 1397, in the darkest hours of the night vigil, brothers observed strange lights moving in the heavens, drifting without order or explanation. Lights brilliant yet silent, neither stars nor meteors. Abbot forbade further public mention, believing it heretical to suggest God's creation could contain such unexplainable wonders. Yet we could not forget what our eyes witnessed clearly."

He felt a gentle chill run through him. The entry closely mirrored other accounts he had found—monks from various monasteries across Europe, each recording identical observations, each incident hurriedly concealed by ecclesiastical authorities fearful of heretical implications.

He shifted another volume into the lamplight, revealing yet another inked record, this one dated 1431, from a Benedictine monastery near Avignon:

"On the Feast of Saint Catherine, several brothers observed strange celestial illuminations, silent yet brilliant, dancing oddly across the heavens. Initially interpreted as divine signs, yet

careful examination revealed no clear religious symbolism. We prayed fervently for understanding, but such remained elusive, leaving many deeply troubled."

IAN SLOWLY LET OUT A BREATH, setting down his pencil. Each discovery reinforced a consistent historical pattern: medieval observers studiously documenting unexplainable celestial phenomena were then promptly silenced by authorities fearful of theological disruption.

Still conflicted between skepticism and curiosity, Ian knew who should see these findings next. He gathered the documents, standing slowly to seek out Father Dominic.

MICHAEL AND SIMON stood quietly beneath the softly illuminated frescoes lining the walls of the private chapel tucked discreetly within Vatican City. The chapel, rarely visited by outsiders, provided the perfect sanctuary for private reflection and sensitive discussion. Michael had purposely selected this location, aware that their current conversation carried profound implications. And also aware that much of their travels and discussions had been compromised throughout this journey.

Simon paced attentively, hands clasped behind him. "Michael, this manuscript consistently defies conventional historical interpretations. Juana's celestial symbolism, combined with Ian's recent discoveries, suggests something far deeper than mere medieval allegory."

The priest's acknowledgment was subtle, almost imperceptible, his gaze thoughtful yet troubled. "I agree. I'm increasingly concerned the manuscript's origins lie entirely outside traditional historical narratives—perhaps something genuinely unprecedented."

Simon paused, meeting Michael's gaze directly. When he spoke again, his voice was cautious yet animated. "You're considering seriously the possibility that these celestial references are literal rather than symbolic?"

Choosing his words carefully, Michael said, "Historically, we've dismissed medieval celestial references as mere superstition or religious allegory. Yet Ian's meticulous research reveals that monks consistently and precisely recorded actual celestial events. Such historical rigor suggests genuinely inexplicable phenomena occurred."

Simon inclined his head, acknowledging Michael's cautious openness. "I've struggled with similar thoughts. Medieval minds tended to explain unfamiliar phenomena religiously or mythically. Yet their careful recordings of silent lights—moving, unfamiliar celestial bodies—suggest authentic observational encounters."

Michael was troubled yet fascinated. "If true, Simon, we must reconsider the entire framework within which we interpret this manuscript."

Simon smiled, sensing Michael's hesitancy. "Medieval history is filled with fear, suppression, even persecution in response to peculiar phenomena. It is no wonder something so disturbing would result in Juana's attempts to conceal it."

Michael gave a slight nod. "Juana clearly understood that risk. She deliberately encoded her discoveries to protect her generation from misusing knowledge they couldn't yet responsibly comprehend, hoping future generations could. Sadly, I fear our generation, although it might not subject such new knowledge to repression, would distinctly exploit it. Both actions are ignorant and dangerous in their own way."

Later that evening, Ian joined Michael privately in the quiet of Michael's modest apartment in Domus Santa Marta, spreading the documented research across the low wooden table between them. Michael reviewed each historical account thoroughly, astonishment deepening with each revelation.

"Extraordinary," he finally murmured, setting down Ian's notes. "Monks consistently recorded these celestial events—silent moving lights they couldn't explain—across monasteries separated widely by geography and time."

Ian nodded, cautiously tempering his own skepticism. "Initially, Michael, I considered these references symbolic or misunderstood atmospheric phenomena—meteor showers, Northern Lights, or simple superstitions. Yet, the consistency and detail with which monks recorded their observations suggest that something genuinely temporal occurred."

"That's my concern, Ian. Medieval monks, knowing the familiar night sky's normal patterns, weren't easily fooled. If they accurately recorded such phenomena, we must take their observations seriously."

Ian hesitated, his tone carefully measured. "Michael, I remain skeptical about suggesting outright extraterrestrial interpretations. Such theories seem too easily sensationalized or misused."

Michael responded with a slight nod, respecting Ian's careful scholarship. "Agreed—caution remains crucial. Yet we cannot dismiss entirely the possibility that these phenomena genuinely represent something not only beyond normal medieval understanding—but perhaps even beyond contemporary scientific explanations."

"Perhaps our role isn't immediate interpretation," Ian said, "but careful documentation, just as Juana herself intended. She deliberately encoded her insights cryptically, suggesting awareness that future generations might approach these mysteries differently."

Michael smiled, appreciating Ian's approach. "Exactly, Ian. Juana anticipated humanity's evolving understanding. She guided seekers toward truth without overwhelming them. Our task is equally dutiful, cautiously stewarding these findings." Michael paused, weighing his words before adding, "And aware always of humankind's dangerous ambition."

CHAPTER

TWENTY-THREE

VATICAN CITY

T he tranquil warmth of morning sunlight spilled through the tall windows of Father Michael Dominic's private study, illuminating rows of antique volumes and casting gentle patterns across the mahogany furnishings. He had chosen this early hour when everyone could gather at once to assess Hana's recent experience. Michael and Ian were already dressed for work, as Hana reclined in casual clothes, needing one more day of recuperation.

Hana sat calmly, a porcelain cup of tea clasped between her hands, gaze distant as she gathered her thoughts. Around her sat Michael, Simon, Ian, and her cousin Karl, each waiting patiently in attentive silence, the air charged with anticipation.

Hana drew a steadying breath, eyes focused momentarily on the steam rising from her cup. "What I experienced during my captivity was far beyond anything I anticipated," she began, her voice soft yet steady. "It wasn't merely a hallucination. Everything felt vivid, intensely real —more like visiting another place entirely than dreaming."

Michael leaned forward slightly, expression attentive but cautious. "Describe again what you saw, Hana— especially the celestial elements. I want all of us to be absolutely clear."

She nodded, gathering her memories. "After they forced the botanical mixture on me, I woke up beneath a sky unlike anything I've ever seen. The colors were extraordinary—deep purples and greens, shifting slowly as if the heavens themselves were alive. And the stars... the constellations were completely unfamiliar. They matched nothing I've seen from Earth. They were intricate, arranged almost artistically, as if deliberately placed."

Michael's eyes narrowed slightly, intrigued yet cautious. "And the figure you encountered? How did it explain these celestial visions?"

Hana set the cup down, then turned directly toward Michael. "It called the place 'between worlds'—a threshold created by Juana's botanical wisdom. It implied that Juana herself had experienced these same visions centuries ago and that her manuscript had deliberately encoded these celestial encounters."

Simon leaned back, hands clasped as he absorbed Hana's words. "Fascinating. Historically speaking, your descriptions echo those of medieval mystics quite closely."

Michael turned toward Simon, eyebrows rising slightly. "Have you encountered similar historical descriptions, Simon?"

"Indeed," Simon answered, his tone cultured but cautious. "Throughout the medieval period, mystics frequently reported vivid visions of heavenly lights, mysterious celestial phenomena that often occurred during periods of intense religious or spiritual experiences. In the twelfth century, Hildegard von Bingen described visions of luminous objects in the sky, which she interpreted symbolically but could never rationally explain. The Cathar mystics in southern France also mentioned seeing 'lights in heaven' during moments of spiritual ecstasy— phenomena they recorded strictly but cautiously, fearful of persecution by the Church."

Ian nodded, shifting in his chair. "I've found similar accounts in various monastic chronicles, as you all know— strange moving lights in the sky, inexplicable celestial occurrences judiciously noted but rarely discussed openly."

"The consistency troubles me," Michael said. "We've previously dismissed these accounts as metaphorical, symbolic, or even superstitious. But Hana's experience aligns closely with those historical records. I'm increasingly convinced these celestial visions may not be merely symbolic."

Simon inclined his head. "Many medieval mystics believed they witnessed literal, though puzzling, celestial phenomena. They lacked rational scientific explanations, so they turned to allegory or theological interpretations. Their careful documentation suggests genuine occurrences, though their descriptions remained necessarily cautious and incomplete."

Hana's eyes narrowed. "The figure also stressed something vital. It warned me that humanity is perpetually at risk—that the knowledge Juana encoded is extraordinarily compelling. It must be approached responsibly, ethically, or it could become dangerously destructive."

Michael offered a quiet nod. "That's exactly my concern. Each step closer we come to uncovering deeper mysteries, we must question whether humankind is genuinely prepared to understand or responsibly handle such revelations."

Simon cleared his throat before adding, "Throughout history, humanity's ethical maturity has always lagged behind its intellectual curiosity. Our ancestors deliberately concealed knowledge—astronomical, botanical, alchemical —not from fear or ignorance, but from awareness of threats and prudence."

Hana said, "I suggest we continue following the map of nodes, the locations Juana mapped out as necessary on this path to the formula she guarded." Then she lifted her cup in a toast. "To the same wisdom and prudence we need to respect as we go forward."

The others nodded in agreement, all likewise lifting their teacup to accept the toast. In the process, Michael's right elbow bumped with left-handed Ian's elbow, and the two men jolted, both teacups tipping, with Ian's spilling its contents on Michael's black shirt. Ian jumped up and swiped at the liquid on his boss's shirt.

"Oh, I'm so—" Ian started to apologize when suddenly his hand stopped, and he stared wide-eyed at the priest, his hand still on Michael's pocket.

"What?" Michael asked, puzzled at his assistant's look. "It's okay. I have other shirts I can..."

But Ian ignored him as he fingered the edge of the shirt pocket, while everyone stared. He stopped, put his finger to his lips, and motioned for Karl. The Swiss Guard approached and likewise felt the edge of the pocket. With a nod of his trusted friend's head, Michael understood to remove the shirt.

Moments later, they all witnessed a tea-soaked shirt, with the pocket edging ripped open, and a small tracking device removed and now sitting on the table. They stared at each other for a moment, each astonished at how devious Blackthorn had been. His operatives had even infiltrated the Vatican at unexpected levels. At least, for the moment, they knew why Blackthorn had kept abreast of their movements so easily. Literally, their tracker had been 'abreast' of Michael all along in his Vatican laundry-supplied shirts.

Karl picked up the device and carefully pocketed it. With a nod from all the others, they began chatting as if each had their own personal agendas for the day, as if unaware of the tracker that had supplied all their findings to their adversary.

"Now I think it's time we get to work," Michael said, speaking to the others as if casually dismissing the group to their normal activities. They all realized he meant more than their daily routines—they needed to get to work to protect themselves and each other from Genetica's long reach.

TWENTY-FOUR

GRANADA, SPAIN

The graceful Dassault Falcon 900 jet descended smoothly through the early morning skies over southern Spain, the Sierra Nevada Mountains silhouetted sharply against a glowing dawn horizon. Hana gazed pensively from her seat by the window, captivated by the dramatic landscape slowly emerging below.

Beside her, Father Michael studied his notes, a sheaf of efficiently organized documents, research summaries, and carefully sketched diagrams spread across the wooden table between them.

Simon sat, his eyes resting for the moment, his age providing wisdom but also the need for the occasional reprieve from gazing at texts few others could decipher.

Karl and Lukas occupied seats across the aisle, quietly reviewing their security arrangements for the upcoming visit. They had researched the most sophisticated tracking detection devices and had recently scoured every inch of the jet, Michael's full wardrobe, and Hana's as well. They had video and audio surveillance in the living quarters for everyone concerned in the operation now. They had assigned a trusted helper of Sister Teri to monitor any activity beyond that of the residents themselves at Michael's quarters in the Domus Santa Marta. Knowing their extended efforts, their vigilant presence was reassuring to the team, a testament to the increased seriousness of the mission following Hana's kidnapping in Rome and the discovery of the latest tracking device.

Hana turned from the window, her gaze settling on Michael as she wrapped her new sweater tightly around her. "Tell me more about this Monasterio de la Cartuja, Michael. You seem convinced it could hold more clues."

Michael's expression grew thoughtful as he assented, setting down his notes and leaning back in his seat, clearly eager to share. "Historically, Hana, the Cartuja monastery —officially the Monasterio de Nuestra Señora de la Asunción—was founded in 1506, during the period relevant to Juana de la Cruz and the original *Voynich Manuscript* context. This makes it incredibly significant for our search."

He paused briefly, eyes distant as he visualized their destination. "The monastery is famous not just for its architecture, but also for its lavish baroque interiors filled with intricate symbolism, complex frescoes, and elaborate iconography. Many historians believe these symbols hold deeper meaning, often hidden knowledge intentionally concealed within religious art."

Hana raised an eyebrow, intrigued. "You mean something similar to Juana's botanical symbolism?"

Michael smiled softly, his brown eyes alight with excitement. "Exactly. Carthusian monks deeply valued contemplation and intellectual inquiry. The monastery's seclusion gave them the perfect atmosphere to pursue scholarly studies far from the prying eyes of the outside world. Given its cultural significance—standing as it does at the crossroads of Moorish, Renaissance, and Baroque traditions—Cartuja became an ideal sanctuary for preserving secret intellectual traditions, from astronomy to botany, and perhaps even alchemy. So it is no surprise that Juana's coded map of location nodes included this institution."

Karl glanced over, curiosity piqued. "You expect we'll find direct evidence of Juana's botanical rituals here?"

Michael tilted his head cautiously. "Perhaps not direct evidence of Juana herself, Karl, but the Cartuja monastery's archives might contain historical documents referencing related celestial phenomena or botanical symbolism, considering its academic legacy. Granada, especially during Moorish times, was a hub for astronomy and botanical research, closely intertwined disciplines historically."

Lukas nodded. "If monks here recorded observations similar to those Ian discovered, we might find stronger historical links supporting Juana's celestial symbolism."

"Exactly," Michael acknowledged. "The monastery archives are extensive, and given their intellectual pursuits, there's a strong likelihood we'll uncover relevant materials."

Hana turned again toward the window as the jet gently touched down, feeling a renewed sense of anticipation mixed with cautious optimism.

. . .

THEIR RENTED vehicle glided smoothly through the outskirts of Granada, soon arriving at the Monasterio de la Cartuja. Situated just beyond the city's busy center, the monastery felt immediately secluded, the quiet serenity of its grounds enveloping them like a protective cloak.

Approaching on foot, Michael paused briefly, absorbing the monastery's imposing façade and ornate architecture, centuries-old stone bathed in morning sunlight.

"This monastery," he explained to Hana and the guards, "has witnessed centuries of intelligent scholarship. From Moorish astronomers to Carthusian monks, generations studied and preserved exceptional knowledge here."

Inside, the monastery's opulence struck them at once—an astonishing fusion of Moorish influence and European Baroque artistry. Gilded altars, intricate stucco carvings, and vibrant frescoes depicting biblical scenes filled the walls and ceilings. The complexity of the artwork suggested deeper symbolic meanings hidden beneath layers of ornate decoration.

Following prior arrangements, the monastery librarian, a quiet elderly friar named Brother Tomás, guided them discreetly into the archive room. Ancient texts and manuscripts, each painstakingly cataloged, rested within wooden cabinets lining the walls.

"Here you will find our historical collection," Brother Tomás said. "Many documents here predate even the monastery's founding—texts preserved from earlier periods, including Moorish times. They have survived countless historical upheavals."

Michael began examining the aged documents, his gloved hands moving delicately through fragile parchment pages. Minutes stretched slowly into hours as the team sifted through medieval texts and chronicles.

Finally, Michael paused abruptly, holding an ancient, delicately scripted parchment fragment from the fourteenth century. "This is remarkable," he whispered, voice filled with awe. "These are letters from Moorish astronomers to their colleagues in Córdoba and Toledo."

Hana moved closer, eyes scanning the Arabic script. "What do they discuss?"

Michael translated the words, excitement building with each newly deciphered phrase. "'In the year 1388, during observation of planetary alignments, we observed unknown celestial objects moving independently, with no discernible path or pattern. These luminous bodies appeared repeatedly across several nights, brilliant yet silent, defying known astronomical explanations.'"

He glanced up, his expression thoughtful. "They go on to discuss similar events in 1392 and 1397—dutifully recorded, yet never openly reported due to fears of religious persecution."

Simon approached, focused on examining the document. "This matches closely the reports Ian found from monastic chronicles across Europe. Moorish astronomers meticulously documented these significant sightings, but were unable to publicly discuss them."

Intrigued, Hana unfolded several reproductions of *Voynich* illustrations she had brought. Spreading them alongside Michael's parchment, she paused, catching her breath. "Michael, look closely—the patterns here are increasingly similar to these illustrations."

Michael leaned closer, attentively comparing the documents.

Hana indicated several botanical symbols, clearly

intertwined with celestial motifs—stars, unfamiliar constellations, luminous symbols—echoing the imagery from her own visions.

"These correspond exactly to what I saw," she whispered, voice trembling slightly. "The arrangement of stars, the strange plants in my vision—it aligns increasingly with the manuscript's illustrations."

Simon nodded. "Historical mystics often described celestial encounters in similar symbolic ways—stars representing wisdom, plants symbolizing earthly receptivity. However, Juana's botanical symbolism could well be more literal than allegorical."

Michael drew a slow breath, privately unsettled yet thoroughly fascinated by these revelations. "It's possible that Juana's manuscript represents not merely mystical botanical symbolism, but actual encoded observations—celestial phenomena she genuinely witnessed or learned about from historical records like these."

Hana glanced toward Michael cautiously. "Are you now leaning toward these celestial sightings being literal? Actual events, possibly even extraterrestrial?"

Michael hesitated slightly, cautious yet open-minded. "It seems increasingly likely these medieval scholars—whether monks or Moorish astronomers—observed genuinely unexplained celestial phenomena. Juana documented similar experiences centuries later, interpreting them through botanical and symbolic frameworks."

Quietly listening, Karl interjected a thought. "But why conceal such observations so thoroughly?"

Simon smiled slightly, offering historical perspective. "Because knowledge that defies existing religious or scientific paradigms historically posed enormous danger.

Medieval scholars feared persecution, suppression—or worse. They encoded their knowledge precisely to preserve it for future generations while avoiding dangerous misunderstandings in their current time."

Michael's head dipped slowly, absorbing the implications. "Then our task remains clear. We must interpret correctly as best we can, always balancing openness to extraordinary possibilities with rigorous historical skepticism. Juana's legacy demands we proceed thoughtfully."

They stood quietly within the monastery archives, absorbing centuries of faithfully preserved wisdom. Michael felt the significance of historical responsibility upon them, guardians now of truths that bridged earthly knowledge and celestial mystery.

As they left the monastery, emerging into late afternoon sunlight illuminating the lush hills surrounding Granada, Michael paused, looking back toward Cartuja's timeless walls. Hana saw his reaction and reached over to take his hand in hers. He looked at her and smiled, his mind suddenly captivated entirely with her loving gaze. "For all the mysteries there are in this world, the one most perplexing is how two hearts and minds can merge as one, as ours have."

She smiled in return with an impish grin that sealed the close bond the two shared.

Then together, they turned away from Cartuja's ancient walls, walking toward their vehicle, each aware of the fascinating historical journey still ahead.

TWENTY-FIVE

GRANADA, SPAIN

S unlight streamed through the leaded glass windows
of the historic villa overlooking Granada, casting a
golden warmth across the spacious salon where
Hana reclined, eyes closed in relaxation. Outside, olive
groves extended toward the distant Sierra Nevada
Mountains, the air faintly scented by blossoms drifting in
from the villa's garden. Michael sat nearby, reviewing
notes collected from their recent discoveries at the
Monasterio de la Cartuja, pausing occasionally to glance
over at Hana with a passive concern.

Hana opened her eyes, blinking against the sun's
brightness. She sat up slowly, offering Michael a reassuring
smile. "I'm better," she said, her voice steadier than before.
"The rest helped."

Michael returned her smile, relief evident in his eyes.
"I'm glad. You've been through a great deal recently."

She nodded in agreement, drawing a careful breath.

"But it was worth it, Michael. Each vision is clarifying something vital about the manuscript, something previously hidden."

Michael set down his notes, leaning forward with cautious curiosity. "In what way specifically?"

Hana hesitated, choosing her words with care. "At first, I believed the manuscript's botanical symbols were purely symbolic allegories of earthly wisdom. But after my recent experiences, especially the visions involving unfamiliar celestial patterns, I'm convinced Juana's symbolism incorporates something distinctly extraterrestrial, or at least deeply cosmic."

Michael's eyes narrowed. "You think the manuscript's botanical symbolism specifically references these celestial encounters you experienced?"

Hana nodded. "I do, yes. The constellations depicted, the arrangements of stars interwoven with plants and botanical forms—everything aligns more clearly now with my visions. In my last vision, I asked if there truly is a connection between plants and stars. The figure told me that all life is interconnected, saying it is 'rooted in cosmic processes that defy conventional understanding.' Juana deliberately encoded something profound—not merely metaphorical, but actual observations she struggled to interpret rationally."

Simon had just joined them, carrying several historical manuscripts from the villa's private collection, then spread them across the large table nearby. He glanced toward Hana with sensitivity. "Your experiences, Hana, correspond closely with historical visionary accounts I've just reviewed—accounts from medieval scholars who similarly struggled to rationalize visions that defied what your visionary being called 'conventional understanding.'"

Michael glanced toward Simon, intrigued. "You found specific parallels in historical texts?"

Simon smiled, selecting one parchment from among several before him. "Indeed. I came across multiple accounts from the thirteenth and fourteenth centuries, written by respected scholars—not mystics or ascetics, but careful, rational observers—describing strikingly similar phenomena."

He translated faithfully, voice quiet and measured. "Listen to this passage from a Parisian scholar in 1342: 'In the depths of an exhaustive botanical meditation, sitting amongst the unusual blooms of newly discovered plants, I perceived a luminous vision filled with unfamiliar celestial shapes—stars arranged oddly, unlike known constellations. They moved silently, purposefully, as if guided by hidden intelligence.'"

Michael sat back slowly, expression cautious yet genuinely intrigued. "Amazing. Possibly, that scholar had encountered the effects of pollen from a plant similar to what Hana experienced in the greenhouse. So, your findings confirm that Hana's visionary experience fits a broader historical pattern?"

Simon nodded. "Yes, it does. Historical records frequently show medieval scholars—rational, cautious men—who privately documented strange celestial encounters, almost universally interpreting them as symbolic or divine signs. Yet their descriptions consistently point toward something overwhelmingly mysterious, even suggestive of extraterrestrial phenomena as we might conceive of them today."

Michael exhaled, his expression pensive, almost troubled. "Yet we must remain cautious about leaping too hastily toward extraterrestrial explanations. Medieval minds naturally explained unfamiliar phenomena in religious or symbolic terms."

Simon acknowledged the point. "Certainly true. Yet their careful observations weren't purely symbolic or imaginative. They genuinely perceived something incomprehensible, something that compelled them toward secrecy and caution, much like Juana centuries later."

Hana glanced toward Michael, her voice quiet yet certain. "Simon's right. What I experienced felt entirely real, vividly authentic, not merely a symbolic hallucination. The figure plainly referenced the world's unpreparedness for deeper truths, suggesting Juana's caution was intentional, responsible, and wise."

Hana watched Michael in silence, sensing his deep internal struggle. Rising, she stepped to his side, sliding an arm around his waist. "I understand your hesitation, Michael. Yet everything we've uncovered so far—my visions, the medieval accounts, Juana's careful encoding—strongly suggests we must remain open-minded to truths beyond conventional explanation."

Michael tilted his chin downward in quiet affirmation, glancing toward her with affection. "Agreed. Yet I remain cautious."

"Michael," Simon interjected, "throughout history, many groundbreaking discoveries began as mysteries dismissed initially as superstition or fantasy. Copernicus, Galileo, Kepler—they all confronted phenomena people initially refused to accept rationally."

Michael smiled faintly, nodding in agreement. "An apt comparison, Simon. Yet even those discoveries were eventually explained through human science. What if we now face truths humanity isn't yet capable of comprehending scientifically?"

Simon shrugged. "One might think then that our task is simply to document mindfully, leaving interpretation open-ended, accepting that some mysteries may remain just that—mysteries—until the time is right."

Privately, Michael's mind turned toward the increasingly unavoidable possibility of genuinely extraterrestrial phenomena, even as skepticism lingered. How would the Church react to that possibility? Where did God's hand, His son's sacrifice, and the Church's most basic precepts fit in with a world beyond our own? Not to mention what the faithful would be forced to grapple with in their own spiritual beliefs. Science and religion have always butted heads... but this? He felt thoroughly torn between fascination and caution, openness and hesitation, conscious always of humanity's ethical vulnerability.

CHAPTER

TWENTY-SIX

GRANADA, SPAIN

I n the shadowed quiet beneath the Alhambra, the majestic Moorish fortress crowning Granada's Sabika Hill, Michael and Hana carefully descended a narrow stone staircase hidden beneath the intricate beauty of the Nasrid Palaces. Above them, ornate arches, delicate stucco carvings, and intricately patterned tile mosaics adorned chambers that had once hosted sultans and scholars, whispered secrets, and echoed with courtly poetry and philosophical debates. Now, beneath this stunning display of medieval Islamic artistry, Michael and Hana moved cautiously downward, their path illuminated solely by the flickering beam of Hana's small flashlight. The air was cool and still, heavy with centuries of silence, as if the very walls had absorbed the whispers of history itself. Above ground, Granada hummed with modern life, but here, concealed beneath the opulent beauty of the great fortress, a deep, timeless silence prevailed.

"You're certain of these chambers, Simon?" Michael called back, glancing toward Dr. Ginzberg, who trailed closely behind, carrying a leather-bound notebook filled with meticulous research notes.

"Quite certain," Simon replied. "Moorish records clearly reference secret chambers beneath the Alhambra, where astronomers recorded their discreet observations away from public scrutiny. If historical accounts are correct, the records we seek are hidden beneath the Court of the Lions."

"I am familiar with various religious sites in many areas throughout Europe," Michael commented, "but not with Moorish fortifications such as this."

He paused briefly, gathering his thoughts before explaining. "The Court of the Lions itself is one of the Alhambra's most celebrated spaces, known for its iconic central fountain supported by twelve laboriously carved marble lions, symbolic guardians of wisdom and power. Historians have long speculated that beneath this famous courtyard lie concealed chambers—spaces once used by Nasrid scholars and astronomers to study celestial phenomena privately, conduct botanical research, and document their discoveries away from prying eyes. These hidden rooms, mentioned fleetingly in ancient texts, were designed not only for secrecy but to ensure that sensitive knowledge was safeguarded from misuse or misunderstanding."

"If these concealed chambers have been speculated about for some time, why haven't they been discovered? And their contents already revealed and potentially taken away or put on display?" Hana wondered.

Simon's eyes twinkled as they walked in the low light of the passageway, which was known to lead to the typical store rooms that provided a cache of food supplies for such a fortress. "Ah, yes, I had a bit of a meditation on that during our journey here. We all see through our own center of focus. I realized the interpretations of certain words would likely be seen by scholars through their academic lens. Yet some words have alternate meanings in light of other vocations.

"A word used to explain the secreted chambers of this monastery has been translated as 'dormant' or 'idle,' leading scholars to consider a quiet area, such as a library, something a scholar would expect. Numerous attempts to find access to those hidden chambers by scholars in the past have been fruitless. I believe they are translating it based on their scholarly viewpoint of that word.

"However, I also considered that those who lived in this fortress, who may stare at the stars at night, could have also been charged with tending to the fortress gardens by day, likely for the sake of preparing meals for their residents. Hence, their awareness of the botanical effects they witness in their gardens by day, and relating that to celestial changes they witness at night. That same word translated by later scholars as 'dormant' could be meant to infer, or be translated as, 'vegetative,' as written by those whose interests lean into the culinary arena. It could literally refer to, well, vegetables. As such, I speculate that the entry we seek likely comes from the very storeroom where the vegetables of the era were kept in dark and cool—in other words, dormant—conditions."

They continued cautiously downward, finally emerging into a large, low-ceilinged storage area, musty with age, and devoid of any goods, vegetative or otherwise. Wooden shelves covered with cobwebs lined the walls, and the scurry of spiders brought motion to every sweep of their flashlights' beams. The thick coating of dust on the shelves and the lack of any prints on the floor made it clear the area had long since been forgotten. The team spread out, carefully reassessing every aspect of the walls, shelves, and other fixtures.

Behind one shelf, Michael noticed a line along the wall, and pulling aside the sticky threads of cobweb, he ran his finger down the line. As he did, he could feel that the one shelf in front of him wobbled ever so slightly.

"Over here," he called, and the others joined him, adding their weight to his along the shelf he had noticed.

A moment later, the shelf began to move inward along that line, opening to a blackened narrow subterranean corridor lined with heavy wooden doors, iron hinges rusted with age. They stepped into the passage. Hana paused before one door, examining faint Arabic inscriptions carved into the weathered wood.

"Here," she whispered, pointing toward the faded script. Simon leaned closer, squinting in the dimness.

"It's Arabic," he murmured, translating the words. "'Chamber of Stars—Protected by Allah's Grace and the Silence of the Wise.'" He glanced toward Michael, excitement tempered by scholarly caution. "We've found the astronomers' secret archives."

Michael cautiously tested the door, relieved as it opened slowly, creaking on rusted hinges. They stepped inside, finding themselves surrounded by shelves holding ancient manuscripts, faded parchments, and stored scrolls, their delicate surfaces coated with centuries of accumulated dust.

Hana's flashlight illuminated delicate celestial charts and Arabic astronomical texts, their careful calligraphy exquisitely precise, exacting even after hundreds of years.

Michael exhaled slowly, eyes widening in awe. "Remarkable. These must date from the fourteenth century —at least as old as the Alhambra itself."

Simon lifted one bound manuscript and cautiously flipped through its brittle pages. "Indeed. Look at this... astronomical observations made by Moorish astronomers between 1370 and 1395, preserved secretly beneath the Alhambra itself."

Hana paused, scrutinizing a fragile parchment illuminated with unfamiliar celestial patterns. "Michael, look closely. These celestial patterns mirror exactly those from my visions—unfamiliar constellations, carefully arranged."

Michael stepped closer, examining the parchment, his heart beating quickly. "You're right. The Moorish astronomers scrupulously recorded these anomalies. Listen —'*Lights appeared again in the heavens, moving silently, intelligently, beyond known celestial bodies. Allah preserve our wisdom as we interpret these sacred mysteries.*'"

Simon nodded pensively. "These astronomers witnessed exactly the same phenomena that medieval monks observed elsewhere. Their observations closely align historically with the manuscript's origins."

Michael read another entry, his voice gentle yet awestruck. "'*These celestial visitors appear intermittently, brightest during unusually rapid botanical growth patterns observed within palace gardens. Surely Allah reveals these heavenly secrets cautiously, protecting knowledge humanity is not ready to possess.*'"

Hana was deeply moved. "Then Juana's manuscript encodes exactly these historical celestial encounters—not merely symbolic allegory, but literal records deliberately concealed."

Simon gingerly gathered documents, his voice quiet yet firm. "We need to document this thoroughly, remembering to interpret with care and avoid making rash assumptions."

As they emerged from beneath the Alhambra into warm evening twilight, Michael scanned Granada's shimmering rooftops, contemplating their extraordinary discoveries.

IN A DISCREET VILLA OVERLOOKING GRANADA, Christophe Vaux paced angrily, frustration evident in every tense movement. Since the failure to contain Dominic's team, Genetica's operations risked complete exposure— everything depended now on quickly neutralizing Dominic and Sinclair, recovering Juana's manuscript, and reclaiming control.

Vaux's encrypted phone buzzed, his chief operator's voice cautious yet firm. "We've regrouped, Monsieur Vaux. Fresh intelligence confirms that Dominic's team has located hidden archives beneath the Alhambra. They have historical documents explicitly detailing celestial anomalies closely linked historically to our botanical studies."

Vaux's jaw tightened, his eyes narrowing dangerously. "Then the priest grows ominously close to truths we alone must control. Mobilize immediately—I want heightened surveillance, armed teams in position throughout Granada. This ends now."

The man's voice hardened resolutely. "Understood, Monsieur. Dominic's team won't escape again."

Ending the call abruptly, Vaux gazed fiercely across

Granada's twilight rooftops, resolution hardening. Dominic threatened everything: Genetica's scientific breakthroughs, proprietary botanical research, powerful pharmaceutical monopolies... Any celestial truths, regardless of their actual origins beyond Earth, on this world needed to belong solely to Genetica, not to idealistic scholars incapable of harnessing knowledge effectively. Blackthorn would stand as the overlord in this world's new era, with the ability to formulate unimaginably powerful pharmaceuticals, which could provide cures that made the cost of existing remedies pale in comparison, let alone that might control the minds of men for whatever purpose desired. Blackthorn could take the credit; Vaux intended to be the instrument of that victory. And to share in the untold wealth it engendered.

He would stop Dominic decisively, no matter the cost.

CHAPTER
TWENTY-SEVEN

GRANADA, SPAIN

The late afternoon sun had already cast long shadows across the winding, narrow streets of Granada's Albaicín district. From their secluded villa near the Alhambra, Michael, Hana, Simon, Karl, and Lukas prepared for their departure. Michael carried a secure case filled with precious manuscript fragments they had collected from beneath the Alhambra—documents rich with delicate botanical illustrations and cryptic astronomical references.

Karl moved cautiously through the villa's courtyard, eyes continually scanning for threats, his posture taut, vigilant. Beside him, Lukas methodically checked the security perimeter, silently confirming their route was clear. Michael glanced toward the guards, comforted by their disciplined professionalism. Yet he couldn't shake an unsettling feeling, a persistent unease he had grown accustomed to trusting.

GARY MCAVOY

As they approached their waiting vehicle—a black Mercedes SUV parked discreetly along the shaded street— Karl abruptly froze, instinctively raising his hand in a silent command for caution. Lukas stepped protectively in front of Hana and Michael, drawing his pistol with practiced ease.

Karl's sharp eyes had detected subtle movement— figures silently emerging from a shadowed doorway ahead. Instantly, he recognized the signature coordinated movements and careful stealth indicative of Christophe Vaux's operatives.

"Ambush!" Karl shouted. "Get down—now!"

Gunfire exploded around them, a sudden storm of bullets ricocheting violently off the cobblestones and splintering the SUV's windshield into shards of glittering glass. Michael instinctively wrapped one arm around Hana as he ducked, clutching the manuscript case closely with his other arm, his heartbeat pounding in his ears.

Lukas swiftly ushered Michael and Hana behind the cover of a sturdy stone wall, his movements determined but strained under the unexpected ferocity of the attack.

Positioned slightly forward, Karl opened fire in disciplined bursts, each shot deliberate and accurate. Yet the attackers surged forward, clearly anticipating the guards' defensive maneuvers, encircling their position from multiple angles.

"Too many of them," Karl shouted urgently, his voice betraying a rare hint of tension. "We need to move— fast!"

As Lukas responded, a sharp cry of pain escaped him, his body spinning abruptly before collapsing against the wall, slipping down behind a solid half wall, his sleeve leaving a trail of blood on the stone wall behind him.

"*Lukas!*" Michael called out, panic surging through him.

"I'm all right... just grazed," Lukas hissed, his breathing labored, eyes pinched with pain. He grimaced, pressing a hand firmly against his wounded shoulder, blood seeping through his fingers.

Karl rushed to Lukas's side, briefly examining the injury with practiced efficiency. The tight line of his mouth spoke louder than words: Lukas's wound could be severe.

"Retreat now!" Karl ordered, urgency sharpening his tone. "I'll cover our exit. Michael, Hana—you must help Lukas. Keep pressure on the wound."

Michael and Hana quickly moved to Lukas's side, supporting him as they maneuvered toward a narrow alleyway nearby. Lukas leaned heavily against Michael, his breath ragged, yet his determination resolute as Karl kept up a barrage of gunfire to cover them.

But enemy gunshots continued to crack around them, closer and more persistent, shattering bricks from nearby buildings and forcing Karl to weave unpredictably, firing quick suppressive shots to buy them precious seconds.

"You won't hold them back alone!" Lukas protested weakly, frustration evident in his strained voice.

"I don't intend to," Karl replied. "You three get out now, Lukas, and I'll catch up."

Michael felt a surge of dread as Karl disappeared into the thickening smoke and chaos, leaving them momentarily vulnerable. Hana locked eyes with Michael, her gaze steady despite the fear they both felt.

"We have to trust him," Hana whispered firmly, adjusting her grip on Lukas. "Come on, we must keep moving."

They staggered through winding streets, Lukas's blood

leaving a stark trail against the pale stones. His breathing grew increasingly labored, each step harder than the last. Michael felt his muscles strain under Lukas's weight, his mind racing for solutions beyond their training or preparation.

Behind them, the echoes of gunfire lessened but didn't cease entirely, a constant reminder that Karl was still desperately engaged.

At last, they reached a shadowed alcove sheltered by thick stone arches, momentarily hidden from pursuit. Michael lowered Lukas gently to the ground, anxiety tightening his throat as he noticed Lukas's face pale, sweat glistening on his brow.

"You must keep going," Lukas insisted, his voice weaker now, eyes defiant despite obvious pain.

"We're not leaving you," Hana said fiercely, tearing fabric from her sleeve to bind Lukas's wound tightly. "Karl trusts us to keep you safe—and that's exactly what we'll do."

Michael's gaze fell to the manuscript case he still clutched protectively. He glanced upward, suddenly struck by a thought. "There might be a safe place for us."

Before Hana could reply, footsteps echoed in the alley, Karl emerging headlong from the shadows, breathing heavily, eyes sharp with urgency.

"They'll find us soon," Karl said, his voice edged with tension. Noticing Lukas, his expression softened briefly. "We have to move immediately, even if slowly. Can you manage?"

Lukas nodded grimly, determination flashing across his pained features. "I'll manage. Just... not quickly."

Michael spoke decisively, confidence returning to his voice as a desperate plan took shape. "There's an old chapel nearby—I noticed it earlier. Narrow doors, thick walls—defensible, at least temporarily."

Karl hesitated only briefly before nodding. "Lead the way, Father."

They moved again, slower but steadier, each step an exercise in quiet resilience and trust. Michael felt the weight of their mission heavier than ever, but also a newfound clarity—the knowledge that victory relied less on flawless strength than on adaptability, resilience, and faith in each other.

Together, they moved toward safety, aware that this night had irrevocably changed them all, forcing them to confront not just physical threats but the depth of their vulnerabilities and the true strength of their bonds.

Several minutes later, they sat in the worn wooden pews of a small chapel tucked between two small business buildings of the district. It was used primarily for roadside worshipers and lunchtime prayers for devout workers, but offered a small room in the back that became their temporary sanctuary.

They had barely caught their breath before a voice rang out, "*Esta es la policía. Salgan con las manos en alto!*"

The four of them looked at each other, aware that the voice was speaking in the local accent of Andalusian Spanish, not English as Vaux's other operatives had used before. After a moment's hesitation, the repeated demand for them to come out moved the foursome to raise their hands and walk into the main chapel area, Karl supporting Lukas.

Two of the local police stood with their guns at the ready. Quickly, the policemen's stern expressions shifted to confused and concerned looks as they noticed Michael's priestly collar and Lukas's blood-stained shirt.

Lukas coughed out a question in perfectly accented Spanish, requesting that he explain their situation. The taller cop agreed and, in a quick exchange of Spanish, he clarified to the officers that they were not, in fact, the aggressors in the gunfight that had alarmed the neighborhood and brought the police to the scene.

At a nod from the tall policeman, his partner signaled for them to lower their hands as he called for an ambulance and motioned for Karl to lower his partner to a pew.

Soon, the two police officers were speaking quickly with Lukas, a bit too quickly for the others to catch it all. But they easily grasped that the police were, in fact, accepting their story. Karl looked over at Michael and Hana and quickly explained that Lukas's grandmother was from this region of Spain, which explained his ease in talking to these two men.

It turned out that the neighbors had recognized the other gunmen as part of a local gang, thugs available for hire for any sort of trouble, but did not recognize this foursome. Not knowing if it was a turf war or something else, the police had been cautious in approaching them.

While they waited for the ambulance, Michael used his best Spanish to try to explain an abbreviated version of his mission as a Vatican archivist to safeguard documents that others would use for profit. He allowed them to think that such artifacts would be sold as historical artifacts, which was close enough to the truth and avoided any deeper explanations. All authorities knew historical artifact thievery was rampant in Europe, so the explanation was sufficient.

When the ambulance arrived and as the medics prepared Lukas for transport, they all discussed how they could have been tracked this time. Karl explained to the police how careful they had been about sweeping for trackers through their clothes and belongings and on the private jet that had brought them here.

It took no more than a look between the two policemen for Karl to realize they had the answer.

"You arrive Federico García Lorca Granada-Jaén Airport?" the taller policeman asked in broken English. Getting an affirmative nod, he then added, "You fly in same jet? All time?"

"Of course, that's what happened!" Hana exclaimed as it hit her. "There are only a few FBOs that support private jet operations in smaller airports. Blackthorn already knows the jet that we use; he only needed to get Intel from the Fixed-Base Operators here to tell them if and when our jet arrived."

Michael asked, "But how would they know to have someone watching Granada in particular?" Then he shook his head, a realization hitting him as well. "Of course, they had listened in on our conversations prior to this and knew about the location nodes in Juana's diary. They have likely hired locals at all of the potential locations where your jet might land."

The medics were moving Lukas to the ambulance, and Karl quickly caught up with the stretcher. Lukas was whisked in through the back doors of the vehicle, Karl jumping up inside as well. Just before the door closed, Karl called out, "Hana, the police will see you are safe." He paused as if realizing something and motioned for the tall policeman to come up to the opened door and conferred with him briefly. The man stepped back, nodding as Karl called out again, "Hana! Call the jet. Tell them to go to one of the other nodes without us. Now!"

The ambulance door swung closed, and the vehicle's lights and sirens swallowed any chance for Hana to ask why. She stood, uncertain what to do, wondering how they would get back to Rome safely without the jet.

She looked at Michael and said, "I don't understand."

Michael shrugged. "He must have a plan."

A COUPLE OF HOURS LATER, the foursome sat in the temporary safety of a discreetly arranged hotel suite near Granada's cathedral. For now, they felt safe with the police on their side in more ways than just the recommendation of this hotel suite. The thugs who had accosted them had been swept up by the police and interrogated. The police had acted chagrined that they could not get charges against them for this crime because their would-be victims had already escaped police intervention by flying off in their jet. When the leader of the villains later made a call, the police recording of it proved the tip of Michael's team's escape was relayed to whoever had hired them. But the thugs had plenty of other crimes already stacked up against them and would be jailed for some time on those charges—time the team needed to finish their work here.

But they knew they had to be more careful, and suspected a mole existed in the Vatican. So, when Karl had rejoined them with Lukas, he'd 'informed' the Vatican they had escaped harm and were jetting their way to another location. Only Sister Teri—contacted on a private and secured line—would know they planned to remain here for the time being.

Karl tended to Lukas in the bedroom, while Michael, in the living area, had reopened the secure case containing manuscript fragments gathered from beneath the

Alhambra. Eventually, they would be cataloged and securely safeguarded in the Vatican archives, far better than deteriorating in a subterranean chamber. Still, for now, they served an immediate purpose for their mission.

"These documents," Michael whispered as he reviewed the delicate script, "contain references not merely botanical or astronomical, but especially mentioning 'heavenly messengers' alongside the plants Juana studied."

Hana leaned forward, eyes tracing the beautiful Arabic script. Michael had spent their first few minutes back at the suite transcribing what he had translated from these fragments. She read aloud, her voice awestruck: *"'In mindful observation beneath Allah's stars, our garden revealed botanical wonders, each herb and flower blooming as if in response to the luminous visitations above. These heavenly messengers moved silently, guiding our wisdom toward sacred truths guardedly hidden from humanity's reckless ambition.'"*

Michael lightly tapped another bit of parchment, translating heedfully. *"'Again these messengers appeared, silent yet clearly intelligent, arranging themselves in diligent patterns above the gardens, illuminating blossoms out of season with their strange celestial glow.'"*

Hana exhaled slowly, greatly moved. "It's brilliant. They confirm exactly what I saw—celestial patterns deliberately linked to botanical phenomena."

Michael's eyes briefly closed, as though internalizing her words. "It matches your visions as you described them, Hana. Clearly, Moorish astronomers and medieval scholars consistently observed these phenomena, interpreting them attentively through religious or symbolic frameworks—never openly acknowledging their possible literal implications. This confirms everything else we've been discovering. And what you experienced."

In one of the rare moments that they could share alone, Hana pressed her cheek to Michael's chest, and he held her tightly, his cheek resting on the crown of her head. The two of them felt their hearts beat as one, as they both faced the danger ahead, knowing their bonds would keep them close.

Meanwhile, in the adjoining room, Karl caringly tended to Lukas. The suite's lighting was soft and muted, lending a calm, quiet dignity to the intimate moment. Karl's face was etched with quiet concern as he set aside the hospital-provided antiseptic and fresh dressings for a later dressing change.

Lukas watched Karl patiently, a faint, reassuring smile softening his features despite the pain. "You don't have to fuss over me so much," he murmured.

Karl paused, meeting Lukas's eyes steadily. "Of course I do," he responded, his voice filled with understated devotion. "I promised I'd always watch your back."

Lukas reached out, placing his good hand over Karl's, squeezing briefly in silent gratitude. "You did more than that today. You risked everything."

Karl exhaled slowly, emotions briefly flickering across his usually composed features. "We both did. And it reminded me how fragile this all is—how easily I could lose you."

"You won't," Lukas reassured him, his voice steady and comforting. "We've faced worse, and each time, we've emerged stronger."

Karl nodded slowly, taking a deep breath as he carefully secured the bandage. "I know," he replied. "Yet every close call makes me realize how precious every moment truly is."

For a few seconds, their eyes met, silently

communicating the depth of their bond, their mutual understanding and quiet devotion, reaffirming the strength that had carried them through every challenge. Without further words, Karl tenderly squeezed Lukas's good shoulder, his presence a silent promise of unwavering care and commitment.

IN THE MEANTIME, back at the Vatican, Sister Teri's fingers moved across her keyboard, cautiously navigating Genetica Therapeutics's encrypted databases. Each digital maneuver required precision; her focus was absolute. Recently, she had uncovered troubling indications that Alton Blackthorn's interests extended far beyond biotechnology and pharmaceuticals into obscure astronomical research.

Teri exhaled, finally breaking through another security layer. The screen filled with complex astronomical charts, intricate data from telescopic observations, and coded references to celestial objects, coordinates unfamiliar even to Vatican astronomers.

"What in heaven's name are you pursuing, Mr. Blackthorn?" Teri murmured, her anxiety rising sharply.

She opened a heavily encrypted folder marked "*Viridis Project,*" containing confidential Genetica documents referencing Juana's botanical formulations alongside detailed celestial maps, diagrams suggesting planetary alignments, and speculative notes about hypothetical interstellar visitors. Blackthorn's obsession was clear—he was pursuing Juana's secrets not merely for pharmaceutical gain, but driven by a conviction that her botanical knowledge was linked to genuinely cosmic phenomena, potentially extraterrestrial in origin.

Teri reached for her own personal and secure cell phone and contacted Michael immediately.

"Father Michael, you must hear this." She spoke quickly, her voice tight with concern. "Blackthorn's research is even more troubling than we imagined. His obsession with Juana's manuscript extends into obscure astronomical and potentially extraterrestrial phenomena. He's pursuing Juana's celestial symbolism, convinced it represents literal alien botanical knowledge."

Michael absorbed Teri's revelations. "Then our situation grows significantly more dangerous. Vaux's renewed attacks confirm Blackthorn's urgency. He believes we've discovered exactly what he already suspects or knows exists, but which he desperately seeks to keep to himself."

"That's right," Teri replied. "Blackthorn won't hesitate now. He genuinely believes Juana's botanical wisdom contains celestial secrets he alone intends to control."

After ending Teri's call, Michael sat pensively beside Hana, reflecting upon their discoveries beneath Granada's historic streets, Moorish astronomers' laborious celestial observations, and Blackthorn's disturbing ambitions.

He felt torn between cerebral fascination and ethical caution.

Hana watched Michael closely, sensing his troubled contemplation. "Your hesitation is understandable," she reassured him, as she snuggled close to him. "Yet historical documents consistently support these celestial phenomena. We can't simply dismiss these accounts rationally."

Michael appeared briefly lost in thought, silently agreeing. Finally, he said, "What properties might these plants, kissed by some cosmic energy, provide to this world? The medievalists listed some of them as toxic, but why? Were they, in fact, dangerous to human life? Something so powerful that Blackthorn could make use of it as a bio weapon? Or was it the visions they experienced from encounters with these plants, such as you experienced, that made them believe in a potency that isn't actually true? Is it, in fact, an opening to new worlds beyond our physical one?"

He paused and held her a bit closer before he continued, "These plants, when under the direct influence of the 'cosmic visitations,' as they are called, need to be analyzed to understand their potential. Blackthorn has been a step ahead of us in some ways. He apparently already understood this extraterrestrial involvement. Is he now pursuing us to stop us from revealing what he is up to? Or is he banking on us to help him somehow discover the last of what he needs for full implementation of the formula?"

Neither of them had answers and found questions swirling, even as they learned more. Quietly reflective, they sat together, arms around each other, consciously aware of the responsibilities now entrusted to them.

TWENTY-EIGHT

GRANADA, SPAIN

M orning sunlight filtered through the tall, stained-glass windows of Granada's university library, casting warm shards of color across rows of heavy oak tables. On one of them lay neatly arranged manuscripts and parchment fragments—some written in Latin, others in Arabic—all sourced from the hidden chambers beneath the Alhambra. Michael Dominic slowly turned a page, his eyes narrowing as they took in the blend of botanical sketches and stylized astronomical charts.

Hana sat beside him, studying an ornate illustration. The image portrayed flowers wrapped in winding constellations, stars blooming from vines as if grown from stardust. She ran a finger lightly across the vellum. "These aren't just decorative. The plants and stars are part of the same language."

Michael offered a small, reassuring gesture, translating

aloud. *"'Travelers from the heavens revealed their truths through blossoms unknown, whose fragrance bore wisdom not of this Earth.'* They shared this with trusted scholars—discreetly, protectively."

Hana leaned back, absorbing the words. "Travelers… these aren't metaphors. They're describing actual contact—intelligences using botanicals to communicate." Her voice held neither awe nor fear, only a growing certainty.

Michael set the page down and folded his hands. "There's a growing body of evidence to support that view. These scholars weren't working in isolation. Letters, diagrams, encrypted glosses—they were in contact with each other across monasteries, libraries, even borders. They knew something unusual was happening and chose to record it, but only in ways that could survive ecclesiastical scrutiny."

Flipping through another manuscript, Hana stopped on a marginal note written in a hurried but precise hand. "This one describes 'lights in ordered motion,' and speaks of 'a harvest prepared under signs not born of Earth.' Michael, it's nearly word-for-word what I saw during the vision."

He didn't speak immediately. Instead, he watched her, noting the steadiness in her eyes. "So, you believe now that Juana's manuscript is more than a spiritual allegory."

"I do," Hana said. "She didn't just encrypt ancient botanical knowledge—she embedded a record of something real. A transmission, maybe. A guidance system encoded into plants from the influence of the stars. Or from beings from the stars."

Michael leaned back in his chair, processing. "That's a hard conclusion for a priest to entertain."

"But you are entertaining it," she probed.

He smiled without amusement. "I'd be a poor historian if I weren't willing to follow the evidence. But also, I'd be a poor priest if I didn't understand the impact it could have on the Church. We have been led to believe that the people on this planet are God's one most miraculous creation, molded in His image, with souls inherent only to us. That God subsequently provided for the salvation of our souls. How do we fit alien life into any of that theology?"

Hana reached over and touched his hand. "That isn't for you to determine. Michael, you are primarily a historian. Presenting the facts to the Church hierarchy is your highest duty. It is up to them to figure out how to interpret it within the light of the Church."

Just then, Simon Ginzberg entered the study, balancing several rolled scrolls and loose parchment in his arms. "More from the university archives," he said. "You'll want to see these."

He spread the texts across the table and pointed to one illuminated page. "This one is from 1423, written by a Jewish scholar in Córdoba. He describes 'correspondence' between monastic figures in southern France and Moorish astronomers here in Granada—exchanges not of theology or politics, but of 'celestial messengers' who appeared during rare astronomical alignments, and whose messages were reflected in plant growth and medicinal potency."

Michael scanned the passage, his brow furrowed. "They were documenting it. Not speculating—observing. And comparing notes across cultures."

Simon nodded. "They saw the same things: unfamiliar constellations, luminous phenomena that behaved with intention, and patterns in botanical development that correlated with their appearance. They recorded these experiences cautiously, always with some plausible theological cover, but the consistency is remarkable."

Hana glanced at Michael. "So, we're not dealing with isolated accounts anymore. This was a network of educated men and women seeing the same anomalies and trying to make sense of them without losing their lives to accusations of heresy."

Michael stepped away from the table and walked toward the tall window. Outside, Granada shimmered beneath a sapphire sky, the distant outlines of the Alhambra just visible beyond the rooftops. "If we accept this premise," he said, still facing the window, "then Juana's manuscript is a chronicle of contact. And not just hers. She was building on generations of protected knowledge."

"And encoding it for us to find," Hana said, joining him. "Or someone like us."

He turned to face her. "But why now? Why us?"

"Maybe because humanity has reached the point where the danger of not knowing matches the danger of knowing," she replied.

Michael didn't answer. Instead, he returned to the table and picked up one of the newer documents Simon had brought. In gold leaf across the margin, someone centuries ago had drawn a vine twisting into a spiral—a perfect echo of a galaxy.

Blackthorn's normally unreadable face morphed between a scowl of anger and a tight-lipped resolve. He was talking to his chief chemist at a laboratory tucked away from the public eye in a small German town.

"What do you mean, you can't replicate it? You have the same plant that the Sinclair woman had ingested."

"Sir, I'm aware we have the same plant, and we have

tested every aspect of it. We suspected the pollen, of course, as it easily could have been inhaled, and a few of the subjects we tested with it reported seeing night skies although, to be honest, they made no sense. Yet none of them had the full experience you were expecting. Could you have been misled into believing that the woman had—"

Blackthorn pounded a fist on his desk, the sound of it cutting off the words of the man on the phone. "I told you, the woman experienced much more than just a night sky. And you did, did you not, require those who did see a star-filled sky to map out exactly what they'd seen?"

"Yes, sir. I've done exactly as you've asked. I will transmit them now for you, if you wish."

"If I wish? You should've sent them already!" Blackthorn allowed a long pause to heighten the tension across the phone line.

To fill in the growing ominous silence, the scientist explained that they had tested every aspect of the plant— leaves, stem, root—and found unusual sequences of cellular combinations, yet none of them resulted in effects on their test subjects.

Blackthorn mumbled more to himself than to the chemist, "The damned timing. Again, this insistence on certain seasons, certain lunar phases, as if I have time for such nonsense. Formulas should work, regardless of such esoteric things."

His boss's comment stimulated the scientist to suggest, "Sir, maybe that is the issue. We were testing at a time different than when this Sinclair woman would have encountered the plant. Maybe, with a bit of patience, we should retest with each lunar phase, testing to determine if the timing—"

"Just do it!" Blackthorn snapped, then clicked off the call. Almost immediately, he saw the mapped constellations appear in his email from the test subjects who had witnessed starry skies.

Moments later, he had confirmed what he suspected. Those constellations coincided with the ones he had from the various medieval manuscripts he had gathered over many long months of research before the interference of Hana Sinclair. To his annoyance, it appeared that those manuscripts, which insisted on such antiquated and superstitious beliefs as lunar phases, had been likely correct after all. He didn't want to admit that patience was going to be required for his people to potentially complete the formula.

He already knew the formula he had given her when he had her abducted had only a limited effect on some of his experimental subjects. Also, it remained in the patient's bloodstream afterward but was inactive. Yet it affected her just as he'd hoped. Meaning something was missing. Why was she affected?

His scientists speculated that the chemical effects—still in her blood, from that specific plant—had triggered full activation of their synthetic serum. Subjects needed to consume one of those cosmically-touched substances somehow. But waiting for some correct constellation or lunar phase didn't work within Blackthorn's timeframe. They needed to add some of that substance into their synthesized serum to complete the formula. But how? Without that additional substance, his synthetic formula had little or no effect. And no chance at being patented, let alone making him money.

He needed that woman or... Then it hit him—the substance circulating through her blood! He sat back, realizing suddenly they could extract whatever latent chemical remained in her bloodstream, replicate it, and add it to his serum to make it viable.

Yes... That's what I need. The woman...

Blackthorn snatched up the phone and made another call—this one to Vaux.

"Do you have them now?" he spat out the moment that the phone was answered.

"They are heading to Provence again."

"I thought they were about to land in Germany?" Blackthorn questioned.

"Yes, they were and they did land, but took off within too short a time for us to—"

"Why?" Blackthorn questioned more to himself than his chief operative. Had there been something they needed to pick up there before jetting off yet again? And why back to Provence? Had they missed something there earlier? It didn't matter now—he knew what he needed. "Do you have your people ready when they land?"

"Of course," Vaux answered as if the certainty was never in question.

"I want the woman alive. And bring her to me." Blackthorne clicked off without another word, a smile finally growing on his face.

CHAPTER
TWENTY-NINE

GRANADA, SPAIN

T he light in the villa study had shifted from sharp Andalusian morning to the soft diffusion of late afternoon. Shadows stretched long across the walls as parchment maps, handwritten translations, and botanical illustrations lay carefully arranged across the long wooden table. A low breeze drifted through the open French doors, carrying with it the distant sound of church bells and the heavy perfume of the garden's orange blossoms.

Several days had passed with no further attacks. Lukas was healing well, gaining some movement in his arm, although still not fully operational. The two Swiss Guards had monitored the activity of Blackthorn's people as Hana continued to send her jet to locations throughout Europe. So far, the ploy was working. They hoped Vaux would wonder where they had been dropped off once he realized they were not on the jet.

Simon was able to access manuscripts kept exclusively in local museums and libraries. Between his academic credentials and Michael's priestly status with the Vatican, they had checked out the documents they needed, borrowing them for analysis at a secured and secluded villa provided by one of Hana's international banking colleagues.

Michael stood over a centuries-old star chart, this one provided from Simon's personal collection of Jewish manuscripts, its fragile parchment protected by a thin pane of archival glass. Across its surface, hand-painted zodiacal symbols curled in elegant detail around unfamiliar constellations. Hana sat opposite him, cross-referencing the star positions against *Voynich* illustrations she had digitized and enhanced on her tablet.

"This symbol," she said, tapping her screen pointedly, "shows up again and again. Not just in Juana's diagrams, but here—in this Moorish chart from 1389, and even earlier, in a Carolingian manuscript we found in Rome."

Michael leaned in, his eyes narrowing. The symbol was simple yet evocative: a central blossom flanked by a crescent moon and a six-pointed star. "I thought it was just a stylized rose, but now I'm not so sure."

"It's not a rose," Hana said, her voice calm but intense. "It's a convergence marker. These manuscripts— European, Arabic, Jewish—all reference a 'flowering' that happens during certain alignments of the moon, Mars, and two unidentified celestial bodies. One of them doesn't exist in any known chart. Or at least," she added with a faint smile, "not any chart recognized by modern astronomy."

Michael smiled warmly, accepting the truth of her words. "And yet they all describe the same effects: a surge in plant vitality, spontaneous blooming, altered chemical properties. All occurring under the same bewildering sky."

"And all marked by that same symbol," Hana said. "It's not ornamental. It's functional."

They had spent days combing through astronomical records gathered from the archives beneath the Alhambra and cross-referencing them with *Voynich* iconography. Juana hadn't only hidden botanical knowledge, she had encoded it into celestial cycles. And those cycles, it now appeared, weren't limited to the stars humanity had cataloged.

Simon Ginzberg entered the study carrying a thick codex bound in cracking goatskin. "You'll want to see this," he said, setting it down. "It's from the Biblioteca de la Sacristía Mayor in Córdoba. Seventeenth-century collection of theological correspondences, mostly responses to ecclesiastical councils convened to discuss 'doctrinal anomalies.'"

He opened to a bookmarked page. "Listen to this. Written by a Dominican Inquisitor in 1494: '*There are some among us—learned and otherwise reputable—who claim that heavenly visitors have walked among men. That these beings come not in glory but in silence, guiding the growth of herbs and whispering wisdom to those who fast and pray. Such ideas, if permitted, would corrupt the foundation of Creation itself.*'"

Michael's expression darkened slightly. "They were afraid of what it would mean—that there are other beings in this universe beyond the biblical progeny of Adam and Eve."

Simon nodded. "More than afraid. They debated whether these so-called beings were angels, demons, or something heretical in between. But they took the accounts seriously enough to keep records—and suppress them."

Hana turned the page of one document, scanning quickly. "Here. A letter from a Cistercian abbot to the Vatican Curia in 1471. He writes: '*If these stars move without God's direction, we are lost. Better they be heresy than reality.*'"

Outside, the faint growl of an engine pulled Karl and Lukas from their conversation on the villa's terrace.

Lukas moved first, scanning the street through binoculars. A black sedan rolled slowly past the villa's gate, the driver just a silhouette behind tinted glass.

"They've found us," he grumbled.

Karl didn't reply immediately. He was already on his phone, sending a secure message to the secondary security team. He turned to Lukas, voice low. "We double the perimeter tonight. Lock down the garden paths, post two at the gatehouse, and prep the extraction plan."

"Understood," Lukas said. "Should we assume they're preparing to move soon?"

Karl nodded. "We've lost our cover. And they've lost the advantage. Michael's too close now to whatever Blackthorn wants. If Vaux is going to act, it'll be soon."

Later that night, Karl moved through the villa with measured steps, checking locks, confirming vantage points, and coordinating shifts with Lukas by hand signal. Vaux had made his intentions clear through action, not words. The ambush in Granada was only the prelude. Their ploy of the jet touching down in various places had lasted only so long. And no doubt had irritated the already frustrated and dangerous Vaux.

Simon entered with a bottle of red wine and three

glasses. "We're either at the end of something," he said, "or the beginning."

Michael took a glass and raised it slightly. "To both."

They drank in silence, each person staring out into the darkened city beyond the balcony windows. Somewhere out there, Christophe Vaux was making his next move. Somewhere above, the stars held their silence.

But here, in the lamplight, surrounded by the work of generations who had dared to document what they saw and feared, three modern seekers prepared to finish what others had only begun.

CHAPTER

THIRTY

GRANADA, SPAIN

T he silence in the villa's study was dense, broken only by the rustle of parchment and the low clink of porcelain as Hana set down her coffee cup. Outside, dawn was just beginning to stretch across the Andalusian skyline, bathing the white walls and red roofs of Granada in soft hues of rose and gold. Inside, the mood was different—quiet, tense, cerebral—as they waited for word from Karl. They'd gone through the night without a problem, but they knew Vaux was watching them, ready to pounce.

Michael sat cross-legged at the far end of the table, surrounded by the pages from Juana's manuscript. He wore his reading glasses low on his nose, murmuring faint Latin phrases to himself as he compared symbols between pages.

"I've been reading it wrong," he said suddenly, breaking the long silence.

Hana looked up from her tablet, where she had been digitally layering overlays of celestial charts onto *Voynich* folios. "What do you mean?"

Michael lifted one of Juana's illustrated pages and rotated it ninety degrees. "These aren't merely ornamental frames around the botanical diagrams. They're directional glyphs. When aligned according to the sequence we discovered in Córdoba, the borders themselves form a layered structure—nested like an encoded map or mechanism."

He pointed to a sequence of repeating symbols—interwoven spirals, triangles embedded within crescent moons, botanical forms intersecting with what appeared to be star positions.

"I think it's a form of instructional language," he continued. "Not written in words, but in layered geometry and symbolism, intended to act as a map."

He gestured to a separate folio filled with star configurations and mysterious glyphs. "This page here, when viewed through the filter of the zodiacal alignment we decoded yesterday, provides a more comprehensive map than what we've used already just from the earlier parchment. The more you understand, the more it reveals. Juana wasn't just preserving data—she was teaching a way of seeing, with each layer assisting the previous one."

Hana returned to her workstation and pulled up a high-resolution scan of one of the manuscript's more abstract folios. She enhanced it, removed the botanical overlays, and then paused.

"There," she whispered. "That cluster—those aren't stars. They're not mapped anywhere in known astronomy. I checked the Hipparcos catalog, the Gaia data—nothing. They're not visible from Earth."

Michael approached slowly, studying the image. The symbols were delicate, precise—like distant constellations seen through a window no telescope could access.

"They're not in the manuscript by accident," Hana said. "Juana—or whoever came before her—had knowledge of star formations we haven't identified yet. That implies either observational technology far beyond her time... or something else."

Michael's expression darkened slightly. "Something beyond Earth."

"I resisted it too," Hana said. "But the evidence is overwhelming. The manuscript is layered with celestial information no human could've mapped from the Earth's surface. Unless we're willing to accept that multiple cultures across multiple centuries were collectively imagining the same astronomical impossibilities... we have to consider the alternative."

Michael returned to the table and picked up a folio he had flagged earlier. It showed a botanical cross-section with vines twisting into a spiral formation. Within the spiral, four concentric circles marked with dots and curves extended outward like orbital paths.

"This isn't a plant," he said quietly. "It's a schematic."

Hana joined him, her eyes tracing the same patterns. "Of a solar system?"

"Or of a conceptual framework," Michael said.

"Or a message," Hana added. "Something non-human, using organic symbolism as a medium. Something reaching across time and space through biology, geometry, and ritual."

They sat in silence for a long moment, absorbing the scale of what they were uncovering. Outside, the church bells of Granada began to ring the hour. Somewhere behind those tones, the ancient city stirred, unaware that inside a secluded villa, two modern scholars had cracked open a manuscript that could rewrite humanity's understanding of its place in the cosmos.

ACROSS THE CITY, in a high-rise overlooking the Genil River, Christophe Vaux stood before a digital display marked with symbols.

He touched a key on the console, bringing up a tactical map of the city. Red markers lit up: the villa, two nearby safe houses, a relay station intercepting local drone traffic, and three routes of retreat blocked off. Once he'd deduced the trick of the jet's maneuvers, he'd zeroed in on finding the priest and journalist, and, once located, he'd arrived to oversee the operation himself.

"We move tonight," Vaux said to the room. Around him, a dozen mercenaries reviewed assault plans and field intel. "Dominic and Sinclair must not leave Granada."

One of the operatives—a wiry man in tactical black—spoke up. "What about their backup team from the Vatican? The Swiss Guards?"

Vaux smirked. "They'll be neutralized. Efficiently. Non-lethal if possible, but we don't flinch if that's not an option. We retrieve whatever documents they have, wipe their drives, and take the Sinclair woman."

"They think they're guardians," Vaux said, almost to himself. "But they're obstacles. This knowledge doesn't belong to the cautious or the faithful. It belongs to those willing to use it."

· · ·

AT THE VILLA, Karl and Lukas prepared for what they now considered inevitable—that Vaux had realized their subterfuge with the jet, and was back on their trail again. Karl had relocated two backup personnel from a secondary safe house and embedded them across the street in a civilian vehicle. Lukas installed additional surveillance in the garden and replaced the security codes on the main doors.

"You think Vaux will try tonight?" Hana asked, watching as Karl tested the perimeter alarm.

"I'd bet my pension on it," Karl said. "He failed in Córdoba, in Avignon, and here in the alley near the archives. By now, we believe he is in town himself and likely knows we are about to leave. This is his opportunity... and ours. That pattern ends tonight."

Michael joined them, his voice calm but serious. "Then we stay ready. And we finish what we started."

Back inside the study, he resumed transcribing a passage that had haunted him since he first discovered it the day before: *"He who reads the stars in silence, and sees the seeds within them, may come to know the gardens of heaven. But let him not pluck too eagerly, lest what blooms become thorns."*

Michael wrote the words in his notebook and paused. "It's a warning," he said.

Hana looked up. "You think Juana feared what this knowledge could do?"

"She feared what people would do with it," Michael replied. "And I think she was right."

Outside, as the final light of day dipped behind the Alhambra's ridge, a faint movement in the street—barely visible—registered on Lukas's handheld display. He stood, silent and still, eyes locked on the screen.

"They're coming," he said.

No one spoke. The room grew still, expectant.

Juana's manuscript had spoken through stars and symbols, through vines and visions.

Now, it would speak through blood.

As THE LIBRARY'S heavy wooden doors closed behind them, the quietude of Granada's nighttime streets settled around Michael, Hana, Simon, Karl, and Lukas like a deceptively comforting shroud. A thin crescent moon hung low above the Alhambra, its pale light casting ghostly shadows upon the ancient cobblestones. The air felt charged, laden with a stillness that pressed uneasily against their skin.

Hana clutched Juana's manuscript protectively against her chest, its worn leather cover a tangible reassurance against the mounting dread that seemed to pulse in rhythm with her quickening heartbeat. She glanced anxiously at Michael, who gave her a reassuring, tender kiss that momentarily softened the harshness of their surroundings.

Karl and Lukas moved ahead, vigilant and poised, their gazes sweeping methodically from side to side. Lukas still favored his injured shoulder, but had no trouble keeping up with his partner. Sensing the tension, Simon stayed close beside Michael and Hana, his expression wary but determined. The Swiss Guards were well aware of the subtle indications of an approaching threat—the all-too-quiet alleys, the unnatural absence of late-night foot traffic, and the way shadows seemed to linger longer than they should.

Their instincts proved correct moments later. Abruptly, bright headlights erupted from both ends of the narrow street, blinding the team in a wash of white light. Tires squealed harshly against stone as vehicles skidded to strategic halts, sealing off escape. Figures emerged rapidly, silhouettes materializing like ghosts from the glare, clearly armed, moving with professional, lethal purpose.

"Get behind us!" Karl barked sharply, his voice edged with protective fury. Lukas instantly shielded Hana, Michael, and Simon, his imposing frame solid, defensive, prepared for violence despite his arm being in a sling.

The attackers surged forward, closing the gap in seconds, their faces concealed beneath dark balaclavas, eyes glinting with ruthless determination. Karl met the closest assailant head-on, his movements swift and brutal. A quick elbow strike shattered the man's composure before a powerful blow to the chest sent him sprawling, gasping, onto the street.

Michael gripped Hana's hand protectively, pulling her toward an opening between two buildings. "Stay near me," he urged, his voice tense yet comforting. Simon remained close behind them, eyes wide with alarm but unwavering in resolve. They dashed through a narrow gap barely wide enough to accommodate them, emerging into the maze-like labyrinth of Granada's Albaicín quarter.

The chase plunged them deep into the heart of the ancient Moorish district, the twisting alleys and hidden courtyards transforming their flight into a desperate, disorienting dash through history itself. The echoing footsteps of their pursuers reverberated ominously off whitewashed walls, blending into a cacophony of shouting voices and panicked breathing.

Hana's breath burned hot in her lungs, each step forward fueled by adrenaline and desperation. The manuscript felt heavier in her arms, as if its weight were augmented by the esoteric secrets contained within its pages. Michael, running closely beside her, reached over briefly to squeeze her hand in silent reassurance, their bond a quiet beacon amid chaos.

The team scrambled through an arched gateway draped in flowering vines, emerging into a small courtyard enclosed by ivy-covered walls. For a heartbeat, a momentary lull enveloped them, but it was fleeting. Behind them, footsteps pounded closer and voices rang out, harsh with fury.

Karl, ever decisive, pointed out a narrow alleyway across the courtyard. "There!" he prompted urgently. As they entered the passage, a steel door on one side swung open, and a man jumped out in front of them.

Hana gasped, tried to step back, but Karl pushed her toward the now-opened door, giving a quick gesture for the others to follow him. The man who had jumped out quickly swung the door closed behind all of them. Hana turned, wanting to see the man, but Karl and the others whisked her forward. She now realized that this subterfuge, which she hadn't expected, had been carefully choreographed by her cousin and his partner; each alley and turn had been well-timed and planned.

The interior of the building smelled dank with age, with just enough light filtering through closed doorways that they soon found themselves exiting another alleyway altogether.

Minutes later, they slipped quietly through Granada's still-darkened streets, reaching a waiting taxi van in front of a local hotel. The drive to Granada Airport was tense, each bump and turn jarring their heightened nerves.

At the airport, the sleek Dassault Falcon awaited them on the tarmac, engines softly humming in readiness and luggage already aboard thanks to Hana's earlier call to the pilots. As they boarded, local security maintained vigilant positions nearby, having been briefed on the gravity of their presence.

Once safely aboard, the cabin door sealed, and the jet smoothly ascended, leaving the ancient city far below in tranquil oblivion of the violent night just endured. Silence lingered densely among them. Michael tenderly entwined his fingers with Hana's, sharing a quiet, reassuring glance.

In the subdued atmosphere, Michael glanced back toward the Swiss Guards and Simon, reflecting on the unspoken depth of loyalty and care binding them all. The night's episode had reminded each of them of their vulnerability, but also of the quiet strength in their companionship, anchored by silent, resilient trust.

Ahead lay Rome, the Vatican's ancient walls promising protection but no guarantee of safety from the enemies determined to silence them. The manuscript, once silent, had indeed spoken through stars, symbols, vines, visions —and now irrevocably through blood. Yet, Michael realized, the darkest revelations were still to come.

THIRTY-ONE

VATICAN CITY

The hush inside the Pontifical Academy's council chamber felt heavier than the carved archways and centuries of dogma hanging overhead. Sunlight spilled through high lancet windows, striking motes of dust that danced like tiny cosmic bodies in suspension—a fitting motif, Michael thought grimly, for a discussion poised to break Earth's self-importance wide open.

Around the oval table, a dozen Vatican theologians pored over stacks of brittle codices, faded astronomical diagrams, and fresh digital scans annotated in the margins by linguists and historians. They had all been admonished that this meeting was to be held in utmost confidence, a warning that a few felt unnecessary, considering all Vatican proceedings are to be held in confidentiality. Yet when a single word—extraterrestrial—became apparent in their proceedings, it hovered over the room like a ghost no one dared invoke too bluntly—and made clear the reason for the reminder of the prudence required of this group today.

Michael shifted in his seat, the weight of his clerical collar suddenly oppressive. He caught the eye of Father Pietro Spada, an older Jesuit whose hands trembled slightly as he traced a line across a parchment charting an anomaly from a medieval monk's night sky log.

"Dominic," Spada rasped, voice cracked from hours of guarded debate, "the evidence bends plausibility but does not yet break it. And if it does... we stand on the edge of rewriting more than theology."

Michael inclined his head just enough to convey understanding, maintaining a neutral expression. "Gentlemen, my role is not to declare doctrine—only to lay out the historical fabric honestly. What we decide to weave from it is a matter for the Curia, the Holy Father, and the faithful—in that order. The Holy Father has been apprised of the situation and awaits the comments of the Curia on how these historic facts might affect faith."

A cardinal opposite him snorted faintly, flicking a dismissive glance at a laptop where digital renderings of a cryptic star map blinked lazily. "History is pliable, Father Dominic. Faith must not be."

An uneasy laugh flickered around the table. Michael absorbed it in silence. He knew too well how brittle truth could become under the grindstone of fear.

Outside the chamber, Ian Duffy leaned against a chilled marble pillar, arms folded tight across his chest as if the stone could brace him against the storm he sensed gathering. Beside him, Sister Teri adjusted the wire-frame glasses perpetually sliding down her nose, tapping through security updates on her phone. Her thumb paused over an alert labeled *Public Disclosure Risk: Medium to High*.

"They'll bury it," Ian muttered, not entirely to her. "Or dilute it until it's safe. And if it leaks—God knows the mob needs no excuse."

Teri flicked him a glance, calm but tinged with melancholy. "Fear does the burying. Faith should do the digging—painstakingly, yes, but without flinching."

Ian huffed a breath, half-laugh, half-sigh. "Easy to say when you're not the guy who has to lock the Archives at night, knowing every crackpot will break in searching for proof that E.T. phoned home."

Teri pocketed her phone and folded her arms to mirror his. "Do you really think this will upend the world overnight? People survive worse truths: corruption, plagues, wars. Maybe an unsettling cosmic neighbor would humble us a little."

Ian's eyes traced the mosaic floor. *Or break us entirely,* he thought but didn't voice it. Instead, he glanced back toward the heavy oak doors muffling the theologians' wary voices.

Inside, Michael rose slowly, sensing the debate drifting into futile loops. He cleared his throat. Conversations stilled.

"Whether we cloak this or bare it," he said, voice carrying just enough steel to hush dissent, "we owe the faithful something stronger than fear. If we conceal too much, we become gatekeepers of terror instead of shepherds of understanding."

No one replied immediately. A breeze rattled a loose pane in the high window, like the soft knocking of the truth wanting in.

· · ·

LATER THAT EVENING, Michael lingered in the dim solitude of the Gregorian Map Room, the frescoed continents around him rendered in muted blues and greens beneath the low, warm glow of inset lighting. He stood alone before Fra Ignazio's fifteenth-century planisphere, its meticulous celestial annotations stark and unsettling in their implications. He wondered, not for the first time, if the hand that inked those careful notes had trembled with awe or dread.

Sister Teri entered quietly, her steps a gentle whisper against marble. She watched him silently for a moment, hesitant to intrude upon his reflections.

"Michael," she finally murmured, approaching slowly, her presence gentle yet firm. "Ian's anxious. The Archives' digital logs show attempts at unauthorized access since your meeting. Someone already suspects something significant."

Turning to face her, Michael sighed, the tension etched clearly across his features. "Blackthorn's people?"

"I think not this time."

"Do we know who?"

Teri shook her head slightly. "Only suspicions of media coverts. Whoever it is, they're scrupulous enough to know exactly what they're looking for, yet careful enough to avoid immediate detection."

Michael's lips tightened. "Then we're already behind. If news breaks without careful handling, it could destabilize more than doctrine. It could fracture trust."

"Or rebuild it," Teri countered, conviction strong beneath her quiet tone. "What if revelation doesn't destroy faith but deepens it? What if seeing ourselves as part of a larger universe encourages humility and wonder, rather than fear?"

Michael exhaled forcefully, conflicted. "Optimism suits you, Sister. But human nature tends toward panic before wonder. We have to consider both reactions."

Teri nodded in agreement, stepping closer to meet his gaze directly. "Then we guide gently, transparently, and honestly. Concealing the truth out of fear only gives ammunition to conspiracy."

Unsettled, Michael rubbed his forehead. "Easier said than done. We have no blueprint for this. We've never confronted such radical uncertainty."

"No," Teri replied, voice steady. "But perhaps the essence of faith has always been just that—standing firm in radical uncertainty."

Michael looked at her, the silence stretching between them dense with contemplation. Around them, the maps lay quiet, mute witnesses to centuries of humanity's bold exploration into the unknown. He straightened finally, decision crystallizing.

"Maybe it's time the Church faced uncertainty head-on," he conceded. "But we must move with utmost speed. Ian's worries are justified—secrets this volatile demand rigorous supervision. Yet at the same time, it is better to head off the storm rather than be destroyed by the winds of public outcry fanned by the purposes of others. And I know just the person who can handle such a diplomatic pronouncement."

Teri smiled. "We'll stand with you, Michael. Whatever comes."

He glanced upward toward the intricately painted ceiling, the celestial imagery above an ironic comfort. "Then let's prepare ourselves—and the Church—for whatever truths the stars might bring."

CHAPTER

THIRTY-TWO

ROME, ITALY

T he grand hall of the Pontifical Gregorian University in Rome was filled to overflowing, a restless sea of scholars, reporters, theologians, and curious members of the public spilling beyond the carved oak doors into corridors where large screens had been mounted. The air was electric with whispers, a murmuring tide of anticipation and intrigue that rose and fell like waves upon an uncertain shore.

At the front of the hall, beneath a towering fresco of celestial beings, Hana Sinclair stood poised at the ornate podium, her slender hands steady against its smooth mahogany surface, though her pulse raced fiercely beneath her calm exterior. Her gaze briefly drifted upward to the fresco's angels, their painted eyes serene, their golden haloes gleaming subtly beneath the vaulted ceiling. She drew quiet strength from their timeless presence.

Michael sat close by, unobtrusively to one side, offering

the quiet reassurance of his presence. Their eyes met briefly, a private communion of love, trust, and mutual resolve passing between them. Nearby, Simon Ginzberg adjusted his glasses nervously, the significance of the moment clearly weighing upon him. At the rear of the room, Karl and Lukas stood with unwavering vigilance, along with more members of the Swiss Guard, their eyes scanning the room for threats, their professional demeanor masking deeply personal stakes.

Clearing her throat, Hana leaned slightly toward the microphone, and the room's whispers quieted into expectant silence.

"Throughout history," she began calmly, her voice clear and resonant, "humans have grappled with visions, symbols, and mysteries that defy easy understanding. Across cultures and eras, the stars have guided explorers, inspired prophets, and comforted those seeking meaning amid chaos." She paused, allowing the gravity of her words to sink in.

"I, too, have sought meaning," she continued slowly, her voice growing subtly stronger, emboldened by the attentive stillness in the room. "In recent months, my journey has involved deciphering symbols etched into history by visionary minds—symbols illuminated by celestial alignments that defy coincidence."

Hana paused deliberately, letting the implications hang in the air. A ripple of excited murmuring spread through the audience before dissipating as she continued. "These visions and symbols have long whispered truths beyond ordinary perception—truths perhaps communicated to humans by entities whose origins remain... uncertain."

She deliberately avoided explicit statements, her choice of words artfully ambiguous yet potent. Journalists in attendance furiously scribbled notes, understanding her guarded suggestion. Scholars exchanged knowing glances, intrigued and startled by implications rarely voiced publicly in such esteemed company.

Hana's heart quickened as she prepared to share something truly personal, her voice softening slightly. "I took part in recent research that covers centuries of documentation, and I've discovered... well, things I cannot readily explain through conventional means." The attendees silently held their breath as they listened to her. "These facts have compelled me, along with my trusted colleagues, to explore the possibility that the world's spiritual and intellectual history may be intertwined with celestial influences we simply do not yet fully comprehend."

Across the room, unseen by Hana but observed keenly by Karl, a dark-haired man subtly shifted in his seat, eyes narrowing, attentively gauging reactions. Blackthorn's agent, disguised as one of the journalists, listened intently, analyzing Hana's every word.

As Hana continued her delicate, thoughtful testimony, public speculation blossomed throughout the audience, her gentle yet daring revelations feeding a wildfire of whispered theories. A journalist near the front boldly called out during a brief pause, "Are you suggesting extraterrestrial involvement, Ms. Sinclair?"

Hana met the reporter's eyes with poised confidence, her smile serene yet enigmatic. "I suggest only that our understanding of divine and cosmic mysteries remains incomplete. These symbols and visions compel us to consider possibilities beyond current paradigms."

The tension in the hall heightened, journalists frantically recording her measured responses. Social media streams buzzed with theories, with debates rapidly spreading across global platforms. Hana's thoughtfully chosen ambiguity had sparked exactly the curiosity and dialogue they had hoped for.

Several hands rose, eager to pose questions. Hana nodded towards one who quickly asked, "What do you mean by symbols and visions?"

She then provided the evidence that had become clear to them, noting the diaries, journals, and documents throughout several centuries, not just from Church sources, but also from others Simon had discovered in Arabic and Moorish accounts. But she did it factually, without speculation as to the source or the intended implication, just the facts of the celestial observations over centuries, their consistency, and the invitation for more scholarly review. She handled questions adroitly, avoiding conjecture and sticking to the facts until those present realized they could not rattle her. As a journalist herself, who had rattled many cages to 'get the real story,' she had anticipated every maneuver and knew how to sidestep them.

Observing from the audience's periphery, Blackthorn's spy discreetly tapped notes into a secure device concealed beneath his jacket sleeve. Hana's strategic ambiguity as she completed her address clearly unsettled the agent, sensing potential trouble in the growing public attention and its possible implications.

In a quiet corner afterward, Michael approached Hana, placing a supportive hand on her arm. "You were extraordinary," he whispered, his voice filled with pride and subtle concern. Hana leaned into his comforting touch, briefly closing her eyes, drawing strength from his quiet presence.

Across the room, Simon joined them, visibly relieved. "Your choice of words was perfect," he whispered earnestly. "Just enough to ignite thoughtful speculation without openly committing yourself to specific conclusions. We've taken the reins of the narrative with your speech."

Karl and Lukas approached cautiously, their vigilant gazes still scanning the departing crowd. Karl's voice was low and controlled. "Someone was observing you closely," he warned. "Likely one of Blackthorn's people. Let's stay vigilant."

Lukas nodded his silent agreement, eyes narrowed in protective concern.

Hana nodded gravely, absorbing their cautious warning with solemn acknowledgment. "We anticipated their interest," she said, her voice tired yet steady. "They will realize that people will now question that whatever formula they come up with may have been obtained from manuscripts that are part of the Church's own documents or historic public records. Now, his capacity to assert any originality will be significantly weakened, potentially even destroyed."

In the distance, outside the university's grand entrance, beneath the gathering dusk, Christophe Vaux himself watched from a discreet, darkened vehicle. His expression, lit faintly by a muted dashboard glow, was calculating and cool. His gaze was fixed steadily on the streaming crowd emerging from the university, quietly contemplating his next move.

Beside him, another agent waited silently, sensing his leader's growing displeasure. "They're dangerously impairing our efforts," Vaux murmured, his voice edged with quiet menace. "Sinclair and her allies have stirred something volatile."

"What would you have us do?" the operative inquired respectfully, sensing his employer's growing resolve.

Vaux turned slowly to him, eyes glittering dangerously. "For now, we must ensure their message remains discredited. Sabotage their credibility—swiftly, decisively. Make certain that whatever legitimacy they've gathered tonight evaporates under scandal and doubt." He failed to state his intention to kidnap the exasperating Ms. Sinclair at some point as well. He realized that doing so now, after this public meeting, would raise too many red flags. That, too, she had spoiled for him.

In the darkness of his vehicle parked in shadows, Christophe Vaux sat in brooding contemplation, patiently crafting plans of sabotage and ruin, determined to extinguish the flame Hana had courageously sparked.

As DARKNESS FULLY EMBRACED ROME, Hana and Michael exited the hall, their hands subtly intertwined, the quiet strength of their bond a comforting refuge against mounting uncertainty. Simon walked beside them, his thoughtful silence underscoring the weight of the moment.

Farther behind, Karl and Lukas continued their vigilant watch, Karl's protective instincts sharpened by recent dangers, Lukas's presence steadfast despite his earlier injuries. Their personal bond, strengthened by recent trials, lent an additional, fierce resolve to their guardianship.

Over the next few days, across Rome and throughout the world, news spread rapidly, speculation burning brightly, echoing through virtual channels across continents. Hana Sinclair had ignited a global conversation

—questions that had been whispered up until now were being shouted boldly into the open.

Questions abounded:

Were these really just astronomical anomalies that could be scientifically proven?

Or were these observations over the centuries the same as those witnessed in recent times?

Didn't this, in fact, reinforce what had been witnessed and documented so well since the 1950s in the United States alone?

Was there, as the conspiracy theorists contended, an unwritten pact among powers that be—religious and governmental—to hide truths that those in power already knew?

The more rational among the voices echoed what Hana had proposed: more research was needed at this point, without a predetermined answer. At the same time, UFO enthusiasts, spiritual leaders, and those with metaphysical ideologies were all stimulated to pursue their own active and latent beliefs. How did these observations reflect their own biases? And how could this reinforce the beliefs of their own adherents?

At the heart of it, Michael and Hana knew that Genetica would be launching its own efforts to undermine what they had shared and reinforce its own agenda. With that troubling awareness in mind, the team met yet again, outlining their next step in the plan they had been formulating ever since the last attack on the team.

THIRTY-THREE

VATICAN CITY - ZÜRICH, SWITZERLAND

The early morning sun bathed Vatican City in a warm, golden hue, illuminating the towering spires and polished marble of St. Peter's Basilica. A press briefing room within the Apostolic Palace hummed with anticipation as journalists, broadcasters, and Church officials gathered, drawn by the urgency and gravity of an announcement leaked hours earlier.

Pope Clement had been apprised of the team's efforts, as well as the Vatican's leaks and the troubles the team had suffered. He had been steadfast in giving them whatever backup and resources they needed, knowing that the basis for everything that resulted was, in fact, part of the Church's own reservoir of knowledge. With the Vatican Archives transitioning into the digital realm of the modern world, he was wise enough to understand that the Church's obligations and operational principles would necessarily require a firm commitment to truth. What form that structure might take, however, was of deep concern to him. He was currently in frequent meetings with the Curia as each new fact was revealed.

Hana's speech to the public had not been a surprise to him, but neither was it one he had been fully prepared for. However, this latest request from the team for a public speech from two of the Vatican staff was one he fully endorsed. If anything, it might help countermand potential public outcry towards the Church and displace suspicion to another avenue.

At the front of the room stood Ian Duffy, tall and resolute, his red hair catching the morning light, standing beside Sister Teri, whose usual buoyant demeanor was tempered today by solemn determination. Behind them, Cardinal Severino offered quiet support, his presence symbolizing the Pope and the Vatican's full endorsement of the disclosure about to unfold.

Ian adjusted the microphone, his deep breaths steadying nerves taut with the significance of the moment. He cleared his throat, voice firm and clear. "We gather today to address grave concerns regarding recent scientific activities conducted by Genetica Therapeutics," he began. "The recent disclosure of manuscripts across centuries that have noted celestial connections to our world has brought to light Genetica's interests in that regard. They have been seizing documents from antiquity in often illegal ways, to use information obtained from them for their own formulas, which they may attempt to claim is proprietary to them. These efforts are not for the good of mankind, but for their own gain. Information uncovered through extensive investigation reveals unethical experiments involving botanical specimens of questionable and potentially non-terrestrial origin."

A stir of excitement rippled through the room, cameras clicking furiously. Ian paused briefly, allowing the magnitude of his statement to resonate. "These experiments have sought to manipulate biological materials in ways that violate ethical and moral boundaries established by both scientific and religious communities."

Ian stepped back momentarily, allowing Sister Teri to approach the podium. Her gentle face radiated seriousness as she spoke. "Documents and digital evidence recovered show Genetica's deliberate concealment of experimental activities. The implications of their work threaten humanity's ethical understanding, particularly if these botanical specimens prove conclusively extraterrestrial."

An immediate eruption of questions surged from reporters, voices clamoring for clarity.

Ian stepped forward again, raising his hand to regain quiet.

"Detailed documentation has already been submitted to international regulatory bodies," he continued firmly. "The Vatican itself strongly condemns these actions, demanding immediate cessation and independent oversight into all research conducted by Genetica."

A flurry of cameras flashed again, journalists rapidly capturing every nuance of his revelation. The weight of Ian's words settled over the room, prompting a hush of startled contemplation. As the press conference concluded, waves of astonishment and speculation flooded digital news platforms, igniting an intense public discourse.

Across the globe, media outlets dissected the revelation, debating passionately the ethical ramifications of potential extraterrestrial botanical specimens being manipulated without transparency. Social media erupted, users demanding explanations, condemning Genetica's actions, or voicing frightened concerns about the broader implications for humankind.

MEANWHILE, within the secretive confines of his corporate headquarters, Alton Blackthorn paced angrily in front of a vast wall of glass overlooking Zürich's pristine cityscape. His carefully manicured image of corporate altruism was rapidly fracturing beneath public scrutiny and growing outrage.

"Do you see this disaster unfolding?" Blackthorn snapped furiously into a secure line. On the receiving end, Christophe Vaux listened silently, a tense muscle ticking at his jawline as he absorbed Blackthorn's blistering rebuke.

"This exposure," Blackthorn continued icily, "jeopardizes everything we've built. The Vatican's meddling and Sinclair's theatrics threaten not just our investments, but my entire legacy."

"I understand the gravity," Vaux replied tersely, barely suppressing irritation. "Sinclair's revelation opened a dangerous floodgate, and now the Vatican has publicly linked us to unethical experimentation."

Blackthorn's voice lowered dangerously, barely above a growl. "Then it's time for decisive action. Neutralize this narrative—now. Destroy their credibility. Make them regret ever mentioning our name."

IN VATICAN CITY, Ian and Teri retreated to the quiet sanctuary of Michael's private study, where Michael and

Hana awaited them anxiously. Simon hovered nearby, visibly strained by unfolding events.

Ian sank into a chair, breathing out deeply, tension visibly easing from his broad shoulders. Sister Teri's hands trembled slightly as she poured tea, her usual steadiness momentarily disrupted by emotional exhaustion.

Michael regarded them with quiet respect, offering gentle reassurance. "You've both shown tremendous courage today," he said warmly. "The world owes you gratitude for uncovering such disturbing truths."

Hana leaned forward earnestly. "Already, your words have sparked crucial dialogue. People are asking important questions."

Teri nodded solemnly. "Yet Genetica's power should not be underestimated."

Visibly tense, Simon spoke cautiously. "We must brace for retaliation. Blackthorn's resources and ruthlessness are formidable."

Michael inclined his head, considering Simon's words. "We anticipated Blackthorn's reaction," he affirmed. "Karl and Lukas will increase security. Our priority remains protecting our findings and ensuring transparency."

As the day progressed, across Rome, news continued to cascade through streets, cafés, and homes. Debates raged passionately about ethics, the possibilities of extraterrestrial life, and humanity's unpreparedness for such profound revelations.

Later, deep into the evening, Hana and Michael stood together overlooking Vatican City from Michael's balcony, hands entwined.

Hana's voice, though weary, was firm. "They'll try to silence us, Michael. But once revealed, they cannot so easily suppress the truth."

Michael gently squeezed her hand, drawing her closer.

As night fell over Vatican City, stars shimmered faintly above, their silent, distant presence an ancient witness to humanity's unfolding drama. Within the Apostolic Palace, Ian, Teri, Simon, Michael, and Hana rested, unaware of the storm gathering rapidly on their horizon—a storm determined to challenge their courage, resilience, and faith in truths still yet fully revealed.

MEANWHILE, in Zürich, Blackthorn's seething instructions propelled Christophe Vaux into action. Alone in a darkened office, illuminated only by screens casting ghostly reflections on his calculating face, Vaux coordinated swift countermeasures.

He orchestrated leaks and misinformation campaigns targeting Hana Sinclair, Ian Duffy, and Sister Teri, crafting diabolical narratives designed to undermine public confidence. Smear articles appeared rapidly, questioning their motivations, their integrity, and even their mental stability, seeking to drown their revelations beneath suspicion and ridicule.

Vaux concluded his preparations with cold determination, knowing Blackthorn's patience was exhausted. The boss still wanted Sinclair, still hoped to use her blood to secure a formula he could replicate consistently and use as the backbone of his new system of drugs. Their next move would need to be brutal, calculated, decisive—a final attempt to crush those who dared threaten their hidden empire.

CHAPTER
THIRTY-FOUR

VATICAN CITY

Morning sunlight poured through the grand windows of the Sala Stampa Vaticana, illuminating a crowded room buzzing with intense conversation. Journalists, religious scholars, and global media representatives filled every seat, spilling into aisles and corridors. The murmur of speculation was fevered, anticipation building to a charged crescendo.

Michael Dominic sat calmly at a long wooden table at the front, alongside Professor Elena Conti, a renowned atheist philosopher and passionate advocate of ethical transparency, and Father Antonio Moretti, a theologian esteemed for his open-minded yet faithfully progressive insights. Beside them were respected religious leaders from multiple faith traditions—bishops, rabbis, imams, and theologians—all of whom carried varying degrees of skepticism, curiosity, or outright concern about recent revelations tied to the *Voynich Manuscript* and the *Hesperides Codex*, and their unsettling implications.

He drew a quiet breath, aware that every word spoken here would ripple outward, amplified by media coverage across continents. But it was time to pull together the scientific and religious communities in a manner that would propel both forward in a positive way. Nearby, from her discreet position beside Ian Duffy and Simon Ginzberg, Hana Sinclair offered a steadying glance to support Michael's delicate task.

A cardinal opened the discussion solemnly, inviting Michael to speak.

Michael rose slowly, his eyes thoughtful and calm as he began.

"We stand today at the intersection of faith, history, and scientific possibility," he said deliberately. "Recent findings surrounding the *Voynich Manuscript* have captured global imagination, raising profound and complex questions— questions that challenge our understanding of the divine, the cosmic, and our place within Creation."

The room was silent now, each journalist's pen poised, microphones angled appropriately.

"As intriguing as these revelations are, it is vital that we approach this knowledge responsibly," Michael continued. "Speculation about the possible extraterrestrial implications of the manuscript is understandable, even inevitable. But we must guard against rushing into hasty conclusions that could lead to confusion or fear."

After this, Professor Conti wasted no time in voicing her pointed concerns.

"Father Dominic," she began directly, her voice clear and challenging, "your recent revelations involving historical celestial phenomena and the Vatican's deliberate concealment present critical ethical questions. Let me be explicit: withholding knowledge from humanity— regardless of motive—is inherently unethical. Secrecy damages trust. Isn't total transparency the Vatican's only morally defensible option?"

Michael listened respectfully, preparing to respond, but Father Antonio Moretti spoke first, his voice gentle yet clear.

"Transparency is unquestionably essential, Professor Conti. However, consider that ethical transparency also requires wisdom and responsibility. Knowledge revealed without adequate preparation or understanding can harm more than it heals. Is it not ethically imperative that we also guard against reckless revelation?"

Conti shifted slightly, her eyes narrowing with intensity. "Father Moretti, I respect your perspective, but history repeatedly shows how institutions justify secrecy as 'prudence.' How do you ensure that your humility isn't simply a cloak for institutional control?"

Father Moretti inclined his head, his demeanor patient and thoughtful. "I understand your concern clearly, Professor. True humility isn't about controlling information —it is about recognizing humanity's vulnerability, our tendency toward misinterpretation or misuse of knowledge. Humility calls us not to suppress truths, but to present them responsibly and factually, guiding people toward genuine understanding. Let me remind you that only in our modern times have we had the ability to carbon date artifacts, to decipher ancient scripts, and to observe the stars in finite ways. Until these functions could come together in our world, how could the events witnessed by those over the centuries and recorded as mysteries be adequately even speculated on, let alone explained?"

Michael interjected calmly, recognizing the tension clearly but constructively. "Both of your points are valid. Professor Conti, absolute transparency is ethically vital. Father Moretti, humility and cautious responsibility are equally necessary. Our goal here, unmistakably, is to balance these truths: to reveal responsibly, honestly, and transparently, but always mindful of potential consequences. Which is exactly what we are doing now."

Professor Conti didn't back down easily. "Transparency must be fully accountable, Father Dominic. Without absolute clarity and open oversight, the risk of misuse grows. Institutions must face scrutiny openly, not defensively."

Father Moretti nodded patiently. "Exactly. Transparency, combined with accountability and self-effacement, creates ethical stewardship, rather than secrecy or reckless disclosure. Let us commit here to transparency that is accountable, careful, and fully open to challenge."

Michael offered a thoughtful nod, genuinely appreciative of their passionate clarity. "Your perspectives enrich the ethical conversation we must sustain. Transparency and humility are not opponents, but partners—together ensuring responsible revelation of unfathomable truths. And may I add that it was only recently, with the ability to index digitized archives and perform computerized searches, that these consistencies of observations are able to be recognized as fitting a pattern. In centuries past, each observation was independent. Some coordination and communication did take place, as witnessed by Juana de la Cruz's attempts to compile such findings, but it is only in the light of today's technology that the full pattern can be recognized."

The symposium hall murmured with agreement, the scholarly audience recognizing clearly the depth and importance of the explicit positions presented and how the use of today's technology had brought these facts into focus. Professor Conti and Father Moretti, now distinctly established, provided clear, memorable perspectives, grounding the ethical discussion in intellectual rigor, transparent accountability, and thoughtful reverence.

Several more religious leaders voiced similar concerns, each questioning how the faithful might respond, the theological implications, and whether public fascination could spiral into dangerous fanaticism.

Throughout, Michael carefully navigated each question, emphasizing caution and responsibility. "Knowledge itself is neutral," he reminded the audience. "Our ethical responsibility lies in how we receive, interpret, and share it. If these findings indeed connect humanity to something greater, our duty is to engage thoughtfully, not recklessly."

Despite his composure, Michael was acutely aware of the moment. The questions he answered publicly mirrored private reflections he grappled with intensely. Hana's gentle presence in his peripheral vision was a steady anchor, steadfastly affirming his path.

As Michael concluded his remarks, the hall erupted in a cascade of questions, camera shutters clicking furiously, reporters clamoring for clarity. The intensity underscored the fierce global interest surrounding the manuscript's celestial connections.

Later that afternoon, as the press conference's ripples spread rapidly through global media channels, Michael,

Hana, and Simon retreated to the quiet sanctuary of the Archives' private study.

Simon's expression was pensive, and he adjusted his glasses nervously. "Public reaction has been intense. It feels as though we've stirred an unprecedented storm."

Hana placed a comforting hand briefly on Simon's arm. "Change always brings turbulence. What matters is our steadfastness in facing these truths responsibly."

Michael responded with a solemn nod. "Exactly. Our challenge remains helping people navigate these revelations with serenity, not hysteria."

In a corner, Ian monitored rapidly evolving online discourse. "Public opinion splits considerably," he reported. "Many embrace these findings enthusiastically, while others denounce them vehemently. Debates are becoming emotionally charged, even volatile."

Nightfall found Vatican City cloaked in tense stillness, streets tranquil beneath heightened security patrols.

Privately, the team gathered again, reflecting soberly on the day's intense global scrutiny. Michael and Hana stepped briefly onto the terrace, overlooking the illuminated Vatican rooftops, the vast sky above glittering with stars. In a private moment, Michael took Hana's hand.

"You were remarkable today," she whispered. "Your calm helped many remain grounded. You fulfilled your purpose—to bring the scientific and religious communities together; not fighting, but discussing the situation."

Michael smiled, his voice steady yet tinged with reflective melancholy. "I pray it's enough, Hana. These truths we approach—are we truly ready?"

She squeezed his hand reassuringly. "Readiness is a

journey, Michael. Our role is simply to guide the first steps with honesty."

Together, they stood beneath the vastness of the night sky, mindful of the thought-provoking mysteries that were both unveiled and yet still veiled, truths tantalizingly close yet still distant.

In the shadows beyond Vatican walls, however, figures moved restlessly, their intentions uncertain, their beliefs inflamed by unprecedented revelations.

CHAPTER

THIRTY-FIVE

VATICAN CITY

E vening shadows had begun to lengthen, draping Vatican City in hues of muted amber and indigo as Sister Teri sat alone in her compact office adjacent to the Vatican's central communications hub. Screens flickered, casting faint illumination across the well-ordered workspace. The soft hum of computers filled the silence, underscoring the gravity of her task.

Teri had spent hours meticulously analyzing internal Vatican communication logs, alert for any irregularities that might indicate leaks or espionage. With growing unease, she finally isolated a series of suspicious encrypted messages originating from within Vatican City, clearly linked to the username "Archive_LVL3," previously identified as a security breach communicating directly with addresses known to be associated with Christophe Vaux's network.

She leaned back slowly, taking a deep, steadying breath

as she realized the implications. There was a traitor—a mole within their very midst—and she had finally pinpointed their identity.

Quickly contacting Karl, she succinctly explained her discovery, her voice steady yet edged with urgency. "We must move swiftly," she emphasized.

Karl assured immediate action. Within minutes, he and Lukas had assembled a discreet team of trusted Swiss Guards. Quickly yet unobtrusively, they moved through shadowed Vatican corridors toward the living quarters identified by Sister Teri as the message's origin point.

Karl motioned silently, signaling his team to hold position. He exchanged a brief, tense glance with Lukas, conveying both confidence and shared resolve. Lukas nodded in return, prepared and focused.

Karl knocked firmly on the traitor's door. After a hesitant pause, footsteps approached cautiously from inside. The door opened slightly, revealing a familiar face —Father Antonio Ricci, a young cleric well-known and respected within the Curia.

"Father Ricci," Karl stated coldly, his eyes flinty and uncompromising. "You're under arrest for espionage against the Vatican."

Ricci's expression flickered briefly with shock, then resignation. He nodded slowly, stepping back from the doorway. Lukas and Karl secured him nimbly, their movements professional and scrupulous, ensuring no opportunity for escape or resistance.

Once safely confined in a secure interrogation room, Michael joined Karl, Lukas, and Teri. Ricci sat silently, hands trembling slightly but eyes defiant.

Michael spoke patiently, his voice heavy with disappointment and sadness. "Antonio, I recall your

GARY MCAVOY

frustration vividly—your passionate insistence that people deserved transparency. But was betrayal truly your only option?"

Ricci lifted his chin defiantly, eyes blazing despite remorse. "You left me no choice, Michael. My warnings fell on deaf ears. The Church refuses to embrace truths openly. Blackthorn understood what you refused to acknowledge: humanity needs transparency, not secrecy."

"And what truth is that?" Michael asked gently yet firmly, sensing the priest's internal turmoil.

Ricci's eyes burned passionately. "That we are not alone. That celestial beings have visited us before, leaving clear evidence. Alton Blackthorn believes seriously in alien visitation; he understands what humans could achieve by embracing this knowledge. He is a visionary, a man with ideals for humanity's future, not a deadwood faith that suppresses its own adherents, keeping them in the past of the dark ages."

Michael frowned, troubled by Ricci's conviction. "Blackthorn seeks personal gain, Antonio. He exploits belief for power, not enlightenment."

Ricci shook his head stubbornly. "No, he sees clearly. He knows humanity stands on the edge of transformation. The Church has concealed truths that belong to all people, truths that could unite the world in purpose and understanding."

Michael felt a soulful sadness, wrestling internally with the unsettling theological implications Ricci's words stirred within him. "The truth has always guided us, Antonio. But the Church's responsibility is safeguarding humanity from truths it might not yet be ready to face fully. Reckless exposure risks chaos, misunderstanding— perhaps even destruction."

266

Karl stepped forward, voice sharp. "You betrayed trust, compromised our security. Innocent lives were endangered by your actions. You claim noble motivations, yet your deeds reflect selfish ambition, nothing more."

Ricci's defiance faltered slightly, eyes wavering. "I... I believed it necessary."

Teri spoke wisely, compassionately, yet unyieldingly. "Belief without interpretation is dangerous, Antonio. True courage means seeking understanding responsibly, not rashly."

Michael stood slowly, feeling the weight of sorrow pressing heavily upon him. "Reflect carefully on your choices, Antonio. The pursuit of truth demands wisdom and integrity—not deception."

Leaving Ricci secured and guarded, Michael and the others reconvened privately, their mood somber.

"It is no wonder that Blackthorn, and therefore Vaux, knew nearly every step in our progress. Ricci had been one of the few confidants within the Vatican aware of most of our movements. Clearly, he believed deeply," Michael murmured sadly, "so deeply he lost sight of the cost of reckless revelation, risking our very lives in the process."

Karl's expression hardened. "Blackthorn exploited that belief, manipulating it for personal gain. And clearly, he gave Father Ricci only what he wished him to believe, that Blackthorn wants transparency of knowledge. Did you notice that Ricci mentioned nothing of the botanicals that we know Blackthorn is replicating for his personal gain?"

Michael nodded and released a tight breath, troubled by the broader implications. "Ricci's betrayal illustrates precisely the danger Juana foresaw. Passion without wisdom risks catastrophe. Our role now is more crucial than ever."

Late that night, Michael sat alone within the quiet solitude of his quarters, cogitating. Theological implications weighed heavily upon him. Ricci's fervent belief—twisted chillingly to suit Blackthorn's motivations —was forcing Michael to confront uncomfortable truths about humanity's spiritual readiness.

Michael prayed quietly for guidance, strength, and authenticity, intensely troubled yet resolutely committed.

THIRTY-SIX

VATICAN CITY

K arl and Lukas maintained heightened vigilance, acutely aware that Ricci's betrayal signaled deeper, persistent threats. Their shared resolve remained unshaken, determined fiercely to protect those truths—and the lives—entrusted to their guardianship.

To that end, Karl and Lukas had coordinated closely with Vatican authorities to strengthen security further, deploying advanced surveillance and increasing discreet guard rotations. The Vatican's visible preparedness reassured yet reminded all within its walls of the seriousness of the circumstances.

Later, in the secure Vatican control room, Karl monitored surveillance monitors closely, occasionally glancing sideways at Lukas. Lukas's complexion remained stoic and determined, but his eyes appeared slightly shadowed.

"Take a break," Karl urged, noting his partner's visible fatigue.

The sound of Lukas's audible sigh betrayed a fleeting moment of frustration. "Karl, I'm fine."

Karl's eyes narrowed with quiet concern. "Lukas, you need rest. Let me handle the heavy lifting today. Trust me —I have this covered."

Lukas hesitated briefly, then finally conceded, sitting heavily in a nearby chair, his good hand absently rubbing the sore muscles around his injured shoulder. "I hate feeling incapacitated," he admitted, his voice tinged with quiet embarrassment.

Karl approached him, then placed a reassuring hand on Lukas's uninjured shoulder. "You are far from incapacitated. You saved Hana's life in Granada. You've backed me up ever since. You've earned the right to recover properly. Don't undermine yourself by pushing too hard."

Lukas offered a faint, grateful smile. "Fine. But I'm still here if you need me."

Karl's voice softened further, eyes filled with quiet affection. "I always need you. But I also need you safe and healthy."

A BIT LATER, Karl stood silently in the darkened control room, the pale glow of multiple surveillance monitors casting eerie shadows across his determined face. Beside him, Lukas studied the screens intently, his eyes narrowed, alert for even the slightest indication of movement. It was late, and Vatican City was cloaked in a tense quietness, as though holding its breath.

For some time now, they had monitored Christophe

Vaux's operatives, mapping every clandestine movement, each covert communication carefully cataloged by Sister Teri's tireless digital investigations. Now the culmination of their efforts approached—tonight, they would decisively dismantle Vaux's dangerous network operating within Rome.

A sudden beep startled them from their vigil. A coded message flashed across a nearby screen.

Lukas decoded it promptly, whispering, "They're moving."

Karl straightened immediately, adjusting his earpiece and addressing the small team of hand-selected Swiss Guards awaiting orders. "Team Alpha, position yourselves at Porta Angelica. Team Bravo, move toward Via della Conciliazione. Hold steady until my command."

Outside, the streets lay quiet beneath lamplit shadows. Moments later, subtle movements emerged, figures slipping discreetly through darkness, unaware their every step was being closely observed. Vaux's men were attempting a final, desperate infiltration into the Vatican Archives, presumably seeking to retrieve or destroy documentation linking their organization to sensitive historical findings.

"Now," Karl commanded. Instantly, both Swiss Guard teams converged with coordinated, silent efficiency, blocking all escape routes. Karl and Lukas moved rapidly from the control room to join the operation directly.

They arrived just as Vaux's team realized their compromised position. A short, fierce confrontation erupted. Karl engaged abruptly, his disciplined training evident in every decisive motion. Lukas moved with equal precision, effectively subduing another intruder who attempted a reckless charge.

Within minutes, the operatives were securely restrained, their mission thwarted before it began. Karl approached the captured leader, his gaze steady and uncompromising. "Your operation here is finished. Tell Christophe Vaux the Vatican's patience has run out. And prepare yourself for a long stint of confinement for your efforts on his behalf."

THIRTY-SEVEN

VATICAN CITY

Across Vatican City, Father Michael, Hana, Ian, and Sister Teri gathered anxiously in the Archives, waiting for confirmation of the operation's success. When Karl's calm voice broke through on the communications device—"All targets secured. Situation contained."—a palpable wave of relief swept over the group.

Michael blew out a quick breath, sharing a look of quiet gratitude with Hana. "We owe them more than we can express," he said firmly, admiration clear in his voice.

Ian stepped forward, placing an ancient, faithfully preserved manuscript on the table before them. "This arrived today from a hidden collection uncovered in Madrid," he explained. "I've been studying it thoroughly, and the documentation is remarkably explicit. It ties directly into Juana de la Cruz's botanical compound and the *Voynich* symbolism."

Michael closely examined the manuscript, his heart quickening as he recognized specific botanical illustrations —exotic plants unmistakably matching those described by Juana and depicted in the *Voynich Manuscript*. More startling, though, were detailed annotations definitely linking these plants' emergence and potency to unusual celestial phenomena.

Ian nodded gravely. "These records go further than anything we've previously encountered. They don't merely suggest an extraterrestrial origin—they explicitly claim the plants appeared following 'visitations from the heavens.'"

Hana leaned closer, her eyes widening as she read passages describing methodical medieval attempts to cultivate these plants under precise astronomical alignments. The section ended with a listing of several monasteries, each of which was safeguarded with one or more of those specific plants within the walls of their private gardens. "This isn't speculation," she whispered in awe. "This is methodical observation and experimentation, centuries before our modern era."

Sister Teri stepped forward obligingly, adding, "The Vatican knew, or at least some within its ranks understood the implications. This explains their anxiety and the aggressive suppression Ian and I uncovered earlier."

Michael turned to face his colleagues, his voice steady yet infused with quiet wonder. "These documents confirm what we've feared—and perhaps secretly hoped. The *Voynich Manuscript* and Juana's own writings aren't merely historical curiosities. They indicate the church has safeguarded and secreted the very plants that represent this influence. Plants that could, in themselves, revolutionize our world in ways we have yet to understand."

Karl and Lukas soon joined them, still alert from the earlier confrontation. Michael greeted them warmly, grateful relief evident. He filled them in on the fact that they now had definitive proof that the Church had both been aware of these plants, and that likely they still existed within the safe confines of gardens. "We owe you both an immense debt. Your courage and vigilance safeguarded truths humanity must now handle judiciously."

Karl inclined his head respectfully. "We're prepared for whatever comes next. The truth, managed wisely, can only strengthen humankind."

Michael looked at those gathered—Hana, whose insight always balanced caution with courage; Ian, whose dedication unearthed forgotten truths; Sister Teri, unwavering in integrity; Karl and Lukas, steadfast guardians. Each had played crucial roles in reaching this pivotal moment.

Late that night, Michael stood serenely outside, gazing upward at the vast expanse of stars above Vatican City. Hana joined him silently, slipping her hand into his.

Beneath the calm, star-studded skies, Vatican City lay peaceful once more, secured by those sworn to protect its secrets. The long-hidden truths now uncovered promised to guide humanity toward greater wisdom, provided those entrusted with this knowledge continued to approach it with the same courage and care demonstrated this decisive night.

THIRTY-EIGHT

VATICAN CITY

Morning sunlight filtered through the ornate stained-glass windows of a discreet meeting chamber deep within the Vatican. Around a long wooden table, a carefully selected committee sat, expressions ranging from curiosity and caution to open apprehension. Father Michael was seated at the head of the table, his demeanor calm yet resolute, reflecting the weight of the decision now before them.

Michael cleared his throat abruptly, gaining the attention of the assembled theologians, medical experts, ethicists, and Vatican authorities, along with his own team seated to his left. "As we all now understand, Juana de la Cruz's botanical compound is far more than a historical curiosity. It represents an extraordinary opportunity—and responsibility. Our research conclusively links these botanicals to celestial events and, possibly, extraterrestrial influences. The question before us today is whether we move forward with controlled trials."

Cardinal Giovanni Severino, sitting to Michael's right, nodded agreeably, though his face betrayed deep contemplation. "The potential benefits are undeniable. Yet we must weigh them against considerable risks."

Sister Teri spoke up with measured assurance. "Exactly why controlled, transparent trials are essential. Managed responsibly, these trials could offer unprecedented healing capabilities, while closely monitoring their broader effects."

Dr. Simon Ginzberg leaned forward, his fingers clasped earnestly. "Historical records describe remarkable spiritual experiences linked to these plants as well. If we proceed, it must be with the understanding that we're venturing into spiritually transformative territory beyond just physical healing."

Michael listened closely, appreciating each perspective. "Agreed. Transparency isn't merely desirable; it's ethically indispensable. We've seen repeatedly that secrecy invites misunderstanding and exploitation. If we pursue these trials, we must commit openly to sharing what we learn with clarity and yielding to greater truths."

Cardinal Severino exhaled slowly, finally voicing cautious agreement. "Controlled trials under stringent oversight, then. Yet I urge absolute caution—our responsibility here extends far beyond Vatican walls."

"And I must warn," Michael stated clearly, "that this needs to be done in secret for the time being. As you are all aware, Genetica Laboratories is racing to produce a synthetic version based on stolen manuscripts and plant species from our own Church libraries and gardens. We know they had no ethics or caution in experimentation in the past, and I doubt that has changed. Plus, their motives are mercenary only, without regard to any sacrifices involved. We must stay ahead of them, and the only way to do that is to do our own formulation and experimentation, so that we can be the first to reveal the formula that our predecessors had safeguarded for the world's beneficial use."

The committee deliberated further, eventually arriving at a firm consensus. Michael's proposal for cautious, monitored trials of Juana's botanical compounds was approved, albeit under strict ethical oversight and continuous monitoring and the utmost secrecy.

In the weeks that followed, meticulous preparations took place.

The plants so well described and illustrated in the various documents were gathered with an orchestrated precision. Careful communiques went to each of the particular monasteries, and teams of botanical experts were dispatched to carefully gather specimens of each of the extraterrestrial-influenced plants. Some could be transplanted near the Vatican, but others were kept intact at each previous location to safeguard their survival.

Michael visited the facility frequently, closely involved at every step. His commitment to transparency was unwavering, and he insisted on periodic public updates, providing expressly worded yet forthright reports on trial progress.

Plants were carefully cultivated, some dissected, with bits of matter from roots or stems or leaves, as noted through Juana's diligent notes or through documentation evident in the *Hesperides Codex*, all gathered appropriately with consideration of the season and lunar phases. Nothing was left to chance. Every step was carefully planned and executed by historical researchers in conjunction with the botanical experts. The *Lumen Viride* formula slowly came to life.

Every form of chemical and spectrographic examination was done to ensure the result was neither toxic nor in any way dangerous. Chemical analysis failed to provide any further useful insight, however. Was it possible that whatever influence this formula had, because of its extraterrestrial origin, failed to be recognized on a terrestrial chemical spectrograph or be beyond our technological review of active compounds?

Laboratory animals showed no response whatsoever to the formula. This brought both relief and questions to the minds of the researchers and team alike. Did this formula have any effect at all? Had this been a lost cause and wild speculation from the beginning? The results of experiments, as documented in centuries past when monks had been researching, were from human trials. The results, though mixed, had all indicated a distinct effect on humans. If that were the case, only human experiments could prove the effectiveness—and safety—of the *Lumen Viride* formula.

A secluded, specially equipped laboratory within the Vatican's medical facilities was designated for the trials. Participation was strictly voluntary, each candidate thoroughly briefed on potential risks and benefits. Comprehensive ethical guidelines were drafted, emphasizing transparency, safety, and spiritual integrity.

Karl and Lukas oversaw security measures, mindful that the trials would inevitably attract external interest. Security checkpoints were tightened, surveillance discreet yet rigorous, ensuring both participants' safety and the integrity of the process.

Finally, the day of the first human trial arrived. Michael and Hana observed quietly from behind a reinforced observation window, watching as Dr. Ginzberg carefully administered a measured dose of the botanical compound to the first volunteer, a middle-aged woman suffering from chronic, debilitating pain unresponsive to conventional treatments. Her despair had been so acute that she had turned to her priest for absolution for her thoughts of suicide. Her dire situation had been brought to the medical team, and she had welcomed the potential of healing, with no fear whatsoever of the serum being potentially fatal.

Minutes passed slowly. The volunteer's initial nervousness visibly eased, replaced gradually by a calm serenity that seemed to radiate through the sterile laboratory setting. Monitors tracking her physiological responses recorded significant changes—lowered stress indicators, reduced pain response, and measurable increases in neurological activity associated with spiritual tranquility. Unlike hallucinogenics, which resulted in marked physical changes with stress on blood pressure, nervous system, and other bodily functions, if anything, the woman's body normalized from its chronic earlier issues even as she experienced something remarkable on another level.

As hours passed, the participant described deep spiritual reflections, speaking softly of visions—comforting experiences filled with imagery of light and an overwhelming sense of connection and peace. And maybe, equally important, her joy at living. Observers documented everything thoroughly, ensuring nothing was overlooked.

Michael watched in awe and modesty, moved by the transformative potential clearly manifesting before them. Yet his excitement was tempered by responsibility, aware of the high-stakes ethical questions inevitably raised.

That evening, gathered again in quiet reflection, Michael addressed the committee earnestly. "Today showed us incredible possibilities—healing not merely of bodies, but perhaps souls. Yet we must not rush forward blindly. These compounds offer spiritual insight, yes, but we are also custodians of a historic mystery."

Hana nodded. "And mystery demands caution. Today's results confirm what Juana hinted at—that these plants might indeed open spiritual doorways humanity must approach with caution."

Cardinal Severino concurred soberly. "Transparency must remain our guiding principle. The Pope has made it clear that the people deserve honesty about what these compounds can do—and what questions they inevitably raise. Yet, at what point do we reveal this to the public?"

Michael looked at his team; it had been a question they had debated for some time. He explained to the Cardinal and committee, "It is too early to document the formula in a way that we can claim any exclusive rights to it, so to speak. Yet, at the same time, we need to put Blackthorne on alert and make the public aware of what we are doing to fulfill our promise of transparency. Plus, this will give us a jump on anything Blackthorn might come up with until the scientific community can properly accept our formula."

He ended with, "I recommend we provide a preliminary announcement, even as we continue our experiments."

Much discussion later, the consensus was that an announcement needed to go out, carefully crafted and artfully delivered. Michael accepted the challenge, aware of the weight of the responsibility given to him.

That evening, Michael stood alone outside the Vatican facility, gazing thoughtfully skyward, the vast expanse of stars sparkling silently above. Hana approached silently, standing beside him in quiet contemplation.

"We've taken an immense step," Michael said, his voice heavy yet undaunted. "But our responsibility now grows even deeper. Transparency requires courage—courage to share truths difficult to comprehend fully."

Hana squeezed his hand, her voice calm yet firm. "And humility. We guide gently, Michael, never forgetting that ultimate wisdom lies not in knowing all answers, but in responsibly pursuing the questions."

Together, they stood beneath the immense mystery of the night sky, united in commitment, knowing their journey was only beginning.

CHAPTER

THIRTY-NINE

VATICAN CITY

T he day of the Vatican's anticipated public
announcement dawned bright and clear over
Rome, the sky an unblemished expanse of deep,
radiant blue. From early morning, an exceptional sense of
expectation permeated the city. Thousands had gathered in
St. Peter's Square, a vast, restless congregation of faithful
pilgrims, curious scholars, international journalists, and
ordinary citizens drawn by the unprecedented event.

Inside his Vatican office, Michael Dominic stood at his
desk reviewing the prepared statement. Hana observed
him from across the room, sensing the weight of
responsibility pressing upon him.

"It's time," she said, stepping closer and placing a
reassuring hand on his shoulder. "You've guided this with
integrity from the start. Trust yourself now."

Michael tilted his head in agreement, his expression
sobered by a quiet resolve firming within him. "I'm

mindful that today's words will ripple far beyond Vatican City. We owe it to humanity to speak honestly, yet with conviction."

They shared a final quiet moment, then stepped into the hallway, joining Cardinal Giovanni Severino and a select group of senior theologians, scientists, and Vatican advisors. Together, they moved toward the vast Pope Paul VI Hall of Pontifical Audiences, which had been prepared for the global audience awaiting them.

Karl and Lukas maintained a discreet yet intense vigilance along the procession, their eyes alert for any sign of unrest or threat. Security throughout Vatican City had never been tighter, with Swiss Guards positioned inconspicuously yet assertively around the gathering crowd.

The hall was packed, its vast space humming with anticipation. Journalists from around the world whispered rapidly into microphones, camera operators adjusted lenses and angles, each striving to capture the perfect image of the historic event unfolding.

Michael took his place at the white podium, a pair of oval stained-glass windows on the wall behind him. A hush fell over the hall as all attention turned toward him. He paused briefly, eyes calmly scanning the expectant faces before him, then spoke clearly, his voice steady yet imbued with great respect.

"Ladies and gentlemen, esteemed colleagues, and guests watching from around the globe," he began, the words deliberate and precise, "the Vatican wishes today to address recent developments and discoveries linked to the historical manuscripts known commonly as the *Voynich Manuscript* and the *Hesperides Codex*, the latter authored by Sister Juana de la Cruz."

He paused again, aware of the expectant silence filling the room.

"These manuscripts contain symbolism, descriptions, and botanical references closely aligned with historically documented celestial phenomena. Extensive Vatican research and thorough historical analysis have conclusively demonstrated that certain plants, described in these ancient texts, appear linked to strange astronomical events."

The room remained intensely silent, with each listener completely absorbed.

"After careful consideration and responsible trials overseen by medical and theological experts," Michael continued, "we can confirm significant therapeutic and spiritual potential within these botanicals. Their appearance and efficacy, historically recorded by observers across centuries, remain undeniably linked to documented, yet unexplained, celestial phenomena."

The hall filled immediately with whispered reactions, reporters hastily scribbling notes, journalists murmuring into microphones.

Michael raised a calming hand, continuing firmly, "Yet we urge caution regarding the interpretation of these findings. While the symbolism within these manuscripts undeniably references celestial events, and while historical accounts clearly describe phenomena beyond our current scientific understanding, the Vatican makes no explicit confirmation regarding their extraterrestrial origin."

A wave of cautious disappointment and increased curiosity rippled visibly through the audience, yet Michael continued, voice measured and deliberate.

"Our responsibility as stewards of faith and truth is to present facts transparently yet responsibly. The Vatican neither confirms nor denies specific theories regarding extraterrestrial intervention. Instead, we openly acknowledge that the world's historical records include encounters with phenomena yet beyond our full understanding. This acknowledgment is neither a challenge to faith nor an invitation to sensationalism, but a humble recognition of humanity's limited understanding within the vast scope of Creation."

Michael glanced briefly toward Cardinal Severino, who nodded slightly, approvingly.

"Our ongoing exploration of these findings," Michael continued firmly, "will remain transparent and responsibly managed. We intend to continue cautious, controlled trials and thorough investigations, sharing openly what we learn. Significant relief of physical maladies accompanied by positive mental and emotional responses has been noted even in the earliest trials. Once the formula is firmly established and replicable, these trial results will be patented by the Vatican."

Anxious hands rose, fearing a Church-held exclusivity of this miraculous formula.

Michael quickly held up his palms to the would-be questioners. "Once properly documented, that same formula will be provided to a worldwide contingent of researchers. The point is to be transparent while remaining cautious as we move forward. As with all clinical trials or significant potential remedies for any situation, all ethical and medical protocols will be handled with extreme care. Humanity deserves truth responsibly delivered—truth that encourages curiosity and unity rather than fear or division."

He stepped back slightly from the podium, voice softening respectfully. "In closing, we urge patience, responsibility, and thoughtful reflection from all those encountering this information today. Our hope is that this acknowledgment fosters respectful, honest dialogue about the vastness of our universe and humanity's humble yet extraordinary place within it."

Michael stepped away from the podium, signaling the formal conclusion of his remarks. The press hall erupted instantly, a torrent of shouted questions rising loudly above the clamor. Michael, Hana, and Cardinal Severino calmly answered select questions, always reiterating their core message—acknowledgment tempered with caution.

Outside in St. Peter's Square, the reaction was mixed yet intense. Some embraced the acknowledgment eagerly, hopeful of new remedies to come from further experiments. Others expressed uncertainty or concern, grappling with the spiritual implications. Yet the dominant mood remained one of respectful curiosity and careful contemplation, just as Michael had intended.

Afterward, gathered privately in a quiet Vatican chamber, Michael, Hana, Cardinal Severino, and their closest advisors reflected soberly upon the day's immense significance.

"You spoke exactly as we agreed," Cardinal Severino assured Michael warmly. "Transparent yet cautious, humble yet firm. Today marked a significant turning point —not merely in Vatican history, but perhaps in humankind's own spiritual journey."

Michael exhaled slowly, visibly relieved yet mindful of ongoing responsibility. "This acknowledgment is a beginning, not an end. Our transparency today was essential—but now the greater challenge lies ahead, guiding people toward responsible exploration and understanding. And, in the process, thwarting any attempts by Blackthorn to monopolize something so precious to the world."

Late that night, beneath a vast, silent sky shimmering brilliantly with stars, Michael and Hana stood together upon a secluded terrace overlooking Rome. The city stretched peacefully below, its lights glittering brightly, as the world's countless lives continued uninterrupted despite the awe-inspiring revelations of the day.

Michael looked upward, voice reflective. "We've taken a significant step. Yet how ready are we as a people to truly embrace such mind-altering truths?"

Hana took his hand, her voice calm and reassuring. "Readiness comes slowly, Michael, built steadily from courage and patient guidance. Our role remains exactly that—guiding humanity thoughtfully, step by careful step."

He turned to her, smiling tenderly, passionately grateful for her steadfast presence. Together, in silent contemplation beneath the boundless mystery of the heavens, they accepted the immense responsibility entrusted to them.

Across Vatican City, beneath the quiet vigilance of Karl, Lukas, and the Swiss Guards, peace prevailed, despite lingering questions and ongoing curiosity stirred by the day's revelations. Humanity stood now at a significant threshold—invited openly yet cautiously to consider truths long hidden, unveiled by responsible stewards committed thoroughly to integrity and compassion.

And as dawn approached once more, the world remained uncertain yet hopeful, united briefly in shared wonder, cautiously stepping together into mysteries vast, beautiful, and profoundly humbling.

After a sleepless night, in the inner office of Genetica

Laboratories, Blackthorn faced a pile of papers, reports, formulas, tests, and contracts that could ultimately prove worthless for his coffers in the future. With the results of the Vatican's initial experiments now public, his millions spent on research and experiments, his intention to make a formula that was proprietary to him alone and reap the benefits of whatever miracles it could achieve, could end up for naught. He still faced numerous lawsuits for experiments conducted beyond all ethical guidelines and had spent millions in attorneys' fees and bribes to stay out of various countries' prisons on those charges alone.

Never again, he had told himself when he headed Zentara, would he suffer at the hands of Hana Sinclair's journalistic tenacity. And yet here he was, with only one last hope to regain the life he deserved for all his foresight and unending efforts. If he could create a replicable formula that could be validated before the Vatican's... all he needed was...

He picked up the phone, and when he heard the voice come online, simply stated, "Get her. Now."

CHAPTER

FORTY

VATICAN CITY

I n the serene tranquility of a bright Roman morning,
Michael Dominic stood at the entrance of a newly
renovated wing deep within the Vatican's Apostolic
Palace. Even as experimentation continued in the Vatican's
medical and laboratory facilities, it was incumbent on
them to document that every source of their resulting
formula had come from direct resources within the Church
itself. This, coupled with a final formula, would safeguard
any commercial interest, like Genetica Therapeutics, from
claiming any proprietary use of the resulting drugs. With
that in mind, a huge undertaking had just been completed.

The subtle fragrance of fresh varnish lingered in the air,
a tangible sign of renewal and purpose. Beside him, Hana
Sinclair gazed thoughtfully at the freshly engraved brass
plaque affixed beside the ancient oak door:

**"Scriptorium Hesperidis: Dedicated to the Cautious
and Responsible Exploration of Celestial Connections."**

The establishment of the Scriptorium Hesperidis was the Vatican's measured response to the global intrigue stirred by fresh revelations surrounding Juana de la Cruz's botanical manuscripts and the celestial phenomena linked to their remarkable healing properties. Michael had spent time in exacting preparation, engaging tirelessly with theologians, historians, scientists, and ethicists to forge the delicate foundations of this singular scholarly institution. In the meantime, the Vatican, unlike its usual functioning under ponderously long timelines, had quickly engaged architects and artisans to create a new space dedicated to this novel endeavor.

As the ornate doors opened for the first time, Michael and Hana entered, gazing up at the vaulted ceiling that rose gracefully above them, supported by sturdy marble columns that echoed centuries of Vatican tradition. Rows of desks equipped with advanced research technology stood respectfully alongside shelves housing ancient texts and fragile manuscripts, their preservation an act of reverent dedication.

"This place embodies our stewardship," Michael said, his voice echoing in the vaulted space. "Here, truth will be pursued with devotion and respect, guided always by the Vatican's commitment to ethical responsibility."

Hana nodded solemnly, her eyes reflecting deep admiration. "It's a delicate balance, Michael. Balancing humanity's thirst for understanding against the weight of spiritual responsibility. But if anyone can guide this venture, it's you."

Already, Michael had assembled a hand-selected team of international scholars, each renowned in their fields of theology, history, astronomy, medicine, and ethics. Their collective expertise represented a careful balance between rigorous scientific exploration and sensitive spiritual inquiry.

The inaugural meeting of the Scriptorium Hesperidis scholars was conducted with quiet dignity. Michael stood before the assembled team, addressing them calmly and clearly. "Our mission here transcends mere academic curiosity," he began firmly. "We are custodians of mysteries, wise and ancient, entrusted with revelations capable of reshaping humankind's understanding of itself and its place in the cosmos."

A respectful silence followed his words, each scholar understanding the depth of their collective responsibility.

Cardinal Severino, seated nearby, nodded approvingly, his voice gentle yet authoritative. "Remember, our work here is not merely scientific or theological—it is fundamentally human. The world watches, hopeful yet apprehensive. Our responsibility is far-reaching."

Work commenced swiftly, the intellectual community within the Scriptorium quickly forming a harmonious balance of intense inquiry and respectful caution. Each manuscript underwent meticulous analysis, with texts cross-referenced diligently against historical astronomical records, and botanical samples studied intimately in state-of-the-art laboratories.

Michael oversaw each phase of exploration, guiding academic efforts and moderating spirited debates, always mindful of their ethical and spiritual implications. Sister Teri supervised digital cataloging and ensured ethical compliance, maintaining utmost transparency in documenting and sharing findings.

Notably, frequent gatherings occurred where scholars openly discussed their work, ethical dilemmas, and spiritual insights. These conversations often ventured into complex philosophical realms, grappling with humanity's readiness for truths implicit in their research.

During one such gathering, Simon Ginzberg spoke, articulating concerns shared by many present. "Our research clearly points to historical encounters with celestial phenomena affecting human health and spirituality. Yet our duty extends beyond simple documentation—we must help the world contextualize these revelations responsibly."

Michael responded agreeably. "Which is our purpose here. Contextualizing truth, acknowledging both its transformative potential and inherent complexities. We offer people insights, not absolutes, guiding them obligingly toward deeper understanding."

Outside the learned enclave, the Swiss Guard maintained vigilant security. International curiosity had escalated dramatically, drawing passionate pilgrims, researchers, and occasionally disruptive enthusiasts attempting unauthorized entry. Karl's disciplined team managed these incidents firmly yet respectfully, their guardianship extending beyond physical security to preserving the integrity of scholarly inquiry within.

As evening fell upon Vatican City, Michael stood quietly within the walls of the Scriptorium Hesperidis, reflecting upon the immense responsibility entrusted to him. Hana joined him, wrapping her arm around his waist, understanding instinctively his thoughtful mood.

Moments later, they strode together outside to the intimacy of the Vatican Gardens, tree-lined with starlight glistening on the damp grass, as they gazed at the cloudless sky. High above, stars glittered in the vast night sky, timeless witnesses to humanity's cautious, earnest exploration, patiently observing as truth unfolded, guided by thoughtful hands within the protective guardianship of those entrusted by history and faith alike.

In the shadows of an olive tree, hidden from the starlight, a man watched the two people walking hand-in-hand. Not tonight, he thought. And he stepped further into the shadows and into the determination that at another time he would make his move.

CHAPTER

FORTY-ONE

ROME, ITALY

ana's life as a journalist took on a new focus with the revelations from the documents she, Michael, and their team had secured. Combine that with the public announcement she made early on about these discoveries, plus the potential of some celestial influence that had brought about potentially miraculous cures, and her recent output of articles had been extensive. At times, she felt they were more promotional, trying to explain to the world things that only those deep in the Vatican would know or find important. Yet the public had responded strongly to everything she'd written, and she felt that the honesty she brought alongside the details of their experiences had given fresh energy to her words. She no longer worked only as an investigative reporter for *Le Monde* in Paris, but was now a writer-at-large for many specialty magazines focused on the scientific and botanical aspects of what she had helped uncover.

Today, she sat in her luxurious apartment, hunched over her computer. She had leased it early in her relationship with Michael, creating a private space for intimate moments as an engaged couple. Sadly, those moments were too few, but today, they provided the quiet she needed for yet another article. This one would capture the essence of her personal journey—witnessing the care and respect of monks in various monasteries, who had cared for the gardens for centuries. These gardens were now recognized as the source of ingredients for the Vatican formula. It was more of a background piece than about a specific plant, a write-up that the longstanding and prestigious *Curtis's Botanical Magazine* had requested.

After working diligently for a while, she leaned back, realizing she needed to stretch her legs. She had plans to meet Michael in another hour, but she really needed to move around. Karl had kept insisting on careful monitoring of their activities so they wouldn't have to worry about Blackthorn thugs or Vaux's operatives returning on the scene. There had been no attempts from them for quite some time, and Karl felt somewhat reassured that when they last imprisoned the entire group of Vaux's thugs, it sent a clear message: Vatican City and the surrounding Rome area would not tolerate more interference.

She sent a text to Karl, informing him that she was about to take a quick walk before meeting with Michael. In the late afternoon sun, she felt comfortable walking alone in this upscale neighborhood. With that in mind, she didn't wait for Karl's response before grabbing her now favorite sweater, slipping on her walking boots, and heading out the door.

Sitting at a barista table across the street from Hana's apartment, a man stubbed out his cigarette as he watched her leave the high-security apartment building.

Finally, he thought. After slipping a few euros under his coffee cup, he exited the coffee shop and surreptitiously began following Hana from across the street.

Hana strode quickly, occasionally glancing at the small neighborhood shops and convenience stores, feeling grateful for the fresh air. Her mind was focused on which monastery to highlight next in her article when suddenly a strange smell hit her nostrils and dizziness instantly overtook her. She reached out for support from a nearby wall, only to realize it was too far away, and she started to fall forward.

Suddenly, someone scooped an arm around her waist and said loudly. "It's okay, *tesoro*, I have you now. Let's take you someplace safe…"

She felt her legs keep moving, but her mind couldn't figure out who was holding her or why she was even moving. What was she doing on the street anyway? Nothing made sense as her thoughts drifted back to how to organize her monastery article, despite the fresh air and brisk walk failing to clear her head.

Sometime later, her mouth dry and her eyes blurring, Hana felt her consciousness and focus returning. She was now strapped into a chair in a dimly lit room, facing a closed door. The only other object in the room seemed to be a small table beside her, with a tray of vials and syringes resting on top. The odd shock of everything pulled her forward as if to stand from the chair, but her wrist straps held tight, and her ankles were taped to the legs of the chair, causing her to nearly topple over in her attempt to move. The clattering of the chair alerted someone outside as the door opened.

"Good," came the voice of one man she recognized: Christophe Vaux. "It's about time."

"What are you doing, Vaux?" Hana exclaimed. "You can't get away with this!" She had no idea what Vaux was about to do, but she feared the worst as she eyed the medical devices again. Whether it was revenge for her efforts against Blackthorn or something else was less important than trying to escape. Maybe if she kept him talking—

"*Shut up!*" he snapped. "I have no use for your warnings. As if you haven't destroyed enough in my life... but this will make up for all of it." He lifted one syringe, flicked the barrel with two quick taps, coaxing a bubble to the surface until a bead of clear liquid trembled at the needle's tip, then plunged the needle into her upper arm. Hana's attempts to move away from him were futile. Almost at once, she felt the heat course through her arm, then climb into her neck. Her mind registered the symptoms with stark precision—every past anxiety trivial compared to the cold, clinical certainty that her heart might stop in the next beat.

Vaux's smile lingered as he lifted the small timer from the table, twisting the dial with deliberate care until the pointer settled on ten minutes. He placed it down with a soft click, the silence that followed more menacing than any words he might have spoken. Then he turned and walked out, leaving her alone with the ticking void. The device gave no sound, yet every thud of her heart thundered like a countdown to her own execution.

"WHERE IS SHE?" Karl barked into the phone, his voice raw with frustration.

On the other end, Teri shook her head, eyes fixed on the glowing monitor. "She's there, Karl. I swear it. The signal is locked—you're right on top of her."

"That's impossible. This is a dead lot—nothing but rusted cars and weeds."

Michael loomed behind Teri, his gaze riveted on the relentless blink of the tracker on the screen. Each pulse was a dagger, mocking him with Hana's absence. He had rushed to Teri's workstation the moment Karl realized Hana's tracker had led him miles from the cheerful "quick walk" text she had sent. Michael's hand tightened on Teri's chair as he jabbed a finger at the map, as though sheer force could bend the machine to yield her location. "Run it again. Triangulate. Do something."

"I'm trying," Teri muttered, her fingers flying across the keys. But even as she worked, dread hollowed her chest— because she already knew the signal was leading them into a void.

HER HEARTBEAT SLOWED, and so did her anxiety. *How can I feel so relaxed in the face of death?* she wondered. Then, suddenly, she was in a completely different place—a realm of light and a shimmering sensation of floating, as if gently balancing on soft clouds. In front of her stood the same luminous being she had seen before. This time, however, the being said nothing and merely pointed upward. Hana's gaze lifted, revealing the constellations she had seen earlier, moving slowly. Superimposed on them this time, she could see the earth's own constellations, layered as if one on top of another, moving in different directions.

Then something changed. She realized the movements had stopped. She heard the being of light call to her, saying, "The window is open."

"Open the window!" she heard a man's anxious voice.

Everything swirled for a moment until she heard again, "Open the window!"

Stars no longer filled her vision; instead, she saw her cousin Karl's worried face peering down at her as he and Lukas untied her. Fresh air suddenly flooded in through a window that had been behind her all along. Several Swiss Guards moved in and out of the room, taking orders from Karl as they made space for a medic. They placed her on a stretcher, and her eyes shut once more. A warm wave of gratitude washed over her for her apparent rescue, even as her mind clung to the memory of the layered constellations.

"Got her," Karl spoke into the phone, and he could hear Terrye's sigh of relief. "In an abandoned building to the side of the lot. We found Hana's sweater snagged on the open door of one of those abandoned cars."

"Is she...?" Michael called out to Karl through the speakerphone.

"She's fine, Michael. Well, alive and sedated, but her vitals looked good. The medics are taking her to the hospital now. We're confiscating whatever was here. Vaux gave her something, and the hospital will be able to analyze the residue from the syringe to identify it." Karl paused, glancing at Lukas before continuing, "More troubling is the empty syringe and vials apparently waiting to be filled. I hate to think what Blackthorn had

Vaux planning on doing… But we stopped them, Michael. We stopped them."

When Michael didn't respond, Teri turned and saw the priest's eyes closed, his mouth moving through a prayer of gratitude. Teri responded to Karl for both of them, "Thank you, Karl. Thank you."

Karl and Lukas finished securing everything at the scene. Vaux had been quickly apprehended outside the room where he'd held Hana. Despite his bravado, he had little fight left when he saw the guns pointed at him. The two Swiss Guards watched as they placed the handcuffed man into a Vatican Gendarmerie vehicle to whisk him away to their private cells for questioning. Later, he would be transferred to the local police on a charge of kidnapping. But until then, Karl looked forward to questioning the man whose thugs had wounded his partner earlier and who had tried to kill his cousin today.

FORTY-TWO

ROME, ITALY

The Vatican's temporary detention facility beneath the Apostolic Palace was a place few ever entered —and fewer still left unchanged. Its corridors were sterile, humming faintly with fluorescent light. White walls, steel doors, the soft hiss of filtered air—it felt more like a research lab than a prison. That stark modernity was intentional, a deliberate departure from the gilded corridors above, designed to strip away pretense.

Michael, Hana, and Karl moved down the corridor in silence, their footsteps echoing faintly on the polished tile floor. Behind them, Cardinal Severino walked with hands clasped tightly behind his back, flanked by a discreet security escort. It had taken considerable persuasion to allow this meeting—no press, no cameras, no Vatican insignia—just one final reckoning.

Christophe Vaux, known provocateur and agent of Alton Blackthorn, waited in a featureless room at the end of the hall, seated at a steel table beneath cold, buzzing lights. He wore no restraints—he had been promised dignity in exchange for cooperation—but the presence of two plainclothes guards behind the mirrored glass reminded him of his reality.

As the door opened, he didn't look up.

"You brought her," he said without inflection.

Hana stepped forward first. "I insisted."

Vaux finally raised his head, eyes landing on Michael with faint amusement. "I expected a confessor. A firing squad, maybe. But not the priest and the journalist."

Michael took the opposite chair without speaking. Hana stood beside him, her expression unreadable.

"How did you know?"

Karl shook his head with a humorless smile. "Used your own methods. That tracker we found on Father Dominic's shirts? That was clever, by the way."

Vaux shrugged. "Your lower staff don't make much for all their work. It didn't take much—"

"To destroy that poor woman's life and toss her in jail? Please. That part was easy. What mattered was the tech—and it worked. When we needed to protect our own, we stitched trackers into their clothes. That sweater you ripped on the car door? All it took was a few extra minutes to follow the signal straight to her room. Your real mistake was simple—" Karl leaned in, voice hardening—"you underestimated us."

Vaux's gaze drifted toward her. "My mistake," he repeated, "was assuming you were only a journalist."

Michael folded his hands on the table, bringing them to the point of their interview. "Your boss wanted control of something that was never meant to be controlled. He saw Juana's manuscript as a key to wealth, power, influence."

"It *was* a key," Vaux replied sharply. "To advancements in healing, longevity, even memory. You saw a miracle; he saw potential. And, sure, advancements of any kind mean huge potential profits. Don't pretend you weren't tempted."

Michael's eyes didn't flinch. "I was tempted. But temptation isn't permission. And potential without restraint becomes disaster."

Vaux laughed, the sound dry and bitter. "You think restraint is a virtue? I think it's fear in ecclesiastical robes."

"And yet you're here," Michael said. "Powerless. Alone."

The words hung heavy in the room.

For a moment, Vaux's mask slipped. His hands trembled slightly on the table, revealing the toll of defeat. He had been entrusted by a man, powerful and wealthy, whose influence stretched across continents. More importantly, his ambitions reached for the stars. Their wealth would have been unmatched, with Blackthorn wielding power and Vaux the strength behind him. Together, they would've ruled the world, quite literally, and done so without regard for their actions. Reckless ambition? He shrugged. Sure. Vaux had been at the center of every murder, every illegal act, and, in the world's eyes, every unethical deed. The influence he provided for Blackthorn—through brute force, blackmail, and torture— had shaped Blackthorn into what he was today.

Now, sitting in this underground cell, Vaux realized his fingerprints on all those actions would be the ones that would condemn him for life. And Blackthorn? The man may have lost his chance at a miraculous drug that could make him king of the world, but he was still rich, still powerful, and more importantly, now determined to destroy the one man who knew enough of the skeletons in his closet to bring him down.

Still, his voice retained the glint of conviction. "Dominic, you think you've protected the world with your hymns and handwritten scrolls, by releasing the truth. But humanity won't settle for minor remedies when people like Blackthorn can give them more."

Michael leaned in. "Juana knew that. So did the monks who buried these texts. That's why they encoded them, guarded them, entrusted them to time. And why only now, in the light of transparency, the formula has been revealed to the world. Scientists, doctors, and the religious will have their miracles, but they will do so with the restraint of ethics and without the greed of those like Blackthorn. Nor will they use tactics like yours."

Vaux's lip curled. "You want control, no different from Alton. History will judge who could serve humanity better."

"No," Hana interjected. "Conscience will judge."

He turned toward her, eyes weary now. "And what does your conscience say, Ms. Sinclair? That my downfall redeems you? That this wasn't personal?"

"I'm not here for redemption," she said. "And it was always personal."

"What happens to me now?"

"That depends on you." Michael looked to Karl, who nodded.

"There are authorities nearby waiting to take you away," Karl explained. "You will be held in the general population of inmates at Regina Coeli prison, transported several times as needed to get you to trials and such." Karl let the implications settle in and saw Vaux's eyes shifting from vain hope of escape to the growing fear that

Blackthorn would have access to him during those transfers or at any of those facilities. Karl then shrugged. "But the authorities have no jurisdiction here in Vatican City, and you can be kept here indefinitely at our discretion."

Moments later, as the door closed behind them, the sterile corridor suddenly felt warmer—Hana perceived it less as a place of punishment and more as a crucible of tough truths. Michael took a quick breath, the weight of finality settling over them like a heavy mantle.

"Is it over?" Hana asked.

Karl looked to Michael, knowing his answer.

Michael shook his head. "No. But it's ended for him."

Far above, the bells of St. Peter's tolled again—low, measured, resonant.

CHAPTER

FORTY-THREE

VATICAN CITY

Under the soft glow of artfully positioned lighting, the Vatican's discreet medical facility exuded an air of reverent anticipation. Within the highly controlled laboratory, a select medical team led by Dr. Simon Ginzberg meticulously prepared a small vial containing the *Lumen Viride*—the unique botanical compound derived from Juana de la Cruz's detailed manuscripts, combined at the right celestial time, treated with profound respect for the formula's careful methods.

Outside Vatican walls, few were aware of the experiment about to unfold inside. Already, the public outcry that resulted from the original announcement of the potential for extraterrestrial influence on Earth had morphed. Skepticism had replaced most fears. Some of the faithful had found even deeper commitment to their beliefs that whatever revelations came from the stars, while most awaited in patient forbearance for the Pope's proclamation. Only the scholars, theologians, and some in the scientific community remained actively discussing the situation and working towards an understanding yet to be achieved. Although it had been known that these Vatican-run botanical experiments were being conducted, they were not widely discussed. As the weeks passed, and with the ever-revolving news cycle now focusing on other international events and local issues, most people had returned to their everyday lives.

Today could change everything.

Behind the glass partition, Father Michael and Hana watched in silence, their faces a careful balance of solemnity and hope. At their side, Cardinal Severino stood with furrowed brow and clasped hands, his posture a wordless prayer. Sister Teresa Drinkwater lingered nearby, her eyes carrying a quiet expectancy that seemed to fill the room with fragile possibility.

On the other side of the glass lay Elena, a nine-year-old girl slowly undone by a ruthless neurodegenerative disease. One by one, her abilities had been stripped away —speech, thought, movement—until little remained but the faintest echoes of the child she once was. Medicine had failed her; every known therapy had been tried, every door closed. Her parents, clinging to a hope as fragile as glass, had placed their trust in this moment, in this unprecedented trial. Elena rested on the table, small and still, a blood pressure cuff around her arm, a sensor at her wrist, a band across her forehead capturing the fragile rhythm of her brain waves—the last signals of a life not yet surrendered.

Simon leaned close to Elena, his voice low and steady, offering reassurance to her and to her visibly shaken parents as he explained the precautions being taken. Every gaze settled on the girl. Her hands, twisted together and trembling in her lap, gave no sign she had absorbed a word. Yet her eyes shifted—first toward her parents, then back to Simon. It was the faintest flicker, but enough to suggest she understood. Michael clung to that fragile gesture, praying it meant consent. Her parents, hearts breaking, saw it too. Remembering the bright, laughing child she had been only a few short years ago, they clung to one another, and through tears, gave Simon a solemn nod.

With steady precision, Simon delivered the measured dose of the vivid green tincture. Then came the waiting—long, unbearable minutes in which every tick of the monitors seemed amplified, each breath in the room held tight with expectation. Anxiety ebbed only when Elena's features softened, her clenched hands loosening, her ragged breathing settling into an even, peaceful rhythm. At last, her eyes drifted closed, as though slipping into a gentle sleep. The monitors remained steady, free of stress. Simon glanced back at the observers behind the glass and gave a small, reassuring nod.

Nearly thirty minutes later, Elena's eyelids fluttered. She looked around with astonishing clarity, her body calm and still, free of the tremors that had plagued her for so long. A faint smile lifted her lips, and then—fragile yet clear—came a single word: "Mama?"

Her mother gasped, tears spilling freely as she pressed trembling hands to her mouth. Her father, voice breaking with gratitude, seized Michael's hand in both of his. "This is beyond anything we dreamed," he whispered. "It's a miracle."

Michael's chest swelled, awe rising within him as he

met Hana's gaze; her eyes mirrored his amazement, tempered with cautious wonder. Behind them, Cardinal Severino crossed himself reverently, murmuring a prayer of thanks. Then the medical team moved in around Elena, screens and instruments obscuring her from view. Through the intercom, Simon confirmed what the monitors already proclaimed: normal function, clear brain activity, stable vitals. Other physicians took over, gently posing questions —and for the first time in months, Elena answered, slowly yet undeniably herself once more.

In the days that followed, Elena's recovery astonished doctors and observers alike. Tests confirmed unprecedented neurological regeneration—healing once thought impossible. News spread rapidly, from Vatican circles to international media, drawing scientists, reporters, and desperate families all seeking answers.

The Vatican suddenly found itself at the center of global attention. Michael managed the response with measured transparency, stressing caution. "This development humbles us all," he told the press. "We remain committed to patient safety and ethical responsibility."

Inside the Vatican, Michael convened an urgent council with Cardinal Severino, Hana, Sister Teri, Ian, Karl, Lukas, and Simon. The dilemma was clear: how to balance stewardship of *Lumen Viride* with the world's urgent demand for access. "We have proof of its effectiveness," Michael acknowledged. "Yet our transparency obliges us to consider broader use. Humanity is watching—and hoping."

Cardinal Severino urged restraint. "Our guardianship of this gift requires caution. Humanity's readiness is fragile." Sister Teri countered that cautious expansion, under strict ethical oversight, was the only responsible path forward. Karl and Lukas emphasized the growing security risks, while Hana pressed the importance of openness. After long deliberation, consensus emerged: expand access under Vatican supervision, governed by rigorous ethical and scientific standards.

The decision ignited global debate. Elena's transformation was hailed as miraculous, sparking both medical excitement and spiritual controversy. Many saw new hope; others feared disruption to traditional beliefs. Michael addressed the world with calm resolve: "Our role is neither to conceal nor provoke. Truth must be stewarded with respect—for knowledge, for faith, and for those this discovery touches."

As carefully monitored trials expanded, the results were extraordinary. Patients experienced dramatic recoveries, often accompanied by profound spiritual awakenings. Each case was painstakingly documented and shared openly, reinforcing credibility. Weeks passed, and reports multiplied, fueling both wonder and unease across the globe.

Meanwhile, Karl, Lukas, and the Swiss Guard intensified security. With swelling public interest came desperate attempts to breach Vatican walls—some seeking healing, others seeking control. Each incident was managed firmly yet respectfully, as vigilance became the new order of daily life.

LONG AFTER HER RECOVERY, Michael visited Elena and her family in their modest apartment. Joyful laughter spilled through the rooms, proof enough of her transformation.

Kneeling beside her, he smiled warmly. "How are you feeling, Elena?"

Her eyes shone, her voice clear and strong. "I feel wonderful, Father. It's like waking from a long, dark sleep into the brightest dream."

Michael tilted his head gently. "What kind of dream?"

She hesitated, her expression thoughtful. "I don't remember it clearly—only that it was vast, like a sky filled with stars. It still lingers, Father, and now every day feels like a blessing."

Michael's heart lifted, filled with quiet joy at her words.

Later, outside beneath a serene evening sky, he stood in silence, the weight of what had unfolded pressing on him as much as it uplifted him. Elena's healing—and the others that followed—were undeniable beacons of hope, but also carried profound consequences he could not ignore.

Hana came to his side, her presence grounding him. "The burden is heavy," she said softly, "but what we've witnessed is real."

Above them, the heavens stretched endlessly, glittering and patient, as if waiting for humanity to step forward— carefully, humbly—into mysteries and miracles it was only beginning to understand.

CHAPTER

FORTY-FOUR

VATICAN CITY

A gentle dawn stretched its rosy fingers over Rome, illuminating St. Peter's Basilica in delicate hues of pink and gold. The city was quiet, as though collectively holding its breath, awaiting the words soon to be spoken. At precisely nine o'clock, the bells of St. Peter's Basilica tolled in solemn harmony, their deep, resonant tones marking a significant event.

Pope Clement, clad in simple yet regal white vestments, stood on the balcony overlooking a vast, expectant crowd that filled St. Peter's Square. Tens of thousands gathered, while millions more watched worldwide, sensing the solemnity of the moment.

"My dear brothers and sisters," he began, "today we recognize an individual whose spiritual insight and ethical courage have completely reshaped our understanding of humanity's relationship with both Earth and the cosmos."

Below, a respectful silence deepened throughout the

piazza, broken only by the quiet rustle of leaves stirred by a passing breeze.

"Juana de la Cruz, long obscured by history's shadows, emerges now into rightful illumination," Clement continued solemnly. "She has long been declared 'Venerable' by the Catholic Church, signifying that she lived a life of heroic virtue. Today, we begin the process of canonizing this remarkable woman as a Catholic saint. Her writings, recently uncovered and painstakingly deciphered, have revealed her as a guardian—one entrusted historically with truths of ethical sensitivity, particularly regarding humans' interaction with God's celestial mysteries and the botanical wisdom bestowed upon our world."

A murmur of awe rippled through the crowd, a wave of whispers reflecting astonishment and curiosity. Clement paused briefly, allowing the gravity of his words to settle among those present.

"It is the newly discovered document, aptly named *Testamentum Caeli*—the Testament of the Heavens—that has significantly guided this recognition," the Pope declared, his eyes earnest and solemn. "In its reflections, we are reminded that God's touch, His wisdom and providence, envelops more than our earthly presence. In His wisdom, when His flock became ready for assistance, He touched our lives through His divine firmament, bringing forth remedies that can both alleviate pain and bring peace to the masses. He used the stars above our heads and the seeds below our feet to bring to fruition plants that will offer us His Grace and Healing. We are reminded by His love of us that what science has brought into our lives does not contradict our faith but broadens it as proof that He rules the universe and has cared for us throughout all time. The Church, as caretaker of His truths and love, will remain the fount by which the faithful can find solace, healing, and peace.

"Yet, our hearts are open to all people of the world, as are God's welcoming arms. As such, although the miracles inherent in the *Lumen Viride* formula have been divinely entrusted into the Church's hands, its benefits will be made open to all people throughout the world."

The Holy Father lifted his gaze toward the sky, momentarily silent, as if gathering inspiration from the infinite expanse above.

"Juana de la Cruz's testament does not diminish our faith; rather, it expands it, challenging us to embrace humility in the face of God's cosmic mysteries."

As Pope Clement concluded his historic announcement, applause gradually blossomed into enthusiastic acclaim. Cameras from global media networks broadcast every nuance of the Pope's expression, every subtle reaction from the deeply moved crowds.

Almost immediately, the reverberations of Pope Clement's proclamation surged worldwide, igniting fervent discussion and debate. Scholars, philosophers, theologians, and laypersons alike grappled openly with the concept that the Church would have jurisdiction over the *Lumen Viride* formula, yet open its benefits to the world at large.

Universities hosted emergency symposia; theological seminaries scheduled urgent dialogues. Newspapers ran front-page editorials dissecting every facet of Juana's testament and its ethical implications. On social media, hashtags proliferated, reflecting global fascination and philosophical engagement.

At Oxford, Harvard, and the Sorbonne, eminent

scholars discussed Juana's testament openly, grappling fiercely with its intellectual and spiritual ramifications. Challenging ethical questions were raised, scrutinized, and debated vigorously.

"Have we, as a civilization, prepared ourselves adequately for the concept that we have been provided a miracle drug from some source, be it God or aliens or a purely astronomical influence?" asked Professor Lydia Marshall during a televised debate at Cambridge. "The *Testamentum Caeli* compels humanity to confront our vulnerabilities and responsibilities—not merely in theological abstraction but in stark, undeniable terms."

Dr. Martin Eckhardt of Heidelberg countered, "Indeed, Professor, and perhaps Juana's testament is exactly the stimulus people require. Ethical growth often emerges most authentically from periods of intense discomfort and self-reflection in the face of others."

Across Rome, Ian Duffy watched these unfolding discussions with deep satisfaction.

Ian stood quietly beside Sister Teri in the gardens adjoining the Archives. They watched the sunset cast long shadows across pathways walked by countless seekers before them.

"Is this how history feels when it pivots?" Ian murmured, his voice quiet and reflective.

Teri nodded calmly, her smile gentle yet wise. "Perhaps. But history, Ian, isn't merely something we observe. It is what we live, what we leave behind."

Ian exhaled through pursed lips, absorbing her words. "It's humbling to consider how profoundly a single voice can echo through time."

"Yet comforting," Teri replied. "It reminds us that none

of us are insignificant, none of our actions meaningless. Each choice shapes our collective destiny."

Together, they turned to watch the fading sunlight, their thoughts joined silently with millions worldwide, all collectively considering humanity's next step forward as part of a greater community of life.

In his private chambers later that evening, Pope Clement knelt in prayerful contemplation. His fingers rested upon a copy of Juana's testament, its pages newly bound with reverent care.

"Guide us, Lord," he whispered earnestly, his heart open to the quiet presence he always sensed in moments of the most profound reflection. "Let these truths we uncover not frighten nor divide us, but unify and elevate us toward wisdom, compassion, and understanding."

Outside, Rome settled, the stars above silent yet watchful, bearing witness to a world forever changed by truths bravely spoken, wisely considered, and finally embraced.

FORTY-FIVE

VATICAN CITY

S ister Teri frowned as she looked over the reports of communications that she had been tracking for some time now. She had followed the trail of Blackthorn's attempt at communicating through different channels, using many clandestine routes for servers and internet addresses. She had been privately proud of her ability to track the man.

But now, her failure struck her pride to the quick. Blackthorn had gone to ground. It was as if he had vanished from the Earth. She chuckled to herself, though without humor, imagining he had headed off for the stars.

"What do you have going, Teri?" Ian asked as he entered her area.

"Thank you for coming by," Teri said. "I haven't come up with anything, and that's the problem."

"What do you mean?"

"I mean, I can't find Blackthorn anymore. I've been able

to follow him for, what, weeks now? Every time he switches servers or uses a different online alias, I've managed to either communicate with him or track him. His people might be competent, but I thought I was better. Until now."

"Lost him?" Ian looked over her shoulder at the reports.

Yes, I'm afraid I have," she replied. "I've reached out to him, as I have ever since we learned that Father Ricci was the Vatican's mole. Impersonating Ricci's syntax and texts was no problem. With Ricci under the Vatican's roof and control, and no public announcement of his incarceration, everything went smoothly. Blackthorn wasn't any the wiser."

Ian nodded. "That sure helped us be prepared for the last attack on Vatican City. Rounding up all of Vaux's thugs that night made a big difference for us."

"Now, I'm worried that Blackthorn has cut off all communication. You don't think he's dead, do you? I mean, with everything else going on..." Teri let the question hang in the air.

Both had been following the recent attacks on Genetica Therapeutics. The news media had been sensationalizing the gruesome experiments that the laboratories conducted on unwilling victims. This had led to the burning of laboratories and the expulsion of unprincipled scientists and medical teams who had performed heinous acts for Blackthorn's experiments. The family members of victims, once they understood what had happened, could not be satisfied with just legal action. Revenge, anger, and frustration spilled over into vandalism and even murder on a scale unseen before against a single company. Not to mention, legal authorities had seized Blackthorn's assets and were seeking to press charges for crimes against humanity.

Ian did not answer her. He doubted Blackthorne could be so easily destroyed, whether by a bullet from an angry father or a knife from a freed victim of his experiment. The man was too devious, too rich, too powerful to be defeated simply by dying.

Finally, Ian said, "Let it go, Teri. There are too many people after him. Too many problems he needs to face, and I have no doubt he'll be buried in his own sins for quite a while."

Teri took a deep breath of relief at Ian's words and got up from her chair to stretch her back. "How about a cup of tea, Ian? And thank you for stopping by. You're right: the man may have had money and power before, but now he's accountable to the public and to God."

FORTY-SIX

VATICAN CITY

Ian sat hunched over an ancient oak desk, surrounded by stacks of fragile manuscripts. Soft lamp lighting bathed the Vatican Archives in a hushed amber glow, their warmth contrasting starkly with the chill of unease that enveloped the young archivist. Alone in the restricted annex, he methodically sifted through archival records, his intuition guiding him as much as his expertise. Since Juana's testament had been canonically recognized, an unrelenting sense of incompleteness had haunted him. Each ancient parchment he touched whispered faint, elusive truths, yet always seemed to stop short of clarity.

His fingers moved across pages worn smooth over centuries. Deep lines of concentration marked his forehead as he deciphered faded Latin and cryptic medieval annotations.

Suddenly, his eyes widened slightly as his breath caught. Carefully, reverently, he examined the page before him, recognizing immediately the significance of the faded ink and delicate script. The manuscript detailed surprising events, chronicling celestial phenomena witnessed centuries before—accounts unmistakably aligned with those described within Juana de la Cruz's *Hesperides Codex* and linked closely to the mysterious *Voynich Manuscript*. But these were not just the observations of unknown constellations in the night sky or seen in the visions of monks affected by the pollen from the spontaneous growth of unknown plants.

Ian exhaled lightly, realization sending a shiver through him. These documents explicitly detailed Vatican encounters with "beings from the stars," describing celestial visitations purposely hidden and suppressed by medieval popes fearful of theological upheaval. Each page documented painstaking attempts by the Church to reconcile or conceal these truths, portraying anxious debates among theologians grappling with implications that utterly shook their faith. These were not random, scattered, largely unsubstantiated accounts as they had been uncovering prior to this. He had uncovered thoroughly transparent and documented extraterrestrial visitations that had been systematically suppressed at the highest levels.

Hands trembling slightly, Ian turned to read further, discovering additional commentary penned by unnamed Vatican scholars of centuries past. Their annotations indicated clear directives—this text had been deliberately concealed, suppressed due to fears it would ignite panic or severely undermine the Church's theological stability.

A chill prickled at the base of his spine.

This provided proof of actual alien visitations, live beings, walking the streets of Rome and various villages throughout Europe. But more than that, it was proof of active concealment by the Church.

Gathering the documents, Ian quickly notified Michael, pushing for an urgent private meeting.

Michael sat in quiet contemplation, a white candle flickering softly on his desk, when the urgent knock disturbed his reverie. He opened the door to his assistant Ian, his expression grave and troubled.

"Michael," he began breathlessly, stepping quickly inside, "I've found something disturbing. You need to see it immediately."

Concern arched his brow as he methodically examining the parchments. His face grew progressively paler, the implications striking him forcefully with each sentence. The candle flame flickered uncertainly, mirroring his own wavering composure.

"Where did you find this?" he finally asked, voice barely above a whisper.

"In the Archives, buried deliberately," Ian replied earnestly. "The Vatican knew—centuries ago—that alien beings walked the face of the Earth."

Michael, profoundly reflective upon reviewing the fragile pages, felt dual senses of awe and unease.

"These accounts," he murmured, his voice barely audible, "confront us with truths the Church has purposefully kept hidden for centuries."

Ian nodded rapidly, eyes wide with restrained excitement. "And perhaps rightly hidden, considering their magnitude. Yet now, the choice has been taken from us. The world's attention, the Vatican's promise of transparency, leaves no place for secrecy."

Michael placed a gentle hand on Ian's shoulder,

reassuring yet solemn. "Our responsibility now is clarity and receptivity. Let's discuss this with our team."

A bit later, Michael assembled Ian, Hana, Simon, and Sister Teri, all gathering around the ancient manuscripts Ian had uncovered. He spoke firmly, calm yet resolute. "We now face an unprecedented responsibility. These documents confirm what many feared or hoped: our ancestors indeed encountered not just celestial phenomena they couldn't explain, but beings from elsewhere in the cosmos. We've recognized that potential in the scattering of sightings and manuscripts that we've unveiled already. But this," he pointed at the proof before them, "this transcends all that by clearly stating the existence of aliens who have walked on Earth. And the Church kept it hidden."

Sister Teri's eyes held deep compassion and understanding. "Their fear is understandable. Confronting such truth requires realism and courage—qualities humanity struggles with all too often."

Hana nodded in solemn agreement. "Yet we must provide leadership now, guiding others through uncertainty rather than denying its existence."

Michael's voice carried quiet conviction. "Agreed. Transparency combined with measured caution will guide our path forward. The world watches closely; our response must reflect integrity, courage, and open-mindedness."

LATE THAT EVENING, under a sky slowly deepening toward nightfall, Hana found Michael alone on the terrace, serenely contemplating the horizon, the distant lights of Rome flickering in the fading dusk. He had an appointment with Cardinal Severino in the morning and knew the night would pass fitfully for him until then.

Hana approached, standing beside him in silent companionship. Eventually, Michael spoke, his voice soft yet burdened. "These truths challenge us, Hana. They compel us to reconsider everything we believe about our place in Creation."

Hana reached for his hand, fingers intertwining warmly. "Perhaps this challenge is our greatest opportunity, Michael. An invitation to embrace groundedness, wonder, and a broader sense of kinship with Creation itself."

Michael turned toward her, eyes gentle yet weary. "Are we truly ready?"

She smiled warmly, her eyes calm and steady. "Readiness isn't about certainty, Michael—it's about willingness. The willingness to seek truth humbly, even when the path feels overwhelming."

A prolonged silence settled heavily between them, each comprehending the magnitude of potential repercussions. Finally, Michael turned decisively.

"I will bring this to Cardinal Severino in the morning," he resolved firmly. "The Church must confront openly what it concealed long ago. Complete transparency is now our only path forward."

FORTY-SEVEN

VATICAN CITY

The predawn hours found Father Michael and Cardinal Severino gathered solemnly within Severino's private chambers. The cardinal, understandably disturbed yet determined, pored over the documents, eyes narrowing with intense concern.

"This revelation," Severino began slowly, "alters everything. It calls our recent decisions into absolute question."

Michael folded his arms, signaling quiet concurrence. "It explicitly mentions living beings walking the Earth who came from the cosmos. This directly confirms speculations that the Church has been wont to admit—that there are other civilizations beyond our world."

Severino's exhaustion was evident in his weary features. "We believed transparency was ethical, necessary even. Yet now we face the possibility we may have acted precipitously, placing humanity in grave spiritual peril."

Michael leaned forward earnestly. "Or perhaps this is precisely why transparency matters most—mankind deserves complete truth…"

Severino regarded him, his expression conflicted yet resolute. "I will attend to this with Pope Clement himself. I trust that you will apprise anyone who is privy to this matter of its sensitive nature and that it is now in the Holy Father's own hands."

Acknowledging the clear warning in Severino's words, Michael added, "Withholding the truth now would compound the original error."

The cardinal nodded solemnly. "I will relay your concerns to the Holy Father."

He rose decisively, ending the meeting. "This decision cannot rest solely upon us. The entire Church must bear this revelation responsibly. However and whenever the Holy Father sees fit."

By the next dawn, Michael, once confident in humanity's readiness, found himself humbled and disturbed, reconsidering whether people would truly understand the gravity of their discoveries. He found himself equally disturbed by the tone of Cardinal Severino yesterday, the implication that, once again, transparency would be an empty promise.

Michael found solace briefly in the gardens, now bathed in morning sunlight, yet felt little comfort.

His reflection was interrupted by Ian Duffy's quiet approach. Ian had heard the words of Cardinal Severino and understood Michael's internal conflict.

"You've always championed truth, Michael," Ian began. "Even uncomfortable truths."

Michael sighed heavily. "Yet now I wonder if our actions have inadvertently placed us at risk? The burden of releasing this truth is no longer in my hands. I have done as I have been tasked, and now Cardinal Severino will leave it in the hands of His Holiness. All we can do now is trust in the process."

The two of them sat quietly, both deeply familiar with the Church's traditional stance in light of revelations that could undermine the faith of the flock. Would the Church, as it has before, hide this most recent revelation? Or would it keep its promise of transparency? And if it did, how would it deal with the idea that God and all their beliefs might relate to an alien civilization? The task seemed too vast for any institution to manage... For any institution to disclose to its followers that we are not alone.

Together, Michael and Ian watched the sun rise higher, illuminating both the Vatican and the conflicting challenges they now faced. Truth, Michael knew, was complex and demanding—yet it was still truth. The Church's response would indeed reveal its readiness, and perhaps its surprising resilience, in the face of uncertainty.

CHAPTER
FORTY-EIGHT

SUBIACO, ITALY

Father Michael Dominic stood at the threshold of the Abbazia di Subiaco, a historically rich Benedictine monastery nestled within the serene Aniene Valley about seventy kilometers east of Rome. Founded by Saint Benedict himself around the year 529, the monastery was home to the sacred *Sacro Speco*, the very cave where the saint spent three years in solitary contemplation. As Michael approached the ancient stone walls perched dramatically on the verdant hillside, he felt the weight of centuries enfold him, the stones beneath his feet worn smooth by generations of seekers and penitents. Here, amid the timeless quietude and metaphysical spiritual legacy, he sought clarity for the internal conflicts that gripped him.

Brother Anselmo, the monastery's elderly prior, greeted Michael at the entrance, his weathered features a testament to decades spent in disciplined reflection. Without unnecessary words, he guided Michael to a starkly furnished room—a bed, a desk, a candle. Here, simplicity invited deep introspection.

Left alone, Michael placed the bundled manuscripts and philosophical texts upon the wooden desk. He lit the candle, the small flame casting long, dancing shadows upon ancient walls.

A cold shiver passed through Michael. Here, in this silent solitude, he hoped to reconcile the intellectual allure of Juana's *Testamentum Caeli* with the disturbing dangers, both from beings unknown and from the masses of panicked humans, that the document starkly unveiled. Where did truth and transparency make sense in such a complex issue?

HIS FIRST DAYS at the monastery passed in quiet intensity. Michael immersed himself in philosophical treatises spanning centuries—from Aquinas and Augustine to Kierkegaard and Nietzsche—seeking threads that might clarify the world's ethical stance toward celestial knowledge. Yet each philosophical perspective deepened his internal conflict rather than resolving it.

He found himself particularly haunted by Kierkegaard's musings on humanity's dread and trembling in the face of divine mysteries:

"Truth is subjective," Kierkegaard wrote, *"but it must be faced alone, in earnest isolation, with absolute inwardness."*

Indeed, Michael felt this isolation acutely, wrestling alone with truths that demanded both courage and self-restraint. His nights were filled with restless dreams—

visions of celestial entities both benevolent and terrifying, silently observing mankind's fumbling search for meaning.

One storm-laden afternoon, Michael wandered the monastery's small yet extensive library, shelves brimming with age-old wisdom. Rain drummed rhythmically against narrow windows as he uncovered historical accounts of celestial sightings diligently recorded by medieval monks. Each sighting had evoked awe and reverence, yet beneath these emotions lay an undercurrent of deep unease, a quiet acknowledgment of the world's limitations and vulnerabilities.

An entry from a fourteenth-century monk particularly struck Michael:

"TONIGHT, a celestial fire blazed across the heavens, filling hearts with awe and terror alike. Do such sights offer revelations, or are they cautionary reminders of our fragility? Perhaps both, and perhaps we are not ready for either."

MICHAEL CLOSED the fragile book slowly, heart heavy with the monk's honest uncertainty echoing across centuries.

On the seventh evening, as the twilight sky turned violet and stars began emerging, Brother Anselmo gently knocked on Michael's door, inviting him to join the monks for their evening chant. Michael accepted gladly, following the prior into the austere stone chapel. There, beneath candlelit icons and soaring arches, their voices rose in resonant Gregorian chant, a collective expression of humanity's yearning for the divine.

The music, ancient yet timeless, pierced Michael's

internal turbulence. He felt something significant in the monks' harmonies—a willingness to accept mystery without demanding certainty, to embrace a sacrificial mindset amid cosmic vastness. Tears welled silently, unnoticed by others, as he knelt in quiet reflection.

Following the chant, Michael lingered alone in the chapel, eyes fixed upon a crucifix illuminated softly by flickering candlelight. Brother Anselmo approached quietly, sensing Michael's turmoil.

"You carry heavy burdens, Father Dominic," the elderly prior observed, his voice gentle yet firm.

Michael bowed his head slightly, solemnity evident in the gesture. "I seek clarity amid significant contradictions, Brother. Knowledge calls to us, yet we've seen warnings against our very nature of relentless curiosity. How do we reconcile such opposing truths?"

The elderly friar considered Michael's words carefully before responding. "Perhaps reconciliation is not the aim, Father. Perhaps our task is to live humbly and responsibly within that tension—acknowledging our immense capacity for both wisdom and folly."

Absorbed in Anselmo's words, Michael asked, "Yet how do we determine when knowledge serves enlightenment or risks destruction?"

The prior smiled faintly, eyes compassionate. "By seeking always with humility rather than pride, compassion rather than arrogance. It is intention, Father Dominic, that ultimately shapes our journey and defines our relationship to truth."

Michael pondered Anselmo's remarks through the long night that followed. As dawn illuminated the distant hills in golden hues, he finally felt a subtle yet significant shift within himself. He realized that humanity's pursuit of celestial truths required not merely intellectual courage but considerable spiritual deference—a balance delicate yet essential.

He rose, determined yet quiet, knowing his pilgrimage here had offered not absolute clarity but essential perspective.

Michael departed the monastery that morning with sincere gratitude, returning toward Rome. The revealed truths had initially shaken him deeply, yet now he recognized their true gift—not of fear, but of caution, not paralysis but mindful discernment.

His journey homeward was marked by silent contemplation, each step reaffirming his commitment to share openly both Juana's insights and the sober cautionary truths that tempered them.

Upon returning to Vatican City, Michael found Ian and Sister Teri waiting anxiously. Their faces showed clear relief at his presence, tempered by cautious concern for his emotional and spiritual state.

"Did your pilgrimage offer clarity?" Ian asked.

Michael smiled faintly, a quiet strength returning to his eyes. "Clarity is perhaps elusive, Ian. But my pilgrimage has offered something equally valuable—acceptance and an attitude free of self-importance. We must continue seeking truth openly, yet with sincere respect for its risks."

Teri nodded thoughtfully, recognizing the subtle yet essential shift in Michael's perspective. "Then we stand together in that commitment."

Michael placed gentle hands on both their shoulders, reassured by their unwavering support. "Indeed, we do. Together, with reverence guiding our courage, we will help humankind navigate truths far greater than ourselves."

As evening descended upon Vatican City, Michael's

quiet resolve felt like a soft beacon amid significant uncertainties—a testament not merely to humanity's potential peril, but to its equally powerful capacity for wisdom, perspective, and growth.

CHAPTER
FORTY-NINE

VATICAN CITY

F ather Michael Dominic sat in the privacy of his study, staring pensively at the aged manuscripts arrayed across the desk, his gaze lingering particularly on the *Hesperides Codex* and photographs of the *Voynich Manuscript*. The mysterious text had defied the world's greatest minds for centuries—its pages filled with enigmatic script, botanical illustrations, celestial maps, and symbolic images that whispered secrets only hinted at, never revealed.

He leaned back in his chair, fingers steepled beneath his chin. Michael had long pursued truth with diligence and courage, yet now, in quiet reflection, he recognized a fundamental limit—a boundary mankind must respect. Recent experiences, from the contemplative isolation of Subiaco Abbey to intense philosophical debates within Vatican walls, had clarified something essential: ultimate truth, particularly regarding humanity's relationship with celestial beings, might need to remain intentionally unresolved. Michael had the duty as a priest in the Church to follow the edicts of the Holy Father and heed his enlightened decisions. Faith and trust, beyond duty, required Michael to accept Pope Clement's decision. And, having heard nothing more from any source about an announcement of the Church's documented and direct contact with aliens, it was clear the decision had been made, at least for now. The Church had changed its perspectives over time as the flock needed new guidance. Maybe in this matter, too, it was simply a matter of waiting for the right moment. A soft knock at the door interrupted his contemplation. Ian Duffy and Hana Sinclair entered, their expressions mirroring Michael's. Ian offered a faint, understanding smile as he noted the manuscripts lying upon Michael's desk.

"We suspected we'd find you immersed in these mysteries," Ian remarked, pulling up a chair and settling beside Hana.

Hana's gaze swept across the manuscripts, particularly fixated on the detailed images from the *Voynich Manuscript*. "After everything we've encountered, it still fascinates me how some secrets elude even the most persistent pursuit."

Michael nodded. "Indeed. The *Voynich*, for instance— centuries of scholarship, infinite intellectual effort, and yet it stubbornly resists revelation. Perhaps deliberately so."

Ian raised a curious eyebrow. "Deliberately?"

Michael expelled a breath, leaning forward. "Yes. But consider for a moment the manuscript's absolute resistance to decipherment—not merely challenging, but seemingly impossible. Some scholars suggest it might be a clever medieval hoax, others an encoded wisdom designed precisely to guard itself. But what if its indecipherability itself holds significant philosophical meaning?"

Hana's eyes brightened. "You mean its mystery could be intentional—a philosophical statement about the limits of human understanding?"

"That's it exactly. The *Voynich Manuscript*'s enduring enigma could be its most meaningful lesson: that society's quest for knowledge is inherently bound. Not through lack of intellect or determination, but through necessity—the ethical and philosophical deference required to acknowledge limits."

Ian leaned back, visibly intrigued by the thought. "Then you believe some truths must remain beyond our grasp by design?"

Michael sighed, his gaze distant yet clear. "Not all truths, Ian, but certainly some. Consider the warnings we've encountered—the *Testamentum Caeli* and its suppressed counterpart. They caution against unbridled curiosity, warning explicitly about the risks inherent in knowledge pursued without sufficient ethical maturity."

Hana nodded reflectively. "Then perhaps the *Voynich Manuscript* is humanity's enduring metaphor—a tangible reminder that some mysteries should remain unresolved. Mystery itself becomes a safeguard, preserving the wisdom to know we're not the ultimate measure in our relationship to the unknown."

Michael's eyes lit tenderly, moved by her insightful articulation. "Exactly, Hana. Mystery isn't merely a puzzle to be solved. It serves a critical ethical function, reminding mankind continually of its place within a vast, complex cosmos—one not fully within our grasp or dominion."

Ian exhaled thoughtfully. "And yet, Michael,

humanity's drive to understand, to uncover, seems equally intrinsic. How do we reconcile these competing forces?"

Michael smiled faintly, acknowledging the sweeping paradox. "Perhaps reconciliation isn't entirely necessary or even desirable, Ian. Maybe the tension itself is instructive —a dynamic equilibrium between curiosity and understanding, driving progress yet restraining hubris."

Hana's gaze turned to the image of a delicately illustrated botanical page from the *Voynich Manuscript*. "Then what of the *Hesperides Codex*? How does its decipherment fit within this philosophical framework?"

Michael considered the codex carefully, eyes tracing the intricate script and imagery. "The *Hesperides Codex* represents a portion of truth that people can responsibly embrace. It was decipherable because we possessed sufficient maturity and context to integrate its revelations with foresight. But what if we're not meant to solve the *Voynich Manuscript*? What if its mystery is the point?"

Ian nodded, his gaze distant in reflection, understanding dawning visibly in his thoughtful expression. "So, rather than a failure, our inability to decode *Voynich* fully might be an intentional success—its ultimate purpose fulfilled precisely because it remains undeciphered."

"Exactly," Michael said. "Its indecipherability maintains a necessary tension, a perpetual reminder of the readiness to learn required when approaching such mysteries."

Hana leaned forward contemplatively. "Michael, after everything we've discovered, experienced, and debated— do you genuinely believe humans aren't ready for certain truths?"

Michael's response was measured, reflective. "Mankind

is capable of extraordinary insight, Hana, but our ethical growth often lags behind our intellectual achievements. Recent events—the global reactions, the intense debates—highlighted the potential turmoil truth can unleash if prematurely revealed. Perhaps some revelations, especially regarding cosmic or spiritual realities, demand an ethical and spiritual maturity that humanity hasn't yet fully attained."

A gentle silence settled comfortably among them, each reflecting on the implications of Michael's observations. The quiet was interrupted only by the subtle rustle of the ancient parchment pages, stirred gently by an almost imperceptible draft.

Ian broke the silence. "It stands to reason, then, that our greatest responsibility, as custodians of these truths, is to guide people gradually toward maturity—never fully concealing but always mindful of our collective readiness."

"I see your point," Michael murmured, reassured by Ian's thoughtful conclusion. "Indeed, our role becomes guardianship rather than gatekeeping—stewarding humanity's gradual awakening, patiently nurturing the ethics required for genuine understanding."

Hana's gaze returned to the *Voynich Manuscript* images. "Then this manuscript, in its refusal to yield its secrets, becomes our silent, constant companion—an enduring reminder of humility, discipline, and respectful wonder in the face of the unknown."

Michael smiled, intensely moved by her poetic insight. "Yes. The lingering mystery serves humanity best not by yielding answers, but by prompting continuous reflection, caution, and awe."

Outside, the evening deepened, stars slowly emerging in the velvet sky above Vatican City. Michael gazed out the window, contemplating the vast cosmos that stretched infinitely beyond human comprehension. The quiet vulnerability he had learned at Subiaco Abbey echoed within him, a reassuring anchor amid exhaustive uncertainties.

Ultimately, he realized, the most significant truths the world might encounter—celestial, spiritual, or otherwise— might best remain just beyond reach, guarded by the foresight inherent in mystery itself. It wasn't ignorance, he reflected, but wisdom that accepted mystery's intrinsic value. Such acceptance would sustain humanity's freedom from self-importance, preserving its ethical core as it journeyed through a cosmos forever richer and more complex than human imagination could fully embrace.

CHAPTER

FIFTY

THE VATICAN GARDENS

The afternoon sun gently warmed Vatican City, filtering golden rays through leafy canopies overhead, painting delicate patterns across the tranquil gardens. Michael Dominic knelt beside Hana Sinclair, their hands immersed together in the cool, rich soil. Between them was a small, carefully prepared garden bed—an empty canvas awaiting the promise of new life.

Michael glanced over at Hana, captivated by the way sunlight illuminated her hair, giving her a gentle radiance that stirred his heart. Her expression, serene yet focused, mirrored the quiet strength he had come to cherish deeply. He opened a small pouch, revealing a handful of delicate seeds.

"Planting seeds always feels symbolic, doesn't it?" he whispered. "Each one represents possibility, waiting patiently beneath the surface."

Hana smiled warmly, meeting his gaze. "Exactly. It's

about trusting nature—knowing that the most beautiful things often take time."

Together, they placed the seeds into the earth, their movements effortlessly synchronized, unspoken harmony guiding their hands. As they covered the seeds tenderly with soil, Michael felt a profound sense of tranquility envelop him, restoring and reaffirming their shared commitment to nurturing life—both in their relationship and the greater truths they had discovered.

Hana brushed soil from her fingers, her voice quiet yet filled with meaning. "We've learned so much, yet maybe our greatest lesson is that some mysteries are meant to remain mysteries, patiently waiting until we're truly ready."

Michael's eyes briefly closed, as though internalizing her words. "Yes, accepting mystery is an act of courage. It acknowledges our limitations and respects the wisdom of patience."

She placed her hand softly over his, a shared warmth radiating through their intertwined fingers. "Patience has certainly defined us, hasn't it?"

Michael chuckled, squeezing her hand. "Patience and a little stubbornness, perhaps. But always guided by love."

The surrounding gardens seemed to whisper in agreement, leaves rustling as if nodding approval. Birds sang in the distance, underscoring the peaceful serenity surrounding them.

Michael glanced down at their hands, fingers interwoven naturally, and felt an unexpected surge of boldness. He looked back up, catching Hana's eye with sudden intensity. "Speaking of patience—I think we've waited long enough."

Hana's eyes widened slightly, curiosity and

anticipation mingling beautifully in her expression. "Long enough for what?"

Michael took a deep breath, his voice steady but his heart pounding. "To set a date for our wedding."

For a moment, Hana stared at him, her lips parting in gentle surprise, before a radiant smile blossomed across her face. "Oh, Michael—really?"

"Yes, really." He laughed, the warmth of her reaction filling him with delight. "We've navigated through so much together. The Church, the manuscripts, celestial mysteries—we've faced them all side by side. And through every challenge, I've grown more certain about us, about our future together."

Her eyes sparkled with tears of happiness. "You couldn't have surprised me more beautifully."

Michael leaned closer, his voice tender. "It just felt right, spontaneous—like everything with us has always been. We've earned this moment."

Hana nodded, her voice barely above a whisper. "We have. So—when?"

Michael smiled, playful yet sincere. "I was thinking spring. When the world renews itself, it seems fitting we do the same."

"Spring is perfect," Hana agreed immediately, her voice filled with quiet joy. "A fresh beginning, symbolic of everything we've discovered, cultivated, and nurtured together."

Michael brushed his thumb tenderly across the back of her hand, warmth and affection evident in every subtle movement. "Exactly. Like planting these seeds—our marriage will symbolize renewal, trust, patience, and love."

Hana leaned closer, her forehead delicately touching

his. "I couldn't imagine sharing this journey with anyone else."

"And I wouldn't want to," Michael murmured. "Our love has been patient, humble, tested by time and challenge. But through everything, it's only deepened, grown stronger."

She closed her eyes briefly, savoring the closeness, the intimacy of the moment. "That's because we've always respected the mystery, never rushing, never forcing—just patiently nurturing what we knew was precious."

Michael lifted their joined hands, placing a soft kiss on her fingers. "And now, it's time to share that beauty, to celebrate it openly…"

As evening fell upon the Vatican gardens, Michael and Hana remained close, savoring their newfound promise beneath a sky turning shades of lavender and gold. Nearby, beneath the cool earth, seeds lay patiently, waiting to awaken—a fitting metaphor for the patient, nurturing love they had cultivated, finally blossoming fully at precisely the right moment.

EPILOGUE

THE VATICAN SECRET ARCHIVES

I n the dimly lit chamber of the Vatican Secret Archives, Father Michael Dominic turned the pages of a delicate manuscript laid across the antique oak table. Each fragile leaf seemed to whisper beneath his fingertips, each line inscribed with ink that had long since faded yet retained its compelling power. Hours had passed unnoticed as he rigorously examined Juana de la Cruz's original documents. Her writings had already unveiled unprecedented declarations, yet Michael sensed something deeper, something carefully concealed beneath layers of symbolic complexity.

Pausing to rub the fatigue from his eyes, his gaze fell on a star chart peeking out from the piles of papers beside him. He remembered that after Hana's vision, she had shared her final vision with him—one induced by Vaux's injection. He shivered at the thought of what Vaux later explained was the plan. Blackthorn believed that Hana, having been exposed to the pollen of one of the rare plants at a critical moment, would have the essential elements in her blood to create a synthetic version of what was needed to perfect their formula. Their scientists had prepared a potion to stimulate the initial influence of that plant, and after a few minutes to circulate, they planned to extract what they needed from her: her blood.

The thought of it made Michael shiver. At least that threat was gone. In the aftermath, relieved that she had been rescued, they hadn't talked much about her vision during that episode. In fact, it was only recently that Hana described it. She recounted the words she'd heard, unsure if they were truly from the vision or from Karl as he revived her, asking someone to open a window. Then she gave Michael a drawing of the constellations she had seen, overlaying constellations from current perspectives on Earth. She told him at the time that she felt she needed to document it somehow, and once she put it on paper, she felt it had no purpose for her.

Which was odd, really. Hana felt purpose in nearly everything in her life. But Michael had accepted it as a way of Hana gaining closure for the trauma she'd experienced.

He sorted through his desk and found the drawing she had made.

Over the next hour, what Michael discovered would stay with the priest for the rest of his life.

Later that night, he stood outside, staring at a cloudy sky with no stars visible. Yet, beyond the clouds, he knew what lay in wait for the world.

And when.

He had studied the star charts, juxtaposed what Hana had given him and realized something profoundly revealing. By using the backtracking method for astronomical events, a program provided early on in their research by the CalTech Astronomical Department, and the recent documents Ian found, he could calculate exactly the constellation positions when the aliens had walked on earth among the monks. By extrapolating that, fast-forwarding astronomical events, Michael realized now what Juana had likely meant about the seasons of time.

She did not only mean spring on Earth bringing a cycle of growth. The thirteenth constellation in the corresponding world of the aliens, when timed properly with our own celestial configurations, provided a different cycle, a time when the two civilizations were open to each other.

The time when the aliens could return again.

And now Michael knew that time.

He closed his eyes in prayer, whispering, "What do I do?"

He looked to the stars, seeking a divine answer, when a passage from Matthew instantly settled his soul:

"But seek first the kingdom of God and his righteousness, and all these things will be given you besides. Do not worry about tomorrow; tomorrow will take care of itself. Sufficient for a day is its own evil."

He knew that when the time came, the voice in Hana's vision would say again:

Open the window.

ANGOLA

In a room barely eight feet square, in the oppressive heat and dripping humidity of jungle air, Alton Blackthorn sat waiting for his next step to freedom. With little more than the case of cash he still clung to at his side, his life had become one anxious day after another, evading authorities, and seeking refuge in the hell holes of the world, where others cared little about ethics or responsibility or international opinion.

Yet for all the worries that beset him, as he waited for his next clandestine transporter to arrive, his mind continued to repeat:

The powerful always prevail. And, given time, I will return.

FACT, FICTION, OR FUSION?

M any readers have asked me to distinguish fact from fiction in my books. Generally, I like to take factual events and historical figures and build on them in creative ways—but much of what I do write is historically accurate. In this book, I'll review some of the chapters where questions may arise, with the hope that it may help those wondering where reality meets creative writing.

GENERAL:
Home of the Voynich Manuscript, Yale's Beinecke Library provides a wonderful online reference to view the entire codex, at https://collections.library.yale.edu/catalog/2002046

Juana de la Cruz Vázquez y Gutiérrez, also known as Blessed Juana de la Cruz, was a notable Catalan mystic and abbess whose life is well-documented in ecclesiastical records, but I've added fictional interests and capabilities to her actual biography. To my knowledge, she wasn't associated with either botanical symbolism or the Voynich Manuscript. (Not to be confused with Juana Inés de la Cruz, the Hieronymite nun and Mexican writer, philosopher, composer, and poet of the seventeenth-century Baroque period.)

Keep in mind that early Church leaders did not shy away from the mysteries of the heavens; in fact, many were steeped in the astrological traditions inherited from the Greco-Roman world during the early centuries of Christianity, roughly between the second and fifth centuries. Tertullian, for instance, railed against the pagan misuse of astrology even as he acknowledged its pervasive influence, while Origen warned of the stars' sway upon human affairs but could not deny the fascination they held. Augustine himself wrestled with astrology in The City of God, conceding that celestial bodies marked the rhythm of earthly life even if he sought to place their power under God's sovereignty. Far from dismissing the stars as pagan superstition, bishops and theologians often interpreted celestial phenomena as signs of divine will, recording eclipses, comets, and planetary alignments with profound seriousness. What is striking to modern readers is that these same chroniclers occasionally described sudden illuminations, fiery globes, and unexplainable lights traversing the skies—accounts that, through our contemporary lens, resemble reports of unidentified flying objects. To the Church fathers, such events were framed as omens or portents in the cosmic struggle between heaven and earth; yet the language they used—mysterious wheels of light, radiant disks, or angelic fire—suggests encounters with phenomena that resist easy explanation even today.

· · ·

CHAPTER 9:

Ramon Llull (1232–1316), the celebrated Catalan philosopher, theologian, mystic, and prolific writer, had only a tangential, somewhat ambiguous involvement with alchemy—an involvement that remains a subject of scholarly debate to this day.

Llull is best known for his ambitious philosophical system, the Ars Magna ("Great Art"), a complex logical framework designed to unify all knowledge and support the evangelization of non-Christian peoples, particularly Muslims and Jews. While alchemy as a defined pursuit—transmuting base metals into gold, searching for the Philosopher's Stone, or creating elixirs of life—was flourishing during his lifetime, Llull's relationship to it was nuanced and largely indirect.

CHAPTER 14:

No plants depicted in the Voynich Manuscript have ever been found on Earth (or anywhere else, one might assume), though some have posited their similarity to certain extant species.

CHAPTER 19:

There is no direct historical evidence that monks at Montserrat Abbey in 1427 specifically observed lights in the sky they called "wandering messengers." This phrase doesn't appear in any extant medieval chronicles, letters, or ecclesiastical documents tied to the abbey or the wider region of Catalonia during that time.

However, a few key historical and cultural points may have given rise to such a legend:

Founded in the eleventh century and later reformed by the Benedictines, Montserrat Abbey had evolved into one of Europe's most spiritually vibrant monastic centers by the fifteenth century. At its heart lay the revered Black Madonna of Montserrat, a Marian shrine whose mysterious origins drew countless pilgrims from across Europe, eager to witness its miracles and seek divine favor. Nestled dramatically amid rugged mountain peaks, the abbey's isolation provided an atmosphere of deep contemplation, where monks pursued spiritual enlightenment beneath expansive Catalan skies. Its elevated location, offering unobstructed vistas, naturally transformed Montserrat into an informal observatory, allowing the community to witness and interpret celestial events, subtly intertwining their devout faith with the mysteries of the cosmos.

During this period, medieval chroniclers frequently interpreted unusual atmospheric or astronomical phenomena—comets, eclipses, auroras—as divine portents or omens, messages signaling God's will or impending earthly events. Notably, in 1406 and again in 1433, bright comets illuminated the European heavens, their appearance meticulously documented by contemporary scholars and chroniclers. Given its strategic mountaintop setting, Montserrat Abbey would undoubtedly have offered a clear vantage point for observing these extraordinary celestial displays, fostering intense spiritual reflection and fervent interpretation among its monks and pilgrims alike, who sought divine meaning in the enigmatic trails of these transient cosmic visitors.

CHAPTER 20:

One of the most enduring and controversial legends associated with Nazi Germany revolves around the alleged secret program commonly known as *"Die Glocke,"* or "The Bell," purportedly spearheaded under Adolf Hitler's regime. According to proponents of this theory, the Nazis were deeply invested in unconventional and esoteric sciences, striving to harness advanced technologies, including anti-gravity propulsion and energy manipulation, to create revolutionary aircraft—effectively early prototypes of what later generations would term "UFOs." Central to these accounts is *"Die Glocke,"* described by some researchers as a bell-shaped metallic craft surrounded by rotating cylinders filled with a mysterious fluid, capable of generating a powerful electromagnetic field. Witness testimonies, disputed documents, and persistent folklore suggest that experiments involving the device aimed not merely at revolutionary propulsion but possibly at breakthroughs in weaponry and energy. Despite extensive debate and widespread skepticism within mainstream historical circles, the myth of "The Bell" has endured, fueled by post-war speculation, conspiracy theories, and ambiguous testimonies from former Nazi scientists and officials. To this day, its supposed existence continues to capture imaginations, inspiring extensive research and frequent appearances in alternative history narratives, prompting persistent questions about the hidden technological ambitions and secretive projects allegedly pursued by Hitler's Third Reich.

CHAPTER 24:

The Cartuja monastery, Monasterio de Nuestra Señora

de la Asunción, was truly founded in 1506. It provides worship services and tours for local residents and is a fine example of architecture from that century.

CHAPTER 30:

The Hipparcos Catalogue is catalogue of more than 118,200 stars that was published in 1997. Its star charts are taken from the Hipparcos, a scientific satellite of the European Space Agency (ESA), launched in 1989 and operated until 1993.

The Gaia catalogues 1.2 billion objects created from the Gaia space observatory telescope, another program of the ESA. It began operation in 2013 and operated until March 2025.

AUTHOR'S NOTES

A word before you go.

Stories that touch on faith, scripture, and the hidden corridors of religious history walk a delicate line—and I've always tried to walk it with care. What you've read is fiction, shaped by oral traditions, historical fragments, and the kind of "what if" wondering that keeps writers up at night.

I hold no brief for any particular belief, and I mean that sincerely. Whether you come to these pages as a person of deep faith, quiet skepticism, or something beautifully in between, you are welcome here. The mystery is the point—not the argument.

Thank you for trusting me with your time and your imagination.

WRITING *The Voynich Codex* was a labor of genuine joy, and

if you've made it this far, you have my deepest gratitude. Readers like you are the reason these stories exist.

If Father Michael, Hana, and the secrets buried beneath the Vatican have captured your imagination, I hope you'll continue the journey. The Magdalene Chronicles—*The Magdalene Deception, The Magdalene Reliquary,* and *The Magdalene Veil*—are where it all began, and more adventures are already in the works across both the Vatican Secret Archives and Vatican Archaeology series.

One small favor, if you're willing: a review on Amazon, Goodreads, or wherever you like to share what you're reading makes an enormous difference to an independent author. A sentence or two is plenty—honest words from a real reader carry more weight than anything I could say about my own work.

I'd also love to hear from you directly. Whether you have a question, a thought about the story, or just want to say hello, you're welcome to reach me at **gary@garym cavoy.com**.

And if you'd like to explore the full world behind the books—series details, historical notes, and early word on what's coming next—please visit **www.garymcavoy.com**, where you can also join my private reader list.

Thank you, sincerely, for spending time in this world I love so much.

With kind regards,

GET YOUR CHARACTER BRIEF

YOUR FREE BOOK IS WAITING

Download your free copy now of **CODEX PERSONAE**, containing comprehensive backgrounds and other biographical details of all principal characters in *The Magdalene Chronicles*, *Vatican Secret Archive Thrillers*, and *Vatican Archaeology* series—with my compliments as a loyal reader!

https://garymcavoy.com/character-brief/

ACKNOWLEDGMENTS

My deepest gratitude goes to a new friend (she knows who she is…), whose careful proofreading and discerning suggestions enriched this manuscript in countless ways. Her attentive eye and generous spirit made a tangible difference, helping me see the work from fresh angles. Thank you, Sue, for your kindness, encouragement, and unwavering support.

Hail to my editor, Sandra Herner, whose editorial mastery and steadfast commitment to excellence have once again shaped this manuscript into its finest form. Sandra's discerning judgment, steady guidance, and deep understanding of my storytelling style have been invaluable—across many books now. Her quiet brilliance brings clarity and cohesion to every narrative thread. I'm deeply fortunate to have her as both a trusted collaborator and a cherished friend.

As always, no manuscript reaches publication without the eagle-eyed rigor of Donna Marie West, my superb copy editor. Her attention to grammar, style, and continuity— along with her ever-reliable instincts—elevates every sentence and ensures the highest standard of polish.

I'm also grateful to Yale Lewis and Greg McDonald for generously reading early chapters and offering wise, candid feedback. Your insights helped shape the arc of the story and refine its direction at key moments—thank you both for your thoughtful engagement.

www.ingramcontent.com/pod-product-compliance
Lightning Source LLC
Chambersburg PA
CBHW021238190726
48289CB00005B/1374